RESTORATION
The Gaia Origin

Book One

Daniel C. McWhorter

RESTORATION

Copyright © 2019 by Daniel C. McWhorter

Published by Underhill Press, LLC.

For more information visit, www.danmcwhorter.com

ISBN: 978-1950282968

For Marcia,
without whose encouragement and support
I could have never seen this through.

"The whole difference between construction
and creation is exactly this:
that a thing constructed can only be loved
after it is constructed;
but a thing created is loved before it exists."
—Charles Dickens

ONE

December 15, 2023 7:15 p.m. Central Daylight Time
New Beginnings Cancer Treatment Center
Kansas City, Missouri

"So, how much time does he have?" Dylan Harris asked. He put his arm around his wife and pulled her close in anticipation of the doctor's response.

Dr. Miles Conley hated that question. He had been a doctor for over thirty years and, despite significant advancements in technology during that time, there were no definitive answers in medicine. So, he did what he always did in these cases—he told the truth.

"Honestly, I just don't know. It could be hours, or it could be days."

Lily Harris burst into tears again. She pressed her face into her husband's chest. Dylan put both arms around her and held her tight. He could feel her shoulder blades pressing against his forearms. Her father's illness had been tough on her and, despite his best efforts, she hadn't been eating or taking care of herself.

"I'm sorry, Lil…at least he's not in any pain," he said.

Dylan felt Lily tense; he should have stopped at *I'm sorry*.

She slid her hands against his chest and shoved until there was an arm's distance between them.

"What does that have to do with anything?" Her voice trembled as she spoke. "I should be happy because they've pumped him full of painkillers?"

"You know I didn't mean it like that," he said, his voice soft but firm.

Evan was like a father to Dylan, but they knew this day was coming. He only wanted to ease his wife's pain—he just wished he could find the right words.

Lily put both hands over her face and cried even harder.

"Dr. Conley," the nurse interjected, "the patient is awake."

Everyone turned to look at Evan. Lily wiped the tears from her eyes and moved closer to her father.

"Dad, it's Lily," she said in the steadiest voice she could muster. "You're alright…you're in the hospital."

Doctor Evan Feldman's eyes fluttered open. The bright light above his head was blinding, but he could just make out the shapes of four people hovering over him.

Where am I? Who are these people? Why do they all look so concerned? Oh yeah, I'm dying.

He vaguely recalled collapsing the last time he got out of bed to use the bathroom, and he remembered the ambulance ride from his home to the nearest emergency center. After that, nothing.

Dr. Conley moved to the bedside and leaned over his patient. "Don't talk, Dr. Feldman. You're on a respirator."

The doctor took a small penlight from his pocket and swept its beam across his patient's eyes. Evan's pupils responded slowly, but that was normal given the medications being used to control his pain.

"Good. Blink once if you recognize this person." He pointed at Lily. "Blink twice if you don't."

One blink.

"Excellent. Blink once if you know where you are."

One blink.

"Do you know how long you've been here?"

Two blinks.

"Not to worry, you were brought in three days ago. You suffered a hemorrhage in your left lung. We stopped the bleeding, but the cancer has spread. You're stable for now but we're running out of options. Do you understand what I am telling you?"

Being diagnosed with lung cancer at age fifty-nine had been a cruel twist of genetic fate for Evan, who had never smoked a day in his life. He had tried every form of treatment, but they had discovered the cancer too late and there was no stopping its deadly rampage throughout his body.

He looked at Dr. Conley and blinked once.

"Well then, I will leave you with your family. I'll be back to check on you later." The doctor turned to Lily and put his hand on her shoulder. "Not too long please, he needs to rest."

"Not too long," Lily promised.

"I'll be at the nurse's station right outside, if you need anything," the nurse said as she followed the doctor out of the room.

Lily wiped her cheeks dry before sitting in the chair next to her father's bed.

He had an IV tube sticking out of the top of his wrist, and there was a spot of blood visible under the clear bandage that held it in place. His skin was so thin and pale that she could see the squiggly blue outlines of the veins running up his arm. She couldn't believe that the thin, frail man lying in this bed was her father.

Just two years ago, he had been in his prime. He was a world-renowned geneticist and CEO of Telogene Life Sciences, Inc., one of the biggest publicly traded biotech companies on the planet. His lean, six-foot, two-inch frame had radiated health and confidence—he looked at least ten years younger than he was. He was a man on a mission, and he had seemed unstoppable. But that was before cancer began destroying his body from the inside out.

She took his hand in hers and rubbed his fingers with her thumb. "How are you feeling, Dad? Can I get you anything?"

Two blinks.

"Aubrey is with Dylan's parents. She wanted to come, but I thought we should wait until after you woke up. Maybe we can bring her for a visit tomorrow, if you are feeling better. Would you like that?"

Yes, he wanted to see her; she was his only grandchild. He couldn't talk to her and reassure her that everything would be okay, but he could hug her and look in her beautiful blue eyes one more time.

One blink.

Dylan stepped forward and rested his hand on the dying man's knee. "You gave us quite a scare there, Evan. But you're one hell of a fighter. If anyone can beat this thing, it's you."

Lily glared at Dylan.

"Will you please stop with the optimistic bullshit!" she hissed.

"What? I mean it. Your dad is tough."

The look on Lily's face told him to stop talking. He decided that she needed to be alone with her father.

"I'll grab a coffee. Do you want one?"

"Yes, please," she said, thankful he'd finally gotten the message.

She loved her husband dearly, but she found his perpetual optimism tiring. She was a pragmatist, like her mother. Dylan was just like her father; he was a dreamer who believed that tomorrow would always be better than today.

Dylan gave Evan's knee a squeeze. "Take care, Evan. I'll see you tomorrow when we bring Aubrey."

Lily sat quietly, stroking her father's hand. He struggled to keep his eyes open, but she caught glimpses of the fire that still burned beneath his heavy eyelids. He was a fighter, he always was. Giving up just wasn't in his vocabulary.

"Dad, do you think you will be with Mom?" She had to ask; this might be her only chance.

He blinked once; a tear slid down his cheek.

Lily's mother, Christina, had died three years earlier in a plane crash. She'd been flying to Hong Kong on a Telogene corporate jet to spend time with her husband at an international conference on genomics, where he was speaking. The plane crashed in the middle of the Pacific Ocean with no survivors. The cause of the crash was never determined; the plane had broken apart on impact, and its pieces were submerged beneath 9,000 feet of water. At least they had found Christina's body. Aubrey was born two months later.

"Will you please tell her I love her and miss her and wish so much that she had met Aubrey?"

One blink. Another tear.

"I love you, Dad. You're my hero and I promise that Aubrey will grow up knowing what an amazing man you are." She sobbed. "What amazing parents you both were."

Lily stood up and brushed the tears from his cheeks. She looked into his blue-grey eyes and smiled before kissing him softly on the forehead.

"I only hope that Dylan and I can be half the parents you were," she whispered as she leaned forward to kiss him again on the forehead.

"Good night, Dad. I'll see you in the morning." Lily squeezed her father's hand one last time before picking up her purse and heading for the door.

She tried to twist the handle, but it was as if every ounce of strength had left her body—it wouldn't open. She took a deep breath and twisted again. The door opened, and she saw the nurse sitting at her station across the hall.

The nurse smiled at her. "Is everything okay?"

Lily tried to take a step forward, but her knees only trembled

What if she never saw her father again? What if she could never be the mother to Aubrey that her mom had been to her? What would her life be like without her ever patient and loving father to guide her?

She willed herself to step forward, but her legs would not support her. She stumbled into the hallway, slamming into a technician who had just exited the room next door. Lily fainted and crashed hard to the floor.

Dylan, who was filling a second cup of coffee at the vending machine, dropped both cups and sprinted toward her. The nurse checked her vital signs and tried to wake her while the technician raced down the hall to retrieve a stretcher.

"What's wrong with her," Dylan demanded. "Will she be okay?"

They loaded her on the stretcher, and the technician wheeled her down the hall toward the emergency department.

The nurse grabbed Dylan's hand. "She fainted, but she'll be fine. Has she eaten anything today?"

"Uh…no, I don't think so. We…we've been under a lot of stress."

She gave his hand a reassuring squeeze. "She'll be okay, I promise. Please come with me."

He followed her to a nearby waiting area. It was empty except for a bench, four chairs, and a coffee table littered with tattered, outdated magazines.

"Please wait here," she said. "I'll come get you in a few minutes."

He shuffled through the magazines. Woman's Day and Good Housekeeping weren't really his thing. He liked National Geographic, Popular Science and Road & Track, but it was the July 2022 issue of Scientific American that caught his interest. Evan's picture was on the cover along with big, bold text that asked: *Can he feed the world?*

He'd seen it before; Lily had a copy on her iPad. She'd tried to get him to read it several times, but he never got around to it. He checked the table of contents and flipped to the story about Evan. Telogene had patented a breed of genetically engineered corn that required a fraction of the fertilizer and didn't deplete the soil like regular corn. It was being touted as the biggest breakthrough since salt-tolerant rice.

It took him just a few minutes to read the three-page article, so he turned his attention to Road & Track. There was a Torch Red, 2023 Corvette Stingray on the cover. His was a 2020, the first year of the mid-engine Corvette, in Rapid Blue with a matching blue on black interior.

The nurse appeared in the doorway just as he reached the last page. It had only been twenty minutes, but it felt like an hour.

"You can see her now," she said. "She's fine. She was dehydrated, so we started an IV. And we've asked her to eat something before we discharge her. They just brought her some soup and crackers, and she should be able to go home as soon as she's done eating."

"Oh, thank God. Thank you, thank you, thank you!" Dylan clasped his hands and bowed his head in silent prayer. He then leapt forward to give the nurse a giant bear hug. "And thank you!"

The nurse was a taken by surprise but smiled politely. "You're welcome. Now please follow me."

The nurse led Dylan to a quiet, curtained-off area near the back of the emergency department. He pushed passed the curtains and rushed to his wife's side.

"Oh, baby," he cried. "I'm so glad you're okay; you scared me."

"It's nothing. I just need to take better care of myself," Lily replied, her voice shaky and weak.

Dylan leaned over, kissing her gently on the lips.

"I'm sorry this is so hard on you. I'm trying, I am really trying." Tears streamed down his cheeks.

"I know you are. It's not your fault. I haven't eaten since yesterday and I guess it caught up with me. I promise to do better; you and Aubrey are too important to me."

"I love you." Dylan gave her another kiss.

"I love you, too." She kissed him back.

They arrived home two hours later. They were both exhausted, and wasted no time getting ready for bed. Dylan started snoring just minutes after his head hit the pillow, but Lily couldn't turn her brain off. The events of the past three days had overwhelmed her. She knew that her father was critically ill, but she had let herself believe that he would get his last-minute miracle. If anyone deserved one, he did!

Dr Conley's words reverberated through her mind. Her father was dying, and there was nothing anyone could do to change that.

First Mom, and now Dad. I can't do this without him!

She turned away from Dylan and buried her face in her pillow. She wanted to cry, but there were no tears left. All she could manage were a few muffled sobs. When sleep finally came, it was the same nightmare-ridden sleep that had plagued her for the past year. But it was better than nothing.

Two

DECEMBER 16, 2023 3:07 A.M. CDT
THE HARRIS FAMILY HOME
KANSAS CITY, MISSOURI

The sound of Lily's cell phone brought her nightmare to an abrupt end. Perfect timing. That shadowy, nondescript thing that nearly caught her would have to wait. Her heart pounded in her chest like she'd just finished a marathon.

The phone rang again; she checked the number on the display. She didn't recognize it but answered anyway. "Hello?"

"Mrs. Harris?" an unfamiliar male voice asked.

"Yes, who is this?"

Dylan heard Lily talking, but he wasn't fully awake yet.

"This is Bruce Wagner, your father's attorney. I'm at the front gate and need to speak with you right away. Will you please buzz me in?"

"Why, what's wrong?"

The panic in her voice brought Dylan to full consciousness. He sat up and rubbed the sleep out of his eyes.

"Mrs. Harris, I am sorry to have to tell you that your father has passed away."

"No, no, no…please no…." She dropped the phone.

Dylan picked it up. "Who is this?"

"I'm sorry to wake you Mr. Harris. This is Bruce Wagner, Evan Feldman's attorney. I need to speak to you and your wife. I am outside the front gate."

"The front gate? Okay, just give me a minute."

Dylan set the phone on the bed and picked up the aluminum cylinder sitting on his nightstand. He released the lock on the side of the iScroll and unfurled the 12 x14 inch flexible display. Dylan tapped an icon on the screen and nine small boxes appeared—each showed a real-time video feed from one of the many cameras located around the property.

He tapped the box labelled *Front Gate*. The image zoomed in on a dark-colored SUV with a middle-aged man sitting behind the wheel. Dylan tapped another icon to open the gate.

Dylan picked up his phone. "Okay, park by the fountain. I'll be right down."

He hung up the phone before tapping yet another icon to disarm the security system.

"Honey, you stay here. I'll see what he wants."

Lily stared at Dylan in complete disbelief. "Are you kidding me? That man just told me that my father died, and you want me to stay here? Wake up, Dylan!"

She leapt from the bed and hurried to the closet where her robe hung. Dylan followed close behind, grabbing her elbow when they reached the top of the stairs.

"Lil, you know I'm here for you. I love you and I want to help however I can. Please let me help."

"I know you do, and I appreciate your efforts. But you can't fix this. The best way to help is to let me do what I need to do."

She pulled her elbow away and continued down the stairs.

Dylan jumped in front of her just as they reached the front door. He twisted the lock and pulled the door open to reveal a man in a dark, pin-striped suit walking up the stairs from the driveway. He carried a black leather briefcase in his left hand.

The man stuck out his free hand. "Bruce Wagner."

Bruce Wagner was a burly man, with broad shoulders and strong beefy hands. He was at least two inches taller than Dylan, which put him somewhere over six feet. He wasn't fat, but he carried the bulk of someone who might have once been an avid weightlifter but who hadn't seen the inside of a gym in several years.

Dylan shook his hand. "I'm Dylan and this is Lily."

"It's very nice to meet you. Evan has told me a lot about you both."

"What do you want, Mr. Wagner?" The harsh words stuck in Lily's throat like glass. She knew this wasn't his fault, he was just the messenger, but the tremendous anger welling up inside her had to go somewhere.

Bruce nodded his understanding. "I'm sorry to be the bearer of bad news. He died in his sleep, a little after 1:00 a.m., cardiac arrest. The doctors tell me that it happened fast; he didn't suffer."

Lily didn't say a word. She just stared past him, like he wasn't even there. Dylan put his arm across her back and rested his head on her shoulder but said nothing.

Bruce gave them a minute to process the news. "I hate to be indelicate, but there is another matter that we must discuss."

"There's nothing to discuss. I am going to the hospital to see my father," Lily shouted at the top of her lungs. "Now get out!"

"Mrs. Harris—Lily—please, that won't be possible. Your father's body has already been moved to another location."

"Where are you taking him?" Lily demanded.

"Lily, I am here at your father's request. This can't wait," Bruce said, his tone firm but patient.

Dylan took his wife's hand in his. "Please honey, let's listen to what Mr. Wagner has to say. He drove out here for a reason, and it's obviously important since it's three in the morning."

She jerked her hand away. "No. I…want…to see…my…father!"

"I understand that you want to see him, and there will be time for that. But, for the moment, I need you here." Bruce held up his briefcase. "I only need fifteen minutes of your time…please."

"What is it that is so goddamned important?" She wiped the tears from her face and straightened her shoulders.

"Your father had very specific final requests, and one of them was that I bring this to you." He tapped his fingers against his case.

Lily stared at the briefcase and thought about it for several seconds before finally stepping aside. The three of them walked the short distance to the kitchen. Lily motioned to an empty chair at the small kitchen table. The attorney removed his iScroll and a sealed folder from his briefcase.

"As the sole surviving heir," Bruce said, "your father's fifty-one percent stake in Telogene Life Sciences now belongs to you. In addition, your father has asked the board to promote you to CEO. Bill Frederickson will stay on as president for the time being."

Bruce opened his iScroll while he talked and slid it in front of Lily.

"I need you to key in your access code and give me your palm print here to acknowledge these changes. There is more signing to do, but this will suffice for now."

She slammed her hands on the table, her last ounce of self-control gone. "Seriously? You came here at three in the morning to get me to sign some bullshit corporate documents? Get the hell out of my house!"

Lily got up from the table and started to leave the kitchen but stopped at the doorway. She spun on her heels to face the lawyer.

"Wait. If I'm CEO, that means you work for me now. I demand that you tell me where they took my father." She stared at him with a glare that would melt most people.

Bruce straightened in his chair. "First, I don't work for Telogene. I'm your father's *personal* attorney. Second, you're not CEO until you sign these documents."

Lily glared at him a little longer before sliding back into her seat.

"You have ten minutes, Mr. Wagner."

Bruce repositioned the iScroll in front of Lily.

She scrolled through the document on the display. It was twenty-two pages long and overflowing with legalese. "What does it say?"

"It gives the company the ability to act on your behalf during the transfer of ownership. It also says that you won't make any public announcements until you've received final approval from the board."

Lily keyed in her Telogene network access code and placed her palm on the display to sign the document.

"What's next?" she asked, her tone hurried.

She would sign anything he put in front of her—the faster, the better. She wanted to see her father one last time, to tell him she loved him and that she was so grateful to have been born his daughter. One way or another, Bruce Wagner was going to take her to him.

The attorney took the iScroll from her and confirmed that she had signed the document. He tapped on the display several times before sliding it back across the table to her. "Your father left this for you."

Evan Feldman's face filled the screen. Her heart skipped a beat and her hand shook as she reached for the device.

Bruce stood up and took a step toward the doorway. "I will step out while you watch."

Dylan joined Bruce at the door. "This way—you can use my office."

Dylan returned a minute later and sat next to Lily. She was still staring at her father's frozen image.

She started the video. The camera zoomed out to show Evan sitting behind his desk. He was in his office at Telogene's headquarters. She knew it well; her office was just down the hall from his. He looked young and healthy. He must have filmed this before his cancer diagnosis, or perhaps shortly thereafter.

Evan stared directly into the camera. "Hi, Lilypad." He'd called her that since she was born. "I know you're hurting and confused, and I wish I could be there with you. Some of what I am about to say will be hard for you to hear, but you're strong…stronger than you know. I know you can do this."

He stood up, walked around to the front of his desk, and started pacing back and forth. She had seen him do that a hundred times before. It usually meant that he was angry or nervous. Obviously, the latter in this case.

"I'm ashamed to admit it," he said, "but I've been keeping something from you. I hope you can find it in your heart to forgive me for what I have done. I have kept it from you because I knew you would have opposed my decision."

He stopped pacing. "Your mother wasn't cremated. I had her put into cryogenic storage…and the fact that you are watching this means I've joined her."

After dropping that bombshell, Evan explained that there was a secret division of Telogene that reported to him and operated with little board oversight. He called it "Project Second Chance," and its purpose was to identify and develop mechanisms to preserve human DNA indefinitely. Over the last three years, the team had significantly improved Telogene's cryogenic storage technology—and it was now possible to freeze human tissue indefinitely with minimal deterioration.

Evan briefly reviewed the backgrounds of the key personnel before sharing details on the various locations involved. The main research lab was in Hong Kong but a network of limestone caves near Kansas City served as the primary cold-storage site. There was an air of pride in his voice as he described the storage facility's geothermal power source. He expected that it would generate power for hundreds—if not thousands—of years.

He concluded with an explanation of his goal for Project Second Chance.

"By now you will have figured out that preserving DNA is only the beginning. I envision a day not too far off when we'll take a sample of every person's DNA at birth. We'll preserve it, store it, and use it to sequence genetically targeted cures for all kinds of diseases. And no one will ever die waiting for an organ transplant again; we'll use their DNA to clone whatever they need."

He resumed pacing.

"And if we can clone organs, then there is no reason we can't clone entire bodies. Of course, cloning a body is just creating another person. They may have the same genes, but they would have their own brains and would develop as unique individuals as they matured—like identical twins."

Evan stopped mid-stride and leaned against his desk.

"Ethical issues aside, what I am really interested in is extending human life and perhaps even…"

Lily paused the video.

She knew where her dad was going, and she wasn't sure if she wanted to hear it. Dylan, to his credit, didn't say a word. He took her hand in his and gave it a tight squeeze.

She tapped *Resume*.

"…the complete elimination of death. That wasn't my main goal five years ago when I started this project, but it became my goal when your mother died. She left us too soon, and she had so much more to offer the world."

He returned to his oversized, brown leather chair, taking a deep breath before he continued.

"We are also working on preserving the brain. Not only the tissues but the knowledge and memories locked inside it. If we can make it work, we will give new lives to all those people who live with perfectly healthy brains trapped inside diseased or broken bodies. And maybe even provide an option for those who are being slowly killed by their own bodies…like me."

Evan clasped his hands together as if in prayer. "I want you to promise me you will continue this work. I believe in you…you're a natural leader. People respect you and they *will* follow you. The Second Chance team will make the breakthroughs required to make this technology viable, I know it in my heart. They just need a leader who can keep them focused…and who can protect them from those that might not understand."

Her father stood up from his chair again. "Lily, I want you to promise me you will bring us back. Give your mother and me a chance to see our grandchildren grow up. We both worked too hard for too long to be denied the opportunity to experience the full fruits of our labor. This is a big ask, and you will probably need time to think about it. Believe me, I understand. Just know that I love you and I believe in you. Bruce is a good friend and trusted confidant. He will help you if you let him. Goodbye, Lilypad, I miss you already."

The screen faded to black. The words *For Lily, April 17, 2021* appeared on the display.

Lily took her hand from Dylan's, wiped her eyes, and stood. She walked over to the kitchen door, took a deep breath, and called down the hallway.

"We're ready for you, Mr. Wagner."

Bruce returned to the kitchen and took his seat at the table.

"So, what do you think?" he asked.

Lily's face turned red as her anger overwhelmed her.

"I think very little of it, Mr. Wagner," she answered. "I just learned that my father is a liar. That he and Mom are stored in some high-tech freezer a hundred feet underground. And that he actually believes that he can bring people back from the dead! What does he think, that he's God?"

Dylan rubbed her shoulders, trying desperately to calm her down. It didn't help.

"Even worse," she continued, "he wants me to promise to carry out this mad scheme of his…which I guess means he that thinks I'm God, too. I should resign right now!"

Bruce responded in his usual calm demeanor. "I understand that this is quite a shock, Lily. Why don't you get some sleep? I can come back in a few hours to help with the funeral arrangements."

Lily couldn't believe what she had heard. "Funeral arrangements? What the fuck do we need to have a funeral for? Isn't he already in the icebox?"

She shoved the iScroll across the table. It would have ended up on the floor if Bruce hadn't caught it.

"Lily," he said, his voice soft and calm, "your father is the CEO of a multi-billion-dollar company. There are lots of people that expect a funeral and it would not be prudent to disappoint them."

Bruce put the iScroll back on the table and leaned toward Lily.

"Look, I know this is hard. And I get that you would have preferred to learn of this in a very different way. But it's what your father wanted, and I am doing my best to carry out his last wishes."

He leaned back and picked up his iScroll.

"Let's do this—you take a few hours to calm down and think about it. You can call me whenever you're ready."

Bruce tapped his iScroll several times.

"I just sent you my contact info. Call me anytime, twenty-four hours a day."

Bruce put the device in his briefcase and reached for the folder he had left on the table.

"There is just one more thing," he added. "This folder contains your new access card and a flash drive. The drive has the video you just watched and copies of your father's private files. They're encrypted but you can access them from any device with a palm reader."

Lily stood up and extended her hand to the attorney. "Thank you, Mr. Wagner. You've been very helpful, and you will hear from me soon. Please show him out, Dylan."

"Goodnight, Lily," Bruce said. "Please remember the non-disclosure agreement, and don't hesitate to call if there is anything I can do for you…anything at all."

"I just need time to think," she replied.

Dylan showed Bruce to the door and thanked him for his patience. He came back to find Lily pacing back and forth across the kitchen floor—a habit she had inherited from her father.

"What are you going to do?" he asked.

"I don't know…"—she spun to face him—"I don't know!"

Lily inhaled deeply before continuing. "On one hand, I am intrigued by this whole idea. But, on the other, it just doesn't seem right. Does anyone have a right to live forever?"

"Well, it's not forever, Lil…"

"Of course it is!" Her hands shot out from her sides like bullets from a gun. "Don't you see? If you can clone someone's body and then transplant their brain once, who says you can't do it two or three or a hundred times? What would this world be like in a decade if the death rate dropped to zero? What about a hundred years from now?"

She resumed pacing.

"We are already approaching nine billion people, Dylan. Do you think this planet can sustain ten or twelve or twenty billion? I don't, and I don't want to be a part of creating the nightmare this world will become if people stop dying."

"Yeah, I see what you mean," Dylan acknowledged. "But what if it was just two people…or ten, or maybe a hundred? Would that seriously unbalance the world? I doubt it. I understand that there are ethical considerations. And it won't be easy keeping this technology away from those who would misuse it, but that's why your father chose you."

She stopped pacing again.

"Don't *you* see?" he continued. "Evan wants you in charge of this project because he knew you would have ethical concerns…that you'd think about the big picture. Your father chose you because he knows you will do the right thing. He believes in you, Lily and so do I."

Dylan took her hands in his. "I know that I am just a has-been game developer."

He was being modest. He created his first blockbuster video game when he was twenty, sold his company for three hundred million dollars when he was twenty-nine, and retired when Aubrey was born at the ripe old age of thirty-seven so he could be a stay-at-home dad.

"But Evan gave you an amazing gift, and I'd hate to see you throw it away."

"What gift?" she asked skeptically.

"The gift of life, the power to decide how long it lasts and when it's over. This isn't just about bringing your parents back. It's about the power to decide when your own life ends…or mine, or Aubrey's for that matter. Just imagine if, heaven forbid, someday Aubrey gets sick and this technology could save her. Would you do it then?"

"That's not fair."

"I know it's not," Dylan agreed, "and that's precisely why your father kept this from you. It's not fair, and no amount of rationalizing will ever make it fair. Dying isn't fair. Getting sick or being born with a genetic defect isn't fair. *Life* isn't fair!"

"You're right," she said, "I'm exhausted and not thinking clearly. Thank you for being there for me."

She threw her arms around his neck. "Please be patient with me. I love you and I promise we will get through this."

Dylan leaned in and softly touched his lips to hers. "I love you, too. Hang in there and give yourself time to think it through. You will make the right decision."

He held her close and kissed her again. "Do you want to try to get a few hours of sleep?"

"Yeah, that's a good idea," she said. "We both should try to sleep."

The couple walked hand-in-hand up the stairs to their bedroom. Lily climbed into bed first and Dylan snuggled up behind her with his arm drawn tight across her chest. Lily closed her eyes and tried to sleep but, as before, her brain would not quiet.

Too much had happened too fast. She couldn't help but replay every moment of the past several days over and over in her head. When she finally succumbed to the dark embrace of sleep, her memories gave way once again to her nightmares.

Lily moaned and whimpered as her brain conjured images of a planet ruled by a small group of wealthy elites. She imagined them as brutal people who lacked empathy and who used their vast wealth and unnaturally long lives to gain an unfair advantage over the less fortunate.

Her tears flowed freely down her cheeks and pooled on the pillow beneath her.

She imagined that she had unleashed the curse of eternal life on humanity. She dreamt of a stinking, decaying, over-populated Earth, with its billions of people all clamoring to live forever—and she screamed.

THREE

APRIL 3, 2075 10:00 A.M. GLOBAL STANDARD TIME
TELOGENE WORLD HEADQUARTERS
LEAD, SOUTH DAKOTA

"Dr. Harris?" A female voice echoed through a partially open office door.

Dr. Aubrey Harris, CEO of Telogene, shifted her glance toward the speaker. "Yes?"

A young woman in a dark blue pantsuit stepped through the door. It was Evelyn Wu, Aubrey's executive assistant. "Dr. Hao says he is ready for you now."

A smile crept across Aubrey's face. "Okay, please tell him I will be right down."

"Is there anything I should know?" Evelyn asked.

"No, I'm sure it's just another one of Chen's experiments. Will you please clear my schedule for the rest of the day?"

"Certainly," the assistant replied as she closed the door behind her.

Aubrey waved her hand to dismiss the holographic projection that filled the air above her desk.

She was reviewing a new genetic enhancement protocol that, once perfected, would significantly increase human lung capacity. This would be a boon to the tens of thousands of space and undersea colonists who lived and worked in low oxygen environments. More importantly, it was exactly the type of innovation the company needed to stay ahead of its competitors.

She would have to come back to that later.

Aubrey stood up and walked across the room to her private elevator. The elevator was an executive perk that allowed her to access any floor in the complex without having to enter public areas. Not only was it incredibly convenient, but it enabled her to get from point A to point B without having to stop and chat, or have people wonder where she was going and why she was going there.

She placed her hand on the scanner inside the elevator and stated her destination.

"Cryonics Lab."

The scanner flashed green.

"Thank you, Dr. Harris," a pleasant female voice replied.

The elevator began its rapid descent to the Cryonics Lab.

Telogene's corporate headquarters was on top of an old gold mine that once served as a government-funded research facility. Aubrey's destination was deep inside the mine, some 500 meters below ground.

A series of devastating earthquakes starting in 2037 had forced the company out of Kansas City. The old mine was a perfect choice for the company because the U.S. government had spent billions turning the site into a high-tech research lab used to conduct physics experiments. That funding had dried up after the global financial crisis of 2025, and Telogene had purchased the property for pennies on the dollar.

The elevator halted, and the door slid open with a soft hiss. Its lone occupant exited into a long, narrow hallway that glowed with a soft bluish light. Aubrey turned down the first hallway to her right and continued past several closed doors until she reached the one labeled *Lab 46-D*.

She put her hand on the scanner next to the door—it flashed green— and the door slid open. The large circular room featured a raised workstation in the middle surrounded by four patient bays. It took a moment for her eyes to adjust to the bright white light that flooded the room.

There were three other people present—one operating a series of holographic displays surrounding the central station and two others standing next to a large sarcophagus-looking glass tube in one of the patient bays. Although made of clear glass, a thick white gas obscured the capsule's contents. The swirling gas looked like a fluffy cloud stuffed into a bottle.

The man working in the center of the room looked up as she entered.

"You're just in time, Dr. Harris," he said.

Dr. Chen Li Hao was Chief Cryonicist, and the best cryo-engineer at Telogene—if not the world. Trained as a physician and geneticist, he specialized in the preservation and restoration of human DNA. He had worked at Telogene for nearly forty years, but you couldn't tell that by looking at him. His appearance suggested a physically fit, Asian male in his mid-thirties, but in reality, he was just two months shy of celebrating his 75th birthday.

Long life and a youthful appearance were among the perks of working at Telogene. Employees enjoyed convenient access to a multitude of discounted, and often free, gene therapies. This unique employment benefit allowed Telogene to attract and keep some of the best scientists and engineers in the world.

Dr. Hao gestured at the holodisplay before stepping down to join Aubrey next to the pod.

"Dr. Berkovic, Dr. Walker, it's nice to see you both again," Aubrey said to the two technicians monitoring the holographic displays projected above the capsule.

The two women smiled and returned her greeting. Both appeared to be in their mid-thirties but, like Chen, they were nearly twice that old.

Dr. Leah Berkovic was the company's Chief Neurochemist. It was her job to oversee the just-completed transcription of the patient's neural pathways. Dr. Tanessa Walker, Assistant Chief Cryonicist, would monitor the restoration process.

It had been many years since this group had performed a restoration, but this was a very special patient and Dr. Harris wanted only her best people working on it.

"We've completed the neurotransfer and are ready to begin restoration on your order," Dr. Hao offered.

"Excellent. How is he doing?" Dr. Harris inquired of Dr. Berkovic.

The neurochemist examined her holodisplay, gesturing several times to confirm the results. Each finger point, hand sweep, and wave caused a different set of data to appear on the virtual display.

"Neurotransfer is complete with 98.7 percent of all engrams successfully encoded. There was some minor degradation of the original data store…probably from a power disruption at the old facility," she said, referring to the company's original storage site in Kansas City.

Aubrey checked the display to verify the results for herself.

Neurological transfers were always a delicate process because every neural structure had to be encoded exactly as it had formed in the donor brain. Any deviation or error in the transfer process could cause symptoms ranging from minor memory loss to total synaptic failure. The system grouped regions of interconnected or related neurons into engrams, which were the higher order brain structures that allowed for persistent memory, motor function, emotions, and personality.

"I was hoping for better but I'll take it. Have you isolated the affected areas?"

"Yes, it looks like most of the memory loss occurred in this region," Dr. Berkovic said, pointing to a three-dimensional image of the patient's brain.

"I believe these are mostly early childhood memories," she continued. "But there may be some bleed-over into later memories built on the affected memory region. He might require some minor reconstruction but we won't know for a couple of weeks, at least."

"Okay, that shouldn't be a problem," Dr. Harris said before turning to her Chief Cryonicist. "You may proceed, Dr. Hao."

Dr. Hao walked over to where Dr. Walker stood and gestured at her holodisplay. A duplicate display appeared in the air next to it. The Chief Cryonicist used hand gestures and voice commands to move the various elements on the display to different locations, and to add a few new ones.

Once he was satisfied with the view on his display, he nodded at Dr. Walker. "Please begin."

Dr. Walker adjusted several virtual dials and slides on her display before issuing her verbal command. "Begin restoration. Authorization Walker 091792."

A digitized female voice echoed from the ceiling above them. "Senior executive approval required."

Dr. Hao looked at Aubrey. "Would you like the honor?"

She smiled. "Why thank you, Dr. Hao, I believe I would. Authorization Harris alpha epsilon zero 10352."

"Restoration approved. Initiating sequence now," the digital voice acknowledged.

The holodisplays in front of Hao and Walker changed to show a three-dimensional image of the person inside the capsule.

Several readouts appeared alongside the image showing the patient's core temperature, heart rate and respiration. Aubrey noted that the patient's core temperature was minus 136 degrees Celsius and all other readings were zero. Perfectly normal for a person in moderate cryogenic suspension.

Full suspension involved temperatures below minus 196 C, but the patient had been warmed slightly for the neurotransfer procedure. Overlaid on the image were graphical indicators for cellular and neural activity. These indicators showed minimal cellular activity but no activity in the brain or nervous system...also normal.

"All readings normal and rapid warming is in progress," Dr. Walker reported.

The temperature reading climbed toward zero at the rate of about one degree Celsius per second. Cellular activity slowly increased with the temperature, but all other indicators remained flat until the first signs of neurological activity appeared in the brain stem. All eyes were on the holodisplays as the subject's core temperature passed ten degrees Celsius.

"Ion exchange returning to normal across all neural pathways." Dr. Berkovic said. She turned her attention to a three-dimensional rendering of the patient's brain. "Synaptic signaling is a little low but within range."

"Increase cortical stimulation by point zero three percent," Dr. Hao instructed. "I don't want to risk any further memory loss."

"Increasing cortical stimulation by point zero three," Dr. Berkovic repeated as she manipulated a set of virtual controls.

"Synaptic activity has stabilized...all readings are normal," she added.

Dr. Walker repeated the information that appeared on her display. "Respiration started and heart rate is ten beats per minute and climbing. Blood pressure is 90 over 50."

The temperature reading stopped at 37 degrees Celsius—normal human body temperature. Dr. Walker watched closely as the patient's heart rate and blood pressure stabilized. Respiration settled in at twelve breaths per minute. All body systems were normal, and the patient was breathing on his own.

"Restoration complete," the digitized voice intoned.

A sucking sound replaced the humming noise as the thick cloud-like gas evacuated from the capsule. It took only seconds for the gas to clear, revealing a physically fit male lying inside. He appeared to be in his mid-thirties, was about two meters tall, and had the physique of an Olympic athlete. He was hairless, except for the close-cropped thicket of brown hair covering his scalp.

Dozens of tubes were inserted into various parts of his body, and he had electrodes attached to his head, chest, and along his spinal column. A robotic arm inside the capsule emerged to remove the tubes from the patient's mouth, arms and legs. A second later, a loud hissing sound signaled the release of the vacuum seal holding the lid in place—a robotic arm descended from the ceiling to remove it.

"Wake him up, two CCs should do it," Dr. Hao instructed.

Dr. Walker selected the specified dose on her display, causing yet another robotic arm to emerge from the side of the pod and inject the high-potency stimulant Adreneron into the patient's neck.

A few seconds later the patient's eyes fluttered but didn't open. His heart rate jumped up to sixty-two beats per minute, and he was breathing noticeably faster.

Dr. Harris stepped closer to the pod.

"What's wrong?" she asked.

Dr. Hao looked at his display. "He's fine. Give him a minute. If he doesn't wake up, we will give him another CC of Adreneron."

Just then a spike appeared on the display showing a big increase in brain activity.

"And here he comes now," Dr. Berkovic said.

The patient opened his eyes for a second but then quickly closed them again.

"Ambient light only," Aubrey ordered.

The light diminished until it was the same soft blue glow as in the hallway.

"There, that's better. Try to open your eyes again."

The patient slowly opened his eyes and scanned the room before locking his gaze on the woman hovering over him.

"Don't try to sit up just yet," she said as she took the patient's hand in hers. "Give yourself a few minutes to acclimate."

The man in the capsule blinked his eyes repeatedly as he tried to focus.

"Lil…li…Lily?" he asked.

She smiled as she put the man's hand to her lips. "No, Papa, it's Aubrey."

Aubrey had only learned to talk a year before Evan had died, and Papa had been the closest she could come to grandpa. A tear ran down her cheek and splashed on the back of his hand.

"Dr. Feldman," Dr. Hao leaned forward so the man in the capsule could see him. "I am Dr. Hao. It is an honor and a pleasure to meet you."

He pointed to the other two technicians. "This is Dr. Berkovic, and this is Dr. Walker. We will do your orientation."

Dr. Evan Feldman nodded politely at the three technicians before turning his attention back to his granddaughter.

"Aubrey," he said, his voice still raspy from the breathing tube, "you're all grown up. It's so good to see you." He squeezed her hand. "Where is your mother? Where's Lily?"

"I know you have a lot of questions, Papa, but I need you to focus on your orientation for the time being. Once Dr. Hao gives the okay, I will come visit you again…probably in time for dinner tonight *if* you follow all of his instructions and don't give him any trouble. Can you do that for me?"

Although he was eager to discover where Lily was—to discover where *he* was—the strong pounding sensation in his head and the extreme dizziness he was experiencing convinced him he should heed her advice.

"All right, Princess. I will be on my best behavior and do as the good doctor asks."

A big smile crept across Aubrey's face. His ability to remember the nickname he had given her was a very good sign that they had achieved a successful neurotransfer.

"Can you give your Papa a hug?" Evan asked. "I've really missed you."

Aubrey leaned forward and gave her grandfather a big hug and a kiss on the cheek.

"I've missed you too, Papa." She wiped another tear from her cheek as she stood. "You are in excellent hands. Trust Dr. Hao and his team, and you will be up and around in no time…I promise."

She reached down and squeezed his hand one more time. "I have to leave now but I will come back and check on your progress in a couple of hours, okay?"

"Please do," he said.

"And don't worry about the headache. It shouldn't last long, and they can give you something for the pain if it's too distracting. That poor brain of yours just absorbed a lifetime of information in less than a day, so it's feeling a little overworked at the moment. But it will pass."

She gave him another kiss on the cheek before turning to leave.

"Please call me once you've completed phase one," she whispered to Dr. Hao on her way out.

Aubrey looked back at her grandfather one last time. The technicians had him sitting up and were helping him put on a white gown.

God, I hope we're doing the right thing.

The door hissed open, and she walked down the long hallway back to her private elevator.

FOUR

APRIL 3, 2075 02:43 P.M. GST
TELOGENE WORLD HEADQUARTERS
LEAD, SOUTH DAKOTA

Phase one of the orientation was designed to help Evan acclimate to his new body. Push-ups, pull-ups, sit-ups, jump rope, and an hour on a treadmill to get started, followed by mental acuity tests and a two-hour-long video that summarized the key events of the last fifty-odd years.

First, there was the global financial crisis of 2025, followed just two years later by a global famine and World War III. The battle for control of the Middle East started in 2027 when a Syrian dissident assassinated the Israeli Prime Minister. Israel responded by invading Syria and things spiraled quickly out of control from there, with the United States, Russia, and China all deploying troops to defend their respective allies in the region.

The war finally ended in August 2032 after China used a low yield nuclear weapon on the battlefield, causing Russia to ally with the U.S. in protest. The combined might of the U.S. and Russian militaries, and the threat of the conflict turning into a global nuclear war, were enough to convince China to withdraw from the region. In the negotiated peace that followed, the Allies gave Israel the Syrian territory south of Damascus that the Israelis had captured at the start of the war.

The much-debated global climate change phenomena of the late 90s and early 2000s became undeniable as lush jungles became desert wastelands, great deserts transformed into grassy plains, and once snowy tundra turned to swampy marshland.

The Northern ice sheets shrank by seventy percent, and the southern half of Greenland and all of Iceland, were now ice-free. Temperate forests grew in fertile volcanic soil where there had once been only ice. The southern pole had experienced similar melting, and the loss of billions of tons of ice had transformed the coastline of Antarctica into a barren, rocky wasteland.

The deluge of fresh water into the oceans had altered water temperature and salinity world-wide, killing off marine life and altering weather patterns. Hurricanes, tornadoes, earthquakes, and volcanic eruptions were all frequent occurrences. The loss of habitable coastal regions caused massive migrations of people and animals to more habitable areas. The planet had experienced a mass extinction of plants and wildlife equivalent to the end of the Cretaceous period 65 million years ago—the same one that ended the dinosaurs.

And then there was the decades-long global drought and famine. Billions had perished from starvation and disease. India was hardest hit, with over seven hundred million dead. China, Indonesia, and Africa also suffered significant reductions in population. Even more might have died had it not been for Telogene and the billions of dollars' worth of drought-resistant crop seed it donated to affected countries.

Not all the news was bad, however. Several private corporations from around the world, including Telogene, had partnered to establish permanent colonies on the Moon and Mars in the mid-2030s. A world government was formed in 2042 with Zurich, Switzerland serving as the capitol for the Global Federation of Nations (GFN). And Telogene Life Sciences had become the world's first multi-trillion-dollar corporation.

Evan found all this fascinating, and he wanted more detail than what was in the orientation video. But Dr. Hao explained that he would have to wait. They would give him full access to the company's information archive, and the global information network known as *GeoNet*, once he completed his orientation. But for now, he needed to learn more about himself and the new body he inhabited.

As shocking as some world events had been, the biggest shock of all came when they finally let him see himself. He had noticed his well-defined musculature and the ease at which he completed the exercise portion of his orientation, but he hadn't given it much thought. He knew they had given him a new body; they had told him that much, and it only made sense that they had made it young and healthy. What he hadn't considered was that the body he inhabited was not his own!

He looked nothing like he remembered. The average looking, bookish body he remembered had been transformed into that of a devilishly handsome actor from one of those action films he used to enjoy. His hair was still brown and his eyes blue, but his jaw was more pronounced and he no longer had an overbite. There was something vaguely familiar about his face, but it most definitely was not the face he had been born with.

It was disconcerting to see another person staring back at him and, to make matters worse, Dr. Hao refused to explain why Evan wasn't in his own body. The doctor said that Aubrey would explain everything and had asked for his continued patience. Then he had excused himself to call Aubrey.

Aubrey was at her desk reviewing the lung enhancement protocol when the image of her executive assistant popped up in the corner of her display.

"I am sorry to interrupt, but Dr. Hao is calling," Evelyn said.

"Please put him through."

Dr. Hao appeared on the display.

"You asked me to call when we finished phase one," he said.

"Yes, thank you. How is he doing?"

"So far, so good…his headache has subsided. There were no problems on any of the body system tests, and he took the world events video in stride. His biggest problem seems to be his appearance…especially his face. I told him you would explain it when you come down."

"Please tell him I will be down in a few minutes. Any flashbacks or recall issues yet?"

"No, and he's not showing any signs of dislocation or spontaneous hallucination."

"Excellent news! I'll be right there."

"Okay, I'll let him know."

Dr. Hao's face faded from the display as the call ended and Aubrey got up from her desk and headed for her private elevator. The news from Dr. Hao was very encouraging, but they weren't out of danger just yet.

One challenge with full body replacements was that a person's brain contains deeply ingrained memories of their original body—not just how it looked but how it worked. These memories are created by physical and chemical changes that occur in the brain throughout a person's lifetime. With every new experience, thousands of new connections are formed between the over one hundred billion neurons that make up the typical human brain. These networks of connections, called engrams, grow and evolve, becoming ever more complex. As a result, each person's brain is unique from birth and becomes more so as they age.

Please let him adapt! Aubrey thought as she began the descent to Sub-level Forty-six.

She had experience with patients who did not accept the transfer, and it was never pretty. Some experienced dislocation, like that of traumatic amputees, while others suffered debilitating hallucinations that lead to insanity. Overcoming these problems required lots of therapy and conditioning to retrain the brain, but even then, there was no guarantee of success.

These were but a few reasons the GFN had banned full-body replacements. That and the fact that several of Telogene's less scrupulous competitors had attempted to clone long-deceased tyrants. Rumors circulated claiming that a German scientist had restored Adolf Hitler. The public outrage was immense.

Aubrey's mother was running the company then, and she refused to allow anyone to use Telogene's technology for that purpose, but that didn't stop a rogue Telogene scientist from trying to clone former President John Fitzgerald Kennedy. They destroyed those clones, along with the source genetic material used to create them. But the GFN remained vigilant and spared no expense tracking down and prosecuting those who violated the ban.

Aubrey and her dedicated team of scientists had just committed that same crime by restoring Evan Feldman.

Although he did not pose the same threat to society as Hitler or Stalin might, the ban made no distinction between resurrecting good people or bad people. Bringing someone back from the dead was illegal regardless of the legacy of the person being revived or the motivations of those performing the restoration. Aubrey and her team gladly took the risk though—the stakes were just that high.

Aubrey exited the elevator and made her way to the recovery area. The recovery area was a suite of small apartments that provided a controlled environment for monitoring patients and helping them adjust to their new bodies.

The company had learned long ago that it couldn't just thrust the newly restored back into society, especially after an extended period of non-existence. It had to give them time to process everything that had changed since their death, and to adjust to their new reality. It was also prudent to keep them under observation until they showed that they were not a danger to themselves or others.

Aubrey placed her hand on the DNA scanner. It flashed green and the door to her grandfather's apartment slid open.

God, I wish Mom was here to help me with this.

Aubrey entered the small, sparsely decorated studio apartment and saw her grandfather sitting in front of a holoterminal. She saw an image of her mother on the display, and she immediately recognized it as the speech Lily had given at the GFN's tenth anniversary. The year was 2052 and Lily was sixty-seven, but she didn't appear a day over forty.

This should be interesting.

"How are you doing, Papa?" she asked.

Evan waived his hand to pause the video and turned to face Aubrey.

"I am fine, thank you," he said. "The real question is, what are you doing?"

"I didn't mean for you to see that just yet," Aubrey said with an exasperated look on her face. "Where is Dr. Hao?"

"He's in the bathroom." Evan stood up and put his hands on Aubrey's shoulders. "Now, please answer my question."

Aubrey removed her grandfather's hands from her shoulders, took a small step back and, still holding his right hand, gestured toward the sofa.

"Come on, Papa, let's sit. I know this is upsetting, but please give me some time to explain. I promise I'll tell you everything." This conversation would be far more uncomfortable than she'd hoped.

Evan pulled his hand away and crossed his arms in an obvious sign of refusal. "I have been sitting since lunch. Please, Aubrey, no games. Tell me what's going on."

The bathroom door hissed open and Dr. Hao stepped into the room. "I am sorry, Dr. Harris, nature called."

"I see you have given him access to the corporate archives already," Aubrey said with a clear note of displeasure in her voice.

Dr. Hao glanced at the frozen image of Lily on the holodisplay. "Ah, well, yes. He is doing well and was keen to learn about his daughter. I'm sorry if I have caused a problem."

"There is no problem, Dr. Hao," Evan interrupted. "I would find out, eventually."

Aubrey nodded in agreement. "There is no problem. I just wish we could have talked first."

She took a seat on the sofa. "Dr. Hao, will you please excuse us for a few minutes?"

"I will be in my office," the Chief Cryonicist gave her a deferential nod as he exited the room.

Aubrey gently patted the cushion next to her. "Come sit next to me, Papa. Please?"

Evan dropped his arms and rolled his eyes as he begrudgingly complied with her request. "Okay, I'm sitting again. Now what?"

Aubrey reached over and took hold of his hand. "Now we talk and get to know each other. I am sure you have lots of questions."

"I sure do…but I don't even know where to begin. I guess for starters you can tell me how long you're going to keep me locked in this room?"

"You're not a prisoner, Papa. They lock the door to keep others out, not to keep you in."

"Then how come I can't go outside?"

"You can just as soon as you finish your orientation. You're adapting well, but you still need time to acclimate. And we need time to be sure that your brain and body are working as they should."

"And how long will that take?"

"Well, it depends on you," she answered. "Usually a week or two... sometimes longer."

"Are you telling me I am stuck here with the good Dr. Hao for at least another week?"

"Not just Dr. Hao. Drs.Berkovic and Walker will also work with you."

"I don't know if I can stay cooped up in this little room for a week."

"You won't just be in this room. There is an exercise room next door, and a rec room just down the hall. You can do this, Papa!"

Aubrey tapped the large, white plastic bracelet she wore on her left wrist, causing a holographic image to appear in the air above her arm. Evan stared in fascination as Aubrey used her free hand to gesture and poke at the floating display, which he guessed to be a control panel of some sort. The image disappeared after several furtive swipes and pokes.

"There," Aubrey said, "look at the wall behind you."

The previously bare white wall disappeared. In its place was a park-like forest with tall, leafy trees and a narrow stream cascading over jumbled boulders.

Evan stood up and crossed the short distance to where the wall had been. A soft breeze caressed his face and the odors of damp earth and grass filled his nose. The sounds of water rushing over rocks and leaves rustling on trees echoed in the background. He put his hand out to see if the wall was still there—it was. The image flickered slightly as his hand brushed against the wall.

"Th...that's amazing," he said.

"Yeah, it's pretty cool. You can control it from your holoterminal, and there are lots of scenes to choose from."

"It's like I am standing there...I can even smell the grass."

"It's but one of many technological advances made over the last fifty years."

"Okay, I guess I don't have to worry about dying of boredom." Evan turned to face her. "Now, tell me why I am not in my body."

"Well, that's complicated. We came as close as we could with what we had to work with. We debated plastic surgery but decided against it."

"What happened to the body I put in cryogenic suspension? You had to have at least some original genetic material to work with if you still had my brain."

"We didn't."

"You didn't what?"

"We didn't have any of your genetic material."

"How can that be? This is my brain, isn't it?"

Aubrey inhaled deeply. "No, Papa, it's not your brain, and that's not your body. The New Madrid quake of 2037 was massive. We lost our primary cryogenic storage facility outside of Kansas City, and the company headquarters."

"Then how am I here?" Evan said, with equal parts confusion and fear in his voice.

"Because before that happened, we figured out how to digitize your engrams, and we stored those in multiple locations around the world for safekeeping."

"You mean you made a copy of my brain and stored it in a computer?" Evan asked incredulously.

"Kind of, but that's also a long story. The short version is that we invented a carbon-based organic storage medium that replicates the function and capacity of the human brain. We still can't achieve the density and efficiency of the brain, but we're pretty darn close. Our storage technology has replaced silicon memory chips and hard drives in computers—it was the product that earned us our first trillion dollars. Even today, organic storage still represents over forty percent of our annual revenue."

Evan was stunned. Not only was he not in his own body but he wasn't even thinking with his own brain! He had envisioned the possibility of memory transference when he had himself cryogenically frozen, but he had always assumed that the technology would involve transferring a person's memories into a clone of their own brain and body. His vision had been to replace diseased brain tissue with healthy brain tissue while preserving memories, not putting one person's memories in another person's brain!

"So, is my brain this organic storage stuff you are talking about?"

"No, of course not. You are one hundred percent human."

Evan paused for a moment as he considered what he'd learned. It comforted him to know that he was human, even if he wasn't inside his own body. His mind shifted to a question that had been roiling inside his mind for hours.

"Where is Christina?" he asked about his wife.

Her untimely death was the reason he had started down this path, and he had to know where she was. Surely, they wouldn't revive him without her!

Aubrey had expected this, but she struggled to answer. "Um, well, I don't know exactly how to say this…"

"Oh, just tell me for fuck's sake!" Evan raised his voice almost to a yell.

His sudden change in demeanor surprised her, but she remained calm.

"She's gone, Papa. It took too long to recover her body from the crash site. I'm sorry."

He slumped into the couch and his face contorted with the pain of profound loss.

"No, no, no," he said, covering his face with his hands. "That cannot be. What about the memory transfer thing, did you at least try that on her?"

"Yes, but her engrams were too degraded. We tried and tried, but she was just too far beyond the reach of our technology."

Aubrey reached over to put her arms around him. "I'm so sorry. I wish I had better news, Papa, but please know that Mom and I tried really hard to bring grandma back."

Evan sat up and wiped his face. "And what about your mother? Where is she?"

Oh shit, now I've done it. Aubrey realized she had said too much.

"Papa, I need you to listen to me. We've already gone too far in this conversation and I need you to focus on acclimating to your new body. You probably feel fine now, but I know from experience that will not last.

The next couple of weeks will be hard on you, and I need you to focus on getting through the acclimation period. Can we please talk more about this later?"

"I need to know if she's alive or not."

Aubrey looked him in the eyes and slowly shook her head from side to side. "No, Papa. I'm sorry, but she's not with us anymore."

She leaned forward and wrapped her arms around him in a tight embrace.

"It's just us, we're all that's left," she whispered. "And I really need you."

Evan stood up, pulling her up with him. He stood a full six inches taller than her, and she had to look up to meet his stare.

"I appreciate that, Aubrey," he said calmly. "But I need to know what happened to my daughter. Don't let me find out some other way, please tell me."

Aubrey took a deep breath, and tears welled up in her eyes. "It was a…it was a plane crash…last year."

Evan looked like someone had just punched him in the gut. He wanted to comfort his granddaughter but he couldn't think of the right words. He couldn't believe both his wife and daughter had died in a plane crash. What were the odds?

"I can't believe it…is Lily in storage somewhere? Can you restore her?" he asked.

Aubrey took a minute to consider how best to respond before answering. "Yes, we have her last engramic archive from the day before the crash, but she made me promise not to restore her."

"Why would she do that? That makes no sense."

Aubrey wiped the tears from her cheeks with the back of her hands. "It will once you learn more about her. And it's illegal, so we couldn't do it even if we wanted to."

"Yeah, I read something about it in the archives. The government banned full body clones decades ago. But being illegal didn't stop you from bringing me back."

"No, but that's different."

"How so?"

"For one, you're not registered in any GFN system. So as far as anyone knows, you don't exist…at least not as Evan Feldman."

"And?"

"And, by bringing you back, I'm fulfilling the promise you asked of Mom."

"What promise? I didn't make her promise me anything. That's absurd."

"You don't remember but, trust me, you did. You left her a video. You recorded it a year before you died, and you asked her to do everything she could to bring you and grandma back," Aubrey said.

"So that's it? You broke the law and brought me back just to fulfill a promise?"

"That's one reason."

"But…"

"No, now is not the time." Aubrey pulled against his grip on her, a look of grim determination replacing the sadness of a moment ago. He relaxed slightly but did not release her.

"Please be patient, Papa," she implored. "I need you to trust me."

Evan pulled her into a tight embrace, locking his arms behind her shoulders. He kissed her cheek several times and stroked the back of her hair with his hand.

"I'm sorry, Princess, it's just a lot to take in. I wish Lily and Christina were here, but I am so happy to see you. I love you more than anything, you know that."

"I know, Papa, I love you too." She kissed him on the cheek and slumped against his chest.

They held each other for several minutes, both wanting to say something but neither able to find the right words.

"I need to go," Aubrey said as she gently slipped from his embrace. "I'll come back and check on you later, when you are ready for bed."

"I would like that."

Aubrey tapped the communicator implanted behind her right ear. "Dr. Hao, will you please return to Recovery Room One?"

"On my way," he responded.

"He's on his way down," Aubrey said to her grandfather.

Evan stood and walked Aubrey to the door. "Okay, I'll see you later."

Aubrey kissed him on the cheek again. "See you later."

Aubrey left the room and headed toward the elevator that Dr. Hao would be using. A few minutes passed before the elevator door slid open and he stepped out into the hallway.

"How did it go?" he asked.

"As expected, he's as inquisitive as ever."

"I am sorry for giving him premature access to the archives. I just thought I'd try a different approach this time."

"No need to apologize, Chen. Do what you think is best, just get him ready to travel."

"You think thirty-six hours will be enough?"

"It will have to be, won't it?"

He shrugged. "I suppose it will."

FIVE

Aubrey returned to her office and spent the rest of the afternoon reviewing the lung enhancement protocol. It looked promising, but she thought they needed to move faster. She called the lead researcher and gave him approval to begin clinical trials on primates.

Unlike the past, when researchers had to rely on animals captured from the wild or bred in captivity for their lab specimens, Telogene's scientist could clone test subjects on demand. The company had achieved complete mastery over the genomes of these animals and could alter them at will during the growth process. Need an animal that can't feel pain? No problem. Do you prefer your test subjects without teeth or claws? No problem. Don't want to deal with fur all over your lab? No problem!

Once the research was complete, all genetically modified creatures were destroyed to avoid any chance of escape and interbreeding in the wild. Although animal rights activists had protested mightily in the early days, nobody seemed to give it much thought anymore. Most people had just accepted it as the cost of progress. Besides, these weren't *real* animals produced by nature—they were organic tools that the company created, altered, and destroyed at will.

Aubrey felt a little pang of remorse every time she saw one of her company's creations used for research. It was why she usually avoided using live animals but, in this case, it was unavoidable. There just wasn't any other way to validate the effectiveness of the genetic modifications without measuring their impact on a living, breathing creature.

Aubrey's holoterminal chimed and Evelyn appeared on the screen. "I'm sorry to interrupt, Dr. Harris, but Secretary General Merkel is asking to speak with you."

The Global Standards and Safety Administration was an independent agency responsible for ensuring that multinational companies, like Telogene, adhered to all global treaties, rules, regulations, and policies. Dianne Merkel was the head of that agency and getting a call from her was never a good thing—especially not on a day like today.

"Put her through; let's see what she has to say."

A second later the image of a forty-something woman with short brown hair appeared on the holodisplay.

"Hello, Ms. Merkel, what can I do for you today?"

"Good evening, Dr. Harris, it's good to see you again," the woman said with a mild German accent. "I am sorry to bother you, but we have had some very disturbing reports coming in from our Overwatch team. I wanted to talk to you in person before anyone overreacts."

Overwatch was the group inside the GSSA that monitored corporate activity across the globe. Its agents were international spies with the power to monitor the business and personal communications of every person on the planet. Their mandate gave them tremendous latitude in their surveillance and crime prevention roles. They even had covert agents embedded inside of the major corporations—including Telogene.

Aubrey had been careful to cover her tracks with Evan's restoration, but receiving this call meant she had missed something.

Aubrey didn't flinch. "Well, I certainly appreciate that. What exactly is so disturbing that warranted this call?"

Dianne Merkel smiled. "I'll get straight to the point then, Dr. Harris. Why did you access your grandfather's engramic archive?"

How did they find out so fast? Aubrey didn't allow her shock to register on her face. "I am not sure I understand, Ms. Merkel. What do you mean by *access?*"

"Okay, let me be more specific. Why did you transfer Evan Feldman's engrams from your storage facility in Xi'an, China to your labs there in Lead, South Dakota?"

Shit, they are on their way here right now!

This time, Aubrey allowed her concern to show.

"I'm sorry, Ms. Merkel, but that is a serious allegation. I'm not sure what to say."

"Yes, it is quite serious. And that's why I am calling you. You and I have known each other for a long time, Aubrey, and I will give you one chance to come clean. One chance…do you understand?"

"I understand what you are saying, but I don't think I fully understand what you are suggesting."

"Yes, you do, Aubrey. Did you restore your grandfather? Tell me the truth now, and I can help you. Lie to me and well… you know the consequences for violating the HDDA."

The Human Dignity and Decency Act (HDDA) was the global law that banned cloning. Passed in 2055, the intent of the act was to protect humanity from rampant abuse of genetic manipulation and cloning technologies, and to ensure their responsible use. It made it illegal to restore a deceased person to life, or to extend a person's life beyond 150 years. Penalties for violating the act ranged from large fines and asset seizure to imprisonment or banishment to a mining colony. As harsh as these penalties were, they didn't stop people from breaking the law. Since the law's passage, the GFN had tried and convicted thousands for excessive life extension, and hundreds for illegal cloning and restoration.

Although Aubrey had thought about moving to Luna or Mars a few years back, the idea of working in a dirty mine for the next quarter of a century was not appealing.

"I'm aware of that legislation Ms. Merkel. My mother was part of the committee that wrote it."

Aubrey threw out that last tidbit for effect. She knew Dianne knew that her mother had been on that committee, but she wanted to remind her, anyway.

She continued. "I did not order the transfer of my grandfather's engrams." This wasn't a lie in the strictest sense because Chen had ordered the transfer. "But, as you know, we are amid a significant crisis here and we are working hard to find a solution. That means exploring every legal avenue available to us. *Including* accessing archived engrams, analyzing stored genetic material, and testing new genetic algorithms and therapies that we hope will reverse the current situation before we reach the point of no return."

That should buy me some time.

"I remember that Lily was on that committee. In fact, you may recall that I was a GFN lawyer at the time and we met frequently." Secretary Merkel leaned back in her large black leather chair and put her fingertips together below her chin. "So, your position is that you have no knowledge of your grandfather's engrams being transferred. Is that correct?"

When Aubrey didn't respond immediately, she added, "Is there someone you need to check with?"

She's throwing me a lifeline. She has me dead to rights, but she is giving me a way out. Why?

Aubrey tapped on the virtual keyboard projected onto her desk by her holoterminal. "Yes, thank you. Let me make some inquiries and get back to you." She calculated the time difference to Zurich. "It must be after midnight there. Would one hour be acceptable?"

"Yes, one hour will be fine. I will await your call."

Aubrey stopped typing and leaned back in her chair. "Okay, one hour then. And thank you, Dianne, for bringing this to my attention personally."

Showing her a little gratitude can't hurt!

"You're most welcome. It's the least I could do."

"Goodbye, I'll talk to you in an hour."

"One hour, Aubrey and not a minute more. Understood?"

That's a warning. I probably have less than that before her agents are banging on my door.

"Yes, perfectly. Thank you again."

"Goodbye, Aubrey."

The holodisplay faded. A few seconds later, Evelyn came through the office door.

"I'm in trouble, I need your help," Aubrey said.

* * *

"Is everything underway?" Aubrey asked as she gathered some of her personal things from around her office.

Her original plan had been to move Evan to a secret location as soon as he was stable enough to travel. But that was no longer possible; she couldn't take the risk that the GSSA would find him. They would destroy Evan if they caught him, and she would go to jail. He wouldn't even get a hearing—an illegal clone has no rights under the HDDA. A simple genetic test would reveal his status as an undocumented clone, and they would terminate him on the spot.

The unexpected phone call had forced her to push her timeline up by more than a day and a half, and Evelyn had spent the last fifteen minutes helping to make that happen. Fortunately, they had a pre-arranged contingency plan in place for just such an occurrence.

"Yes, your jet is being readied now," Evelyn answered. "The GSSA isn't here yet, or at least it hasn't announced itself. The lab and recovery rooms are being scrubbed as we speak, and I have wiped all records related to your activities over the past twenty-four hours."

"Dr. Hao gave the test subject access to the corporate archives. Please make sure you purge his access credentials and activity logs."

Aubrey trusted Evelyn, but not with everything. She hadn't told her that the *test subject* was her grandfather. All Evelyn knew was that Aubrey had allowed the restoration of an important scientist that had once worked for Telogene.

"Understood," Evelyn acknowledged. "Where should I say you are when they ask?"

43

"Tell them I went to talk to someone in Neural Analytics to find out what's going on. It's a big facility; run them around for as long as you can."

"Not a problem, I am sure I can keep them busy for at least an hour." Evelyn gave Aubrey a sly smile.

"Thank you, Evelyn. I will never forget this. You are a great friend and I couldn't do any of this without you." Aubrey gave Evelyn a hug and patted her gently on the back.

"You're welcome, Aubrey." Evelyn figured now was not the time for formalities. "You stay safe and focus on what you need to do. I will take care of things here."

"I know you will."

Aubrey reached into her handbag and pulled out a small black case. Inside the case was a silver data cube. She handed it to Evelyn.

"This has everything you need if things go bad; it's encrypted with your DNA signature. To anyone but you, it's just a bunch of unclassified research files."

Evelyn took the case and slid it into the inside pocket of her blazer. "Things won't go bad. At least not as long as you are not here when they arrive. Now go!" She pointed toward Aubrey's private elevator. "I will recall the elevator and wipe the access log."

God, she's good.

Aubrey had long admired Evelyn, but today she was going well beyond the call of duty of a loyal employee. They had worked together for nearly a decade, and Aubrey considered her to be a friend—one of a small group of people she trusted implicitly.

A tear rolled down Aubrey's cheek. "I love you, Ev, please be careful."

"I love you too. Now get out of here before they show up."

Aubrey entered her elevator and specified her destination as sub-level five. That level was mostly storage, and it was unlikely that she would run into anyone she didn't want to see. An old mining tunnel exited that level and ran nearly a kilometer to the other side of the complex. From there, it was just a few hundred yards to the landing pad where she would meet up with the others and catch her ride out of here.

She exited the elevator to find herself in a large, rough-hewn cavern—a remnant of the old gold mine. It was relatively small and close to the surface, so they had relegated it to serving as storage for old equipment. Aubrey crossed the dimly lit cavern to the tunnel entrance.

The normally locked, steel gate was open and a brand new hoverbike was waiting just on the other side. The hoverbike looked like an old-style motorcycle with a two-foot wide inflatable skirt around the bottom instead of wheels. Aubrey had it parked here a few days ago just in case she needed to make a quick escape.

Aubrey slung her bag over her shoulder and slid her leg across the seat. She pushed the start icon on the handlebar-mounted console and the bike hummed to life. The skirt inflated, and the bike rose about a foot off the floor on a cushion of air. Aubrey turned on the headlights and pressed the accelerator knob with her right thumb. The bike leapt forward.

The tunnel was about three meters wide and a straight shot to the surface. She jammed the accelerator all the way forward. Her hoverbike gained speed rapidly, and it took just minutes to reach the surface. An exterior gate had been "accidentally" left open.

Thank you, Ev! Aubrey pointed the bike toward the landing pad and accelerated hard.

She slowed as she approached the aircraft, stopping just under the tail. She got off the bike and walked to the left side of the plane where the access ramp was down and waiting for her arrival. The engines were idling, but it surprised her that nobody was waiting at the top of the ramp to greet her.

They must be on board, she thought.

The aircraft was a Gulfstream G1450 supersonic jet airplane capable of vertical takeoff and landing. It looked like a cross between an early twenty-first-century business jet and a helicopter. It had two jet engines mounted on the tail, and two large turbofans underneath the retractable wings. The rear engines could rotate a full one hundred and eighty degrees, allowing the pilot to direct his considerable thrust down, forward or to the rear of the craft.

With all four engines turning at top speed, the craft could travel at almost 2,500 kilometers per hour, or more than twice the speed of sound. Very convenient transportation for the wealthy businessperson who wanted to get somewhere in a hurry!

She walked up the ramp, looking behind her as she went. There were a few people walking to their personal transports in the nearby parking lot, and a few more milling about the hangar, but nobody seemed to pay any attention to her.

She climbed the top stair and ducked through the open doorway. "Okay, lets g—"

The last word stuck in her throat. There were three people sitting in the cabin—none of whom she expected to see. A woman sitting in Aubrey's seat swiveled the chair around to look at her. Aubrey's heart skipped a beat and her words stuck in her throat. It was Dianne Merkel.

"No, Aubrey, everything is not *okay*," Dianne said with a cold scowl.

Aubrey heard movement behind her and felt a sudden sharp pinch on her neck. She felt lightheaded, and her vision faded. Her legs crumbled beneath her, but the man who had just injected her caught her before she crashed to the floor. The General Secretary loomed above—her stern, disapproving eyes following Aubrey into the darkness.

Six

Evan Feldman glanced out the window of the Gulfstream G1450, a twin of the one Aubrey had planned to make her escape in, as it roared west across the Pacific Ocean at almost twice the speed of sound. It was after seven p.m. in Zurich, the home of the global standard time system, but here the morning sun was still rising in the sky behind them. They were barely 100 meters above the water and, to Evan, it seemed like a tall wave might sweep over the jet's wings at any minute. Looking out the window for too long made him nauseous, so he closed the shade and turned his attention back to the holoterminal mounted on his armrest.

He worried about Aubrey. Dr. Hao had tried to reassure him, but their departure from Telogene's research facility had been unplanned and somewhat chaotic.

Evan had just sat down for dinner when Drs. Berkovic and Walker burst into his apartment. They pulled Dr. Hao out into the hallway for several minutes before returning with worried looks on their faces. The Chief Cryonicist told the other two to go on without them, and they would catch up. He asked Evan to change into a blue jumpsuit while he worked on Evan's holoterminal. It looked to Evan like he was locking the terminal down or deleting files—or both. After changing clothes, Dr. Hao led Evan down the hallway to a bank of elevators that took them to the ground floor lobby.

Once outside, they had hurried across the parking lot to the doctor's car. Vehicles of all shapes and sizes filled the parking lot. Chen's hovercar was a silver, minivan-sized, tube-shaped vehicle with turbofans instead of wheels. The front and rear doors slid open to reveal a luxuriously appointed cabin equipped with a black leather sofa and four black leather captain's chairs. Each seat had its own flip-up, mahogany drink table and holodisplay. Evan found the whole idea of a car without wheels somewhat disconcerting, but he got in anyway.

The entrance to the expressway was just a few minutes from Telogene's headquarters, and from there it had taken them only another ten minutes to the airport. When they arrived, Dr. Hao drove through a private security gate and into a large hangar. They parked next to the hoverjet, and the doctor told Evan to get on board. Dr. Hao boarded a few minutes later and surprised Evan by sitting in the pilot's seat. He reassured Evan that he had been a Chinese Airforce pilot during the last war and had been an avid private pilot ever since.

They taxied quickly to the runway and, less than thirty minutes after leaving Telogene, they were airborne and flying west across Wyoming. Thirty minutes later, they were just south of Seattle and starting their five and a half-hour flight across the Pacific Ocean to China. They flew close to the ground the entire time, dropping even lower after they crossed the coastline. Dr. Hao said something about flying "nap of the Earth" and "avoiding being tracked by ground sensors".

Evan used the flight time to catch up on world events. Dr. Hao had just given him access to another set of historical archives before their unexpected departure, and he was curious to see what new information they might contain. He activated the holodisplay, and a 20" wide by 16" tall virtual display screen appeared in the air two feet in front of him. He selected the first archive and told the holoterminal to display all content. A video documentary titled *Long Term Impact of the 2027 Famine* started to play.

The first of several global famines began two years after the 2025 financial crisis. The proliferation of genetically modified seed had caused farmers to become dependent on the large, multinational agribusiness that produced the seed stock—Telogene among them. The seeds wouldn't reproduce on their own and farmers had to buy new seed every year—a very profitable arrangement for the seed producers. Eventually, hyperinflation caused the genetically modified seed to become so expensive that nobody could afford to buy it. Millions of acres went unplanted.

Five years into the crisis, global food production dropped by over fifty percent, and within ten years it was down over eighty percent. The world's inability to produce adequate grain supplies led to massive shortages of livestock feed, which resulted in the loss of billions of pigs, goats, sheep, cows, and chickens. The situation got so bad that incidents of human cannibalism became too many to count, and more than a billion people died of starvation and disease.

Thankfully, a few enterprising governments and individuals had the foresight to stockpile large caches of unmodified seeds. The largest of these was the Svalbard Global Seed Vault in Norway.

The Norwegian government created the seed stockpile in 2008, and accumulated over two billion unique seed samples from around the world in the subsequent decades. Although the Svalbard facility was the world's largest seed repository, it had nowhere near enough to supply global demand—but that's where Telogene came in.

Thousands of researchers had requested samples from Svalbard, hoping to discover a means of mass-producing economically viable seeds for the world's farmers. But Telogene's scientists perfected a method of cloning seeds that didn't require the comparatively long germination times of other methods.

Rather than seeking a patent for its seed cloning process, Telogene gave it away for free. Within two years, global seed production surpassed one trillion seeds a day, and Telogene went from being hated and despised for its role in helping create the famine to revered as the planet's savior. Three years later, the world was once again producing adequate supplies of food for its diminished population, and the famine was over.

One year after later, the nations of the world set aside their differences and formed the Global Federation of Nations. Since the end of the twentieth century, the world had endured extreme climate change, devasting financial crises, and conflict. It couldn't withstand the global outbreak of famine and disease that swept across the planet. It took over three billion deaths and a mass extinction on a scale not seen since the Cretaceous period, but the nations of the world finally realized that humanity's survival depended on their ability to work together.

The GFN's first official act was to ban the creation of genetically modified plants and animals. Although popular at first, it soon became clear that the conditions that encouraged genetic manipulation, like drought, blight, and insects, were still problems. After just two years, the GFN revised the law to allow for "minor" genetic enhancements of seed and livestock. This opened the door for companies to create genetically modified seed stock again, but the law still prohibited them from creating crops that could reproduce on their own. That prohibition would have dire consequences later.

The problem with allowing genetically modified crops to reproduce is that they can cross-pollinate with compatible species—both domesticated and wild. Cross-pollination was mostly a good thing (like rice that required less water and yielded two to three times more grains per acre than any previous breed), but there were also occasions when certain undesirable traits would appear (like unusual smell, color or taste or lower than expected crop yield). When that happened, the only option was to destroy those crops to prevent them from spreading. Unfortunately, that didn't always work to prevent the spread of undesirable strains and, by 2050, it had become clear that preventing unwanted hybridization would be an ongoing challenge.

It was these consequences and the fear of what might come next that prompted Lily Harris to give her speech against cloning and genetic manipulation of the food supply to the Global Federation of Nations in 2052. Given her role as Telogene's CEO, it was a brave (although some would say stupid) thing for her to do. Her company's stock had taken decades to return to its previous highs from before the famine, and Lily's speech slashed it in half almost overnight. It would take another decade for it to recover once again.

Lily's warning went largely unheeded, and the GFN did not ban cloning or genetic manipulation of the world's agricultural food sources and livestock. It did, however, place limits on genetic manipulation and cloning of humans—including an outright ban on full-body replacements—when it passed the Human Dignity and Decency Act of 2055.

But the famine and its aftermath were not the worst plagues to affect humanity. A new, even more devastating crisis began on January 4, 2063, when scientists discovered that a significant portion of the population could not conceive children by any known means—including in-vitro fertilization. Although birthrates in some regions had increased slightly since the famine, the global birthrate was nowhere near high enough to offset the rate at which people were dying.

Many people viewed cloning as the only way to save humanity, and protests against the HDDA erupted all over the world. In response, the GFN considered amending the HDDA to allow cloning for reproductive purposes, but the sudden appearance of random genetic mutations caused it to abandon that effort.

The first case of genetic mutation occurred in Rio de Janeiro in June 2064. A girl of Portuguese decent had been born with mottled green skin and golden eyes with vertical slits for pupils—similar to those of alligators and other reptiles. Shortly thereafter, the number of random genetic mutations in newborns spiked worldwide. It was almost as if all of humanity had become infected by some unknown, highly virulent virus.

At first, the scientific community thought fertility treatments or genetic enhancement therapies were to blame. But, although they had likely played a role, the real culprit turned out to be the food supply. Humans had been consuming genetically modified crops and meat products for over six decades, and many scientists believed that long-term exposure to GMOs had activated otherwise dormant genes. The recent outbreak of mutations was the result.

The situation grew progressively worse after that first case in Rio. People were afraid to have children, and birthrates declined rapidly. Even more devastating, scientists discovered that most of the people born in the last thirty years were sterile. Of the few children born, six in ten had some kind of a genetic defect, and the rest died within their first year.

The last normal, healthy child was born in August 2069 to a couple in Japan.

Evan turned off the holodisplay; he'd seen enough.

My God, what have we done?

SEVEN

Aubrey woke up in a dimly lit room with a splitting headache. The room was three meters square with white walls, floor, and ceiling. There were no decorations, and it was sparsely furnished with a small table and two chairs, a sink, a toilet, and the cot-sized bed she was lying on. There were no windows and only one door, which was closed.

Oh God, I'm in a cell.

She tried to stand up, but it took a minute of sitting on the edge of the bed before she felt stable enough to try. Once up, she stumbled the few steps to the table and sat down in the chair. In front of her was a glass of water, a spoon, and a packet containing a white powdery substance. There was no label, but Aubrey assumed the powder was a protein supplement of some kind. Her mouth was dry, and she was ravenous since she hadn't eaten since breakfast.

Was that yesterday?

"Date and time?" She asked the personal communicator implanted behind her right ear.

No response.

Aubrey rubbed her fingers over her skin to confirm that it was still there. It was, but her jewelry was missing, and she wore a white jumpsuit instead of her designer skirt and blazer. To make matters worse, they had replaced her expensive black pumps with white slippers.

Oh shit, this is bad.

She toggled her communicator off and then on again, but the device did not respond.

Damn, she swore to herself. *They must have disabled it.*

Aubrey gulped down the glass of water and then took the empty glass with the spoon and the packet of powder over to the sink and refilled it from the tap. One good stir and the powder dissolved. She sniffed it—it smelled like strawberry—and then gulped that down too.

Yep, strawberry-flavored protein shake. I hate these things!

She refilled the glass one more time, drank about half of it, and then set the glass down on the small counter next to the sink.

Okay, let's review the situation. Dianne Merkel set a trap for me, and I walked right into it. I am now in a cell God-knows-where and have no way to communicate with the outside world.

Just for good measure, she tried opening the door.

Locked…what a surprise.

Her headache was fading, and she was no longer dizzy. She scanned the room again and confirmed there was nothing else in it except for two little black domes mounted in opposite corners of the ceiling.

Cameras, they are watching everything I do.

Aubrey sat in the chair facing the door and tried to relax. She didn't have to wait long; only a few minutes passed before the door opened. Dianne Merkel stood there with two men dressed in black suits.

"Wait here," Dianne said as she entered the room.

The door hissed shut behind her.

"Oh, Aubrey," she said, "what a mess you've made. I gave you a chance to come clean, but you decided on the hard way instead. May I?" Dianne sat in the chair across from Aubrey without waiting for a response.

"Where am I?" Aubrey asked.

"You, my dear, are in a holding cell at GSSA Headquarters in Zurich."

"On what charge?"

"Violating the HDDA. I am sure your motives were honorable. But you broke the law, Aubrey."

"That's a bold statement," Aubrey said. "What proof do you have?"

"Let's just say that I have everything I need to make a case against you and your cohorts. Drs. Berkovic and Walker are in custody, and I have issued a warrant for Dr. Chen Hao. I assume that he has your grandfather with him?"

They don't have him. Way to go, Chen!

Aubrey made the most distraught look she could muster to mask her joy. "I don't understand what you are talking about."

"And so, the lies continue." Dianne looked disappointed.

"I also have this." The Secretary General placed a small silver cube on the table in front of Aubrey.

Damn, they must have grabbed Evelyn.

"And what is that?" Aubrey asked coolly.

"That is the data cube you gave Evelyn; we've already retrieved its contents. We're also seizing your assets, including those you transferred to Evelyn."

Fuck!

"We have also frozen your shares of Telogene and have suspended your voting rights pending the outcome of your trial." Dianne waited a few seconds for her last statement to sink in before she continued.

"Now, as a gesture of goodwill, I would like to give you one more chance to tell the truth. Where is Hao taking Feldman?"

There is no way I am giving them up. They don't have proof until they have Papa.

"As I said before, I appreciate your good will, but I can't give you information I don't have. Are you sure that this isn't a big misunderstanding? Isn't it possible that someone accessed my grandfather's engrams but that no cloning took place?"

Aubrey paused for a response, but all she got back was a disapproving glare.

"Regardless," she continued, "I am not saying anything else until I speak with my attorney, Geoffrey Wagner. I would also like to speak to Evelyn Wu at the earliest opportunity."

Dianne Merkel grimaced and stood up from her chair.

"Okay, Aubrey," she said, "we'll do it your way. Your attorney is already here, but Evelyn is busy and doesn't have time to take your call. You wouldn't want to hear what she has to say, anyway."

Dianne placed her hands on the back of her chair and leaned forward. "She works for me, Aubrey, and she has for a very long time."

That last statement pierced Aubrey like an arrow. Her face turned ghostly white, as if the last drop of blood had leaked from her body.

"Tha…that can't be."

"Oh yes, my dear, it can and is—Evelyn Wu is an Overwatch agent. I was thrilled when you promoted her after your mother died. I always knew you would need someone to keep you on the right path."

"But…I thought she was my friend."

"Oh, but she is. She has been a great friend to you, probably in more ways than you'll ever know. But she had a job to do…and this time you crossed the line one step too far."

Aubrey slumped in her chair. *Oh God, this can't be happening—it can't be true.*

Dianne took a few steps toward the door before turning back to face Aubrey.

"And one other thing. I lied to you earlier when I said I had met your mother just a few times—she and I were friends for over three decades. It breaks my heart to see you in this situation…just as I know that it would break hers. That is why I gave you every opportunity to make this right, Aubrey. I don't want to see your mother's legacy ruined any more than I want to see your career destroyed. I am trying to help you, but you have to help me first."

Dianne knocked twice on the door.

"Give that data cube to your lawyer so he can see what you gave us— it's unlocked and decrypted," she said as the door slid open. "You have until midnight tonight to give me Feldman and Hao. After that, I can no longer help you. Nor can I help you if they get caught before you turn them in."

Dianne stepped into the hallway.

"Think about it if you must…but think quickly," she added.

The door closed behind her with a hiss and a whir as the locks engaged.

Aubrey sat there for several long minutes considering her situation and the revelations that Secretary Merkel had just made.

Her mom and the Secretary General friends? She had known they knew each other, but she had never heard her mother call Dianne Merkel her *friend.*

And Evelyn Wu an Overwatch agent? If that was true, then why hadn't she informed on her before? This wasn't the first time Aubrey had pushed the boundaries of the HDDA.

I have to talk to Geoff.

She wasn't sure how much time passed while she waited, but it seemed like forever.

The cell door hissed opened.

Finally!

The two men in black suits escorted her down a long hallway to an elevator. It was a quick ride up to the 14th floor from the basement sub-level where they had been holding her. They exited the elevator and walked down another hallway to a big set of double doors. Inside was a large conference table surrounded by tall-backed, black leather chairs.

The wall opposite her was glass, and it perfectly framed the Zurich skyline outside. It was a bright, clear day, and she was happy to see the sun; especially since, until just a few minutes ago, she was unsure whether she would ever see it again. There were two sets of double doors, the one through which she had entered and another to her right at the other end of the room. Besides her and her well-dressed escorts, there was one other person in the room. She immediately recognized the strikingly handsome man with sandy brown hair sitting at the conference table. Geoff Wagner, Telogene's Chief Legal Counsel.

She didn't even know Geoff Wagner existed until he called to offer his condolences two weeks after the crash that killed her mother. They bonded immediately over their shared grief—his father, Bruce Wagner, had died in the same crash.

Like her, he was an only child (the product of Bruce's first marriage) and was well off financially. He was a corporate attorney and had gone to work for a boutique firm in Zurich immediately after earning his law degree. He didn't need to work; he had a substantial trust fund, but he had the same strong work ethic as his father. He also had a strong sense of justice, and he especially enjoyed helping those who lacked the knowledge or financial resources to help themselves.

After the plane crash, he and Aubrey spoke via video call almost every day for several weeks, and she found she enjoyed talking to him. Not only was he good-looking, he was also a good listener. And he had the same calm and consoling demeanor as his father. Aubrey offered him the Chief Legal Counsel job at Telogene almost on a whim, and it pleasantly surprised her when he accepted. Since then, they had become best friends. And if Aubrey had ever needed a best friend who was a lawyer, it was now.

Aubrey rushed to greet him. "Geoff! Oh God, I am so glad you're here!"

He stood up from his chair as she approached. She threw her arms around his neck and he returned the hug, lifting her slightly off the ground. After a few seconds, he let her down.

"It's good to see you, too. But Aubrey, you are in one heck of a mess here. Take a seat and tell me how this happened."

After a quick survey of the room, the black-suited escorts returned to the hallway and closed the door. Aubrey and Geoff sat down at the conference table. Geoff took a holocube from his briefcase and sat it on the table in front of him. A virtual display appeared in the air above the cube.

"I'm recording this, okay?"

Aubrey nodded. "Go ahead."

She glanced around the room looking for recording devices, even though she knew she would never see them if they were there.

"Do you think they're recording?" she asked.

"That's unlikely. That would violate attorney-client privilege, and they can't use anything you say to me in court. That said, it wouldn't hurt to be thoughtful about your statements. Understand?"

"Perfectly."

"Okay, so why don't you start from the beginning. Just assume that I know nothing."

Aubrey took a deep breath and then began her story. "Well, this all started last year when Mom died…"

She spent the next thirty minutes recapping her decision to bring back her grandfather.

They had been working on the global fertility and mutation problems for a decade with no success. It was possible that there was a flaw in the cloning process that was the basis for all genetic enhancement technologies. She believed that they were missing something, and she thought a new perspective might help. The only way to find a cure was to go back to the beginning—to the days when her grandfather, and others like him, were just beginning to understand the human genome.

She believed that her grandfather, a geneticist and pioneer in his field, might have first-hand knowledge of events and decisions long forgotten by modern scientists. In addition, his lack of exposure to the breakthroughs and scientific advancement of the last fifty years made him a true outsider, without bias toward long-accepted practices and methodologies.

"Think about it like this," she said. "You work every day within the boundaries of an international legal system that didn't even exist fifty years ago. If there was something fundamentally flawed with that system, who is more likely to see it—someone who has spent his entire life practicing law within the boundaries of the current system, or someone who is looking at it for the very first time?"

Geoff thought about it for a moment. "Well, I could argue that the insider is better able to find flaws in a system that he knows intimately… but I understand your point. Sometimes a fresh perspective can lead to a breakthrough."

"Exactly," Aubrey replied.

"But that still doesn't explain why you brought back your grandfather, Aubrey." Geoff could tell she was holding something back, and he needed to know what it was. "There must be dozens, maybe even hundreds, of scientists—living or dead—that are as smart and talented as your grandfather was in his day. Why not bring in one of them? Or heck, why not bring them all back and increase your odds?"

Aubrey leaned forward in her chair and flexed her index finger a few times to signal him to move closer. When their faces were just a few inches apart, she leaned forward and put her arms around his neck, pulling him even closer.

She put her lips to his ear and whispered. "We have assembled a team of the world's best geneticists and bio-engineers at a secret location, and Dr. Hao is taking my grandfather there now." Aubrey let that sink in for a second before continuing. "But, more than that, he's the only family I have left…and I need him."

Aubrey slowly removed her arms from around his neck and slid back in her chair.

"First things first," she said for the benefit of anyone who might be listening. "You need to get me out of here, so we can work on my defense."

Geoff swiveled his chair, and tapped out a few commands on a virtual keyboard. In addition to responding to voice commands and gestures, the holocube could project a keyboard on any flat surface. He reviewed the information on his display before turning back to Aubrey.

"I already requested an expedited arraignment," he said, "but they won't hear us until tomorrow. So, I am afraid that you will have to spend at least one more night in here."

The door at the end of the room opened, and one of the dark-suited men entered the room.

"Time's up," he said curtly. "Let's go."

Aubrey and Geoff both stood. Aubrey gave him a firm hug and a quick kiss on the cheek. "I appreciate that you came."

He took her hands in his and gently squeezed. "I will do everything I can to get you out of here."

"I know you will." She did her best to force a smile before turning toward the door.

She stopped and turned back toward Geoff after just a few steps. "One more thing," she added. "You'll need this, it's the data cube I gave Evelyn. They unlocked it."

Geoff took the cube from her and twirled it between his fingers. "What's on it?"

"My last instructions to Evelyn and updates on all current and pending initiatives at Telogene."

"And…" Geoff prodded.

"Nothing noteworthy, just a few housekeeping items in case I'm never heard from again."

Geoff scowled. "Well, that's a grim thought. Did you update your archive?"

It was common practice for corporate executives and senior government officials to maintain current, archival copies of their engrams. The HDDA provided limited exceptions for cases of accidental death or disability, so long as the individual was less than 150 years old and deemed important for the welfare of society. A high standard and a loophole for the wealthy elite that had caused much public debate over the years.

"Yes, and I created backups of all sensitive material in my possession… as required by the board and our business continuity plan."

Geoff raised an eyebrow. "How current?"

"April 2nd at 11:13 p.m."

"Hmm, I guess that will have to do."

"It was the best I could manage given the circumstances."

"Okay, I will look when I get back to my hotel. Take care of yourself until I can get you out of here."

"I will, and when you have a minute, will you please find out what's going on with Evelyn? I would like to talk to her, and please also check in on Leah and Tanessa?"

"Will do. I am scheduled to meet with Berkovic and Walker at 1:00, and I will try to get a meeting with Evelyn. You know she is an Overwatch agent, right?"

"Yes, Dianne told me…but I still want to talk to her if I can," Aubrey said as she moved toward the exit. "And thanks for getting here so quickly."

Geoff replied with a slight nod and a smile. He gathered up his things and headed for the door. Leah and Tanessa were being held in another building a few blocks away, and he had a little under an hour before he was to meet with them.

It's time to call in some favors, Geoff thought as he hurried toward the elevator.

As soon as he was well away from the GSSA building, he made his first call. The image of an attractive blond appeared on his retinal display.

"Alexei Dumanov, please," he asked politely.

"I'm sorry, Mr. Wagner, but you don't have an appointment," she replied with a heavy Ukrainian accent.

That was the downside of modern communications technology—everyone knows everything about you before they answer.

"I understand, would you please tell him that today is the day that the sun rises after midnight?"

The woman raised her eyebrows. "Just one moment, please," she said.

The image projected on Geoff's retina showed random nature scenes, and soft music played in his ear. He had requested a taxi during his elevator ride down to the lobby, and it pulled up to the curb in front of him. The door slid open, and Geoff climbed in, placing his palm on the DNA scanner mounted on the center console.

"Number Twelve GFN Plaza," he said to the driverless hovercar.

"It will take ten minutes to reach your destination, Mr. Wagner," the car replied in a pleasant female voice. "The fare will be ten Globals. Should I proceed?"

Global was the common name for the worldwide currency implemented by the GFN. Some countries, like the United States, still supported their own currencies, but Globals were used for all international trade. Every member nation had to accept Globals as legal tender within its territory. After Zurich became the capital of the GFN, the Swiss people voted to replace the Frank with the Global as a show of solidarity and commitment to the new government.

"Proceed," Geoff replied.

Money transferred, the autonomous vehicle left the curb and merged into traffic.

A minute later, a man in his late forties or early fifties appeared on Geoff's retinal display.

"What can I do for you, Mr. Wagner?" he asked, his accent even heavier than the woman who had first answered the call.

"Ah, Alex. It's good to see you, old friend. How are Svetlana and Mikka?" Geoff asked politely about Alexei's wife and son.

"They are well, thank you. Svetlana still loves shopping, and Mikka is enjoying his assignment on Mars…but of course, you already know that." A thin smile spread across his face. "Thank you for asking, but I am sure that this is not just a social call."

"No, it's not. Let's go secure." Geoff said before giving him the access code for his private encryption key.

A moment later, an icon appeared on his retinal display informing him they had a secure connection. Secure was a bit of a misnomer because all civilian encryption schemes included a built-in back door for easy access by law enforcement. But at least they would have to get a warrant if they wanted to hear Geoff's conversation—and that would take time.

"Now, what do you want?" Alexei said curtly.

"I need an extraction."

"Who is the target?"

"Aubrey Harris, CEO of Telogene."

"Current location?"

"GSSA headquarters in Switzerland."

"Is she in custody?"

"Yes."

"Of course she is," Alexei said with a note of disdain in his voice. "Destination?"

"Mars."

"Are you out of your fucking mind?" Alexei's Russian accent became noticeably more pronounced as he swore in frustration. "You have the nerve to call me out of the blue after all these years, and this is what you ask for? I am hanging up now. It was nice hearing from you; please don't be such a stranger."

"You owe me, Alex. Please don't make me remind you of just how much you owe me. I wouldn't call you if I had any other choice."

Alexei sat back in his chair and folded his arms across his chest. Several seconds passed before he said anything.

"So, there it is," he finally said.

"Yes, Alex, we both knew this day would come, and here it is. Please don't make it any harder than it needs to be. I am not asking you to go out of pocket on this; I will cover all your expenses. But I need you to do this, and please don't ask me anything you don't need to know. Understand?"

"Yes, I understand, but now you understand something—if I do this, then we are even. You will never call me again. I don't want to see you or hear from you ever again, are we clear?"

"Agreed. I will send you an address where you can retrieve the data file that will give you the pertinent details."

"What's the time frame?" Alexei asked.

"How quick can you have your team ready?"

"Twenty-four hours, maybe less."

"Perfect. The hearing is tomorrow at 3:00 p.m. I am not sure of the location yet but I will let you know. Assuming it goes against us, I want you ready to go on a minute's notice."

"Okay, Geoff, whatever you say. We'll be ready." Alexei paused. "That is what you are calling yourself these days, isn't it? Geoff?"

"Just be there, Alex. Don't make me regret saving your life."

"Don't worry, we will be there. Enjoy the rest of your day." Alexei ended the call.

Geoff leaned back into the plush leather seat and took a deep breath.

"It's going to be a long week," he said out loud.

The taxi's lifting fans hummed as it made its way through Zurich traffic.

EIGHT

Evan Feldman looked out the window of his hotel room on the fourteenth floor of the Xi'an Marriott. His room looked down on a narrow green space that divided his hotel from a nearby cluster of other tall buildings. The streets were crowded with throngs of people trying to get to wherever it was they were headed. Pedestrians scurried from one side of the street to the other in between signal changes, and cyclists (both pedal and motorized) jockeyed for position in their designated lanes.

From his vantage point, the scene looked surprisingly calm and orderly considering the sheer number of people involved. Every few minutes, a line of flying hovercars would zip by his window—a sight he didn't think he'd ever grow accustomed to seeing.

They had landed at the People's International Spaceport on the outskirts of Xi'an a little over fourteen hours ago. Prior to landing, Dr. Hao had informed him that his DNA belonged to one *James Evan Richardson*. Mr. Richardson was a Telogene researcher who worked at the company's Xi'an lab. His duties required him to make regular trips to Telogene's headquarters, which accounted for the friendly "Welcome back, Mr. Richardson" he had received from the customs agent.

It had been dark for several hours by the time they finally reached their hotel. Evan was exhausted from the day's events, but he stayed awake long enough to enjoy a late-night dinner in his room—steak and eggs, one of his perennial favorites. He slept soundly for a solid nine and a half hours, and he would have likely slept longer had his bladder not vigorously protested the amount of fluid it had stored.

When he awoke, he found that Dr. Hao had left him a message saying he had an errand to run and he would be back around noon. Since he had time to kill, Evan had ordered a heaping plate of pancakes and a pot of fresh-brewed coffee. He relished the slightly acidic flavor of his first cup of coffee before adding cream and sweetener. It had been a long time since he had enjoyed a morning coffee, and the cup in his hand was the last of the pot.

"What time is it?" he asked.

"It is 11:55 a.m. GST", an unseen female voice answered. Every room came with its own digital assistant—basically an artificially intelligent butler that attended to the guest's every need.

"What is the local time?" he asked.

"The current time is 11:55 a.m. Global Standard Time", the voice intoned.

Evan was struggling with the whole concept of Global Standard Time. He had grown up under the old Coordinated Universal Time (UTC) regime, where each region had its own localized time zone. That wasn't the case with GST, which was calibrated to a day in Zurich, Switzerland —the home of the Global Federation of Nations. He wasn't sure whether there was such a thing as local time anymore but, so far, he had seen no evidence that there was. Every time display he had seen had shown GST.

That meant that, in Xi'an (which had been six hours ahead of Zurich under the UTC system), the sun was just starting to set in the western sky and most people were ending their work day. He assumed that everyone must have adapted their lives to GST, or perhaps they had another system of local time that he just hadn't seen. Regardless, he preferred it when noon on the clock meant it was the middle of the day.

It's almost noon! He suddenly realized that Dr. Hao should have been back an hour ago.

He slipped out of the courtesy robe the hotel had provided and hopped in the sonic shower. The sonic shower worked by vibrating water at extremely high frequencies. The combination of ultrasonic sound waves and water quickly stripped the accumulated dirt and oils from his hair and skin—no soap necessary! It's biggest advantage over an all-water shower was a ninety percent reduction in the amount of water required.

It took him less than ten minutes to shower and dress. Unfortunately, the blue jumpsuit he had fled Telogene in was his only clothing option.

He walked two doors down the hall to Dr. Hao's room and knocked. There was no answer, so he continued down the hallway to the elevator and waited for it to open.

The door slid open to reveal Dr. Hao standing inside.

"Chen, you're late! I was worried," Evan said. He had decided they would be on a first-name basis going forward since they were now both fugitives from justice.

"Good, you're ready. Let's go," the doctor replied. He grabbed Evan by the elbow and hurried him down the long hallway.

"What happened?" Evan asked.

"I apologize; I was being followed and had to lose them before I could attend to my business."

"Who's following you?"

"Probably GSSA agents but—"

"What's the GSSA?" Evan interrupted.

"The Global Standards and Safety Administration—it's the branch of the GFN that monitors illegal cloning activity."

"Are they going to arrest us?"

"Only if they catch us, which is why we are taking the stairs. Come on, pick up the pace. We have to hurry."

Both men sprinted the length of the hallway and ducked into the stairwell. They hurled themselves down the stairs as fast as they could. They were alone in the stairwell, and nobody interrupted their descent to the ground floor.

Evan was out of breath by the time they reached the bottom. Chen wasn't even breathing hard.

"Wait here." The doctor signaled for Evan to stay in the stairwell while he checked the rest of their exit path.

Only a few seconds passed before he came back.

"Okay, Plan B. There are GSSA agents in the lobby and I am sure there are more agents upstairs banging on our hotel room doors as we speak." He pointed at the stairs. "That way."

The two men continued down another two flights of stairs and exited on the top-most level of the underground parking garage.

"This way." Chen jogged down a long line of vehicles toward a downward sloping ramp.

Evan could see daylight coming from the street exit and moved toward it.

Chen stopped him. "No, this way."

They ran across the garage, trying to use the parked vehicles for cover as they made their way to the opposite side of the structure. Chen stopped when they reached a door marked "Emergency Exit" in several languages.

"An alarm will sound when I open this door. There's an alley to the right; run as fast as you can to the street and then turn left. Keep running until you get to the restaurant at the end of the block and then go left down the next street. You'll see a black hovercar about halfway down the block…it's much sportier than mine. There will be a woman in the front seat. Get in and do exactly what she tells you. Understand?"

"What about you?" Evan asked.

"I will be right behind you. Just keep going no matter what happens, understand?"

"Got it."

"Okay, let's go."

Chen pushed the door open, and a loud alarm blared throughout the garage. Both men ran down the alley at top speed. Evan glanced back briefly but saw no one chasing them.

Chen gave Evan a gentle shove, "Keep going. Just because you don't see them doesn't mean they aren't there!"

There were too many people to run. They barely managed a fast walk as they pushed and shoved their way through the throng. Several people shouted rude slurs as they passed, and a few shoved back, but nobody made a serious effort to impede their progress. The crowd thinned once they turned down the side street behind the restaurant.

Evan could see the black car parked right where Chen had said it would be. It looked like a high-end sports car with turbofans instead of wheels. Bumper-mounted winglets protruded at the front and rear of the vehicle. The driver's side front and rear doors were open—they hinged up and away to provide unfettered access to the vehicle's interior.

"Come on, Evan, run. We are almost there!"

When they were about twenty meters away from the car, the woman sitting in the driver's seat stepped out and pointed a large shotgun-looking thing at them.

"Down!" she yelled.

Chen tackled Evan to the ground just as she pulled the trigger. Evan saw a bright flash of light and felt a jolt of static electricity ripple across his back.

"Get up, run!" Chen pulled Evan to his feet and pushed him forward.

"Glad you made it." The woman said, holding the rear door open for the men as they piled into the back seat of the car.

"You've got trackers," she said as she slid into the driver's seat.

She powered up the hovercar, and the doors hissed shut as she made a tight U-turn in the middle of the street. The vehicle leapt into the air as she slammed the throttle forward.

"Hang on," she yelled back to the men. "It's going to get bumpy!"

Evan heard a loud whining noise and felt the car shake as the large turbofans mounted at each corner of the vehicle roared to full power. The vehicle climbed rapidly, and within seconds they were several hundred meters above the city. There was more rumbling and shaking as wings unfolded on either side of the vehicle. Evan saw Chen strap on his safety harness, and he did the same. They gained altitude quickly, and it wasn't long before the city disappeared in the distance behind them.

Once they were cruising at altitude, the woman in the front seat turned around and handed Chen a small silver case.

"Here, do it now," she commanded.

He opened the case and took out a device that looked like a small handgun with three thin prongs sticking out of the barrel.

"Give me your arm," he said to Evan.

Evan rolled up his sleeve and extended his arm.

Chen took the device and pressed the prongs against Evan's skin.

When he pulled the trigger, Evan felt a sharp sting as something shot out from between the prongs and slammed into his skin. He expected to see blood, but there was only a faint red mark on the skin where the injector had hit. The doctor rolled up his sleeve and used the gun on himself.

Evan rolled his sleeve down. "Now, will someone please tell me what just happened?"

The woman in the front seat responded. "Yes, I just saved your life. My name is Yin Li. It's very nice to meet you, Dr. Feldman."

Not the answer he was looking for, but Evan decided it was better to be polite. "Um, thank you for that, and it's nice to meet you, too, but…"

Chen interrupted, "Yin is a very good friend of mine. We're safe for now." He put the injection device back in its case. "I just injected you with nanites that will hunt down and kill the trackers in your bloodstream."

"You injected me with what?"

"Nanites…microscopic robots that swim through your bloodstream looking for and destroying foreign bodies, including the trackers."

"What are trackers?" Evan said with a look of alarm on his face.

"Relax. Trackers are just another kind of nanite. The surveillance drones probably released them into the air when we ran out the garage door. We inhaled them into our lungs and, from there, they migrated into our bloodstream. They are most likely harmless tracking devices, otherwise, we'd already be dead."

"But I didn't see any drones in the alley. Where were they?"

"They were there, trust me," Yin said. "They are no bigger than a mosquito, so I'm not surprised that you didn't see them. My sensors detected more than a dozen of them following you as you approached. That's why I fired."

"The pulse rifle Yin fired emits a powerful electromagnetic pulse that incapacitates or destroys electronic devices," Chen added. "It knocked out the drones long enough for us to get away."

"Why didn't that pulse destroy the trackers in our bodies then? I felt a burst of static on my skin when she fired so I know I was inside the blast radius."

"The trackers are too small and they're organic, not electronic—they're powered by the flow of your blood and your body heat."

"How do we know when they're gone?" Evan asked.

Yin picked up the thin silver box on the seat next to her and tapped on it a few times. She examined the holodisplay that appeared in the air above the box for a moment before answering.

"They're gone. The nanites got them," she said.

"What happens to the nanites?" Evan asked, directing his question to Chen.

"They will keep doing their job for about a week, then they'll deactivate and flush out of your system with other body waste," he answered.

Evan thought about that for a few minutes. He wasn't particularly fond of having little robots swimming around in his blood, but better that than going to prison.

He finally asked the obvious question. "So, what happens now?"

"Now," Yin replied, "we get you somewhere safe."

"And where might that be?" Evan asked.

"Mars," Chen responded.

Evan's jaw dropped; he couldn't believe what he had heard.

"We are flying to Mars in this thing?" he asked incredulously.

"Christ, Chen," Yin said with more than a hint of exasperation in her voice. "I thought you said this guy was smart?"

The doctor ignored her. "No, Evan, this vehicle can only take us so far. We have a launch facility nearby, and from there we will catch a ride to Luna…and then on to Mars."

"Why Mars, Chen?" Evan asked.

"Because the GFN has no jurisdiction on Mars. We'll be free to do our research in peace if we can get off this planet before they find us. And all will be forgiven once we find a cure," Chen said, "or at least I hope it will."

"What is Mars like?"

"It is cold, windy, and dull. But the colony is well established, and we'll be quite comfortable."

"Is Aubrey meeting us there?"

"That is the plan," Chen replied.

"I hate to interrupt, gentlemen, but we have company. They are eighty kilometers out and closing fast," Yin said, with more than a hint of anxiety in her voice.

"How far?" Chen asked, leaning forward to look at the holodisplay projected in front of Yin.

"Twenty kilometers. But we're not going to make it; they are much faster than we are."

Chen activated the communicator implanted behind his right ear.

"This is Dr. Hao. Initiate response plan Delta."

Evan could not hear what the person on the other end of the conversation said, but he assumed that they understood what Chen was asking for.

"Take us down, Yin," Chen said after disconnecting his call.

"Tighten your harnesses, it's going to get bumpy again." She shoved the control yoke hard forward.

The ground filled the windshield as the vehicle plummeted through the air, picking up speed as it dove. Evan sat back in his seat and tried to not get sick from the rapid turns that Yin was making as they descended.

They were just a hundred meters above ground when Yin shouted her first warning.

"They have missile lock! We are still ten kilometers from the base's defense perimeter."

"Keep going," Chen encouraged her. "They've got us covered."

The four turbine fans screamed as the vehicle raced forward at top speed.

"They fired. Two missiles inbound!" Yin said as she twisted the vehicle hard to the right.

A second later, six silver drones blew past the hovercar at an almost unimaginable speed. Each was roughly the size of an eagle, and they moved with incredible speed and agility.

Evan looked out the side window as they turned.

He saw several of the craft launch missiles at the attackers while the others filled the air with flares and small silver pods dangling from parachutes.

"Missiles down, they've engaged the attackers. Twenty seconds from base perimeter," Yin said as she steered the craft toward a large silver and glass building that loomed in the distance.

A few seconds later, she gave another warning. "Two of our Raptors are down. One of theirs is down but the other one is evading our drones and is heading straight for us. It's on a collision course!"

"Keep going, do not deviate from your approach, Yin," Chen instructed.

"I think it's got us!" Yin yelled.

"Stay on course!" Chen yelled back.

Evan turned his head to look out the rear window and saw a small, black drone less than one hundred meters behind them—it was closing rapidly.

It was slightly larger than the silver Raptors, which were nowhere in sight, but it was every bit as fast and agile as the smaller drones. A few seconds passed and Evan was sure the drone would get them. He figured it must have run out of missiles fighting the Raptors or they would be dead already.

Another more few seconds went by and the drone was just twenty meters behind and slightly above them—the drone was aiming for one of the hovercar's engines.

The hovercar dropped sharply and Evan hit his head on the roof. Not hard—the shoulder restraints kept him in place—but he definitely felt it.

There was a loud explosion behind him and the hovercar's engines screamed. He looked forward and saw they were mere meters above the ground and still racing along at an insane rate of speed. Evan leaned back in his seat, closed his eyes and got ready for the crash he knew must come. Several seconds went by with no jolt or tearing of metal.

Then he felt the hovercar slow. He opened his eyes and saw that they were still flying. They were heading toward one of a half dozen massive hangars that lined the several kilometers-long runway.

"We're clear," Yin said calmly. "Alpha reports no hostile contacts in this sector. We've been directed to hangar four."

"Well, that was exciting," Chen smiled at Evan. "How are you doing?"

"I think I'm going to throw up," Evan replied. "But I'm otherwise fine, thank you. What happened to that drone? I was sure it had us."

"The base defenses got it," Yin said. "We were lucky."

"It wasn't luck," Chen countered. "We have been planning for this day for a long time, and we have accounted for every contingency."

"Whatever you say, Chen. I say it was luck, plain and simple," she retorted.

Evan's stomach churned, and he vomited on the floor.

Yin made a disgusted groaning noise. "You're cleaning that up, Chen."

"Sorry," Evan said as he wiped his mouth on his sleeve. "I was trying to hold it, but your flying finally got the best of me."

"Get used to it, Evan," Chen grabbed a tissue from the armrest and handed it to him. "The ride to Mars will make this look like a kiddie ride at the amusement park!"

NINE

April 4, 2075 2:13 p.m. GST
Telogene Special Projects Facility
Shaanxi Province, China

Yin piloted the hovercar into the hangar bay and turned off the engines. The hangar was empty except for three men standing in front of them. One man wore a white and blue jumpsuit with a large Telogene logo emblazoned on the left breast pocket. The other two men sported full sets of black-on-black combat gear. Each man carried a weapon (Evan thought they looked like submachine guns but with faintly glowing red lights along each side), and had several grenades hung on his utility belt.

Chen pushed a button on his door. It swung up toward the rear of the vehicle. He got out and signaled for Evan to do the same. Evan paused a moment to wipe away a few stray bits of vomit on his pant leg before exiting the hovercar. Yin joined them as they walked up to the three men.

The man in the white and blue jumpsuit spoke first. "Those were GFN drones we just shot down. I hope to hell that you all know what you're doing!"

"So do I," Chen replied. "It's good to see you again, Max, thanks for the assist." He turned to Evan. "Evan, this is Dr. Maximilian Ramos."

Evan stepped forward to shake Max's hand.

Chen continued, "And this is Dr. Evan Feldman."

"It is a great pleasure to meet you, Dr. Feldman," Max smiled as he accepted Evan's hand and gave it a firm shake.

"And you know Yin," Chen added.

"I certainly do. That was some nice flying up there, Yin." Dr. Ramos shook her hand. "We will probably need your piloting skills a time or two more before this is over!"

"Let's hope not," she replied. "We should all get the hell out of here before the GFN comes looking for its drones."

"Agreed," Chen said. "How long until we can take off?"

"We are at T-minus thirty minutes and holding. Were you able to pick up the package in Xi'an?" Max asked Chen.

Chen reached inside his blazer and pulled out a small silver data cube. He held it out for Max to take it.

"I did. My contact assures me that everything is in place. All you have to do is load this into the ship's command console and execute it. The AI will handle the rest."

Max took the data cube and examined it as though he was reading its digital contents.

"Excellent! You two go change and have a quick snack if you are hungry. I will finish the pre-launch checklist and get this loaded. You need to be at hangar seven in twenty-five…no, make that twenty-four minutes. These two men will ensure that you get there without difficulty. Now, if you will please excuse me."

Max put the data cube in his pocket and left the hangar through a nearby door.

Chen turned to Yin. "We really appreciate your help, Yin. We wouldn't have made it without you."

"You're welcome. Now do me a favor and get the hell off this planet before you get caught!" she gave Chen a warm hug before turning to Evan.

"Listen, Evan, I know that everything is happening at lightning speed, and you probably don't have a clue what's going on, but you need to keep doing exactly what Chen tells you. We have all taken significant risks and made huge sacrifices to bring you back…a lot is riding on you. Not to put too fine of a point on it, but it's game over if you get caught—and all of us end up dead or spending the rest of our lives on some God-forsaken rock in the asteroid belt. Understand?"

Evan stared at the woman for a moment before answering. She was a full foot shorter than he was, but he could tell there was more to her than her lithe five-foot-two frame might suggest. This woman was clearly much older and wiser than she looked.

"Yes, I understand," he finally said. "Trust me. I will do whatever Chen asks."

"Fair enough," she said before giving Evan a quick hug and a pat on the back. "Now get your asses out of here before I shove my size-seven boots up them!"

"This way, gentlemen," one of the armed guards said, pointing to the door that Dr. Ramos had just exited from.

The guard led the way with Chen and Evan close behind. The other guard followed just behind them as they exited the hangar into a long hallway. They got into an elevator at the end of the hallway and rode it down three floors. From there, it was a short walk down another hallway to the large, well-lit room.

Inside the room were three men and a woman wearing the same white and blue jumpsuits that Dr. Ramos wore. The guards directed Evan and Chen inside and closed the door behind them. The woman stepped forward to greet them.

"Well, it's about damn time!" she swore in Chen's direction. "What took you so long?"

"Sorry, Meili," Chen replied. "We ran into trouble getting out of Xi'an and it slowed us down a little."

Meili Yang was a short woman, barely over a meter and a half tall, and her white lab coat hung loosely on her thin frame. Her short black hair was held behind her ears by a pair of black, thick-framed eyeglasses.

"Well, never mind about that," Meili said. "I am just glad you made it. Now let's get you two into your flight suits, shall we?"

She led them to a screened-off area at the back of the room.

"Strip, shower, and put these on," she said as she handed them each a garment that looked like a form-fitting, full body swimsuit.

Evan took his and headed for the area behind the screen. He examined the outfit as he walked and noticed that there was a mesh of microscopic tubes or wires woven throughout. The fabric was very soft and elastic, like silk, but it had a synthetic quality to it. Evan tugged on a sleeve to see how far it would stretch; it nearly doubled in length before he released it, allowing it to snap back into its original shape.

Chen noticed Evan's fascination with the material. "It's synthetic silk. It's almost impossible to puncture or tear it and it molds itself to your body. You won't even know you are wearing it."

"What does it do?" Evan asked.

"It's the innermost layer of our flight suits; it monitors and regulates body functions and temperature."

"Hmm, interesting." Evan said. He started to unzip his jumpsuit. "I just took a shower thirty minutes ago; do I have to take another one?"

"Yes, this one is special. It preps your skin to receive for the nanosuit. It's not required, but you won't itch as much if you do."

Chen showed Evan how to operate the wash and dry features of the shower. Once started, the rest of the cycle was fully automated and Evan just had to stand there while the shower did the work. It took just two minutes for the wash and dry cycles to complete, leaving Evan clean and dry without even a hint of moisture anywhere on his body. He felt a strange tingling sensation rippling across his skin.

He stepped out of the shower and sat on a nearby chair.

The suit went on easily, but it was skin tight. He stood up once he had the suit on up to the top of his thighs, and he continued wiggling it up his body until it encased him from the neck down. There were no fasteners of any kind on the garment, but it needed none since it stretched and conformed to each part of the body as it went on.

After a bit of tugging and stretching to get everything in the right place, Evan searched for something reflective to see what he looked like in his new outfit. There were no mirrors in the room but the parts he could see told him that the nanosuit was not designed with modesty in mind as it showed every curve, bulge, crack and crevice on his body.

Thank God for good DNA! he thought, appreciating how the garment showed off his well-formed physique.

Chen finished squeezing himself into his suit. Evan noticed that he was also in exceptional shape. He was a little shorter than Evan but no less muscular or well-formed.

"Let's grab a quick bite to eat and then we will finish suiting up," Chen said, ignoring Evan's stare.

"Don't worry," he added, "the rest of the suit is considerably more concealing."

"God, I hope so," Evan replied. "I am not sure how well I could focus on my work if everyone was running around in one of these things!"

"Oh, you'd get used to it. People are much freer with their bodies these days. They spent their hard-earned money on looking perfect, so why not show it off?"

"Are people really that vain?" Evan asked.

"Not so much anymore—we're in the midst of another body positivity movement. People used to want DNA modifications to improve their looks but, over the last decade, they've shifted to wanting things like improved senses, enhanced strength, and better stamina."

Evan kept his hands folded in front of him as they walked back into the main room.

"That may be true. But I grew up in the late twentieth century, and back then we were taught to cover ourselves up." He nodded toward the woman Chen had identified as Meili before whispering, "And especially in front of the opposite sex."

"Now, now," Meili smiled. "There is no reason to be self-conscious here. You are among friends."

She handed each a large plastic glass filled to the rim with a substance that looked and smelled like a watery vanilla milkshake.

"I'm not hungry; I had a late breakfast," Evan said as he handed the glass back to her.

"Sorry, Evan," she said, "but you have to drink it. There is stuff in there you need before you take off. Bottoms up!"

Evan smelled it again and then took a small sip. Thankfully, it tasted better than it looked or smelled. He downed the rest of the glass and handed it back to Meili.

"Okay, now how about some clothes?" he pleaded.

"These men will help you get into your suit." Meili pointed to the other side of the room where Evan could see two space suits hanging on a rack.

The suits were similar in overall appearance to the large, bulky space suits that Evan remembered, but these were smaller, lighter and far less cumbersome to get into. With a little practice, Evan figured that he could get in and out of one on his own, but he appreciated having two of the three men helping him on his first go around. The other man helped Chen into his suit.

In less than ten minutes, both men were fully suited with helmets in hand.

Evan rubbed his hand over the fabric and found it had a similar texture to the under suit. There were differences, though: the fabric was not as smooth, nor did it have the same elasticity, and it moved as an exterior garment should rather than something molded to his skin.

He appreciated that it adequately concealed all the appropriate parts.

The three helpers led the men to a door at the back of the room where Meili was waiting.

"Comfy?" she asked Evan.

"Yeah, it feels pretty good, actually. I feel a slight tingling sensation every so often but it's not uncomfortable."

"That would be your nanosuit integrating with your body. It sends out microscopic fibers that plug into your nervous system…so it can monitor and respond to physiological changes. The tingling sensations you feel are new connections being made. It should subside in a few minutes once they're fully integrated."

"You mean this suit is literally fusing with my body?" Evan asked, his eyes suddenly wide with fear.

"Sort of," Meili replied. "You can easily remove the suit without risk of harm to yourself or the suit. The nanofibers are harmless, and will cease functioning within a few hours of removing the suit. In the meantime, they serve the valuable function of providing your suit with all the information it needs to ensure that you have a safe and comfortable trip."

Evan looked at Chen. "I am not sure how I feel about all these nano-things being injected into my body. If these things are this pervasive in the rest of society, who can say that they aren't causing the mutations?"

Chen paused for a second to consider Evan's comment before responding. "I seriously doubt it, but we can certainly investigate that possibility once we get to Mars."

"Please tell me you thought about the nanites as a possibility?" Evan persisted.

"Believe me, Evan, when I tell you that we have investigated every possible cause. Although I personally have not pursued nanites as a causal factor, I am quite confident that someone on the team has."

Meili stepped between the two men. "I am sorry, gentlemen but you will have to continue this later if you want to catch your ride."

An assistant stepped forward and put his palm on the scanner next to the door. It slid open with a soft hiss to reveal another long corridor. Meili led Evan and Chen into the hallway and down a short flight of stairs to a platform with a hovercar sitting on it.

"This car will take you to hangar seven. It's on the other side of the complex but it will only take a few minutes to get there."

Chen signaled for Evan to get in first. While Evan was climbing in, Chen turned back to Meili.

"Thanks to you and your team for everything you've done. It couldn't have been easy pushing the launch schedule up by two weeks, but you came through. You're amazing."

He embraced her in a warm hug and then shook hands with the assistant standing next to her. "You guys did a fantastic job getting everything ready on such short notice."

"No problem, Dr. Hao," the assistant replied. "I'm glad we could accommodate you and your guest."

Meili gave Chen a soft pat on the back. "I'm afraid that we had the easy part. Now it's all up to you and Dr. Feldman. Good luck, and Godspeed."

Chen slid into the car next to Evan and said, "Hangar seven, please."

TEN

APRIL 4, 2075 2:37 P.M. GST
TELOGENE SPECIAL PROJECTS FACILITY
SHAANXI PROVINCE, CHINA

The car hummed to life and lifted into the air. "Time to destination is one minute forty-two seconds."

The hovercar shot down the long tunnel like a bullet fired from a gun. The rapid acceleration sucked Evan deep into his seat, and he felt the now familiar tingling sensations as his suit adjusted his posture to compensate. The thought that his suit was interfacing with his nervous system unnerved him. If it could cause him to sit differently, what else could it do?

The tunnel angled upwards with the occasional dip and turn but the hovercar didn't slow down until the last few seconds of the ride. Evan saw a large door appear in the dim light of the tunnel. He thought they might not stop in time. Fortunately, the door slid open as the car approached. Once inside, he saw a large aircraft sitting in the middle of the hangar.

The spacecraft was seventy meters long and ten meters wide at the fuselage—about the same size as a commercial airliner. The top of the craft was about ten meters above ground at the cockpit, but the V-shaped tail soared another seven meters above that at the rear of the craft. The delta-shaped wings folded into the rear of the craft, but Evan could see that their length would easily double when fully extended. Two large engines were mounted under each wing with two more mounted at the rear of the craft underneath the tail structure.

Damn, I bet this thing chews through fuel! Evan thought.

The hovercar continued to slow down as it approached the craft, finally coming to a complete stop near the stairs on the left side of the spacecraft. The hovercar doors opened automatically, and Chen leapt from the vehicle. Evan followed closely behind as Chen led them up the stairs to a platform about seven meters above the ground. There was a ramp spanning the short distance between the platform and the aircraft door. There were two people just inside the craft and they turned when they heard Evan and Chen approach.

"Miss me?" the shorter of the two said. It was Yin.

"What are you doing here?" Chen asked with a note of alarm in his voice. "What happened?"

"The GSSA identified me during our little escape, and I am now a wanted woman. So, I decided that it would be prudent for me to tag along a while longer. If you don't mind?"

"Oh, Yin, I'm so sorry that happened; I was hoping we might get lucky and make a clean getaway."

"No such luck. There are pictures of us all over the net. We are the top three on the GSSA's most wanted list."

Chen frowned. "Bounties?"

"Yep, one hundred mil for him and twenty-five mil for each of us."

"Shit. Are you kidding?" Chen scowled. "Every bounty hunter between here and Mars will be after us now!"

The man standing next to Yin spoke. "Welcome aboard, Dr. Hao. Captain Dieter Bauer at your service."

After a quick handshake with the doctor, he continued, "The crew and ship are ready to depart on your command, sir."

"Thank you, Captain. We are ready to leave when you are."

Chen turned back to Yin. "I'm sorry you got caught up in this…but I'm glad you're here. Please help Evan get buckled in so I can have a quick word with the captain?"

"Sure." She turned toward Evan. "Come on, let's get you situated."

Yin led Evan into the ship. To his left were stairs leading to the cockpit, and to his right were two rows of egg-shaped pods. Each pod was about 2.5 meters long and a little over a meter wide, and each contained what looked like a very comfortable leather recliner. The pods angled toward the central walkway so that thirty of them fit on each side of the aisle.

"Wow," Evan said as he took in the full length of the cabin.

"Yeah, wow," Yin replied. "This is the latest and greatest in near-Earth space travel. It takes off like a jet plane but is capable of interplanetary space flight. It used to take two days to get to Luna. Now we can get there in about ten hours—faster if we really push it. I am not sure what the passenger craft speed record is, but I suspect that our pilot will do his best to beat it on this flight."

"I thought you said we were going to Mars?"

"We are but we have to get to Luna first. As fast as it is, this craft would take weeks to get to Mars and we don't have that kind of time. Once we get to Luna, we have to catch a ride on another ship that will get us to Mars in about three days."

Just then a young woman appeared at the end of the walkway coming toward them from the rear of the craft.

"Good afternoon," the woman said. "I am Elise and I will be your attendant on this flight. It's just your group today, so please choose any pod you'd like. Is there anything I can get you before we depart?"

"No, thank you. I'm fine," Evan said.

"I'll take this," Elise said as she took Evan's helmet and stored it in a drawer underneath his pod.

"I'll have some water, please," Yin said as she stored her own helmet.

"Certainly…I'll be right back." The attendant headed back the direction she came.

"Now, let's get you strapped in." Yin grabbed Evan's elbow and guided him toward the closest pod.

"Does this thing close?" Evan asked as he eased into the pod.

"It can for long trips or emergencies, but this is a short flight. The pilot will probably leave them open unless we run into trouble."

"What kind of trouble?"

"You know, space trouble. Micrometeorites, space junk hitting the ship, engine malfunction, that kind of stuff. It rarely happens, but once you get out of the atmosphere anything is possible."

"Well, let's pray for smooth sailing on this trip," Evan said hopefully.

"I'm sure we'll be fine. Now sit back."

Yin helped Evan with the padded safety bar that came up over his head and settled softly on his chest. Another bar swiveled across his legs. Evan felt like he was being strapped into a high-speed roller coaster.

"Here's your console," Yin pointed to a glass panel built into the chest restraint. "You can also use voice commands. Just say *release* if you want to get up, *entertainment* if you want to watch some video or listen to music, and *service* if you need the flight attendant."

"Release," Evan said. The restraints retracted back into the pod.

"You'll get a warning message if the captain has the pods locked because of turbulence or something, but you can override it. I wouldn't recommend it but it's up to you. Just say *ready* or *restraints* when you want the restraints."

Evan leaned back in his seat. "Ready."

The restraints slid back into place.

"Entertainment," he commanded.

A holodisplay projected above his chest and presented a selection of video and audio entertainment options, including several games.

"Cancel," Evan said.

The holodisplay disappeared.

"Good, you're getting the hang of this." Yin nodded her approval.

"Yeah, Chen let me poke around a terminal at Telogene. It worked the same way as this one."

"You know you can get an implant that gives you full-time access to the GeoNet, right?" Yin asked.

"No, I didn't know that. I suspected that might be the case, since I've seen several people interacting with something I couldn't see. I assumed it was some type of ocular implant."

"You should consider getting one. I have one and couldn't live without it; you can do some really cool stuff with it."

"I'll think about it," Evan said. "I'm not sure how much technology I want inside my body. To be honest, the whole idea of nanites and implants unnerves me."

"I understand, it's all new to you…no worries. Take your time and think about it. I am sure Chen can arrange it for you if you change your mind."

"What can I arrange?" Chen said from behind Yin.

"I was just telling him about ocular implants. I said you could arrange it for him if he decides he wants one."

"Oh," he replied. "Well, let's give him more time to acclimate before we start suggesting enhancements, shall we? It's only been two days, and getting an implant may be a little ahead of where he is in his recovery process."

"You can say that again," Evan said. "When do we leave?"

"Now," Chen answered. "Let's get into our pods, Yin. You take that one, and I will take the one across from Evan."

The flight attendant brought Yin her water and asked Chen if he needed anything—he didn't. A few minutes later, Evan felt the ship rock slightly as it taxied out of the hangar and onto the runway.

"What are the odds we will encounter more of those drone things?" Evan asked Chen.

"Low. But we have numerous surveillance drones up, and interceptors are on standby, just in case. They are probably on their way but they won't be able to touch us once we get airborne. This ship is way too fast for them."

"Doesn't the GFN have anything bigger they can throw at us?"

Chen took much longer than Evan would have liked to answer. "Well, there is no point lying to you. They have a large array of aircraft and spacecraft that can take us out. But *only* if they can find us. Do you remember that errand I ran this morning?"

"Yes. Is that where you got that data cube I saw you hand to Max?"

"Yes, that was it."

"What's on it?"

"Well, it's kind of complicated to explain to you…but let's just say that it's a very special computer program—an artificial intelligence, really. It's designed to send false signals to the GFN's global surveillance network, and it should make us invisible to their sensors. It won't help us if a human-piloted craft finds us. But it will keep the drones away, at least long enough for us to get out of the atmosphere."

"Can't they follow us into space?"

"They can but I'll be surprised if they do."

"Why?"

"Because the GFN's jurisdiction ends at the upper boundary of the atmosphere, and any action by them beyond that point would be a treaty violation with the colonies."

"Yeah, I remember seeing somewhere that the space colonies were independent. Wasn't there a threat of war at some point?"

"Kind of, the GFN tried to annex Luna a few years back, and it caused quite a stir. Both Luna and Mars threatened to embargo any country that voted for annexation. That would have meant no new colonists from those countries and restricted raw material sales from all space mining operations."

"That sounds bad."

"Yeah, it would have been. The vote was close, but the measure was defeated in a general session of the GFN assembly. It's been tried twice since and defeated handily both times—nobody wants to disrupt the status quo."

"I sure hope you're right," Evan said with more than a hint of anxiety in his voice.

The pilot's voice echoed from the headrest-mounted speakers in each pod.

"Ladies and gentlemen, this is your captain speaking. The tower has cleared us for takeoff and we are ready to go. Please follow all directions from your flight crew and sit back and enjoy our approximately nine-and-a-half-hour flight to Luna."

A female voice came over the speakers as soon as the pilot finished. "We will begin taxiing momentary. Your seats and safety restraints will automatically adjust throughout the flight, and we ask that you please do not override them except in case of an emergency or when instructed to do so by your flight crew. I'm Elise, and you also have Anika and Talia on board today to assist you during the flight. Up front, we have Captain Bauer, First Officer Antonelli, and Navigator First Class Panagakos. Please don't hesitate to let us know if there is anything we can do to make your trip more comfortable. Flight attendants, please secure the cabin."

Two flight attendants that Evan had not seen before walked down the aisle to check on each occupant and and ensure they were secure in their pods. They read through a checklist, double-checking each step as they went, to ensure that the cabin door was secure, the cabin pressurization system was functioning properly, and each pod was working correctly. Once satisfied, they took their seats in two slightly smaller pods located behind the stairs leading to the cockpit.

Evan tried to relax as his pod adjusted to a partially reclined position. The chest and leg restraints inflated, so that he was locked firmly in place, but not uncomfortably so. The wing-mounted engines screamed as the spaceplane surged down the runway. The pilot pulled the nose up, and the plane leapt into the air. It gained altitude quickly.

On a whim, Evan said, "Show position."

A display appeared that showed a satellite view of the aircraft, along with readouts for altitude, heading, and speed. They were already at 7,000 meters and climbing fast. Their speed was 2,000 kilometers per hour and increasing. Their heading was roughly due north, which meant they were flying toward Mongolia, Russia, and the North Pole.

Over the next fifteen minutes, the plane continued to gain altitude and speed, and Evan couldn't help but be amazed at how fast they were flying. In that short amount of time, they had climbed to twenty-five kilometers and were traveling at over 7,400 kilometers an hour. That was over six times the speed of sound—fast enough to fly from New York to London in under an hour!

Chen saw him watching the display and called over, "So far so good. Get ready, the fun part is about to begin!"

Five minutes later, Captain Bauer's voice came over the speakers. "Ladies and gentlemen, we are at 45,000 meters and are ready to transition to orbit. The upper atmosphere is pretty stable today, and we don't expect a lot of turbulence along our flight path, but please make sure you do not remove your restraints until instructed to do so. If you direct your holodisplays to the exterior cameras, you will get some great views of the Earth and space as we make our roll. Enjoy the ride."

Elise came back over the speakers. "Okay folks, for those of you who haven't taken this trip before, this is the fun part. When the pilot starts the burn, you will experience approximately three Gs of force pushing your body into your pod. That means you will weigh three times what you do now, and you might find it difficult or uncomfortable to lift your head or arms during peak acceleration. We don't recommend that you try, but knock yourself out if you want to give it a go. If you check your holodisplays, you'll see that a countdown has started—the fun starts when it hits zero. Enjoy the ride!"

Evan watched as the countdown timer worked its way down from sixty to zero. When the counter reached thirty, he heard a noise he interpreted as the wings being retracted into the fuselage. Everything went quiet at ten seconds. Even the loud droning sound of the engines had died down to a low hum.

Five…four…three…two…one…zero!

Evan heard an explosive roar from the tail-mounted engines. The speed readout climbed rapidly and, in just a matter of seconds, they were traveling at over 10,000 kilometers per hour. Evan felt the pod adjust to compensate for the increased G-forces, and he also felt his suit subtly adjusting his body. The tingling sensations were less than before, but he still felt the occasional tinge as his suit fully integrated with his nervous system.

The craft continued to accelerate, and they were now experiencing three times the Earth's gravity pushing their bodies into the seats of their pods. Evan felt parts of his seat inflate and deflate, conforming to his body and easing pressure points as they developed. The angle of the seat had also changed so he was laying almost flat with his head just slightly above his chest.

Out of curiosity, he raised his right arm and found it felt dull and heavy, like lifting a 30-pound dumbbell. The same was true when he tried to lift his head and look around the cabin. He could do it, but it felt like he had a giant weight strapped to the top of his head. It strained his neck muscles to lift his head more than a couple of inches above the headrest.

He decided it was better to relax and let the equipment do whatever was necessary to keep him comfortable.

It took only a few more minutes for their speed to reach 16,000 kilometers per hour at an altitude of just over sixty kilometers above sea level. He checked the moving map and exterior camera views, and saw they had crossed the North Pole, flown briefly over Greenland, and were now somewhere high above the Atlantic Ocean. Their trajectory showed that they would soon fly over the southern Caribbean Islands and Central America. From there, they would pass over the wide-open spaces of the Pacific.

The flight had been smooth so far, with only the occasional jostle as they hit pockets of unstable air. Things got progressively rougher, however, as they climbed higher, and the atmosphere became progressively thinner. The space plane shook so hard at times that Evan thought for sure he would be thrown out of his pod, but the active restraints and his neurosuit did their jobs keeping him in place. He was, however, feeling sick again.

The nausea came in waves and Evan was sure he would lose his lunch if the shaking didn't stop soon. Just when he thought he couldn't take any more, the jostling subsided and Evan felt the pressure on his restraints ease.

The plane rolled over onto its back.

The bottom-mounted cameras now showed the blackness of space, and those on top showed that they were somewhere over Indonesia flying west along the equator.

The readout on his holodisplay showed that they had just passed 110 kilometers and were now well beyond Earth's atmosphere. Their speed had climbed to 32,000 kilometers per hour, and they were still accelerating.

Evan glanced over at Chen, who gave him a thumbs up. Evan attempted to return the gesture but was overcome by a sudden wave of nausea. He reached for the vomit bag and put it to his mouth, just in time.

ELEVEN

APRIL 4, 2075 4:00 P.M. GST
GSSA HEADQUARTERS
ZURICH, SWITZERLAND

"Madam Secretary, I am sorry to interrupt but Captain Bachmann said it's urgent." The speaker appeared to be a six-foot-tall man wearing a blue-grey, custom-tailored suit. But the dull white color and too-round shape of his bald skull betrayed him for the artificial being that he was.

GSSA General Secretary Dianne Merkel was sitting at a large oval table with a half-dozen GSSA executives, all of whom were staring intently at charts and graphs being projected in the air above the table.

"Keep working," Dianne said to the group as she stood up. "I want revised projections within the hour."

One of the two women at the table replied on behalf of the group, "Yes, ma'am."

"I'll take it in my private office," Dianne said to the man who had just interrupted her meeting.

He nodded. "Will there be anything else?"

"No, my order stands. No interruptions unless it involves the Telogene case."

The young man nodded as he exited the room.

Dianne walked down a short hallway to her private office, stopping briefly at a mirror next to the door to check her appearance. She wasn't a vain woman, but she had been working for forty-eight hours straight and was feeling a little worse for the wear. She could safely take stimulants for another twenty-four hours, but then she would have no choice but to sleep.

Dianne walked over to her desk and said, "Accept call."

A holodisplay appeared above her desk and resolved into an image of a man wearing the black and gray uniform of a GFN peacekeeper.

"What is it, Captain? You had better be calling with good news," Dianne said curtly.

"I wish that was the case, ma'am," he replied. "We lost them."

Dianne's face flushed, and she raised her voice well above her usual mild and measured tone.

"How is that possible? We knew exactly where they were and where they were going. You had every possible resource in position and at your disposal. And yet you are calling to tell me they got away? You had better have a very good explanation, Captain!"

"I am sorry, Madame Secretary. They planned well and prepared for us. We almost had them in Xi'an, but they had help."

"So where are they now?"

"Our agents on the ground have reported that they left the planet about an hour ago. We tracked them into orbit but have since been unable to locate them."

"Telogene has invisible space planes now…is that what you are telling me, Captain?"

"No, ma'am. Even if it was a stealth craft, we should have been able to track them on GeoNet. I am not sure how they slipped through, but our best people are working on it."

The GeoNet was an array of satellites and ground stations around the planet that provided every GFN citizen with access to the global telecommunications network. GFN traffic controllers also used the network to monitor every vehicle on the ground, on or under the sea, and in the air. Each craft broadcast a unique identifier that allowed controllers to track its movements, and to coordinate its path of travel with other craft in the area. Any craft not broadcasting an identifier was flagged as a potential threat and drones would be dispatched to intercept it.

"Do you realize what is at stake, Captain? These people represent an extreme threat. It is imperative that we take them into custody before they cause themselves or others harm. Is that clear?"

She continued without waiting for his response. "I don't want excuses and I don't want to hear about who's working on what problem. I want results, plain and simple. Now, are you the man who can get me those results or do I need to put someone else on this, Captain Bachmann?"

"No, ma'am. I will get it done. You have my word on that."

Dianne took a deep breath to calm herself. "Very well. This is your last chance, Captain. If you don't get them before they leave Luna, then there will be no more chances. Are we clear?"

"Yes, ma'am. Our team is in en route to Klaproth, and we believe we have identified the transport ship they intend to use to get to Mars. We've also dispatched two interceptors to orbit Luna. There is no way they will slip by us this time."

"Just make sure you get them back here as quickly and quietly as possible. Do everything you can to avoid confrontation with the colonists but arresting these people is your top priority. I will deal with any political fallout if it comes to that."

"Understood and thank you for your support. Will there be anything else?"

"Just one thing, Captain. Which ship is it?"

"Ma'am?"

"The transport ship, which one is it?"

"Oh, it's the *Endeavor*—Admiral Gbadamosi's flagship."

"I've heard of him, CEO of the Galileo Group. He was one of the first Lunar colonists as I recall—a geologist before he became a spacer. Didn't he discover the helium three deposits below Casatus?"

"Yes, ma'am, that's him. He made a fortune on that find and a few others that came after it. He used his profits to build the first transport for hauling ores from the Asteroid Belt. Since then, he's branched out into passenger and cargo service between Luna and Mars. His fleet numbers at least a dozen ships with *Endeavor* being the newest and largest."

"With all that success, why isn't he retired somewhere enjoying his money?"

"He did an interview a few years back and said he fancies himself an explorer, and that space is home. His stated goal is to make enough money to fund the first interstellar flight, and he supposedly has a facility on Ceres that is researching faster-than-light travel. He's a bit strange, but we expect that he will cooperate fully."

"Okay, keep me posted, Captain." Dianne waived her hand to disconnect the call.

"Christian?" she said into the air.

The door to her private office opened a few seconds later. The android who had interrupted her earlier walked into the room. His movements were natural and fluid, and his silicone skin looked impressively real. It wouldn't take much more than a wig and some makeup to make him look human.

"Yes?" he said as he crossed the short distance to Dianne's desk.

"Get me everything you can find on Adekunle Gbadamosi. He owns the transport ship *Endeavor* and a bunch of other stuff. I want to know if he has any affiliation with Aubrey Harris or anyone else from Telogene."

Christian nodded his understanding. "Do you want me to send it to you, or deliver it personally?"

His masculine voice was strangely warm and soothing.

"You can send it."

"Right away, ma'am." Christian turned to leave.

"And get Counselor Birchmeir on the line. I want to talk to him about the hearing tomorrow."

"Yes, ma'am." Christian closed the door behind him.

A few minutes later, GFN Chief Legal Counsel Johannes Birchmeir appeared on her holodisplay.

Johannes Birchmeir was a thin man, with wispy blond hair, pale skin, and thin lips. He looked like someone who should spend less time in the office and more time at the beach.

"Thanks for getting back to me so quickly," Dianne said. "I'd like to change the venue for tomorrow's arraignment of Aubrey Harris. I am concerned about her safety and would like to keep her out of the public eye."

They went back and forth for several minutes while Counselor Birchmeir questioned her rationale for the last-minute change, but Dianne Merkel eventually persuaded him to see things her way.

"I'll see to it. But the judge will not be happy, Dianne," Birchmeir said with begrudging agreement, his English thick with a Swiss German accent. "You know she is old-fashioned and likes to have defendants appear in person whenever possible."

"Don't you worry about that. I will talk to her. Just make sure that Aubrey doesn't leave that building."

"Understood. What about her lawyer?"

"I will call him and explain. I am sure he will agree that his client's safety is more important than her right to appear in person before the judge."

"Good evening, Madame Secretary."

"Good evening, Counselor." Dianne ended the call and headed back to her meeting, pausing only briefly at the mirror as she passed by.

Twelve

Evan marveled at how small the world looked from outer space. The last of the sun's rays had fallen below the horizon, and darkness had fully enveloped the ancient continent that was Australia. The brilliantly lit cities of Sidney and Melbourne in the east, and Perth in the west, stood in stark contrast to the pitch-black interior region.

Incredible, simply incredible! he thought.

Much had changed over the last fifty years, including the coastlines of every continent. Rising seas and surging tides had inundated most of the low-lying coastal areas and islands of the world. Australia, having the dubious distinction of being the lowest continent, had lost nearly a tenth of its landmass, and its coastline looked radically different from how Evan remembered it. Brisbane and the Gold Coast had been hardest hit, the crushing waves having forced more than a million people from their homes. But even that number paled with the nearly seventy million who had been affected worldwide.

"Dr. Feldman?" Evan looked up from his display to see Captain Bauer bobbing next to him.

"Yes, hello again, Captain. I am sorry that I lost my lunch earlier. I guess I am just not cut out for space travel."

"Well, normally your suit should have compensated for any disorientation or nausea, but please don't worry…it happens to the best of us," the captain replied with a friendly smile.

"In any case," he continued. "I was wondering if you would like to see the view from the cockpit before we initiate our transition burn. We have about fifteen minutes before the Hellfires are ready."

Captain Bauer had come by shortly after they entered orbit to check on his passengers. Evan had used the opportunity ask the captain about his ship.

The captain had explained that the ship had two sets of engines—four wing-mounted Synergistic Air-breathing Rocket Engines (called "SABREs" for short) and two helium-3 fusion rockets (these he called "Hellfires") at the rear of the craft. The hydrogen-burning SABRE engines could get the craft into the orbit but they burned too much fuel for interplanetary travel. The Hellfires lacked the raw power of the SABREs, but they provided the high-efficiency thrust required to propel the craft out of Earth's orbit and beyond.

Each Hellfire engine consisted of a helium-3 closed cycle fusion reactor coupled with a Variable Specific Impulse Magnetoplasma Rocket (VASIMR) capable of producing exhaust velocities up to 50,000 meters per second, or nearly 180,000 kilometers per hour. The downside of the VASIMR engine was that its fusion reactors required a fair amount of warm-up time to reach the high temperatures required for operation.

They had spent the last hour and a half orbiting the planet while they waited for the reactors to reach full power.

"I'd love to," Evan replied. "I am just worried that I might become disoriented and get nauseous again."

"Well, it's up to you but I think you'll be fine."

Evan thought about it for a minute. "Okay, let's try it."

"Excellent. Elise, will you assist Dr. Feldman, please?"

"I'd be happy to," she said as she floated toward Evan's pod.

It took Evan a moment to acclimate to the low gravity, but Elise made sure that he made it to the front of the plane uninjured and with no disorientation or nausea.

Chen and Yin were having a lively conversation with the other flight attendants in the forward lounge area, and Chen gave Evan a thumbs-up as he floated by.

Evan pulled himself up the stairs using the handrails.

The captain helped stabilize him once he reached the top. They floated together into a small cockpit, where a young woman sat in the right front seat and a similarly aged man sat immediately behind her.

"Dr. Feldman," the captain said, "May I introduce First Officer Melania Antonelli and Navigator First Class Sam Panagakos—two of the most talented spacers in the fleet...and I don't just mean the Telogene fleet."

Evan smiled and gave them a polite wave, "It's a pleasure to meet you both."

"The pleasure is all ours," Melania replied. "Welcome aboard."

"Have you enjoyed your flight so far?" Sam asked.

Evan smiled. "Well, other than a bit of upset stomach during the turbulence, it's been great. It's hard to believe going to space is so easy."

"This is Dr. Feldman's first time," Dieter added.

"Wow, a virgin, huh?" Marissa snickered. "Well, if you thought orbital insertion was fun, just wait until we start the deceleration phase!"

Evan looked at Captain Bauer with more than a hint of concern in his eyes.

"Now, now. Let's not be scaring our VIPs, shall we?" Dieter scolded his first officer.

He turned to Evan. "Do not worry, Dr. Feldman. All she means is that we will make a rapid deceleration as we enter orbit around Luna. Some say it feels a bit like a roller coaster because we lose speed so quickly as we move to shallower and shallower orbits around Luna. It is perfectly safe, I assure you, and there won't be any atmospheric turbulence to worry about."

"That's good to know," Evan replied dryly.

The captain patted Evan's shoulder reassuringly and directed his attention to the front of the cabin.

"Quite a view, isn't it?" he asked.

The Moon filled the viewscreen, appearing far bigger and brighter than Evan remembered. Of course, he was also much closer to it than he had ever been before.

It's called Luna now, Evan reminded himself before verbalizing his amazement. "Wow, it's so bright…and so big!"

"If you look closely, you can just see Casatus City," Captain Bauer said as he pointed to an area near Luna's south pole. "And just north of that is our destination, Klaproth Spaceport."

"Should I magnify, Captain?" the navigator asked.

"Yes, please. Let's give our guest a closer look."

Evan watched as the image in the window zoomed in on the area the captain had identified as Casatus City.

"How are you doing that?" he asked.

"The windshield is actually a holodisplay. You may not have noticed, but there are no windows in this craft. All view ports render in real-time based on the viewer's perspective. It gives the appearance of looking out the window but without the challenge of integrating large transparent surfaces into the skin of the craft," Dieter explained.

"And since it's just a holodisplay, we can manually change those views if we want to, just as I am doing now. This is coming from a Lunar satellite," Sam added.

It took a second for the zoomed image to focus and stabilize but when it did, Evan saw a collection of small domed structures tightly grouped around a larger dome.

"Most of the city is underground," Dieter said. "Those are for food production and above-ground recreation."

After a short pause, he continued, "An underground high-speed rail system connects the city to the spaceport. You won't have time to ride it this trip but perhaps on your next visit."

"How many people live there?" Evan asked.

The captain thought for a moment. "Oh, I think its somewhere north of 35,000 these days, which is about a third of the total population on Luna."

Evan raised his eyebrows at the much larger than expected number. "What do all those people do there?"

"About half are miners, the rest are researchers and support personnel. Mining on Luna is big business. The colony ships tens of billions of dollars' worth of helium-3 and other rare elements to Earth every year."

"Yeah, I read something about the vast fortunes that have been made mining the Moon…I mean Luna."

The captain nodded. "Indeed. But the mines on Luna are nothing compared to those in the Asteroid Belt. That's where the real money is. We're talking about tens of trillions of dollars' worth of rare elements and metals that are basically free for the taking to anyone with the necessary equipment and courage."

Evan considered that for a moment. "I would imagine it is very expensive to mine and ship all that material back to Earth."

"It is," Dieter acknowledged, "which is why a lot of production has moved to Mars. It's much cheaper to build a spaceship in orbit above Mars than it is to haul all the materials back to Earth. They even have orbital refineries now. If you think Luna is something, Mars will blow you away!"

Evan smiled. "I am looking forward to it."

Dieter gave Evan another moment to examine the image before asking his navigator to zoom in on the spaceport.

"This is the recently expanded spaceport," he said.

The screen moved across the surface of Luna and resolved on another collection of domes; these were arranged in a star pattern with various-sized platforms circling each dome.

"This is the gateway to the solar system. Pretty much everything that comes or goes between Earth, Mars and the Belt passes through here—people, supplies, minerals, you name it," Dieter added.

"Yeah, and they don't hesitate to let everyone know it either," First Officer Antonelli chimed in.

The captain gave his first officer a scowl. "No, they don't. But let's not burden our guest with a political debate."

The first officer rolled her eyes. "Aye, aye, Captain."

Dieter ignored her and turned back to Evan. "That's the problem with these civilian ships. If this was a combat vessel, I'd just have her shot out the airlock for insubordination."

Evan could tell from the rather large grin on the captain's face that he was mostly kidding.

"T-minus five, Captain," Antonelli said.

"Engines at ninety-eight percent and course plotted," Panagakos added.

"Very well," Bauer acknowledged. "I'm sorry, Dr. Feldman, but I must ask you to return to your pod. Thank you for coming up."

"Of course, Captain. Thank you for letting me meet the rest of your crew."

"It was our pleasure," Antonelli and Panagakos replied in unison.

Elise, who had been waiting patiently at the top of the stairs, floated forward and took Evan's arm at the elbow.

"Just grab the handrail and pull yourself down. I will be right behind you," she said.

It took several minutes for Evan to get back to his pod and get settled in.

"Thank you," he said once he was secure in his pod.

"You're welcome," Elise replied with a friendly smile. "You probably won't need them, but I tucked a couple of extra bags into the console."

Evan gave her an embarrassed smile and a hushed "Thanks."

She patted his shoulder and then turned her attention to Yin and Chen, who had already returned to their seats. "Everyone all set?"

"Yep," Yin replied.

Chen nodded. "Ready."

"Great," Elise replied. "In about two minutes, the captain will engage the Hellfire drive system, and you will experience roughly twice the rate of acceleration you felt during our orbital insertion burn. Just relax and let your suits and pods do their jobs. The initial burn will last for about twenty minutes, and you'll be unable to move during that time. Don't even bother to try because your suit will keep you locked in place until we drop below three Gs.

"Also, you won't be able to exit your pods until we drop below one G of acceleration, but I recommend waiting until we stop thrusting. Once that happens, we'll have about two hours of zero G if you'd like to experience that. In any case, we'll let you know when it's safe to move about the cabin. Please feel free to avail yourself of our entertainment system in the meantime. Our media library is quite extensive, and we have all the hottest VR games and video content to keep you entertained. We will also serve refreshments and a couple of light meals before we start our deceleration burn. Any questions?"

There were none.

"Okay then, just sit back, relax, and enjoy the flight!" she concluded.

Just as Elise finished securing herself in her pod, a digitized voice sounded over the craft's sound system.

"Lunar transfer burn in 15…14…13…"

The voice counted down to one before saying "Ignition."

During the countdown, the passenger pods rotated so that each passenger faced forward in a head-high, feet-low position. A second after the electronic voice stopped, Evan heard a massive roar emanate from the rear of the craft—it sounded more like an explosion, really—and found himself pushed deep into his seat by the sudden burst of acceleration. For the first second or two, Evan grew lightheaded and feared that he might lose consciousness, but his suit compensated, and the feeling quickly faded.

Evan closed his eyes and tried to relax. Five minutes later, he found that the pressure pushing on his body had eased considerably. The craft was still accelerating, but the suit and pod had positioned him to reduce the effect of the extreme G-forces on his body. He couldn't move; his suit was disrupting his nervous system. He was paralyzed, but otherwise comfortable. Not being in control of his own body was somewhat disconcerting, but he understood that it was for his own protection. They were accelerating so hard that the force would crush his body like a grape if the pod wasn't actively positioning and supporting him.

Oh well, I guess this is as a good a time as any to catch a quick nap.

He quickly realized that there was too much adrenaline pumping through his body for him to sleep. So, he resolved himself to listening to the pulsating roar of the Hellfire engines instead.

THIRTEEN

APRIL 4, 2075 7:22 P.M. GST
TELOGENE SHUTTLE
EARTH-LUNA TRANSITION

"Dr. Feldman?"

Evan opened his eyes to see Yin floating next to him.

"Yes?" he replied groggily.

He had fallen asleep once the engine noise diminished, and been resting comfortably for the last two hours.

"I am sorry to bother you," she said, "but I thought it better to wake you before we start our deceleration burn. I hope you don't mind?"

"No, not all. Thank you." Evan rubbed the sleep from his eyes and adjusted his pod to a sitting position. "What time is it?"

"The current time is 19:22 Global Standard Time," a digitized female voice announced from unseen speakers.

"We are about five hours out," Yin added. "The captain burned a little longer on the acceleration leg to get us there faster, but that will mean a harder deceleration."

"I see. Do we have time for me to use the restroom facilities?" Evan asked.

"Sure. Let me get Elise or one of the other attendants to help you."

Yin made her way to the back of the craft and soon returned with Talia, who helped Evan float his way back to the restroom and showed him how to use it. Five minutes later, all three of the passengers were back in their pods, and the flight attendants had assumed their usual positions at the front and rear of the craft.

"Well, that was interesting," Evan said to Chen after returning to his seat.

"Yeah, it's a little awkward using that suction thing…but at least it makes aiming easy!" Chen retorted with a boyish grin on his face.

"Yeah, there's that," Evan chortled.

"Ladies and gentlemen, this is your captain speaking. We are about to begin our deceleration burn and it will get a little bumpy. Same as before though—just relax and let your pods do their jobs. We'll experience approximately six-Gs of deceleration for approximately fifteen minutes, followed by about an hour at three-Gs. From there it will be a one- to two-G glide into orbit. I will let you know what our landing approach will look like once I get our final vectors from Klaproth Control. Please sit back and enjoy the ride."

As soon as the captain stopped speaking, the electronic female voice began another fifteen-second countdown, and the pods rotated so the passengers faced the rear of the craft.

Evan wondered why the pods had changed their orientation, but he quickly understood once the countdown reached zero. Both Hellfire engines ignited with the same explosive roar as before, and Evan felt himself slammed into the back of his pod seat with considerably more force than he had felt during the acceleration burn. His suit and pod did their jobs though, and it wasn't long before they had him in a reasonably comfortable position.

The six-G deceleration burn felt like it took forever, and he welcomed the sound of the engines throttling back to a dull roar. The pods adjusted into a slightly more horizontal position and he found he could roll his head and lift his arms a bit. He also found that if he tried to move his arms or legs too much, the suit would override his nervous system and force him to lie still. He wasn't excited about being frozen in place for the next hour, but he listened to some music and tried to relax.

"Play music, late twentieth or early twenty-first-century smooth jazz," he instructed his pod.

A moment later, a playlist appeared on his holodisplay and "Anything's Possible" by Dave Koz started playing through the speakers mounted in Evan's headrest. Evan closed his eyes and listened to some of his time's best jazz musicians do their thing. He even dozed off again.

He woke up an hour later when the constant roar of the engines suddenly stopped. He looked around and saw that Yin and Dr. Hao were both asleep. Elise and the other flight attendants were at the back of the craft doing something in the crew area. Although Evan couldn't tell what they were up to, he assumed that they were preparing another in-flight service—like the one they had offered during the acceleration phase.

A few minutes later, Anika and Talia came down the aisle on a moving platform. Between them was a four-foot-high by two-foot-wide cart containing several food and beverage choices.

Evan still had not fully adjusted to the rules of space travel, and the sight of the two women standing on the platform caused him to become disoriented.

He was no physicist, but he understood that acceleration, or deceleration in this case, caused an effect akin to gravity on objects inside the craft. The craft's current rate of deceleration meant there was roughly one-G of inertial force pushing everything toward the rear of the craft. Without the platform, the attendants would fall down the aisle until they hit the divider between the main cabin and crew area. The effect would be like jumping off a fifteen-story building—and most likely fatal.

Being closer to the rear of the ship, the attendants reached Yin's pod first. Evan watched as they positioned the pod so that the top of Yin's head pointed toward the rear of the craft. Talia helped Yin open the table that folded out over the top of the lap restraint and then served her from the cart. Evan couldn't tell what she ordered, but she ended up with several white plastic containers on her tray.

When the platform carrying the two attendants stopped at his row, Evan selected cranberry juice (he would have liked it with some vodka, but there was no alcohol served while in space for the safety of passengers and crew), a fruit and nut energy bar, and chicken and rice with mixed vegetables—the other meal choices were beef with potatoes and carrots or a vegetarian medley. Anika helped him position his pod and open his tray table before placing each of his selections in front of him. Talia did the same for Chen.

"Anything else?" Anika asked.

"No, thank you, this will be fine for now," Evan replied.

"Okay, call us if you need anything."

The platform reversed direction and headed back "up" the aisle toward the rear crew area, eventually disappearing behind a sliding door.

Evan looked at the assortment of plastic containers in front of him and picked up the one with a picture of a basket of cranberries and the words "Cranberry Juice, made from concentrate" printed on it. He removed the straw stuck to the side of the container and inserted it into the designated spot. But there was no risk of the juice floating away, they served everything in zero-G compatible containers. To drink, he had to squeeze the package and suck through the straw simultaneously.

Boy, does this bring back memories! Evan recalled the countless juice boxes he had consumed as a child.

Next, he turned his attention to the chicken and rice. Anika had activated the built-in warmer before handing him the container, and Evan could see that the contents were steaming beneath the clear plastic lid. He peeled open the lid, removed the combination spoon-fork attached to the side of the package and dug in. The food tasted surprisingly good, and not just because he was hungry. The chicken was moist and nicely seasoned, and the rice and vegetables were a perfect al dente—not raw or the least bit soggy.

Evan ate his meal, sipped his juice, and chatted with Yin and Chen. The engines still blasted away, but they were just a distant hum now and it was easy enough to talk over them.

Their dinner conversation was mostly just friendly chit-chat with Evan asking most of the questions. He learned that Chen had just turned seventy last month and that he had worked at Telogene for the last forty years. He had also been a pilot in the Chinese Airforce during World War III.

Yin was forty-four but looked at least ten years younger. She had been born in London but moved with her parents to Denver, Colorado when she was ten. As soon as she turned twenty-one, the minimum age to enlist, she signed up as a GFN Peacekeeper and served for twenty years. She now worked as an independent contractor, providing executive protection services to the highest bidder.

Her father had worked at Telogene for thirty years before retiring ten years ago, and he and Chen were close friends—the only reason she had accepted Chen's request to help get Evan out of Xi'an. Her parents now lived in Adelaide, Australia, and Yin tried to visit them at least a couple of times a year. They were retired now, but they lived very comfortably on the money her father had made during his years at Telogene.

"Wow," Evan said to Chen. "If her dad is doing so well after thirty years, I can only imagine the fortune you've amassed in forty!" he added.

Chen smiled. "Yes, the company you founded has been very good to me over the years, Dr. Feldman. I guess I should thank you for that."

"Not at all. I am just thrilled to have been a part of creating such a long-lasting company that has bettered the lives of so many people. I know that things haven't always gone as I would have liked, but it seems to me that Telogene has done more good in the world than harm. Wouldn't you agree?"

Chen nodded. "I would not work for Telogene if I thought otherwise."

"Oh, come on, Chen," Yin interjected. "I've heard the stories from my father...and you were there. You know as well as I do that Telogene played a huge role in the famine, and some would say they pretty much caused it. Is that your definition of doing less harm??"

Chen frowned. "No, of course not. But great scientific achievement rarely happens without risk."

"That's right," Evan added. "Nuclear power is a perfect example. This ship would not be possible without it, but today's achievements came at the cost of hundreds of thousands of lives lost to nuclear detonations and reactor meltdowns. Not to mention the ongoing threat of the complete annihilation of humanity in an all-out nuclear war."

"Yes, Dr. Feldman, but the famine killed billions," Yin replied, her tone stern and disapproving. "We know that nuclear power is inherently dangerous, and we do our best to protect ourselves. Genetic engineering is a different beast altogether. It can take generations before we even realize we've made mistakes, and our world is proof of that!"

Chen replied before Evan could respond. "You sound like your father, Yin. He and I have had this debate countless times, and it always ended the same. Humans are curious creatures, and we will always probe the limits of what we know and what we can do. The problem is that evolution has ill-prepared us for the rapid pace of our advancement. We lack the wisdom to understand the difference between whether we *can* do something, and whether we *should* do something."

He let that sink in for a second before continuing. "Our insatiable curiously makes it almost inevitable that we *will* make mistakes and that we *will* use new technologies in inappropriate and dangerous ways. And that is unfortunate. But I believe that the unknown is no reason to forsake scientific advancement. Humanity is doomed if we don't colonize space, and it's only a matter of time before—"

"I've heard that argument before, Chen," Yin interrupted. "I don't agree that our only choices are continuous technological advancement or going the way of the dinosaurs. Technological innovation is fine, but when are we going to learn patience? Must we rush to put everything we learn into immediate use? What's wrong with taking decades, or even centuries to study and test our discoveries before deciding whether they are safe? Shouldn't our longer lifespans allow us at least that luxury?"

"Yes," Chen said calmly but firmly, "I would agree with you...*if* we lived in a perfect world where everybody played by the same rules. But we don't. Unfortunately, we live in a world where there are just as many people intent on doing evil as there are those intent on doing good. Just imagine what would have happened if Hitler had developed the A-bomb first? We will never know for sure, but I suspect he would've used every single one he managed to build. Russia, the UK, and possibly even the United States would have been wiped from the map. Thank God that never happened!"

"I understand your concerns, Yin," Evan interjected. "I have asked myself these same questions countless times, and especially during the early years...when we knew almost nothing about how DNA worked. We couldn't help but think we were crossing a line we weren't meant to cross. But here's the thing...I believe nature is self-limiting, and that our species' survival depends on our ability to advance scientifically and technologically. The Earth is littered with the fossils of extinct species that could not adapt and evolve. Without technological advancement, we are all just one unforeseen plague, famine, super-volcano, or asteroid away from extinction."

Yin shook her head. "That's fine, but building spaceships and playing God with genetics are not the same thing. I am all for building cool machines to take us to the stars, but I am not for messing with Mother Nature."

Chen tried to speak but Evan cut him off. "How is it different, Yin? We're nothing more than biological machines—our cells have power sources that require fuel, we have parts that can wear out and break, and we can be copied and recreated indefinitely. If that's not a machine, then I don't know what is."

Yin considered Evan's words for a moment. "There is one thing you are forgetting, Dr. Feldman—machines aren't alive. They can't procreate on their own, they don't feel pain unless we program them to, and they certainly don't fall in love. Machines are tools that enhance and extend human ability, plain and simple. Like this ship, they exist to serve a purpose and they will never become more than what we make them to be. I don't know about you, but I am not just some tool that exists to serve someone else's purpose."

"Not yet," Chen whispered in Yin's direction.

"What?" Yin asked.

"You said that machines aren't alive, and I said *not yet*," Chen clarified. "But it's only a matter of time. I agree with Evan that we are machines— I have been a geneticist for way too long to not understand that basic truth. And I also agree with you that our thoughts and feelings make us different. But it's only a matter of time before we create an artificial intelligence that can endow mechanical forms with the same independent thought and will to survive that we possess. I am certain that time is coming and, when it does, I think you will be hard-pressed to define us as anything other than highly advanced, organic machines."

"Well, I'll believe that when I see it," Yin retorted, undaunted in her argument. "But until then I think we need to stop playing God and stop messing with things that we clearly don't understand."

"Your point is well taken, Yin," Evan said. "But the damage is already done, and there is no putting that genie back in the bottle. Our only choice now is to fix what's broken or risk extinction. While it's true that a genetic mutation that causes mass infertility and cancer is essentially a killer asteroid of our own making, the difference between us and the dinosaurs is that we don't just have to sit by and watch it happen. We can do something about it. And I intend to make sure that this event becomes a near miss rather than a direct hit on our planet."

"And that's why I am helping you, Evan," Yin said casually. "Although we disagree on several key points, I do believe we share the same goal and that you are highly motivated to help solve a problem that you helped create. I only hope that, once this is all over, people will take a hard look at what we are doing to ourselves and perhaps reconsider our current position on genetic manipulation."

Evan smiled. "I can't disagree with you there."

Chen raised his hand toward Yin, "Okay, Yin, I think that's enough for today. Evan hasn't had a lot of time to process all this yet, and you are pushing a little hard. We appreciate your help more than you know. But please remember that your job is to protect him—not to chastise him or act as his conscience."

"It's okay, Chen," Evan said. "I appreciate her sharing her views with me. It helps me to better connect with the reality of what's going on and how I fit in."

"You're very kind, Dr. Feldman, but Chen is right. I shouldn't have expressed my views quite so strongly. As you can probably tell, I am very passionate about this issue."

"May I ask you a personal question, Yin?" Evan asked.

"Sure, what is it?"

"I hope this doesn't sound too indelicate…but are you sterile?"

Yin looked down. Evan could barely hear her answer, she said it so softly. "Yes."

"I'm very sorry, Yin. Have you tried to have children?"

Yin looked up with teary eyes. "Yes, about ten years ago. My ex-husband and I tried for several years but the fertility treatments didn't work for us. We eventually gave up, and it wasn't long afterward that our marriage ended. He didn't want to believe he was just as sterile as I was, so he left. I haven't talked to him since the divorce, but I am sure he is out there somewhere still looking for that one person who can have his baby. His loss."

"I'm sure that was very difficult, and I understand why you feel the way you do," Evan said. "Thank you for sharing that with me."

"Look, Evan, I know you didn't do this…and I don't blame you. You may have helped start the ball rolling but there have been many people pushing it down the hill since then. I just hope you all can figure out some way to stop it."

"Me too, Yin, me too."

FOURTEEN

APRIL 4, 2075 7:45 P.M. GST
THE DOLDER GRAND HOTEL
ZURICH, SWITZERLAND

After leaving Aubrey at GSSA headquarters, Geoff met with Assistant Chief Cryonicist Walker and Chief Neurochemist Berkovic to discuss their cases and prepare them for their arraignments, also scheduled for the following day. As with Aubrey, it was unlikely the GSSA would release them, but Geoff assured them he would do everything he could. He had to tell them he wouldn't be able to represent them himself because he needed to focus on Aubrey's case, but he had assigned two of Telogene's best lawyers as their council. They seemed reasonably comfortable with his decision.

Next, he attempted to call Evelyn Wu, but she wasn't taking his calls. Evelyn's assistant had referred him to her GSSA lawyer, Heinz Mast, but calls to his office were equally unproductive. He would have to wait until after the arraignment before speaking with Evelyn or anyone from the GSSA.

With nothing left to do, Geoff returned to his suite at the Dolder Grand Hotel.

Located on the outskirts of Zurich, the Dolder Grand was a Swiss hospitality icon, having been in nearly continuous operation for over 175 years. Geoff stayed there whenever he was in town because he preferred quiet seclusion over the hustle and bustle of downtown. He also enjoyed walking in the lush, wooded areas behind the resort.

Geoff's hovercar deposited him at the main entrance to the hotel, where an impeccably dressed man greeted him.

"Welcome back, Mr. Wagner."

"Thank you, Fritz," Geoff replied to his butler, one of the many perks the Dolder afforded its high-end clientele.

"A pleasant day, I hope?"

"More busy than pleasant, I'm afraid."

"Sorry to hear that, sir. Is there anything I can get for you?"

"Just dinner in my room at nine, please."

"Of course, sir. Any special requests?"

"Surprise me, chef's choice."

"Very well, sir. May I escort you to your room?"

"No, I'm fine, thank you."

Fritz nodded slightly, "My pleasure, sir."

A short time later Geoff was sitting out on his balcony overlooking downtown Zurich in the distance and Lake Zurich beyond. The sun was just setting, and the city below twinkled in the cool dusk air.

Man, this view never gets old.

He took another sip of his forty-year-old, single malt Scotch whiskey.

And there is no such thing as a too-old Scotch!

Geoff lingered over his Scotch until the last of the sun faded away before turning his attention to the work that awaited him inside.

"Let's see what I have to work with," he said out loud as he examined the contents of the holocube Aubrey had given him earlier that day.

He spent the next hour pouring over the contents of the cube, but he found nothing of immediate value.

"Come on, Aubrey, it's got to be here somewhere. Where did you hide it?"

He poured over the cube's contents for another half hour and was about to hurl it across the room when Fritz appeared in the doorway across the room.

"I'm sorry to interrupt, but dinner is served."

"Thank you, I'll be right there."

Fritz left Geoff staring blankly at the holodisplay flickering in the air in front of him.

What did she say to me? Data file backups as required by the board and…that's it!

For the past three decades, the company had required that a backup of all corporate documents be maintained at the company's facility on Mars; this included the engramic archives of all senior executives.

She would have known that the GSSA would secure our primary backup locations, and she would have had a contingency.

Geoff activated his personal AI and asked it to query the company's research lab on Mars.

That will take a while. Might as well eat something, I'm starving.

Geoff left the holocube to do its work while he enjoyed a five-course meal that started with a creamy Swiss onion soup, worked its way through salad, beef and fish courses, and ended with a slice of chocolate cake that ranked among the best he had ever had.

Fritz appeared at Geoff's side just as he finished his last bite of cake.

"I'm sorry to interrupt, sir, but you have an urgent call. Would you like to take it upstairs?"

"Who is it?"

"The Secretary General's office."

"Great. Yes, I'll take it in the office."

"Will there be anything else this evening?"

"No, thank you. Please send my compliments to the chef."

"Very well, sir. Have a good night."

"You, too."

Geoff walked up the stairs to the office located just off the master bedroom. The GSSA logo was visible on the holodisplay, and Geoff gestured to accept the call.

General Secretary Merkel's face replaced the logo. "Good evening, Mr. Wagner."

"Hello, Madame Secretary. What can I do for you this fine evening?"

Geoff could see that Dianne Merkel had been burning the candle at both ends. Her face was drawn, and he could see dark shadows beneath her normally youthful-looking eyes.

"There has been a change of plans for tomorrow. I just got off the phone with Justice Salamanca. She has agreed to allow your client to attend the hearing remotely—for her protection and safety."

Geoff could tell from the sly smile that crept across her face that the sarcasm he heard in her voice was intentional. He wished that he could reach through the holodisplay and slap it off her but, since he couldn't, he returned her smile with an ear-to-ear grin of his own.

"Okay, I'll let her know," he said without the slightest note of surprise or aggravation in his voice. "Is there anything else I need to know?"

"You're not going to lodge a protest?" Dianne asked, somewhat surprised.

"What's the point? It's just an arraignment, and I've been doing this long enough to know that my client isn't getting out on bail."

"Well, I'm glad to hear it. I appreciate you not making this any more difficult than it needs to be."

"You're welcome. But please don't mistake my acceptance of this little ploy as resignation. We will fight, and we *will* win. I'm just picking my battles."

"I take offense to that, Mr. Wagner. This is no *little ploy*…I am sincerely concerned about your client's safety," Dianne said with more than a hint of indignation in her voice.

"Yes, I am sure you are. And it's especially convenient that your concern for her safety will have the secondary benefit of keeping her away from the dozens of reporters who I am sure will camp outside the courthouse."

"So, that's your biggest concern? Getting her in front of the press? Don't worry, Mr. Wagner, I am sure you will more than adequately represent your client's interests in that venue as well."

"I will do my best. In any case, it's getting late, and I need to call my client. Are we done?"

"Yes, I thought I would do you this courtesy and tell you in person. Good night, Mr. Wagner."

"Good night, Madam Secretary, and thank you for the call."

Geoff ended the call and dialed GSSA Headquarters to speak to his client. It took several minutes of pleading and more than a couple of threats, but he finally got to talk to her. He explained that he would appear in court on her behalf, and that she would be present only as a holographic projection. She didn't seem to mind and thanked him for letting her know. He told her to get some sleep and then disconnected. He hoped he hadn't seemed in too much of a hurry, but he had other urgent business to attend to.

Geoff went back downstairs to where he had left Aubrey's holocube. He activated the display and was pleased to see he had received the answer he had hoped for.

Good girl!

Aubrey had, as he expected, uploaded her last engramic archive to Telogene's lab on Mars. She had also provided several documents that outlined her plans for Evan and her rationale for bringing him back. Geoff didn't bother reading them; he already knew what she was planning and why she did what she did.

I better make a copy just in case.

With a few gestures, Geoff instructed the remote lab's AI to create a copy of Aubrey's engrams and transmit them to another secret location —this one known only to him. Once satisfied that the transfer was in progress, he activated his communicator implant.

The person who answered wasn't happy. "So much for *don't call me again!*"

"I am sorry to bother you at this hour, Alex, but there has been a change of plans," Geoff said.

Alexei listened quietly for several minutes as Geoff explained his new plan.

"So, let me be sure I understand," Alexei finally said. "First, you ask me to extract a high-profile target in GSSA custody, the difficulty of which would be extreme...to say the least."

"Alex—"

"Let me finish," Alexei continued. "And now you want her terminated? That is no simple favor that can be exchanged between friends, Bruce...excuse me, I mean Geoff. That is a service that comes at a very high price, were I to even consider doing it at all."

"Look, Alex, you and I have known each other for a very long time, and you know as well as I do that this was standard executive protection protocol until the HDDA. I am simply asking you to do something that we've done dozens of times before."

"Yes, that is true. But those things just are not done anymore…at least not publicly. Besides, she'll be scooped up the minute she shows herself. And she'll have no rights—the GSSA will do whatever they want with her, and there will be no courts to stand in their way."

"As I said at the beginning…we will get her to Mars, and she will never come back. Her life here is over. Do you think that Merkel will ever allow her to walk away from this? She brought her grandfather back from the dead for fuck's sake, and the story is already hitting the news feeds. Aubrey will be locked up for the rest of her life, only to be hauled out and put on display whenever the GSSA needs to remind people of the consequences of illegal cloning. She will lose everything, and she will spend the rest of her life in some prison camp. I can't let that happen."

A long moment of silence passed before Alexei finally spoke.

"If I do this," he finally said, "then whoever I send will need a new life. There can't be any ties back to us…and that will be very, very expensive, my friend."

"I already have that covered. You secure an engramic archive from your operative before informing him or her of the job. Once it's done, I will ensure that they get a new face, a GFN registered identity, and plenty of money to start a new life."

"And what about you, Mister Wagner, where will you go?"

"I go where Aubrey goes. I promised an old friend that I would protect his family no matter what, and I can't stop now."

"That's what I've always envied that about you, Bruce."

"What?"

"Your dedication and sense of purpose in life. You've always been someone who knows exactly why you are here and what's expected of you. That is a great gift, my friend. I have learned the hard way that living a long life loses its luster when you lack purpose."

"We all have a purpose, Alex."

"That may be true in the beginning, but I am turning one hundred and five years old next month. And what do I have to show for it? More money than I can ever spend, more ex-wives than I can count, and a circle of friends who I only hear from when they need something—present company included."

"You know I'd call more if I could."

"That's not the point…besides, I told you I never wanted to hear from you again. Remember?"

"Alex, I—"

"The point is that my only purpose in life is to be available for those rare occasions when my erstwhile friends call asking for favors. Otherwise, I'm just bored out of my mind because I have nothing left to do."

"Well, we—"

"Except one thing!" Alex interrupted.

"Which is?"

"I want to be on the ship."

"What ship?"

"Come now, Bruce, don't be coy with me. The ship going to Alpha Centauri. The one that the Galileo Group is building in orbit above Ceres."

"Adekunle Gbadamosi's company?"

"The one and only."

"What's that have to do with me or my request?"

"Please, don't insult me. I know that Telogene has pumped hundreds of billions into that ship. There can only be one reason you are so eager to get your asses to Mars, and you are taking me with you."

"Now wait a minute, Alex. I don't know where you are getting your information, but you've got it wrong. There is no…"

"Stop! I don't want to hear your lies! These are my terms. You want my help with Aubrey, then you take me with you. Otherwise, no deal!"

"You got to believe me, Alexei, I know nothing about that ship beyond what we've all seen in the news. We are going to Mars so that Aubrey and Chen can find a solution for the mutation problem. That's it."

Alexei laughed hard. "Oh, that's rich. Is it possible that little Aubrey has not been completely honest with you? Can it be that she has excluded you, her ever faithful friend and protector, from her plan? I don't believe it. The great Bruce Wagner—master of disguise, corporate espionage agent extraordinaire, terror of the courtroom, and trusted adviser to the CEO of Telogene—knows nothing he hasn't seen on the news? I love it!"

He continued before Bruce could respond. "Well, I guess it's only fair since you've hidden your identity from her all these years. I wonder what she'd say if she found out that Geoff Wagner is really Bruce Wagner, her grandfather's best friend and the designated guardian angel of his children and grandchildren?"

"You're out of line, Alexei."

"No sir, I am only stating the obvious. Either what I say is true, or you are lying to me, and I know when you are lying, my friend—you are *not* lying. You really don't know what her plans are, do you?"

"What I know is that she needs my help, and that is all I need to know. If what you say is true, then I am sure she will tell me when she's ready. In the meantime, I need to hear you say you will help me. Will you help, Alex?"

"Yes, Bruce. I will help you. *But you must promise to get me on that ship.*"

"I can't promise to get you on a ship I know next to nothing about. But what I can promise is to find out what's going on and share with you anything I learn. Fair enough?"

"Well, I guess that will have to do, my friend. I will do as you have asked."

"Thank you. I've always been able to count on you."

"But after this, we are even. I have paid my debt in full, understood?"

"Agreed…goodbye, Alex."

"No goodbyes. I will see you again soon my friend…on Mars!"

The display went dark, leaving Geoff—or Bruce, as he was once known—to ponder what Alexei had said.

That was unfortunate. I wonder how he found out.

He went downstairs and poured himself another drink before returning to his favorite balcony. The lights of downtown Zurich were glowing in the distance, but it was the light of the stars above that drew Bruce's gaze. He took another sip of his Scotch.

I wonder which one of those is Mars.

FIFTEEN

APRIL 4, 2075 10:30 P.M. GST
TELOGENE SHUTTLE
LUNAR ORBIT APPROACH

"Dr. Feldman?"

"Yes?"

"I am sorry to interrupt, sir, but can I speak with you outside, please?"

Evan stood up from the conference table and excused himself. The young man who had just interrupted his meeting led him out into the hallway.

"How can I help you?" Evan asked.

"Dr. Feldman, I am Jakob Nielsen from the U.S. Embassy. I am sorry to pull you away, but I need you to come with me immediately."

"What is the problem, have I done something wrong?"

"No, sir. There has been an accident…a plane crash. One of your corporate jets went down in the Pacific."

"Oh, my God! Is everyone okay?"

"No sir, I am afraid not. There is a search and rescue team on-site now, but they haven't found any survivors."

Evan's heart pounded so hard that he could barely hear what the man said next.

"Sir, I need you to come with me now. There is a car waiting downstairs."

Evan suddenly felt lightheaded, and he stumbled backward into the wall. Jacob caught him under his arms and held him up against the wall.

"Chr…Christina?" Evan stammered out his wife's name. The tears welled up in his eyes and rolled down his face.

Jacob steadied Evan and eased him off the wall. "I'm very sorry, sir."

"Nooo!" Evan sobbed. "It's not possible."

"Please, Dr. Feldman, not here. Let me take you someplace more private."

"Christina!" Evan screamed as his knees gave out, almost taking Jacob down with him.

"Are you alright?" Chen asked from across the aisle.

Evan opened his eyes. The hallway in Hong Kong was gone, replaced by the white and blue interior of the shuttle. He had been dreaming.

"I'm fine, I was just dreaming." He wiped his wet cheeks with the back of his hand.

"That sounded more like a nightmare to me…you called out Christina's name."

"Yeah, it was the day she died. That's the first time I've dreamed since…" Evan fumbled for the words. "…since you brought me back."

"Is everything okay up there?" Yin called from behind him.

"Yes, I am fine, thank you. Just a bad dream," Evan called back.

Chen rotated his pod so he could get a better look at Evan.

"That's a good sign," he said. "Dreams mean that your brain is processing memories normally."

"Great," Evan said sarcastically. "I can think of a bunch of other things that I would rather dream about."

"Not all memories are equal," Chen said as he rotated his pod back to its rearward-facing position. "It's not surprising that such a traumatic event is one of your strongest memories. I am sure that your brain allocated a great many neurons to it."

Evan turned off the music playing in his ears and adjusted his pod to a more upright position.

"Evan?" Chen called across the aisle.

"Yes?"

"I'm sorry. I know that was hard for you. Please let me know if there is anything I can do to help."

Evan gave him a slight smile. "Thanks, Chen, I appreciate that. I'll be fine."

A door slid open at the rear of the cabin. Evan watched as a platform carrying Elise and Talia descended slowly toward him. It stopped next to him, and Elise asked if he needed anything. He said he was fine and explained that he had been dreaming.

"Yeah, I noticed your heart rate spike for a few minutes," Talia said. "Are you sure I can't get you anything?"

"You're watching my heart rate?" Evan asked.

Elise nodded. "Yes, your suit monitors your vital signs, and it notifies us when anything abnormal occurs."

"Are you experiencing a headache?" Talia asked as she reached into the food and beverage cart.

"Yeah, and it's getting worse. I figured it would go away once I got some rest."

Chen rotated his pod again to face Evan.

"How long?" he asked.

"Since I woke up," Evan replied.

"Here, take this." Talia handed him a small pink pill and a pouch of water. "It's a mild analgesic and endorphin booster."

Evan swilled the pill with a gulp of water before handing her back the half-empty pouch. "Thank you."

A warm smile spread across Talia's face. "You're welcome."

"Do either of you need anything?" Elise asked Yin and Chen. "We are about to start our final deceleration into orbit, so now is your last chance."

"No, thank you," Yin and Chen said in unison.

"Okay. We should be on the ground in about thirty minutes."

The platform continued to the front of the ship and Evan watched as Elise and Talia settled into their pods.

"Please keep an eye on those headaches, Evan," Chen said. "You need to tell me if they get worse, or if you experience any disorientation or hallucinations. Those may be symptoms of a problem with your engramic transfer, and we need to jump on it right away if that happens."

Evan nodded. "What would you do if that happens?"

"Well, it depends on where we are and what equipment we have available."

"Is it fatal?"

"Not usually. It just means that your brain is struggling to assimilate all your memories, and it may need a little help. Everything usually sorts itself out after a few days."

"What happens if it doesn't?"

Chen paused for a second to consider his answer. "Let's cross that bridge when we get there. I oversaw the transfer personally, and I am confident that you aren't going to have any problems."

"If you say so."

"But, please let me know immediately if you have any symptoms. There is no sense taking any chances."

Evan smirked. "No worries, Doc, I will let you know the minute I feel like I am going crazy."

Captain Bauer's voice echoed in Evan's headrest. "Attention, please. We are about to start our final deceleration into Lunar orbit. We've been cleared to land and will be making a rapid descent to slide in front of a cargo freighter coming in from the Belt."

Evan assumed correctly that "the Belt" referred to the asteroid belt between Mars and Jupiter.

The captain continued. "For those of you that haven't done this before, we land backwards. Your pods are going to stay as they are until we are on the Lunar surface."

"You should get a glimpse of the Tycho mines and Clavius Base as we de-orbit," the captain resumed after a short pause. "And, you should have some pretty good views of Casatus City as we make our final approach to Klaproth."

Another short pause. "There may be a few bumps here and there as we adjust our landing vector and rate of descent, but nothing as severe as what you experienced during launch. Otherwise, just sit back and enjoy the ride, and we will have you down shortly."

Elise's voice came over the sound system seconds after the captain finished.

"Our trip is just about over, and we'd like to thank you all for your cooperation and patience. You were a fantastic group and we look forward to serving you on a future flight. The current time is 22:35 GST, and we should be down in just about twenty minutes. There's a short tow to the airlock after touchdown, so please remain in your pod until the craft comes to a complete stop."

She drew in a breath before continuing.

"Please exit your pods slowly—lunar gravity is just one-sixth that of Earth. We recommend that you take a few minutes to acclimate yourself before you go bounding down the ramp. And we strongly encourage you to take advantage of the handrails that run the entire length of the gangway. Thank you again for flying with us today, and welcome to Luna."

A few seconds after Elise stopped talking, the ship's SABRE engines sprang to life. Evan felt his pod shake slightly as they added their thrust to that of the Hellfires to slow the craft. Their speed had dropped below 20,000 kilometers per hour and was falling quickly. Evan's holodisplay showed their position a little south of the equator and just crossing the boundary between the light and dark sides of the moon.

An "Area of Interest" message flashed on the screen as it automatically zoomed in on the Sea of Tranquility. Soft music began playing as a male voice narrated a description of the Apollo 11 landing. A montage of old video clips and images appeared next to indicators of where they were taken on the lunar surface.

This happened several more times as the shuttle continued its descent. There was the Apollo 16 landing in the Descartes Highlands, the Chinese research stations at Kepler and Letronne craters, and the helium-3 mine in Grimaldi Crater. As the craft rocketed toward the far side of Luna, the automated narrator highlighted the Mare Orientale basin and the large mining consortium that operated there…followed minutes later by descriptions of various research stations and mining outposts, including the Mendeleev Deep Space Telescope.

The Mendeleev radio telescope was an array of telescopes spread over nearly 320 kilometers of crater floor on the far side of Luna. Construction on the facility began in 2033, just two years after the first colonists landed on Luna. It took nearly five years to complete. The narrator noted that the Mendeleev telescope had accumulated more information on deep space than all other Earth and space-based telescopes combined.

The space above the facility was restricted to preserve its unobstructed view of the universe. Evan noted that their current track was taking them 800 kilometers south of the crater. The plot on the display showed that they would make a large arc around the southern pole before descending into the Klaproth Spaceport. As they approached the pole, a magnified view of the Cabeus Research Station appeared on Evan's holodisplay.

The narrator explained that Cabeus Crater was the site of the first lunar colony, having served as home to the two dozen intrepid men and woman who volunteered for the first mission in 2031. They had selected that site because of an abundance of water, in the form of ice, trapped beneath the crater's surface. Early life for the colonists had been difficult because of the extreme cold and lack of sunlight on the crater floor. For power and heat, they relied entirely on two prototype helium-3 fusion reactors, which proved to be difficult to maintain and operate. The colonists also learned the hard way that extracting helium-3 was not as easy as they first thought.

They decided to relocate the colony to the Casatus Crater, some 300 kilometers to the north. Unlike Cabeus, Casatus offered a large, relatively flat area that received significant sunlight throughout most of the lunar year. There was water under Casatus, but it was nowhere near as abundant as at Cabeus. And it was nearly a mile below the surface, which made extraction and processing far more difficult. Transporting the abundant water of Cabeus to the more hospitable Casatus—first with tankers and later an underground aqueduct—solved the problem.

Evan heard the Hellfire engines cut off as the ship made its final turn toward Klaproth. A few seconds later, Elise's voice echoed over the sound system.

"Attention, please. We've been cleared to land. Your pods will rotate forward once we are on the ground, but please remember to remain seated until we have stopped moving and the airlock is sealed. Don't forget to retrieve your helmets and other personal belongs from the under-pod storage compartment on your way out. Thank you again for flying with us today, and may the solar wind be ever at your back."

Evan watched his display intently as they descended into Klaproth. The part of Casatus that he could see consisted of one large dome surrounded by six smaller domes. The large dome was about a kilometer-and-a-half in diameter and over ninety meters high at its peak. According to the narrator, Casatus was home to 35,263 colonists, of which nearly half had been born on Luna. They were largely self-sufficient food and energy-wise, but they still imported most of their manufactured goods from Earth and Mars.

Luna was the hub of a robust trade network between Earth and the colonies; its location made it the ideal trans-shipment point for goods and materials. Like Mars, the lunar colony had an independent democratic government that was organized like a typical Earth corporation—with an elected board of directors and a president who served as chairman of the board. Together, they provided direction and oversaw the colony's day-to-day operations.

A public referendum decided non-routine issues, with anyone over the age of twenty years able to vote. The president and board members stood for election every twelve years on an alternating basis, which meant that either the president or half the board was up for election every four years —with no term limits. The current president, Andrea Renee Duchon, was in her twelfth year and up for re-election in November.

Evan heard a loud roar from the SABRE engines and felt the shuttle's forward motion slow considerably. The craft was now at 3,000 meters above the surface and descending at ten meters per second. The visual display switched to Klaproth Station, which consisted of another dome surrounded by a dozen well-lit, circular landing pads.

About half of the pads were occupied—two by ships similar to the one he was in, and four by larger ships that he guessed to be cargo transport ships, due to their boxy shapes. His ship was headed toward an empty pad on the northeast side of the dome.

The SABREs roared again as the craft descended below 1,000 meters, and Evan watched intently as their descent rate dropped to five meters per second. He switched his display to a rearward view so he could watch the thrusters fire. He adjusted the viewpoint to just under the nose of the ship, looking toward the rear. From this vantage, he could see the thrusters mounted along the bottom of the craft, the four SABRE engines on the wings, and the spaceport just ahead.

He watched with rapt attention as the thrusters and engines lit up in seemingly random patterns. The ship coasted gently toward the landing pad, where a six-wheeled vehicle sat off to one side. They were just meters above the lunar surface, and Evan could see grains of sand and small rocks being tossed around by the ship's downward thrust. A few seconds later, they floated across the landing pad threshold. Evan again adjusted his display, allowing him to look rearward from a point at the top of the fuselage in between the craft's V-shaped tail.

They were now over the landing pad.

The SABREs roared one last time to bleed off the rest of their forward motion. The underbelly thrusters fired as the ship floated lazily down onto the center of the pad. He switched his view to the nose of the craft just as the thrusters went quiet.

"Wow!" he said out loud.

"Yeah, wow," Yin said, "I never tire of seeing that."

The passenger pods rotated forward, and Yin was once again behind Evan.

Evan watched as the six-wheeled vehicle rolled up to the front of the ship and attached itself to the forward landing gear. Once connected, it hauled them across the pad toward the terminal. It took several minutes to get them off the pad and aligned with the airlock. As soon as they stopped moving, Elise and the other flight attendants got out of their pods and moved toward the forward hatch. Evan noticed that they took slow, steady steps to minimize bouncing in the low gravity. Several minutes passed while the flight crew secured the main hatch and opened the airlock.

Elise's voice sounded over the intercom. "Please be careful when exiting your pods and watch your step. You will bounce if you step too hard. And it will hurt if you bang your head against the ceiling, so please proceed slowly and carefully."

There was another short pause.

"And please let us know if you need help with your belongings or exiting the craft."

Elise stayed by the hatch, but Talia and Anika moved down the aisle in case anyone needed help. Evan removed his restraints and slowly stood. He felt light-headed and had to wait a few seconds to regain his balance. Yin and Chen leapt from their seats and gathered their things from the storage bins beneath their pods. They had done this before.

Chen offered Evan his arm, Yin grabbed Evan's helmet from under his pod, and the three of them drifted toward the front of the ship together.

Anika and Talia smiled as they walked past, and Elise gave one last, "Thank you," as they entered the airlock.

The door slid shut as soon as they were inside the airlock. An obnoxiously loud hiss emanated from somewhere behind them as the pressure equalized. The airlock walls, floor, and ceiling glowed with a faint bluish-purple hue.

"Decontamination," Chen said, sensing Evan's puzzlement.

A few seconds went by before the lights turned white and the opposite door slid open. Evan could see a long, well-lit hallway leading away from the ship.

Chen urged Evan forward. "There's a changing room just ahead. We'll want to get out of these suits before we meet our contact in the main terminal."

The three ambled down the hallway as Evan adjusted to the low gravity environment. Chen was no longer holding his arm, but Yin walked a few steps behind, just in case.

Sixteen

April 4, 2075 11:07 p.m. GST
Klaproth Spaceport
Luna

Evan took a few timid steps to test the loaner pair of magnetic boots Chen had given him. Walking in them felt natural as sensors in the boots adjusted the magnetic force with each step. Evan had only to make sure that at least one foot was on the floor at all times, which still took a little practice.

"Looks like you've got it," Yin said.

"I'm getting there," Evan acknowledged.

"No worries. We'll take it slow."

"So, how long are we here?" Evan asked.

"Not sure," Chen answered. "It depends on the location of our transport ship, and when the captain will be ready to go. This isn't our original plan, and we are now relying on the goodwill of others."

"What do you mean?"

"Well, our original plan was to keep you on Earth for two to four weeks while you adjusted. We didn't want to risk restoring you off planet, and we hoped that our little scheme would go undetected. But it didn't, so now we improvise."

"What would be the problem with reviving me on Luna or Mars and avoiding this whole situation in the first place?"

"It's complicated, but we've had problems with that in the past. The human brain doesn't do well when time, gravity, and place vary too greatly from what the person last remembers. We think it involves how circadian rhythm is encoded in our brain and nervous system, but nobody is quite sure. What we know is that slow acclimation in a familiar environment produces the best results."

"So, what does that mean for me?"

Chen shook his head. "To be perfectly honest, Evan, I'm not sure."

Evan's facial expression made it clear that this new revelation was more than a little disconcerting.

"But don't worry about it," Chen added. "You are in the best hands, and we will have everything we need to ensure that you have a successful recovery once we get to Mars."

"I understand, but isn't it going to take us several weeks to get to Mars? What happens in the meantime?"

"More like hours, at least once we are on board the *Endeavor*."

"Hours? How is that possible? We took hours to get to the Moon!"

"Different technology. *Endeavor* is equipped with a gravity pulse engine, which allows the ship to travel at relativistic speeds."

"So, it has a warp drive then," Evan stated matter-of-factly.

Chen thought a moment. "Not exactly, but you need to ask someone who knows about the stuff. I'm just a cryonicist, remember?"

"Okay then, Mister Cryonicist, can you at least tell me what kind of brain problems you are expecting me to have?"

"I am not expecting any problems," Chen reassured him. "More than likely, you will experience nothing more than the occasional headache or bizarre dream, which we can mitigate with drugs if required. The main things you must watch out for are feelings of extreme disorientation and hallucinations. If that happens, you must let me know right away."

"What will it mean if I experience those things?"

"Well, it can mean several things—most of which are minor problems we can easily deal with but…"

"But what?"

"But they can also be symptoms of a breakdown in your synaptic processes. If that happens, we will need to begin aggressive brain stimulation therapy right away or put you into stasis until we get somewhere where we can deal with it."

"Brain stimulation therapy?" Evan grimaced. "That sounds decidedly unappealing."

"It's not that bad. We inject you with special nanites that will reinforce and reconstruct your synapses using your baseline engrams as a pattern."

"My baseline engrams?"

"The copy of your brain we used to restore you."

"Which means that I will forget everything that has happened in the last thirty-six hours?"

"Not everything. It depends on how much your engrams degrade from the baseline. It's possible that the procedure could restore normal brain function with minimal memory loss. But it is unlikely that will happen, okay?"

"If you say so."

"I do. We had a great baseline to work with, and there were no issues during the encoding procedure. I will bet my reputation on the fact that your brain is as stable as if you were born with it!"

Evan nodded and said nothing more. He could see they were nearing the end of the tunnel, and it looked like there were three people standing near the entrance to the terminal. A tall man with light brown skin, dark hair, and wearing a white jacket, shirt, and trousers, stepped forward to meet them. Two other men, dressed in all blue, stood on either side of the passageway.

"Welcome to Klaproth Station," the man in white said. "I am Administrator Nayak, and I am responsible for this facility. Is this your first trip to Luna?"

Chen stepped forward to shake the man's hand.

"Happily, no," Chen replied. "We have made this trip many times, but I don't believe we have met. I am Dr. Chen Hao, Telogene's Chief Cryonicist, and these are my assistants, Drs. Li and Richardson. We are just here on a brief layover. How can I be of service?"

"Well, Dr. Hao, I am sorry, but we have received a request from the GFN to detain you. They claim you are fugitives and are demanding your immediate return to Earth. Will you please come with us?"

Yin took a few steps forward to stand next to Evan. Chen put his hand behind his back, palm out, to signal her to stop.

Chen feigned ignorance. "Are you sure you have the right people? There must be some mistake."

Administrator Nayak frowned. "I am sure there is. But, in the meantime, would you be kind enough to accompany me to my office so we can get this sorted? I prefer to avoid confrontation whenever possible."

The men in blue stepped forward to block the hallway on either side of the administrator. Evan noticed that they both had large pistols strapped to their thighs.

"Why would there be a confrontation? I would be happy to come with you, but we are meeting someone in just a few minutes. Would it be possible to send one of my assistants to find him and let him know we will be delayed?"

The administrator looked the three fugitives up and down several times. "Very well. You can send Dr....Li, was it? The two of you will come with me."

"If you insist," Chen replied. He turned to Yin and handed her something that Evan thought looked like one of those data cubes he'd seen earlier.

"Meet us at the administrator's office after you've made the necessary arrangements."

Yin nodded and slipped the data cube into her jacket pocket.

"And not too long, please," the administrator admonished Yin. "I'd hate to have to send a security detail to retrieve you."

"It should only take twenty or thirty minutes, at most," she replied.

"Very well." The administrator gestured for Chen and Evan to follow him. "Right this way, please."

The guards waited for them to fall in line before stepping in behind them.

The Klaproth terminal comprised a large open area in the middle of the dome surrounded by a handful of glass-walled buildings, several of which were three and four stories high. Dozens of people milled around the central concourse, and they could see dozens more walking between the hallways that led to and from the landing pads.

The administrator led them across the concourse toward the largest of the multistory buildings. Along the way, they passed several holodisplays that advertised the various concourse vendors, including a couple of food stands, and offered directions to customs and the tramway. Evan thought he glimpsed Yin on the far side of the concourse, but he wasn't sure.

None of the people in the concourse seemed to pay any attention to Evan's group as it made its way past the food court. Evan had just eaten a couple of hours ago, but the idea of a "food court" brought on a sudden craving for a double cheeseburger with French fries.

I wonder if they still have that kind of stuff? he thought.

"Any chance we can get a bite to eat while we're here?" he asked the administrator. "I am a little hungry."

The administrator stopped and turned back to him. "Didn't they feed you on the shuttle?"

"Yes, but that was several hours ago, and it's worn off."

"I will order you something once we get to my office. What do you want?"

"A cheeseburger and fries would be great, and a chocolate milkshake if you can swing it."

"Hmm, interesting choices. I will see what I can do." Administrator Nayak turned to Dr. Hao. "Anything for you, sir?"

"The same please," he replied.

"You Earthies and your junk food. We don't get too many requests for that here, but we might find you something passable. This way, please."

They left the concourse and proceeded down a narrow alleyway. The passage zigzagged between several of the smaller buildings before depositing them at the entrance of a much larger four-story building. They marched single file through the glass doors toward a nearby bank of elevators. The group stepped into the first one that opened, and the administrator ordered it to take them to the fourth floor.

They exited the elevator and walked down a short hallway to a suite of offices. An attractive brunette with mocha skin sat behind the half-wall that divided the lobby from the rest of the office. She glanced up but said nothing as the group passed by. Evan turned back to look at her, but she acted as if she hadn't seen him.

The group walked approached a row of U-shaped desks, where a team of eight people were hard at work managing the spaceport's affairs. None of them acknowledged Evan or Chen as they walked past. The administrator's corner office looked out over the concourse below.

The office was a simple affair with a desk, a small table with four chairs, and a sofa. There was a holodisplay above the sofa showing scenes from various locales on Earth, none of which Evan recognized. A few reminded him of India, but nothing stood out as any place he had been. There was another holodisplay floating in the air above the administrator's desk. It showed a slideshow of images of an adult woman and two young children. A few of the images looked like they were taken inside of Klaproth terminal.

"Your family?" Evan asked.

"Mmm, yes, my wife and children. Do you have children, Dr. Richardson?"

Evan wasn't sure how to respond and glanced over at Dr. Hao, who just stared back at him.

"Umm, yes. A daughter. She's grown though, and I have a granddaughter."

"Oh, very exciting. These are my first children. I look forward to having grandchildren one day." He walked over to the table and pulled out a chair for Evan. "Please have a seat."

Evan sat in the offered chair and Chen sat in the one next to him. The administrator sat across the table from them both.

"So, what exactly is the nature of the trouble you two have gotten into?"

Chen sighed. "As I said, Administrator, we do not know what you are talking about."

"Well, it must be something significant. GFN Secretary General Dianne Merkel called me herself a few hours ago to request my help. Of course, I had to refer the question of your extradition back to Earth to President Duchon. My instructions are to hold you here until we get a decision, which shouldn't be too much longer."

"Who is Di--"

Chen interrupted Evan and finished his question for him, "Deciding our fate, the president?"

Evan took the hint and decided it was safer to let Chen do the talking.

Administrator Nayak smiled. "President Duchon is meeting with the board to discuss your situation. They will decide together."

Chen continued, "And did the Secretary General say why she wanted us so badly?"

"No, she did not give me any specifics, except to say that you were fugitives from justice. I assume that she has provided more details to the board."

Chen nodded. "I see."

"She mentioned that they had one of your colleagues in custody though. I believe she used the name, Aubrey Harris. Does that name mean anything to you?"

Evan did his best to hide his emotions, but the thought of Aubrey sitting in jail somewhere overwhelmed him. "What? They have Aubrey?"

Chen reached under the table and patted Evan's knee.

"That's what the Secretary General said. I take it you know her then?"

Chen answered first. "Of course we know her. As I am sure you are aware, Administrator, she is the president of Telogene—she is our boss."

"Well, then. If you truly don't know why you are in trouble, then I would suggest that perhaps your boss is to blame. Very unfortunate."

The three sat in silence for several minutes.

Administrator Nayak spoke first. "Let me check on your meal and see if we've heard anything back from the board yet. Please wait here. There are guards in the hall, and there is nowhere to go."

"Understood," Chen replied.

Evan waited until the administrator left the room before leaning over to whisper in Chen's ear.

"What is going on? I thought you said Aubrey would meet us?"

Chen whispered back. "That was the plan, Evan, but something went wrong."

"I have to turn myself in. We can't let this happen to her. I just got her back...I can't lose her again."

"I'm sorry, Evan, but that won't work. Bringing you back was a crime, and a very serious at that—they aren't just going to let her go because you turn yourself in. If you want to help her, stay on mission and do your job; our only way out is finding a cure for the genetic mutations that are plaguing humanity."

"We have to do something. We can't just let her rot in jail while we're traipsing around the solar system!"

Evan's voice was a little louder than he'd planned, and a guard poked his head into the room to see what was going on.

"We're fine." Chen waived him off.

The guard stared at them for a moment before returning to the hallway.

"Please keep your voice down. I am sure there are recording devices in this room and they are listening to everything we say. I am also sure that Aubrey is in good hands. She's probably got every one of Telogene's three thousand lawyers working on this, and it's only a matter of time before they get her out on bail or released on some technicality—they are very good at that sort of thing."

Evan leaned back in his chair. His face looked like he was trying to recall something important but couldn't quite remember what it was.

"What's wrong?" Chen asked.

Evan leaned forward and put his lips next to Chen's ear. "I just remembered someone. I can see his face, but I can't remember his name. He was very important to me. He was the last person I remember seeing before I died, but I just can't remember his name."

"Do you remember anything about him?"

"No, but talking about lawyers made me think of him. I wonder if that's who he was?"

"It's possible. Does the name Bruce Wagner mean anything to you?"

Evan searched his memory for a name. "I don't know. It sounds familiar, but I just can't remember."

"Bruce was your personal attorney. Lily hired him as Chief Legal Officer after you died."

Evan's eyes lit up as the pieces came together. "Yes, that's him—I remember now. He died in the crash that killed Lily. I didn't remember that he was my personal attorney, though."

"Lily told me about the night you died, and how Bruce was there to help her through everything. Bruce was a great friend to you and Lily. He played a big role in saving the company after the famine scandal, and some would say that Lily could have never accomplished what she did without him. He was a great man and losing them both was a horrific tragedy."

"Were they…romantic?"

"No, I don't think so. They treated each other like family. She and Dylan were married until the end and Bruce was married at least twice that I know of—maybe three times, I'm not sure."

"Whatever happened to Dylan, anyway? I can't believe I never thought to ask about him. He and I didn't always get along the best, but he was my son-in-law."

"Nobody knows. There were rumors that he committed suicide after Lily died, but Aubrey didn't believe that. She thought he might have bought a remote island off the coast of Nova Scotia somewhere. All I know is that he said goodbye to Aubrey at Lily's funeral and she never heard from him again. She searched for a couple of months but gave up once she realized that, wherever he was, he didn't want to be found."

"Did he have any children?"

"Dylan?"

"No, Bruce."

"Oh, I was worried there for a second. Yes, a son, Geoff. And you won't believe this, but Geoff is Telogene's current Chief Legal Officer. He joined the company at Aubrey's request a short time after Lily died."

"You're kidding, I can't believe it! What are the odds?"

"I don't know, but I do know that Geoff is every bit the lawyer his father was. And I am confident that he is doing everything he can for Aubrey. She is in very good hands, Evan."

Evan searched his mind for everything he could remember about Bruce Wagner. He mentally compared the picture he saw in the news story about the plane crash with the face he remembered being with him at his deathbed, but he wasn't sure. They looked similar, but it was as if all his memories about Bruce had been erased or buried some place deep in his brain, currently beyond his reach. He just couldn't remember, and it concerned him.

"Have I forgotten a lot?" he finally asked Chen.

"What do you mean?"

"Well, I'm having a hard time remembering Bruce. And it occurs to me that if I can't remember such a good friend, then there are probably lots of other things I can't remember."

Evan could tell that Chen was choosing his words carefully. "Look, Evan, memory restoration is an imperfect science. There is still a lot about the human brain we don't understand and restoring memory is a traumatic process. It is perfectly normal for you to not remember everything right away, but there is a high probability that your memory will improve with more time. You just have to be patient."

"I hope you're right. It's hard enough being in this body, but to think I don't even have all my memories is a little tough to swallow. Am I even me? Or just a flawed copy?"

"You are not a flawed copy. Those are your memories, your feelings, and your personality inside that brain. Everything that Evan Feldman was is in there…you are still the person you were. Give it more time."

"If you say so." Evan lowered his voice to a faint whisper before asking his next question. "Who is this 'Dr. Richardson' whose body I seem to inhabit?"

"That's…complicated."

"Well, can you at least tell me if he is still alive?"

"What I can tell you is that there is not another copy of you walking around somewhere. The body you inhabit is yours alone but, according to GFN citizenship and employment records, you are an Earth-born Telogene researcher assigned to our facilities on Mars."

"How do you create records for someone who doesn't exist?"

"But you do exist."

"Yes, but only since yesterday."

"Like I said, it's complicated. But trust me when I tell you you've been around much longer than just since yesterday, at least officially."

"What kind of world is this? Planting people's memories in other people's bodies? Manufacturing fake identities for clones? That is far from what I ever imagined when I founded Telogene. My goal was to make people's lives better and help them live longer…not for people to live forever by hopping from one body to the next! Hell, it's not even people that are living forever—it's just their memories!"

Dr. Hao sat back in his chair and folded his arms across his chest. "Do you believe in the soul, Evan?"

"What?"

"The soul…that part of you that makes you unique. A part of us that lives on after death?"

"I haven't thought about it."

"Sure, you have. When you were laying in that hospital bed all those years ago, you didn't think about what comes next?"

"I guess so. I remember not wanting to die and wondering if my life to that point was all that there was."

Chen grinned. "Well, my grandfather was a Daoist from Fuzhou, and he taught me that every person has a soul with two parts—the hun and the po. The hun is your spiritual soul—the part that leaves your body after death. The po is your corporeal soul—the part that remains with your corpse after you die. He believed Tian, the divine spirit, could punish bad people by taking away their po—depriving them of their memories and mental ability. This is how people went crazy; they lost their po. If you lost your hun, you would die. Together they form the hunpo, or the complete soul, and we require both for life.

"He also believed you could restore the dead to life by returning their hunpo to their body. Ancient Daoist priests had a magical pill that would cure disease and illness. It could even cause the hunpo to re-enter a dead person's body and restore them to life. They believed that this was possible because the hun and po are an intrinsic part of who we are— you cannot have life without a body, and a body cannot live without its hunpo. Understand?"

"I don't know, maybe. But what does that have to do with me?"

"Don't you see, Evan? My grandfather and his Daoist traditions were right! As a scientist, I have struggled with this for a long time, but I know in my heart there is more to us than just our physical form. Our memories, our personalities, those are the essence of who we are. If I were to chop off your arms and legs, you would still be you, right?"

"Yes, of course."

"And what if I used someone else's DNA to grow you some new arms or legs, would you still be you then?"

"Yes…I think so."

"What if I removed your heart, your lungs, your liver, and all your other organs and replaced them with those from another person—would you still be you then?"

"Absolutely! I would still have my brain and that's what makes me unique," Evan answered.

"But your brain is just another organ, a mass of tissue that stores information. Is it the mass of tissue, or the information it contains, that makes you unique?"

"I would say it's both. Every brain is unique because of the neural pathways that form over our lifetimes."

"Yes, and those pathways form to store information. If I create an exact copy of your brain, even if from someone else's DNA, haven't I recreated the unique storehouse of information that makes you who you are?"

"I see where you are going, but I am just not sure, Chen. I just can't get past the fact that this brain inside my head is just a copy of the one I carried around for the first fifty-nine years of my life. It's not mine, it's just a facsimile."

"You're wrong, Evan. Don't you see? We gave you that magic pill! Your hunpo found its way back into your body the instant we restored your consciousness. You are the person your mother gave birth to, and everything you became thereafter. You are you! You had a full body transplant but, just like the amputee who receives a new arm, you are still the same person."

"Did you really give me a pill?"

"No, I am just extending the metaphor."

"Oh, just curious. So, what you're saying is that memory, personality, and spirit are all the same thing…and that, together, they add up to the soul?"

"Not quite. We are born with a soul, and our personalities and memories are forever bound to it…and our soul forever bound to them. What I am saying is that we are beings of energy that take physical form for a time. Our physical form can change, but the energy imparted to us at the moment of our creation defines who we are forever."

Chen leaned forward again to whisper in Evan's ear. "What I am saying is that you didn't really die, Evan. Your energy left your old body, but our technology—the technology you helped to create—allowed us to capture and store that energy until we could return it to a new body. I'm saying that our technology gave you the second chance you always wanted. There is a reason you're here, Evan—embrace it."

"Having a lively conversation, I see?" Administrator Nayak said as he walked into the room carrying a dome-shaped plastic container.

Chen and Evan sat back in their chairs and stared at the administrator, wondering how much he had heard.

"Don't worry, we aren't listening. That may be commonplace on Earth these days, but we still respect the right to privacy here."

The administrator sat the container in the middle of the table. "Here is your meal. Hamburgers with French fries and…" He removed the lid from the container. "Chocolate shakes."

The contents of the tray looked nothing like hamburgers and French fries as Evan remembered them. On one side were two multi-layered cubes about four inches square. Next to the cubes were two piles of orange strips that vaguely resembled sweet potato fries. Next to those were two boxes that looked like the beverage containers on the spaceship.

"Thank you," Evan said as he reached for a cube.

His cube had white, brown and green layers that, when viewed from the side, somewhat resembled the bread, meat, and lettuce of a hamburger. He turned it over in his hands several times and sniffed it before taking a timid bite.

"Is anything wrong…can I get you something else?"

The bite dissolved in Evan's mouth and he was pleasantly surprised at the taste of bread, beef, lettuce, tomatoes, ketchup, and mustard—it tasted like a hamburger! And not a bad one at that.

"No, this is great. Thank you."

"Wonderful." The administrator turned toward Chen, "Can I get you anything else?"

"No, thank you."

"Then I will let you two get back to your conversation. I haven't heard from the council yet, so we are still waiting. Do you expect Yin to be here soon?"

"It depends on whether our contact is here."

"Well, if you will give me his name, I am sure that I can find him for you. It's my job to keep track of people in this facility."

"Um," Chen hesitated, "his name is Adee…Adekunle Gbadamosi."

"Ahh yes, I'm quite familiar with Admiral Gbadamosi. I wasn't aware that *Endeavor* was on its way back. Last I knew, it was cruising the Inner Belt and wasn't due back here for at least another two weeks. I will check into it for you and see if I can't have the admiral come pay us a visit, if he's here. And we'll find Yin and bring her here as well."

"I would appreciate that," Chen said as he took a bite of his burger.

Evan shoveled a handful of fries into his mouth as the administrator left the room. Like the burger, they tasted surprisingly good, although they had a slight flavor that Evan didn't normally associate with French fries—the first thing that came to mind was parsnips.

Opening the boxed beverage revealed a cold—but not frozen—liquid that tasted as good as any chocolate shake Evan could remember. Within minutes, Evan had gulped his food down and was staring at Chen's fries.

"Help yourself," Chen said. "You seem to be hungrier than I am."

Evan grinned as he helped himself to a handful of Chen's fries.

"Hey, what do you expect? It's hard work moving into a new body."

Evan slurped his shake. "Plus, I think my hunpo has a monster sweet tooth."

SEVENTEEN

APRIL 4, 2075 11:30 P.M. GST
KLAPROTH SPACEPORT
LUNA

After separating from the group, Yin quickly made her way across the market area to one of the side tunnels that led to the outer docking ring. Chen had filled her in on his plan during the transit to Luna, and it was up to her to make sure that there were no more unplanned diversions. Her objective was to meet up with one of Gbadamosi's men who, she had been assured, would help them get off Luna within the next twenty-four hours. She only hoped they had that much time.

The holodisplay at the entrance to the tunnel projected a friendly looking female face and asked, "Destination?"

"Docking Ring C, Gate Three," Yin replied.

A map of the station appeared, showing Yin's current location and the path to her requested destination.

"Please proceed along the designated path."

"Thank you," Yin replied as she headed down the tunnel toward the first intersection.

A series of yellow dots appeared on the tunnel floor, guiding her to her destination. When she came to the intersection, a yellow arrow directed her to the left passageway.

There were a few others walking the hallway but they didn't have colored dots and arrows guiding their way.

They must know where they are going, Yin mused.

She continued down the long tunnel until she was just outside the entrance to Docking Ring C. She had a feeling she was being followed, so she stopped to check her surroundings. Dozens of people passed through the area as they made their way between the concourse and the docking rings. A few of the passers-by smiled at her, but nobody appeared especially interested in her, or out of place.

But her years as a GFN Peacekeeper had taught Yin to trust her instincts. She played it safe and abruptly changed direction toward docking ring B, which was just another thirty meters down the tunnel.

As she walked, she slid a small plastic container from a pocket on the left arm of her jumpsuit. She pushed a tiny knob on the top of the container, and a button-sized disk slid out into her palm.

She ducked around the nearest corner, tossing the disk in the air as she moved. The micro-drone hummed softly as it made its way up to the ceiling.

The drone was connected to Yin's optical implant, and it immediately started sending her data about her environment and everything in it. Yin noticed a restroom sign up ahead and moved calmly toward it.

As she continued down the hallway, she ordered the drone to monitor the area around her for 30 meters in all directions, and it flew off to begin its scan. Once inside the restroom, Yin checked for other people and, finding none, ducked into the nearest stall.

Her implants allowed her to see and hear everything the drone observed while simultaneously viewing its other sensor data. The drone completed its initial scan in the short time it took her to get to the restroom.

Atmosphere normal, no contaminates or toxins detected.

No other drones or airborne nanites detected.

Multiple scanners embedded in the hallway walls, floor, and ceiling.

Six unidentified targets in search area.

Four of the targets continued down the tunnel, away from her position. But two people, one male and one female, were standing at the end of the hallway ten meters from the restroom door.

"Got you," Yin mouthed as she ordered the drone to identify the targets. A few seconds passed before she acquired the loiterers' names and occupations.

As she suspected, both were GFN Peacekeepers. They were members of Epsilon Six, an elite special operations team that specialized in off-Earth missions. Her AI virtual assistant identified the male as Petty Officer Second Class Tadeas Durand and the female as Petty Officer First Class Marcia Bianchi. They had arrived on Luna roughly three hours ago, along with a contingent of ten other Peacekeepers.

Well, they're definitely not rookies, Yin thought. *I wish I had something more than a surveillance drone on hand. I've got maybe thirty seconds more before they come in here looking for me.*

Yin left the stall and started looking for another way out of the restroom. There was one small vent in the roof, but she would never fit through it.

Oh well, the direct approach it is then.

Yin set her drone to orbit the Peacekeepers at ten meters—far enough out they aren't likely to notice it, but close enough to listen in on whatever they might say to each other.

She washed her hands and face to keep up the '*I must go to the bathroom*' charade before heading back out into the hallway. The Peacekeepers walked toward her, but they moved casually and acted uninterested in her.

Let's see how this plays out, Yin thought as she moved to the side to let them pass.

The Peacekeepers continued down the hall toward docking ring B while Yin moved the opposite direction, back toward Docking Ring C.

So, they are here to observe only. I can work with that.

Yin picked up her pace a little as the little yellow dots on the floor once again guided her to her destination. The video feed from her drone showed that the Peacekeepers had walked only a few steps past the restroom before turning back to follow her.

I wonder why they don't have their drones out. They must have tapped into the station security grid and are watching me that way. I bet that changes when they decide it's time to take me.

Yin overlaid the station map on her right eye to confirm where she was and how much further she had to go.

A little over a hundred meters to go. They probably want to grab me and my contact at the same time. That can't happen.

With her left eye, Yin checked her drone to confirm that the Peacekeepers still followed her. Satisfied they were still at a safe distance, she focused on the station map in her right eye.

I need a blind spot.

Yin zoomed in on Docking Ring C, looking for any place she might shake the peacekeepers. But, other than another restroom, a utility closet and a couple of maintenance hatches, there was only straight tunnel between her and her contact.

She closed the map so she could focus her attention on the tunnel ahead and quickened her pace. Her only hope was to surprise them as they came out of the tunnel behind her but, if they were monitoring station security feeds, they would probably spot her the minute she stepped to either side of the exit.

Yin checked the drone feed and noted that her pursuers were closing —they were now only twelve meters behind her.

I've got one chance at this.

Yin recalled her drone as she approached the end of the tunnel. It hovered a few feet above her head.

As an unarmed surveillance drone, it offered limited functionality, but it did have a built-in holoprojector. The projector was normally used to display surveillance data or relay messages to someone without optical implants. The resolution wasn't as good as a full-size holographic projector, but it might buy her a few seconds of surprise if she timed it right. She quickly queued up a command sequence and instructed the drone to stand by.

The Peacekeepers were only five meters behind her and closing quickly. Durand pulled his weapon from his holster just as Yin activated the pre-programmed command sequence.

The drone emitted a bright flash, and Yin disappeared—at least from the Peacekeepers' point of view.

Yin ducked unseen through the docking ring entrance, the drone's holographic projection of an empty hallway covering her movements.

Peacekeeper Durand entered the hallway, still disoriented from the flash. Yin grabbed his right arm and wrist and stomped hard on his right foot. She pivoted her body across his, locking his arm with her elbow. Yin pointed his hand, along with the weapon it held, toward peacekeeper Bianchi and pressed the firing stud. A burst of blue energy engulfed Bianchi, and she crashed hard to the floor.

Yin spun around and kneed Durand in the groin as she stepped around him, twisting his arm behind his back as she moved. As his hand approached the back of his head, he reflexively released his grip on his weapon. Yin stepped back and kicked him hard in the tailbone, sending him flying face-first across the hallway. She thumbed the firing stud before he hit the floor—the blue flash again reassuring her that the weapon was set to stun, and not to kill.

Red means dead, she recalled the words she had heard so often during basic training.

"Well done," a voice echoed from the hallway to Yin's left.

Yin raised her weapon toward the sound but didn't pull the trigger.

A tall, dark-skinned man stepped forward with both of his hands crossed behind his back, as though he were inspecting a new cadet at a military academy. He wore a dark blue, button-down jacket with thick gold stitching on the collar, lapels, and sleeves. A ruffled, white satin collar covered his neck, and his dark gray pants were so tight that she could see the outlines of his bulging thigh and calf muscles. The overall look was reminiscent of British naval officers in the 18th century.

It wouldn't surprise her if he styled himself as a naval officer. After all, he did own the largest, private space fleet in the solar system. And his reputation for being an intrepid risk taker and explorer had earned him the honorary title of "Admiral" from the men and women who crewed his ships. It was an honor that he seemed to embrace wholeheartedly.

"I hope you don't plan on shooting me. Because I won't be able to get you out of here if you do," he said.

Yin lowered her weapon. "Sorry, Adee, you surprised me."

The man smiled as he slid his hands from behind his back. His left hand held a gun identical to Yin's.

"One can never be too careful," he said.

He slipped the gun into the holster on his left thigh as he closed the distance between them.

"It's good to see you again, Yin, it's been way too long. Although…I have to say that I am surprised to see you here. Dr. Hao said your job ended planet-side."

"An unfortunate change of plans. I got identified in Xi'an, and I didn't want to hang around to see what they'd do to me if they caught me."

"Well, that is unfortunate. The good news is that I have room for one more, and you are more than welcome to come along," he said, extending his hand to hers.

Yin let him take her hand and laughed as he bent over to kiss it.

"Oh Adee, you always were the charmer, weren't you?"

"Only when in the presence of beauty such as yours." He winked at her and released her hand.

Yin had met Adekunle Gbadamosi, known as "Adee" to his closest friends, over two decades ago. This was long before he built his own private fleet of spaceships, but well after he had made his first fortune on Luna.

It was during Yin's time as a Peacekeeper. It was 2052, three years before Mars declared its sovereignty, and she was serving as a customs and border patrol agent. Adee was there trying to recruit a crew and miners for a new venture into the Asteroid Belt.

They both ended up in the same bar one evening (not an uncommon occurrence back then, since the Martian spaceport had only one bar), and one thing led to the next. They ended up dating for about a year before she was recalled to Earth. They had seen each other only intermittently since, but they were both content with their status as friends with benefits.

"Mmm," Yin purred. "As much as I'd love to stand here and listen to your flattery, we should probably move before company arrives."

"Don't worry, I reprogrammed the security grid in this docking ring so they can't see us. Although," Adee glanced toward the downed Peacekeepers, "those two probably have friends looking for them."

"Yep, at least ten more, based on their arrival logs," Yin said.

"Interesting. Six are on my ship lying in wait for you, so that leaves four more wandering around the station somewhere.

"On your ship? Why did you let them on your ship?"

"I didn't want to encourage their suspicions…I'm just an innocent bystander in all this—and a very cooperative one at that!" His thick lips spread into a wide grin. "Besides, if I hadn't let them on, we'd have a lot more than a dozen Peacekeepers to deal with."

"Don't worry though," he continued. "We'll handle the Peacekeepers, but I am afraid that we will have to push up our timetable a bit."

"Do you have a plan?"

"No, I was hoping Dr. Hao had one. Will he be along soon, with our other passenger?"

"Well, that's another problem. Administrator Nayak detained them as soon as we stepped off the ship. I am supposed to let you know that we will be delayed, and then meet them back at the administrator's office."

Adee frowned. "Now *that* is unfortunate."

"I don't suppose we can just bust them out of here?" Yin asked.

"Smuggle them out, maybe. Bust them out, not likely. That would take more weapons and manpower than we have at our disposal."

"So, what do you propose, Adee? I know you always have a backup plan."

His grin returned. "Let's do this…you go back to the administrator's office and tell them you couldn't find me. I will clean this mess up and see if I can't figure out a way to get you three out of here without raising too much of a ruckus."

Yin nodded her approval.

"Oh, I almost forgot," she said, "Chen asked me to give this to you."

Yin handed him the data cube.

"Thanks, I'll make sure this gets relayed to Mars as soon I get back to my ship."

"You know what's on it?"

"No, but I assume it's something important since he went to a lot of trouble to deliver it personally."

Yin threw her arms around Adee's neck and kissed him on the cheek. "Thanks, Adee, I know we can count on you."

"No promises that this will go easy, but I am sure I can come up with something. Now you better get going before they come looking for you."

"Okay, see you soon…and thanks again."

Yin retrieved the drone hovering just above her before starting back toward the concourse.

Adee called after her, "The station's scanners will pick you up when you turn the corner, so act normal."

Yin spun around, her broad smile showing off her brilliant white teeth. "Now, Adekunle Gbadamosi, when have you ever known me to act normal?"

"Good point. How about be careful, then?"

"I'll try," as she continued down the hallway. "But no promises."

Eighteen

Dianne Merkel intended to go home and get some sleep, but she was too worked up over the Telogene matter and her mind refused to quiet long enough for her to get any rest. She had forced herself to take a thirty-minute power nap after the executive council meeting concluded, but it hadn't helped.

The holodisplay in front of her contained a summary of the events of the last two days. It included details of how Dr. Hao escaped, and an assessment of the fugitive's likely objectives. The doctor's ingenuity, skill and tenacity were impressive, so it didn't shock her to learn that he had bribed a GeoNet flight controller to assist in their off-world escape.

The controller had added the Telogene shuttle flight to the GeoNet's classified flight database and provide Chen with the AI response codes necessary to avoid raising suspicion. Once tagged as a classified flight, the craft's location and flight path would not be logged or relayed to other GFN controllers. This made it effectively invisible to the GFN drones dispatched to intercept them.

The master flight control AI had periodically challenged the Telogene shuttle, but the pilfered AI response codes allowed it to continue its stealth escape unmolested. The shuttle's unscheduled departure from the

Earth's atmosphere raised a flag at the control center that monitored all interplanetary travel, but by then it was too late.

Dianne had issued an arrest warrant for the flight controller hours ago, but he too had seemingly disappeared. Her agents investigated the links between Dr. Hao and the controller and discovered a large fund transfer from Dr. Hao's personal bank account on Earth to an account on Mars. She tried seizing the funds, but someone had emptied it several days earlier. There was no record of who withdrew the money or where it went.

That wasn't the worst of it, though. Even more worrisome was the assessment of Dr. Hao's objectives and the tactical analysis of his chance of success. The GSSA agents working the case gave Dr. Hao and his co-conspirators a better than ninety percent chance of achieving their objectives if they got off Luna. And, given the poor state of diplomatic relations between GFN and the colonies, it was fifty-fifty at best that President Duchon would hand them over without a fight.

In addition, Dianne's team of investigators had discovered that Adekunle Gbadamosi and Lily Harris were close friends, with a relationship that went back decades.

The rumor was that Lily had secretly invested in Gbadamosi's first mining venture in the Asteroid Belt. There were also rumors that she had sold him restricted Telogene technology. What technology and to what purpose no one knew, and no hard evidence ever surfaced to prove that the transaction had taken place. But given his rather timely appearance, it was clear to Dianne that there was a connection.

These people have thought of everything. How long have they been planning this? What is their end game? They must not get off Luna, no matter what!

Dianne gestured at her holodisplay. Christian's face appeared a few seconds later.

"Yes, ma'am?"

"I need to speak with the E-Six team commander…now," she demanded.

"Of course, I will contact Captain Bachmann immediately."

"No, I don't want to talk to the Captain. I want to talk to Epsilon Six directly."

Christian stared at her.

"I…I don't think I understand, ma'am," he said. "Protocol dictates that all orders to the recovery team come from Captain Bachmann and…"

"Stop right there, Christian. I know you're only looking out for me, so I will let this insubordination go. But if you don't get me on the line with the ground commander in the next two minutes, I will have to reconsider that decision. Are we clear?"

"Yes, Madame Secretary. Please stand by."

Dianne knew that Christian was correct, she had no business contacting Epsilon Six. And the orders she was about to give contravened the GFN chain of command, but she had to act before the fugitives made good their escape.

"I have Epsilon Six Alpha, Lieutenant Commander Luanne Wilkes, on the line. Connecting now."

The face of a young woman of Western European descent replaced Christian's image on Dianne's display.

Her blond hair was close cropped, and she was dressed in the black and grey fatigues commonly worn by GFN Peacekeepers on non-combat missions. She wore no insignia or badges, except for the GFN emblem sewn above her right breast. The emblem was embroidered with black thread and portrayed a double-headed eagle with a bundle of arrows clasped in its left talon, and an olive branch in its right. The eagle hovered above a stylized Eye of Providence—a human eye inside a pyramid surrounded by rays of light.

"Reporting as ordered, ma'am," the soldier stated.

"Yes, thank you. What is your status?"

"The subjects are being held by the facility administrator pending a final decision by the council. Our team is in place, and ready to go once the prisoners are released to our custody."

"Lieutenant Commander Wilkes, do you understand the importance of your mission?"

"Yes, ma'am, we were briefed en route."

"Good. Then you'll understand why I must ask you to retrieve the subjects now and evacuate them from the lunar surface with all due haste."

"I'm sorry ma'am, but with all due respect, I have orders from Captain Bachmann to wait until the council has reached a decision. He believes they will turn them over to us without a fight."

"I understand, Commander. My concern is that, while you wait for the council's decision, the fugitives will escape. That must not happen…they must not be allowed to reach Mars!"

"I appreciate that ma'am, but I will have to call the Captain to confirm your orders."

Dianne pushed the commander's image off to one side of her display and opened an encrypted file on the other.

"I am invoking GSSA Directive Seven, Commander. Prepare to receive your authentication code."

Dianne manipulated the display several times before placing her palm on the DNA scanner embedded in the top of her desk. A second later, a long string of letters and numbers appeared at the top of the encrypted file.

"I am transmitting authorization now, Commander. Please confirm and authenticate."

"Receiving and authenticating; stand by."

Several seconds passed while the commander validated the encrypted authentication sequence with her onboard operational support AI.

"AI confirms, your message is authentic."

"Very well. Your new orders are to use any means necessary to extract the subjects, preferably alive but dead works, too. I want them off the lunar surface within one hour, no excuses. Understood?"

"Yes, ma'am. We will get them out."

"And one other thing, commander…"

"Yes?"

"Under no circumstances are you to respond to any order that contravenes mine. I am exercising GSSA authority to assume full control of this operation until its conclusion. Are we clear?"

"Understood, ma'am."

"Very well. I look forward to hearing from you in one hour, Commander Wilkes."

"Wilkes out."

The display faded and Christian's face reappeared. "Will there be anything else?"

"No, that's it for now. I am going home to get some sleep. Tomorrow will be another very busy day, I'm afraid."

Nineteen

April 5, 2075 12:30 a.m. GST
Klaproth Spaceport
Luna

Lieutenant Commander Luanne Wilkes glanced over at the Peacekeeper standing next to her.

"New mission, Sam. Immediate exfil, dead or alive."

An exfiltration order was one thing, but the stakes just went up now that the powers-that-be no longer cared whether the targets left Luna on their feet or in body bags.

"Fucking fantastic." Master Chief Samuel Washington pointed at the stun pistol hanging on his right hip. "Does that mean we can trade these in for our suits and some real weapons?"

Luanne smirked. "I'm afraid not, Sam. The Lunar treaty says holstered energy weapons and working uniforms only."

"So, what happens if things get hot?"

"It's our job to make sure they don't!"

"Hmm, should be fun. What's next?"

"I'll assemble our team; standby one."

A faint green glow emanated from Luanne's eyes as she activated her operational support AI, which she called *Emma*.

"Emma, burst to Alpha team. Disengage target Yin and assemble my location. Our new orders are to interdict primary targets and exfil immediately. Send."

"Burst transmission sent," Emma replied via Luanne's audio implant.

"Request status Bravo team. Instruct them to hold position but be ready to move on my order."

A few seconds passed while Emma queried the Bravo team AIs.

"Bravo team reports standing by; they are moving to *Endeavor's* shuttle bay now. Alphas Three and Four are en route. Alphas Five and Six are off-grid."

"Off-grid? Did you try using the station relays to boost your signal?"

"Yes, Alphas Five and Six are not transmitting. Scanning for last known location."

Luanne glanced over at Sam. "We have a problem."

Sam was monitoring Luanne's tactical feed and had seen and heard everything.

"I'm seeing it. You want me to go check it out?"

"It's probably just interference, but we need to check it out. I will have Ryan and Jaime rendezvous with us at the outer docking ring."

"Transmitting new orders to Alphas Three and Four," Emma said, anticipating Luanne's next command.

"Orders acknowledged," Emma confirmed a few seconds later.

The Peacekeepers rushed toward the tunnel leading to Docking Ring C.

As much as she would have liked to run, Luanne didn't want to attract too much attention from the station authorities. While they walked, Luanne asked Emma to replay the last two minutes of signals she had received from the missing Peacekeepers.

It looked like everything was normal. Tad and Marcia followed Yin at a safe distance, and Yin acted as though nothing was wrong. Yin picked up the pace as they approached Ring C, and the Peacekeepers matched her. Tad pulled his stun pistol as they reached the end of the tunnel. The last thing he saw was a brilliant flash of blinding white light.

"Analyze flash."

"I already have." Emma adjusted the holodisplay in Luanne's right eye and zoomed the last image recorded by Marcia's AI. "The flash was a high-intensity photon burst emitted by a micro-drone hovering above the target."

"Goddamnit," Luanne said.

"Bloody hell," Sam echoed.

"Double time, try not to attract too much attention."

Luanne and Sam hurried as fast as they dared through the tunnels to Docking Ring C. Thankfully, they encountered only a few civilians along the way, and no one got in their way. Alpha team members Three and Four, a.k.a. Ensign Ryan Randolph and Senior Chief Petty Officer Jaime Gonzales, caught up just as Sam and Luanne approached the intersection at Docking Ring C.

Randolph spoke first. "Any word from Tad or Marcia?"

"No…it looks like Yin might have taken them out."

"Dead?" Ryan asked.

"Presumed missing," Sam quickly replied.

"Let's split up," Luanne said. "Sam and I will take the left tunnel. You two take the right, and we'll meet up on the other side. Keep comms open, and weapons on stun unless you receive hostile fire. If anyone opens up on you, take them out. But please don't kill any civilians…the last thing we need is a diplomatic incident."

"Got it," Ryan replied.

"Drones?" Jaime asked.

"Surveillance and defense only unless I give the order. Now move out."

"TacNet Emma, active scan," Luanne instructed her AI.

It took just seconds for Emma to establish a real-time tactical network, or TacNet, between the four remaining Alpha team members and their operational support AIs.

Once active, each team member could see and hear everything that any other team member saw or heard. He or she could also monitor each other's biometrics, and view data feeds from any drone.

It took years of training to learn how to manage the overload of sensory data but, having mastered it long ago, the AI-driven tactical network gave Alpha team a significant advantage over its opponents.

No more surprises, Luanne thought as she drew her weapon.

It took less than five minutes for the paired-off soldiers to meet up on the opposite side of Docking Ring C, and neither group had seen any evidence of their missing squad members. A quick review of the station logs showed two vessels parked on the docking ring—a short-range shuttle used to move people between Lunar stations on pad three, and a maintenance drone on pad one.

The Commander glanced up at her three team members.

"Pad three," they said in unison.

The squad double-timed it to pad three, only to find it empty.

"No departure record," Sam said, having queried the station's flight tracking system.

Ensign Randolph slammed his fist into the wall. "What the fuck? That's impossible!"

That earned a stern glance from his commanding officer.

"Easy, Ryan," she said. "Somebody must have hacked the logs."

Ryan took a deep breath to calm himself. "But who has that kind of access? The AI that runs this station is supposed to be impervious to that crap. Unless—"

Sam finished his sentence for him, "Unless they have top-level security clearance with override authority."

"Or have someone on the inside helping them," Luanne added. "There is nothing more we can do here. Let's go pay the station administrator a visit."

"What about our team?" Ryan asked. "We can't just abandon them!"

"You know me better than that, Ryan," Luanne scowled. "They aren't here, and we can't go after them until we know where they went. So, we can either stand here being pissed off, or we can go talk to someone who can shed some light on the situation. Clear?"

"Yes, ma'am. Sorry, ma'am. I just didn't expect to lose anyone on a simple snatch and grab."

"They're not lost, just missing...and we *will* find them. Are you with me?"

"Hooyah!" the three team members shouted in unison.

"Good, now move out," Luanne ordered.

TWENTY

APRIL 5, 2075 12:41 A.M. GST
KLAPROTH SPACEPORT
LUNA

Yin made her way past the Peacekeepers and station security personnel without being seen and now stood in front of Administrator Nayak's receptionist.

The receptionist pointed Yin toward the administrator's office. "Please go in; they are expecting you."

Yin nodded slightly. "Thanks."

Evan and Chen stood up from the couch as soon as they saw Yin standing at the doorway. Administrator Nayak remained sitting behind his desk.

The administrator spoke first. "Welcome back, Dr. Li. I see that you have been busy."

"Yeah, sorry for the delay. I got lost, and it took longer than I expected to find my way back."

"Sorry to hear that. Had you spoken with any of my security team, they would have been more than happy to escort you."

"It's fine—they were busy, and I didn't want to bother them. It seems like a busy day around here."

"Busier since the three of you arrived, I think. We are expecting to hear from the president shortly. Her assistant just notified me that the board has adjourned, and she is on her way here now." Administrator Nayak pointed to a nearby chair. "Will you please sit while we wait?"

Yin gave Chen a slight nod as she took her seat. Chen and Evan returned to their previous positions on the sofa.

"So, the president is coming here now?" Chen asked.

"Yes, she should be here momentarily."

The next five minutes passed in awkward silence, with only an occasional glance between the three fugitives as they waited to learn their fate. Evan was about to ask a pointless question just to break the silence when the administrator suddenly stood up from his desk.

"The president is here," he announced, "please stand."

Everyone stood as the door hissed open and two armed guards entered the room, taking up positions on either side of Yin and Evan. A woman with an athletic build and flame-red hair followed close behind them.

"Madam President," Administrator Nayak said, with a deferential bow to the red-haired woman. "May I present Drs. Li, Hao and Richardson."

President Duchon looked them over for several seconds before speaking.

"You look harmless enough, but you sure have created quite a mess." She spoke with a noticeable accent, probably Slovak or Czech. "Now, which of you wants to tell me who you are, why you are here…and why I shouldn't put your asses on a shuttle back to Earth right now?"

Chen started to answer, but the president cut him off.

"And no bullshit. I've been in three hours of meetings because of you, and I have no patience for bullshit. You've got two minutes to convince me to deny the extradition request…and I strongly suggest that you do not waste it."

Chen continued, "Yes, Madam President, and thank you for your time. We apologize for the inconvenience, and we wish merely to resume our trip to the Telogene research facility on Mars."

"And why Mars?" the president asked.

"There is a team there working on the genetic defect problem, and we hope to provide some hands-on assistance."

"And what role, precisely, will Telogene's Chief Cryonicist play on that team?"

"Madam President, I have had many roles at Telogene over the years, and my current job title is not why I am going. I am going both as a geneticist and as the senior executive in charge of this project."

The president smirked as she turned her attention to Evan.

"And what about you, Dr. Feldman? What is your role in all this?"

"Um, my name is Richardson. Dr. James Richardson, Madam President."

"Oh? I was told that you are Dr. Evan Feldman, recently brought back from the dead. Was I misinformed?"

"It appears so, ma'am. I work at our research lab on Mars. I have been through here several times before…I'm sure your records will confirm that."

"Yes, well, I'm sure they do. We spent the last hour reviewing your travel logs, in fact."

Evan glanced at Chen and did his best to suppress the choking sensation in the back of his throat.

The president continued, "I noticed that you spent nearly a week with us during your last trip. Hopefully, you had a good time."

"Uh, yes, thank you. I had some time before the next scheduled transport and figured I'd take in the sights."

"And the woman you were traveling with on that trip, what was her name?"

Shit, she's got me, Evan thought.

Chen interjected before Evan could answer. "President Duchon, with all due respect, can we please get to the matter at hand? It is imperative that we be on our way."

"I'm sorry, but your time is up."

The president turned toward the security officer on her left. "Arrest them, put them in separate cells. And no contact without my authorization."

"Yes, ma'am," the officer replied as he signaled to four other guards waiting in the hallway.

The four armed guards entered the room. One stood just inside the doorway as the other three moved to restrain the fugitives.

"Madam President!" Chen said with more than a hint of desperation in his voice. "On what grounds are we being detained?"

"You and Dr. Richardson are accused of violating the Human Dignity and Decency Act and will be held pending extradition to Earth. Yin Li is accused of aiding and abetting your escape."

The president turned to Yin. "And Miss Li will also be charged with assault, kidnapping two GFN Peacekeepers, tampering with station security monitors, and unauthorized use of a surveillance drone."

Yin said nothing as the guard searched her. When he found the drone case in her sleeve pocket, he held it up for everyone to see before securing her arms behind her back with plastic restraints.

President Duchon added, "Those are, or course, Lunar offenses and will be tried here. So, it is unlikely that she will be joining you for the return trip back to Earth."

Chen pulled away from the guard attempting to restrain his hands and took a few steps toward the president. "President Duchon, please give us a chance to—"

His last words were abruptly cut off by a guard jamming a stun wand into his side, dropping him to the floor.

"You will all get your chance to explain…just not to me. We have judges for that. Now, if you'll excuse me." She turned to Administrator Nayak. "Thank you for your service, Administrator."

He nodded. "Madame President."

The president and her personal security officers left the room, leaving the chore of moving the prisoners to the remaining guards. Chen was semiconscious and couldn't stand on his own, so two guards each grabbed an arm and lifted him to his feet. The other two guards took turns shoving Evan and Yin down the hallway and into a nearby elevator.

"Now what?" Evan asked Yin.

"We wait," she replied as the elevator doors slid shut.

TWENTY-ONE

APRIL 5, 2075 01:34 A.M. GST
KLAPROTH SPACEPORT
LUNA

Commander Wilkes and her team arrived at Administrator Nayak's office just minutes after the fugitives were taken away. A brief, but loud, conversation ensued between the commander and the administrator. The news wasn't good—the team would have to wait until President Duchon authorized the release of Evan and Chen.

The team weighed its options and decided that Luanne would wait in the administrator's conference room while Sam, Ryan, and Jaime resumed the search for Petty Officers Durand and Bianchi. Another search of Docking Ring C turned up nothing new. Sam called the head of station security for a status update, but he had nothing new to offer.

Having hit another dead end, Sam contacted Bravo team and requested that they conduct a stem-to-stern search of *Endeavor*. Bravo team had acknowledged, and Sam searched Docking Rings A and B while he waited to hear back. Not that he expected to find anything but, given *Endeavor's* size, it would take at least a couple of hours for Bravo team to complete its search. And Sam hated waiting.

Besides monitoring her team's progress via TacNet (she had turned off the sensory inputs to limit unnecessary distractions), Luanne used the downtime to review every piece of information she had on this mission, hoping to find something they had missed.

Recovering her missing team members was her most pressing concern, and she would not leave Luna without them.

They must be here somewhere! Where did they go, and who is helping them?

Adekunle Gbadamosi was the most likely answer to the second part of her question, but there was no evidence that he or any of his crew had arrived at Klaproth Station.

There were two GFN space fighters in orbit, one holding station 100 kilometers above Klaproth and the other shadowing *Endeavor*. Neither fighter had reported seeing any shuttle craft leave or approach *Endeavor* since arrival, which meant that whoever was helping Chen and Evan had been here for a while. It also meant that they hadn't left yet and were likely still at Klaproth Station or somewhere nearby.

"Emma, give me a list of all Lunar facilities. Highlight those owned by or affiliated with Adekunle Gbadamosi, GFN Citizen ID Gamma Six Delta Five Niner Zero Six One One Four Alpha."

"Processing," Emma replied.

A few seconds later, a map of Luna appeared in Luanne's right eye with a list of facilities in the left. There were seventeen sites total, with ten on the light side of Luna and seven on the dark side.

That will take a while if I have to search all of those! she thought.

"Show only sites with shuttle traffic within the last twenty-four hours."

The list of sites on Luanne's retinal display shrank to six, with corresponding indicators on the lunar map.

"Is there any record of a shuttle from *Endeavor* landing at any of those sites?"

"No, all shuttle traffic has been between points on Luna."

"Any traffic from those sites to Klaproth station?"

"Yes, there was a supply of helium-3 from Mare Orientale delivered yesterday at 2117 hours."

"Where?"

"The shuttle landed on Pad Three, Docking Ring C."

"That has to be it; where did it go?"

"There is no record of departure. Lunar traffic control says the transport is scheduled for departure at 0730 hours."

"We checked Pad Three; it was empty. Any record of it stopping anywhere else before it arrived here?"

"No," Emma responded. "It was direct from Mare Orientale."

"Check arrival records from Mars or Earth for the last ten days. Did any craft land at Mare Orientale before *Endeavor* entered orbit?"

"Yes, a private transport landed at the Mare Orientale station two days before *Endeavor* entered Lunar orbit."

"Passengers?"

"One passenger."

"Let me guess," Luanne interrupted Emma, "Adekunle Gbadamosi?"

"That is correct."

"Current location?"

"His location is unknown. I do not have access to the Mare Orientale security network."

"And there is no record of him here at Klaproth, I assume."

"Correct."

"Condense and relay this information to Alpha and Bravo teams. I want Bravo to confirm that Gbadamosi is not on-board *Endeavor*."

"Done," Emma replied.

Luanne initiated a direct comm link to her second in command. "Sam?"

Sam quickly acknowledged. "I read you. What's up, boss?"

"Did you see the last package?" Luanne asked.

"Yeah, just scanned it. What's Gbadamosi's stake in all of this?"

"I don't know but get your ass back here. I don't think Tad and Marcia are here, and I want to be ready to roll as soon as we have Hao and Feldman in custody."

"Copy. Want me to send Ryan and Jaime to recon the Mare Orientale station?"

"Negative. I believe that Gbadamosi will be back. Leave some drones patrolling Ring C, I want to know the second that shuttle comes back."

"Roger. What about rings A and B?" Sam asked.

"Yeah, better safe than sorry. Deploy drones on your way back. Give me full coverage."

"Full coverage, aye." Sam acknowledged.

Luanne scanned Admiral Gbadamosi's file while she waited for Alpha team to return. There wasn't much in it she didn't already know. The admiral's exploits and accomplishments were regular features on the global news networks, but a recent story caught her attention.

It was a press conference from early last year. A Martian astrophysicist named Elena Ramirez announced that her team had confirmed the presence of liquid water and a thin atmosphere on Proxima Centauri B. Even more exciting was the discovery of an Earth-like planet orbiting Alpha Centauri A. She named it Gaia, after the Ancient Greek goddess of Earth.

While Proxima B orbited a red dwarf star and was more like Mars than Earth in its composition and habitability, Gaia appeared to have Earth-like continents, oceans, and an atmosphere.

What interested Luanne most, however, was the part where Dr. Ramirez introduced the project sponsor—it was none other than Adekunle Gbadamosi.

Luanne listened as Gbadamosi thanked Elena and her team before extolling the virtues of interstellar travel, and the opportunity for mankind to spread beyond the bounds of our own solar system. What really got her attention, though, was the journalist Q&A at the end. She played it back several times to make sure she had heard it correctly.

Journalist A: "This question is for the admiral. Admiral, how long will it take to reach Gaia and when do you plan to leave?"

Gbadamosi: "With our latest advances in gravity pulse propulsion, we believe we can attain orbit around Gaia in less than thirty years. As to when we plan to leave…there are several other technical hurdles we must first overcome, but we believe we will launch the first colony ship sometime within the next few years."

Journalist A: "And can you share some of these hurdles?"

Gbadamosi: "Well, first and foremost is keeping a large group of people alive and sane during the long journey. But, beyond that, it's food and supplies for when they get there. Just because the planet is Earth-like does not mean we can assume a ready supply of edible food and building supplies."

Journalist B: "So, Admiral, when you say 'a large group' of people, how many people do you mean? And how big of a ship would you need to house them for that long?"

Gbadamosi: "We believe we need at least 300 people to establish a self-sustaining colony. As far as ship size, let's just say that the ship would have to be at least ten times larger than the biggest ship ever built in order to provide adequate space for fuel, habitat, and supplies."

Journalist B: "What are you saying, Admiral? Are you planning to keep everyone in cryogenic suspension? Is that even possible?"

Gbadamosi: "We will share more details soon. But for now, I will just say that storing the contents of people's brains for long durations has proven far easier and more reliable than storing bodies. Thank you, everyone."

Luanne paused for a minute to consider Gbadamosi's words.

He must be talking about cloning. He plans on storing the colonists' engrams and implanting them in cloned bodies once they reach Gaia.

She asked Emma to search for any other announcements from Gbadamosi or Dr. Ramirez, but there were none.

"So much for sharing more information soon!" she said out loud.

Administrator Nayak quietly entered the room through the doors behind Luanne.

"Who's not sharing information?" he asked.

Luanne stood. "Oh, it's nothing. I was just watching a news conference from last year."

"I see. Well, in the vein of sharing information, I am here to tell you that President Duchon has agreed to release Hao and Feldman to your custody."

"Finally. Where are they now?"

"They are in holding cells on sub-level three. Would you like them brought to your vessel?"

"No. We will escort them ourselves."

"Very well. Your team is on its way back here, I assume?"

"Yes. They should be here momentarily."

A quick check of TacNet confirmed that Alpha team was crossing the concourse from Docking Ring A and would reach her position within three minutes.

"Okay, can I get you anything while we wait?"

"No. I am fine, thank you."

The two sat in silence while they waited for the rest of Alpha team to arrive. It wasn't long before Luanne stood up and moved toward the door as her team approached.

"They're here," she said.

She opened the door and stepped into the hallway to join her team.

"Welcome back," she said. "I want everyone on high alert. If Gbadamosi is going to try to snatch our prisoners, it's going to have to happen between here and our ship."

"Roger that," Sam replied. "Randolph, you're on advance once we've made the pickup. Make sure nobody sets up on us. Gonzales, you take the rear."

"Aye, aye, Chief," both men replied in unison.

Luanne gestured toward the elevators at the end of the hall. "Administrator, if you please."

Administrator Nayak led the team to the middle elevator. A minute later, they were on sub-level three and jogging toward the holding cells.

"Goddamnit!" Sam exclaimed as they entered the side passage leading to the cells.

Four Luna security officers lay sprawled across the hallway. Petty Officers Randolph and Gonzales checked each one for a pulse. They were unconscious but breathing.

The administrator took a few steps back before calling station security.

"Code red. Lock down the station. Nobody in or out. Hold all traffic until further notice," the administrator said to whoever had answered.

A second later, strips of lights running the length of the hallway flashed red, and a klaxon sound blared from unseen speakers.

The administrator signaled Luanne to follow him. "This way; let's check the cells."

As expected, the cells were empty.

"Where could they have gone from here?" Luanne asked.

Administrator Nayak thought for a moment before replying. "They had two options. The elevator bank, which has access to the seventeen levels below us and the seven above us, or the stairs located on either end of this level."

"What else is on this level?" Sam asked.

"Administrative offices and storage areas."

"Security monitors?"

"Station security personnel are checking the surveillance logs now."

"Why didn't they see the guards lying in the hallway?"

The administrator tilted his head as if listening to someone whispering in his ear.

"Video surveillance of this hallway shows the guards standing post outside of the cells," he said, relaying what he was just told. "Someone has bypassed the system. My people are working to trace the source now. This whole level appears to be compromised."

Sam slapped his palm hard against the wall.

"Fucking great!" He turned to face Administrator Nayak. "You people need to work on your goddamned security around here. That's twice today that those fuckers have gotten the jump on us!"

The administrator didn't respond, instead focusing his attention on the sounds of several people rushing toward them.

Alpha team drew their sidearms, but it was a six-man security team escorting four medical personnel to attend to the unconscious guards.

Administrator Nayak greeted one of the security officers. "Situation update, please."

"We've swept this level and found nothing. My teams are moving outwards from here, but it's going to take a while for us to clear every level. It looks like the bastards have disrupted the entire security grid—we are flying blind."

The administrator gestured toward Luanne. "This is GFN Lieutenant Commander Luanne Wilkes, and this"—he gestured toward the newly arrived security officer—"is Watch Commander Chumak."

"Nice to meet you. Any word from your missing team members?" the watch commander asked.

"Unfortunately, no," Luanne replied. "We've been spread too thin to conduct a full search. We think they're off-station but still on Luna."

"I am sure that they are unharmed," Chumak offered. "If Admiral Gbadamosi is leading this, he will ensure that no one gets hurt."

"I hope you're right, Watch Commander but, regardless of whether anyone gets hurt or not, he will pay for kidnapping my people!"

"I understand, and I offer my sincerest apologies for your inconvenience. It is highly unusual to have these kinds of disruptions on Luna."

Luanne had little patience for people who talked more than they acted and as far as she could tell, Chumak was one of them.

She turned her attention to the administrator.

"We need to coordinate our efforts, Administrator. I've got a team sweeping *Endeavor*, and you have yours sweeping the station but so far neither has turned up anything. Where else could they be? And how are they moving undetected?"

"Our opponents caught us unprepared, and I agree that we need to better coordinate our efforts. As to your first question, I can only assume they are trying to leave the station or have already done so. As to the second, it would seem that the admiral is using his extensive knowledge of this station and his vast network of contacts and operatives to ensure that the fugitives leave Luna in his custody rather than yours. Honestly, I'm not sure there is anything we can do to stop him."

Sam exploded. "Are you fucking serious? You're telling me that this one guy has completely compromised this station, and all you can say is you don't think you can stop him? Fuck you and fuck this backwards-ass place!"

Luanne held her hand out in the universal "stop" position. "At ease, Sam, that isn't helping."

"Might I suggest, Administrator," she continued, "that we move this to your operations center where we can better monitor the situation."

"Agreed. Commander Chumak, take the injured men to the infirmary, and see that a forensic team gets down here immediately. I want every sensor inspected, every log examined, and every bit of hair, skin, or dirt collected. I want to know exactly what happened, how it happened, and who did it within the hour. Do you understand?"

"Yes, sir. Right away, sir."

He gestured toward the elevators. "This way."

"One sec," Luanne said. "Jaime, stay here and do a full scan. Work with the tech team and try to stay out of their way, but I want confirmation of whatever they find."

Jaime nodded. "Roger, I'm on it."

"Any concerns, Administrator?" Luanne asked the administrator.

"Not at all."

"Heads-up, Lu, we've got activity in Docking Ring C. That transport just landed on Pad Three. There's also a shuttle inbound for Pad Seven, but it was ordered to hold just short of the station," Ensign Randolph said.

Since it was his job to monitor the drones, Ryan saw the activity alert a few seconds before the rest of Alpha team.

"Got it," Luanne acknowledged. "Jaime, stay here. Sam and Ryan, you're with me."

Luanne grabbed Administrator Nayak's elbow to get his attention. "Now's the time to coordinate and cooperate, Administrator. I need real-time feeds from your op center, and every security officer you've got in the area to Docking Ring C now."

The administrator pulled away from Luanne's loose grip. "I understand, Lieutenant Commander Wilkes. We will do all that we can to assist you."

Luanne, Ryan, and Sam started down the hallway toward the elevators with the administrator close behind.

"I have one request, Commander," the administrator said.

"What is it?" Luanne asked.

"Please keep your weapons on stun, and please, no matter what happens, do not shoot any innocent civilians."

"No promises. We'll do our best, but I am not letting them get off Luna."

The elevator door slid open and Alpha team piled in.

Administrator Nayak stood back. "You go, I would only be in your way."

Luanne selected the concourse level, and the doors slid shut.

"This is a cluster-fuck-and-a-half, Lu," Sam said as the elevator began its ascent.

"Yes, it is. But we need to stay focused, Sam. I know that you hate this entire mission, but I need you fully engaged. This isn't the typical snatch and grab, and we are clearly up against a superior opponent. It's time for us to quit playing catchup with this guy and get out front." She glanced over at Ryan, "Are you with me?"

"Hooyah," both men said in unison.

"Good. Sam, get the op center feeds integrated with our TacNet. I want to see what they see. Ryan, stay on those drones. I want to know the second any of our targets show up."

"On it," again in unison.

"Great. Now, I've got to make a call I should've made an hour ago. Emma, get me Secretary Merkel."

TWENTY-TWO

April 5, 2075 03:14 a.m. GST
Klaproth Crater
Luna

"Where the hell are you taking us, Adee?" Yin called out, her voice echoing inside her sealed helmet.

Evan and Chen were just in front of her, with Adee and two of his men in front of them.

She had to hand it to him—Adee had probably engineered the fastest prison break in Luna history. She had spent a grand total of seventeen minutes in her cell before the door suddenly whirred open. When she stepped out, she found Adee waiting there to greet her. The four security guards were unconscious on the floor.

They fled toward a nearby stairwell and descended two levels before Adee led them to a locked maintenance closet. There, they found six space suits hanging on racks, along with the tools they would need to pry open the sealed door that led to a network of seldom used maintenance tunnels—tunnels that ran for kilometers underneath Klaproth Crater.

They had trudged through the cold, dark tunnels for nearly an hour, and Adee showed no signs of stopping.

"Patience, Yin, we are nearly there," Adee replied.

"That's great! But where, exactly, is there?"

"*There*," he said with more than a hint of agitation in his voice, "is one of my old hydrogen mines. It was the primary source of water and power for Klaproth Station, before we discovered some better sites."

"Nobody comes down here?" Evan asked.

"Not for years…nobody except me."

Chen joined in the conversation. "And I assume that you have a plan for getting us off Luna once we get there?"

"I do indeed, my good Dr. Hao. Fear not, we have considered every contingency, and we will be Mars-bound within the hour."

"Glad to hear it." Chen replied. He tapped Evan's arm twice. "How are you doing, Evan? Are you holding up okay?"

"Yeah, I'm hanging in there," Evan said. "I'm hungry, exhausted, and being in this suit is freaking me out, but otherwise I'm good."

"No headaches or unexplained sights or sounds?"

"I have a little headache and I'm a little short of breath…and my ears are ringing. But that's probably because of the lower atmospheric pressure."

Klaproth, like most stations on Luna, maintained an atmospheric pressure equivalent to about 2000 meters above sea level on Earth in order to conserve fuel. It also had the benefit of putting less strain on the station's bio-dome and surrounding support structures. Environmental suits were typically set to the same pressure to minimize the time required to enter and exit pressurized areas.

"You should have said something sooner, Evan," Yin said. "That's an easy fix, hold up a sec."

The group paused for a minute while Yin reprogrammed Evan's suit to increase the air pressure and the amount of oxygen he was receiving.

"There, that should help," she said.

She monitored the results on Evan's arm-mounted control panel until the air inside his suit achieved the desired levels of pressure and oxygen saturation.

"You'll burn oxygen faster, but you should have plenty…assuming Adee doesn't keep us wandering in these tunnels forever."

"Thanks, Yin. My headache is going away already."

"Okay, friends," Adee prodded, "we need to hustle if we're going to make our launch window. Everyone good?"

"I'm good," each replied in turn.

Adee proceeded down the tunnel at a fast walk, with the rest of the group close behind. Seventeen minutes later they emerged in a large, dimly lit cavern.

"We're here," Adee announced. "Let's have some more light, please."

Adee's men split from the group, heading for opposite sides of the cavern.

The cavern was large, over one hundred meters across and nearly as high—although it was too dark to know the exact dimensions. There was a large rocket-shaped structure sitting in the middle of the visible area, which was dimly lit by a ring of lights mounted on scaffolding.

The vehicle stood over thirty meters high, was ten meters wide, and consisted of a long central cylinder surrounded by six smaller cylinders.

"Is that what I think it is?" he asked.

Adee smiled. "Yes, and no. It's technically an IPD Seven ballistic missile that I modified with a gravity pulse drive of my own design, and therefore not a rocket ship per se."

"What's it doing here?" Chen asked.

"One of Luna's dirty little secrets. Several of Earth's nations deployed thousands of these after the war. This was before they formed the GFN and banned space-based weapons. My company got the contract to dismantle the ones deployed by the former United States of America."

Yin took a few steps toward the rocket and made a sweeping gesture with her arms. "Well, if you dismantled them, why is this one sitting here, Adee?"

"Well, let's just say that we destroyed the warheads but kept a few… souvenirs."

"So, assuming this forty-year-old missile doesn't blow up on launch, just how do you plan to dock with *Endeavor*?" Yin asked. "Surely you're not expecting us to do an EVA!"

"No, a spacewalk is way too dangerous…especially for someone who has never trained for such a thing. No, we will launch from this silo, fire the pulse engine once we've cleared Luna's orbit, and *Endeavor* will pick us up as we hurtle toward Mars at over 8,000 kilometers per second."

Chen did some rough calculations in his head. "That's almost three percent of the speed of light Adee! How long is it going to take *Endeavor* to catch up with us?"

Before Adee could respond, a new bank of lights came on, and a large section of the scaffolding moved across the floor toward the rocket.

"Ahh, good, my men have activated the primary generators and restored full power. Right on schedule! Please follow me."

Adee hurried toward the rocket.

Chen hurried to catch up. "You haven't answered my question."

"I will explain all the details once we are safely off Luna. Until then, all you need to know is that *Endeavor* is the second fastest ship ever built and catching us will not be a problem."

Adee stopped at the top of the first set of stairs and signaled for everyone to continue up. "Right this way, please. Each of you will enter an acceleration pod when you get to the top. It doesn't matter who sits where. I will be right behind you."

Yin was the first to reach the top. She paused at the rocket entry hatch and signaled for Evan to go first. Evan ducked through the hatch and found a cluster of eight pods that were very similar to those on the Telogene shuttle. He climbed into the closest pod, and the automated restraints secured him in place. Once locked in, his pod rotated away from the hatch and an empty pod slid into place for the next passenger.

Chen entered next, followed by Yin, then Adee and his two crewmen. The last crewman secured the hatch before securing himself in his pod. The pods moved in unison, forming two rows that stretched from the middle of the rocket all the way to the top. Adee and one of his crewmen were in the first two pods, each with their own set of controls.

"Okay, everyone," Adee said, "get ready. Suit interfaces will be active in three… two…one."

When the count reached "one", Evan felt a now-familiar tingle as his spacesuit interfaced with his pod. A wave of nausea swept over him but quickly passed.

Adee noticed a big jump in Evan's heart rate on his monitor. "You alright, Evan?"

"Yeah, I'm fine. I got a little nauseous for a second, but it passed."

"Ahh, yes. Well, I'm sorry about that. I forgot it's only been forty-eight hours since your restoration. I should have given you something," Adee said.

"Let's just hope that's the only thing you missed Adee," Yin replied.

"Me too," he said dryly.

Everyone waited quietly while Adee and his co-pilot worked feverishly at their controls.

"Here we go," Adee announced several minutes later.

A few seconds later, the rocket engines flared, and the ship shot like a bullet up the tunnel above it. In the blink of an eye, the ship cleared the silo and accelerated rapidly into space. The roar was deafening inside the ship, and Evan felt as though he was being crushed under two tons of bricks. The suit and pod were adjusting to compensate, but this ship was accelerating much harder and faster than the Telogene shuttle when it left Earth.

Although it seemed like forever to Evan, only ninety seconds passed before Adee's voice sounded inside his helmet.

"I'm sorry, everyone, but this will hurt a little. Stand by for first gravity pulse in thirty seconds."

The rocket engines shut off, their deafening roar replaced by a high-pitched whine. Evan couldn't tell where the sound was coming from, as it seemed to be all around him. He tried to raise his arm to activate the pod's holoterminal but found he couldn't move. He tried to say the words that would cause the holodisplay to appear, but he couldn't speak.

His breathing became more rapid with each passing second. He looked over at Chen in the pod next to him, hoping to get his attention, but all he could see was a tiny speck of light at the far end of a black tunnel. He thought he would pass out.

But the intensity of the next whine, this one much louder than the last, caused him to hold his breath in anticipation of whatever came next. His vision cleared for a second, but then the whine stopped.

He started to fall—or at least it felt like he was falling. His vision blurred and a wave of nausea crashed over him, but he couldn't vomit.

Evan tried to cry out, but he managed only a soft grunt before a sudden darkness swept over him.

Time slowed, but the sense of falling grew more intense. His mind struggled to comprehend what his senses were telling him—he should have been crushed against the back of the ship long ago.

He tried to cry out—but only a faint, whimpering moan escaped his lips.

Twenty-Three

April 5, 2075 3:37 a.m. GST
Klaproth Spaceport, Docking Ring C
Luna

"Well, that was a real joy," Luanne announced to her team.

"The Secretary?" Sam asked.

"Yeah, she chewed me a new asshole and then some. She said that we shouldn't come back at all if we don't come back with Feldman and Hao."

"That's harsh. Did you explain to her we haven't even had them in sight, let alone in our custody?"

"Yes, and she didn't give a shit," Luanne scoffed. "Although I suspect that she gave President Duchon the same ass-reaming she gave me."

"Fucking bureaucrats."

"Yep. But they pay our salaries, so let's get back to work. Where are we with securing this docking ring?"

"We've deployed every drone we've got, and station security is covering every gate," Sam answered. "They're letting that inbound shuttle land, but everyone onboard will be held and screened."

"What about the transport on pad three and the maintenance drone?"

"The drone has been disabled and the cops are going over every square inch of the ore transport now."

"Was there a pilot?" Luanne asked.

"Not that we can tell; it's fully automated. Its logs show that it's been doing nothing but running back and forth with cargo between here and Mare Orientale."

"Any explanation for the unlogged trip it took an hour ago?"

"Nope. Both the station traffic control logs and the ship's record agree that it went nowhere."

"Which we know is flat wrong because our drone saw it leave and come back."

"Yes, ma'am," Sam acknowledged. "And according to the drone's video logs, nobody got on or off of that ship."

"So, we have no idea what it did."

"Right."

"What about Redstar Two-One?" Luanne asked about the GFN space fighter hovering 100 kilometers above her head.

"I called her. She's scanning for orbital launches, not surface traffic."

"Bummer. Was any cargo unloaded after the last trip?"

"Not that we saw, but we can't see the cargo doors or the loading bay from here."

"And no record on the station security grid, I assume?"

"That is correct."

"I think we are wasting our time here," Luanne said "Ryan, Jaime, get your asses back to the ship and get it fired up. We're airborne in ten."

Both men acknowledged Luanne's order before departing at a swift jog.

Luanne activated her comm implant.

"Bravo One, this is Alpha One," she said.

No response.

"Bravo One, this is Alpha One, respond."

The TacNet display showed that the six-man team was on the network, but she couldn't connect with any of them.

"Emma, why can't we connect with Bravo team?"

"Someone is jamming our communications frequencies."

"Then why aren't they showing as on-grid?"

"Unknown."

"Solution?"

"I have tried all available frequencies," Emma answered. "Protocol is to cycle encryption codes."

"Do it."

"What do you think happened?" Sam asked.

"Hopefully, it's just a temporary blackout as they transit the dark side."

Sam asked the orbiting fighter to confirm *Endeavor's* location.

"Redstar Two-One confirms," he said. "*Endeavor* and Redstar Two-Two will transition in two minutes seventeen seconds."

Luanne nodded. "It's too bad we can't relay TacNet signals through Luna's comm satellites."

"Yeah, they do that on purpose—they don't like the GFN playing in their backyard. They let us come visit, but only if we stay in tourist-mode."

Sam held his hand up to pause the conversation. "Stand by one."

"Two-Two just reported that *Endeavor* broke orbit. Two-One reports that someone fired off an IPD Seven from an underground launch site on other side of the Klaproth crater."

The launching of a forty-year-old Interplanetary Defense Mark Seven ballistic missile from the surface of Luna caught Luanne and the rest of her crew by surprise.

"An IPD Seven? Where the fuck did that come from?"

"Unknown Lu. Hang on…"

"I'm seeing it," Luanne replied.

Sam continued. "Two-Two confirms. *Endeavor* ejected a cargo container before she took off. All six Bravo team members are on board and healthy. Bravo One is transmitting his mission log now."

"Got it. Do you see that?"

"Yep. Two-One is relaying TacNet signals from Alphas Five and Six."

"Is that the launch site?" Luanne asked.

"Confirmed," Sam acknowledged.

"Ryan?"

"We're ready when you are, Lu," Petty Officer Randolph replied.

"Come on, Sam. Let's go get our people."

"What about the missile?" Sam asked.

"Can the fighters catch it?"

"No, it's going way too fast."

Luanne shrugged/ "Then that missile will have to be someone else's problem. Let's go."

Two minutes later, the GFN troop transport ship was off the pad and moving at high speed to pick up Petty Officers Durand and Bianchi. They were stuck inside a pressurized cargo container surrounded by vacuum, just like Bravo team, so they weren't going anywhere on their own. Everybody had plenty of air, so the lieutenant had Redstar Two-Two track Bravo team in orbit while she recovered the rest of Alpha team.

Unfortunately, the troop transport was too big to fit down the IPD Seven launch tube, and Luanne and Sam ended up having to change into EVA suits.

They exited the transport and walked the short distance to the top of the stairs that circled the outer edge of the launch tube. Each packed an extra spacesuit so Tad and Marcia could make the trip back with them under their own power.

The dark cavern opened before them as they descended.

"What happens if there's no airlock?" Sam asked.

"Well, then I hope they remember their vacuum training!" Luanne replied.

"Ugh, that will suck."

"We heard that!" Tad said over TacNet.

"Standby, we're almost there. Give us a minute to scout the surroundings," Lu replied.

Once they were in range, Luanne and Sam activated their TacNet interfaces so that Tad and Marcia could get a better look at their situation; they had awoken inside the container and had no idea where they were. Everyone was relieved when Sam discovered that the control center airlock was still functioning, and that the cargo container would fit comfortably inside. The only challenge was getting the container inside the airlock.

Sam looked at Luanne and shrugged. "I guess we push."

"Hang on, guys, it may get a little bumpy while we push you into the airlock," Luanne said.

Thankfully, the container wasn't that heavy, and the thrusters built into the spacesuits made short work of the twenty-meter distance to the airlock. Ten minutes later, Tad and Marcia were suited up and the four Alpha team members were working their way up the stairs toward the surface. A few minutes after that, all six Alpha team members were reunited on board the transport.

Luanne gave everyone a minute to say hello and get seated.

"Okay, Ryan, it's time to recover Bravo," she said.

The transport leapt into space and accelerated hard to catch up to the orbiting cargo container, which was still circling Luna at nearly twenty thousand kilometers per hour.

Sam waited until they were in orbit to ask the obvious question. "So, what's the plan, Lu?"

"Well, the cargo container is small enough to fit into the bay if we drop the ramp. So, I'm thinking we take another walk."

"That's what I was afraid of."

"You and I are on tether duty. Jaime, get the ramp. Tad and Marcia are on the arm. And, Ryan, you'll be up here flying your ass off."

"Hooyah!" Alpha team replied in unison.

Luanne released her restraints and floated toward the back of the ship. "Let's suit up and get locked in, people."

"Standing by for intercept burn, Lu. It will take some serious delta-v to get us in position. If I overshoot, we will have to make another full orbit before we get another shot," Ryan said.

"Roger. How long do we have?"

"Ten minutes twenty-seven seconds."

"We'll be ready."

The team spent the next ten minutes putting on their EVA suits and making room in the cargo hold for the container serving as Bravo team's lifeboat.

"Thirty seconds," Ryan called out just as they were locking themselves into their acceleration pods.

The ship Ryan piloted was a state-of-the-art, military-grade troop transport designed to deploy troops on a moment's notice anywhere on

Earth or Luna. Although it wasn't as fast as the larger ships in the GFN fleet, it could make the trip to Mars and back in a pinch.

The spacecraft was equipped with four Hellfire engines, each one powered by a military-grade, high-density, high-output helium-3 reactor. These reactors required specialized equipment to operate and were far more powerful than their civilian counterparts. Their primary benefit was quicker acceleration, but they also allowed for faster warm-up times. The ship's engines could go from cold-start to full power in less than thirty minutes—and Ryan had been warming them up since they left Klaproth.

Ryan counted down the last ten seconds. When the count reached zero, Ryan called out "Ignition!" and the craft accelerated at nearly thirty times the force of Earth's gravity.

Within seconds, the craft had climbed the 500 kilometers of space between it and the cargo container's orbit. If Ryan's calculations were correct, the ship would be five kilometers in front of the cargo container and traveling at roughly the same speed. A few more seconds went by before Ryan killed the Hellfires and confirmed his trajectory.

"We are right on target. The container is five clicks behind us, but we're a little fast. Engaging reverse thrust now."

Ryan directed the thrust from the Hellfires toward the front of the ship, which was the space equivalent of "tapping the brakes."

"That did it. Everyone into position. The container is closing at thirty meters per second. I'll drop that to ten when it gets within a kilometer, and we will shoot for zero closure at fifty meters."

Luanne released the restraints on her acceleration pod. "Okay team, we're up. Ryan did his part and now it's up to us."

The team members took their places in the cargo bay, with Luanne and Sam standing on either side of the ramp.

"Blowing the bay now," Jaime said as he activated the sequence to evacuate the cargo bay's atmosphere into space. It took less than twenty seconds to go from one Earth atmosphere to vacuum.

"Opening ramp."

Jaime disengaged the clamps holding the ramp closed, and it swung slowly open, giving Luanne and Sam an amazing view of space and the lunar surface below.

"Redstar Two-Two is shifting orbit," Ryan called over TacNet. "The container is two clicks out."

All six Alpha team members watched intently as the tiny silver dot behind them grew larger with each passing second.

"Five hundred meters," Ryan called out.

A formality, since everyone was seeing the same information on their holodisplays. But, as highly trained military professionals, verbal call-outs and acknowledgment were still deeply ingrained habits. Not only did verbal call-outs enhance team coordination and discipline, they also served as a necessary redundancy in case of technology failure.

"I've got comms," Luanne announced. "Bravo One, this is Alpha One. It's great to see you."

"Alpha One, Bravo One. We are looking forward to being out of this box, Lu. Try not to break it, will you? We're not wearing suits."

"Roger that, Bravo One."

Luanne disconnected the safety harness that held her in place.

"Let's do this, Sam," she said as she pushed herself out into space.

Sam grabbed the other tether cable and followed her out the back of the transport.

"Fifty meters," Ryan called out, "zero closure."

"Roger," Sam replied.

Sam and Luanne closed the remaining distance to the cargo container and attached their tether cables.

"Tethers locked. Reel us in, Marcia," Luanne ordered.

Marcia engaged the electric motors connected to the tethers. When the container was within ten meters, an articulating arm swung down from the roof of the cargo bay and extended out the back of the ship. Tad waited until the container was within three meters of the cargo ramp before clamping the arm's claw down on the container.

"Container is locked," he notified the team.

"Retracting," Tad replied.

Luanne and Sam floated with the container as the arm pulled it into the cargo bay. Marcia engaged a set of locking clamps that came up from the cargo bay floor to secure the container in place.

"It's locked in," she said.

It took another five minutes to pressurize the cargo bay and open the container.

"Welcome back," Luanne said to the Bravo team members as they exited the container.

"Thanks, glad to be back," the Bravo team leader acknowledged.

"You know there will be hell to pay, right?" Sam asked.

"Yeah, those bastards were ahead of us every step of the way," Luanne said.

"I hate to say it, but I don't think we ever had a chance," Jaime added.

"It sure didn't seem like it. The brass will be looking at this one for quite some time, I think," Sam replied.

Luanne laughed. "I'm sure they will. Take us home, Ryan."

"Aye, aye skipper," Ryan called back from the flight deck.

TWENTY-FOUR

**APRIL 5, 2075 7:30 A.M. GST
GSSA HEADQUARTERS
ZURICH, SWITZERLAND**

Aubrey woke to the sound of her cell door hissing open, and a guard bringing her a tray containing an assortment of small cartons.

"Good morning," the guard said curtly as he set the tray down on the small table. "I will be back with your lunch around noon, and they scheduled your hearing for three. Your lawyer will call you before the hearing to brief you on the procedures. If you need anything else between now and then, just ask and we will see what we can do."

Aubrey sat up in bed and wiped the sleep from her eyes. "Thank you, I'm good for now."

The guarded nodded and exited the room, the door hissing shut behind him.

Aubrey forced herself from bed and meandered over to the table to examine the tray's contents.

"Let's see what we have here," she said out loud as she picked up the largest of the three containers on the tray. "Eggs, ham, and onion potato bake with a slice of bread with jam. That sounds good; I wonder if it's real food?"

"Probably not," she said as she moved on to the remaining cartons. "Hmm, milk and coffee. That's a nice touch." Until now, they had only given her water to drink.

Aubrey set the cartons back on the tray and turned her attention to the sink and toilet.

She despised that toilet—there was no privacy divider, and she was under constant surveillance. She had used it only twice in the past twenty-four hours because she hated being on full display. But, the discomfort in her bladder convinced her that modesty was no longer her most immediate priority.

She took her time with her morning routine and did her best to make herself presentable with the limited selection of hygiene products arrayed on the sink counter. Once she was satisfied with her hair, she turned her attention back to the breakfast tray.

To her surprise, everything was still warm and tasted like real food, which meant that she was receiving first-class treatment. Since the last global food crisis, most of the food produced planet-wide was grown in a lab rather than on a farm or in a field. A handful of mega-corporations controlled the food supply, and Telogene was among the largest.

Aubrey was proud that Telogene's animal protein and vegetable products were the safest (and some said best-tasting) but, for all their technology, they still couldn't make meat grown in a vat taste like that of free-range, farm-raised animals. The meat of a living, breathing creature developed textures and flavors that just weren't possible in a lab. The same was true of fruit and vegetables grown the traditional way—over a period of weeks or months in a field or greenhouse rather than the few days it took to go from seed to harvest in the lab.

Several years ago, her mother had asked the company's lead botanist to come up with a solution to the quality problem. What she got back was a report with lots of numbers and data, but no solution. The executive summary summed up the team's findings in a single sentence: *There is no substitute for natural development when producing high-quality fruit and vegetables.*

And that was that. The old maxim, "you can have fast, cheap or high quality, but not all three," still held true. As much as Aubrey would have liked to prove the naysayers wrong, feeding the planet's billions required companies like hers to produce as much food as possible, quickly and inexpensively. That meant that quality was often relegated to a distant third priority.

Of course, those with enough money could still enjoy the taste of naturally grown food. But the costs had become so extreme over the past decade that only the very wealthy could afford to eat naturally grown food regularly.

This meal is probably worth more than most people earn in a week, Aubrey mused as she wolfed down the last of her eggs and coffee.

Being wealthy all her life, Aubrey had never thought about the privileges her wealth afforded her—until now.

It's amazing how often we fail to appreciate things until they're gone, she mused.

A short time later, the guard came back to recover the tray and used containers.

"Did you enjoy your breakfast?" he asked as he cleaned up after her.

"I did. It was superb, thank you."

"Good, I'm glad you enjoyed it. Secretary Merkel asked me to remind you that you are entitled to far less, and that this is the last time she will extend you any courtesy if you do not give her what she wants. She said you'd understand."

"I do. And please tell the Secretary that I sincerely appreciate her goodwill, but I have nothing more I can offer her."

"As you say," the guard grunted. "I will be back with your lunch in a few hours."

Aubrey sat at the table a few minutes longer before deciding the bed was more comfortable.

"Well, nothing left to do now but wait," she said for the benefit of her unseen observers.

She spent the next several hours pondering her choices over the past year and wondering if there was anything she could—or would—have done differently if given the chance. She went over each scenario again and again in her mind, searching for some decision that, if altered, might have changed everything. But she realized that all she could do was accept the choices she'd made, and to face the consequences of her actions with conviction and courage.

Reviving Evan on Mars just wasn't an option. The team would still be wanted criminals on Earth, and the risks of an off-Earth resuscitation were just too great. Growing a human body was possible on Mars, but the weak gravity caused abnormal cellular growth that was extremely difficult to mitigate. Even children conceived naturally on Mars were born with very different bone and muscle structures than Earth-born children.

Mars-born children were taller, thinner, and physically weaker than their Earth-born counterparts, but their brain mass was about ten percent greater on average. Weak gravity explained the height and muscle mass differences, but nobody could explain why the Mars-born children had enlarged brains and skulls.

Some scientists theorized that it was evolution and natural selection at work. Since most of the early Mars colonists were brilliant scientists and engineers, it was reasonable to assume they had passed on their capacity for genius to their children. But that theory didn't explain why clones grown on the surface of Mars also developed enlarged craniums and increased brain mass.

The same clones grown on Earth—using the same DNA—would develop normally. It was almost as if low gravity triggered something buried deep in the human genetic code. It was obvious to those researching the problem that certain genes were expressing themselves differently in the Martian environment. But decades of research had yielded no conclusive explanation as to why human genes behaved differently in low gravity.

Years ago, one of Telogene's top geneticists had, to the great dismay of the scientific community, theorized that the human genome contains remnants from some long-lost, space-faring civilization, and that the Martian environment must closely resemble the conditions of their home world. That geneticist, Dr. Dalena Kamdar, had done a reasonable job of making her case, but she failed to prove her hypothesis to the satisfaction of her peers and the scientific community at large. In the end, she was discredited, and Lily had no choice but to dismiss her from the company.

But that wasn't the worst of it. A team of scientists on Mars tried to transfer engrams from people born on Earth into Martian-grown clones.

Every attempt resulted in the test subject going insane within days (or, at most, weeks) of regaining consciousness. No matter how much training, conditioning, and socialization the subjects received, the outcome was always the same—their brains simply could not accept the signals their bodies were sending them as reality.

Some researchers believed the test subjects would adapt to their new environment given enough time, but they halted the experiment when one of them stole an emergency escape pod and shot himself into space. Thankfully, a freighter picked him up before his pod ran out of air and he, along with the rest of the surviving clones, were returned to Earth a few weeks later. Most of them acclimated well enough, but a few became dangerous to themselves or others and had to be terminated.

There had been hell to pay for that! Aubrey recalled.

That was an understatement. The GFN General Assembly had listed Telogene's failed experiments among the most egregious abuses of cloning technology when it passed the Human Dignity and Decency Act. Those failed experiments, along with her desire to save the company, were what motivated Lily Harris to speak out against full-body replacements and restoring deceased people to life.

Her speech to the General Assembly also cited the negative impact of cloning on the global food supply, but it was Telogene's experimental cloning of people that kept her up at night. Giving the order to terminate one of the Martian clones was one of the hardest things that Lily ever had to do, and she swore to never have to make that decision again…a promise Aubrey had willingly supported until now.

No, there was no other way to guarantee success…he had to be restored here. We… I…did the right thing. Now it's up to Papa and Chen to prove that to the world. If they fail, then what happens to me will not matter.

Content with her choices, Aubrey resolved herself to staring at the walls and ceiling of her tiny cell until it was time for whatever came next.

TWENTY-FIVE

APRIL 6, 2075 10:47 A.M. GST
GSSA HEADQUARTERS
ZURICH, SWITZERLAND

"Madame Secretary?" Christian called through the doorway separating his office from Dianne Merkel's.

"What is it?"

"Captain Bachmann is here to see you."

"Give me five minutes, then send him in."

Dianne Merkel had slept for a few hours, but the effects of being awake for two days straight were still visible on her drawn and tired-looking face. She went into her private bathroom to touch up her makeup and make herself appear as well-rested and ready to do battle as possible.

The facial cream she applied contained nanites that would smooth out the wrinkles, even out her color, and give her skin the subtle, healthy glow of someone who spent more time at the beach than stuck in an office. The effect would usually last for a few days, but stress and lack of sleep were causing her to have to apply it more frequently.

Dianne stared at herself in the mirror as the unseen army of microscopic robots went to work. Within a minute, she saw the effects as her worry lines softened, her cheeks puffed and reddened slightly, and her lips went from being drawn, dry and stiff to plump, moist, and supple.

Satisfied, she patted her face with a dry towel to remove any excess cream and returned to her office.

Once ensconced behind her large desk, she signaled Christian to send in the GFN officer.

"Good morning, Madame Secretary," Captain Heinrich Bachmann said as he entered the room. "Thank you for seeing me in person."

The captain walked stiffly, as though he was marching in a military parade. His dark blue dress uniform was immaculate, without a crease out of place or a spot of unwanted lint anywhere. Dozens of military decorations covered his left breast, and his epaulets bore a captain's insignia sewn in heavy gold thread. His black, patent leather shoes were so highly polished they could be used as a mirror.

"Have a seat, Captain." Dianne pointed at one of the overstuffed leather chairs opposite her. "There is nothing good about this morning."

The captain settled into the chair, trying his best to not look like a scolded child—even though that's exactly how he felt.

"First, let me apologize for losing the fugitives," he offered. "Gbadamosi caught us completely unprepared."

Dianne scoffed, "That's an understatement."

"However," the captain continued, "I must inform you that I have lodged a formal complaint with Command and have requested a full review of your use of GSSA Directive Seven to override my authority."

"I assumed as much, Captain. Is this what you wanted to tell me in person?" Dianne leaned forward and clasped her hands on the desk. "Please tell me it's not."

"It is in part. We have always worked well together in the past, and I hope that we can work together now to ease this situation."

The captain leaned forward, clasping his hands on the edge of Dianne's desk, mirroring her pose almost exactly.

"You know that you overstepped and had no legitimate reason to cut me out."

"Captain, please." Dianne unclasped her hands and reclined back into her chair. "That is your opinion, and I obviously felt differently. Debating the point now is a waste of time."

The captain continued, unfazed. "But I know that losing them in Xi'an upset you and, given the nature of this event, Command will probably do little more than give you a slap on the wrist."

"Well, we have that view in common, then. So what? Get to your point."

The captain reclined back in his chair. "My point, Madame Secretary, is that we cannot afford to spend time battling each other when the real enemy is still out there somewhere."

Dianne crossed her arms. "Go on."

"I want to help you get these guys, but I can't do it if you don't trust me. And, quite frankly, you need my help."

"And exactly how can you help me? You haven't been especially helpful thus far. In fact, I would say you have been exactly the opposite of helpful since you lost them not once but twice in the last twenty-four hours!"

"Yes, I agree that was unfortunate, but that was before we knew what we were up against. Now that I know this involves Gbadamosi, I will handle things quite differently going forward, I assure you."

"So, what do you propose, Captain?" Dianne uncrossed her arms and leaned slightly forward in her chair. "You have something you want me to hear, so just spit it out."

"I believe I know what they are planning, and I have a pretty good idea why they brought Feldman back."

"Okay, I'll play along. Let's hear it."

The captain stood, pulled a data cube from his jacket pocket, and placed it on the desk in front of Dianne.

"GFN Command has been watching both Gbadamosi and Telogene for some time now. I made a few calls after you took me out of the loop on the Luna operation."

"Calls to whom?"

"Not important. But you are not the only one with friends in high places. I may just be a captain, but that's by choice."

"I'm fully aware of your distinguished service record, Captain."

"Well, then you know that I have refused promotion to admiral on several occasions because I like what I do and, quite frankly, I am very good at it."

"Fine, I'm happy for you. Now, what's on the cube, Captain?"

Captain Bachmann leaned against the edge of Dianne's desk as he gently slid the cube across the expansive top until it was close enough for her to take it.

"These are plans for an interstellar starship that is being constructed in orbit above Ceres. It also contains classified intelligence that the GFN has collected on both organizations over the last five years."

Dianne picked up the cube and slid it into the reader interface on her desk. The holodisplay prompted her to identify herself, which required both an AI authentication sequence and a DNA scan. A few seconds later, a three-dimensional diagram of a massive ship appeared in the air in front of her.

"Damn," Dianne said, "that's a big ship. Why am I just now seeing this?"

"This is need-to-know material, and neither of us needed to know before now."

"Well, I need to know now…tell me everything. What's their plan?"

"They have scheduled a full briefing for us, and I am to escort you to Command headquarters now."

"Come on ,Captain, you said you know what they are planning and why they brought Feldman back."

He took a step back and crossed his hands behind his back. His pose was almost statuesque. "My friends and I have concluded that Feldman, Harris, and Hao are little more than rats trying to get off a sinking ship."

"In plain language, Captain."

"What I mean to say, Madame Secretary, is that, according to those intelligence files, the Earth is dying much faster than anyone knows. In fact, my friends believe that we'll all be dead within a decade."

"By what cause?" Dianne asked incredulously.

"Genetic mutation. It is apparently far more widespread than generally reported. And it's not just children anymore…the mutations are spreading to the adult population. Based on current projections, we can expect to see widespread outbreaks within a matter of months—a year or two at most."

Dianne already knew the mutations were spreading. She received daily reports from the GSSA Overwatch team, and there was an entire section devoted to genetic anomalies in the population. She kept this information to herself, however, and let Bachmann think he was bringing her new information.

"Assuming your…friends are right," she said haltingly as she considered her words, "we're all screwed anyway, so what's the point? Leaving the planet isn't likely to stop whatever is happening to us at the genetic level."

"That's probably true, it won't. But I don't think Aubrey Harris and her co-conspirators are worried about that. In fact, I think their entire plan is contingent on *not* bringing any contaminated DNA with them. Their goal is to colonize a new planet that's free from genetic contamination, and I suspect that Miss Harris suffers from the misguided belief that she can ensure that whatever went wrong here won't happen again."

"And Feldman?"

"Feldman is a test case—an experiment to prove that they can survive the journey to another world as archived engrams."

"You mean…"

"I mean that they aren't planning on transporting thousands of potentially defective human bodies to this new world of theirs."

"So, they have built this giant ship to transport their engrams across space? Then what?"

"Look at the design plans. That ship has very little interior space allocated to living quarters, maybe enough to house a couple of dozen people at most. It's mostly organic storage media, redundant power systems, and cargo space."

"And what's special about Feldman that makes him the perfect test subject?" Dianne asked.

"It's simple, really. One, his engrams were in storage for more than fifty years. Two, he was one of the most brilliant geneticists of his time. And three, he's family."

"That's right, I remember Lily Harris telling me about that. His was the first successful engramic transfer from a deceased brain. There probably aren't any engrams that have been in storage longer than his."

The captain relaxed a little and let his hands fall to his sides. "Which is why the elaborate plan and extreme lengths to keep us from getting our hands on him. They need to know how long they can keep themselves in storage and remain viable."

"But that doesn't answer why Aubrey let us catch her. Why didn't she just escape with Feldman and Hao?"

"She must have suspected that she was being watched and created a diversionary plan so that Feldman could escape."

Dianne smirked. "They wouldn't just leave her behind, and you said it yourself, she wants...no she needs to be there—wherever there is—to make sure that the colony doesn't repeat the same mistakes she's made."

"Isn't it obvious, Madame Secretary? They don't need her body, just her mind. I'm sure you remember that this kind of thing happened all the time pre-HDDA. A wealthy executive gets sick, taken hostage, whatever, it didn't matter. The company would simply restore the exec using a recent engramic archive and go on like nothing happened."

"Hell," he continued, "I remember when an exec was taken hostage and released something like two years later after the company refused to pay up. They terminated him when he showed up because they couldn't very well have two versions of the same person running the damn company!"

"That's why we created the HDDA in the first place," Dianne agreed.

"Exactly. These people look at their bodies as disposable, and I promise you that Aubrey Harris is no different. You can keep this version of her locked away for the rest of her life, but she will never give you anything because she knows that a copy of her is living out there on some other planet fulfilling whatever God-forsaken mission she thinks she's on."

"I'm following you up to a point, but we're still missing something. Where will they find clean DNA? And how did they choose the colonists?"

"Which is why we need to get to that briefing," Bachmann replied. "I have a car waiting downstairs."

"Alright, but Aubrey's hearing is at three and I may need to step out."

"I'm sure that won't be a problem," he assured her.

"Very well," Dianne said. She activated her communicator. "Christian, please clear my calendar of everything except the Harris hearing."

"Yes, ma'am. Would you like me to go with you?" Christian asked.

"No, I will call you if I need you."

The Secretary grabbed the data cube from the reader as she headed toward the door.

"Let's review this on the ride over," she said.

Captain Bachmann said nothing as they entered the Secretary's private elevator. After a short ride to the parking garage level, the elevator doors hissed open to reveal a GFN-marked hovercar parked a short distance away.

"You know, that assistant of yours is exceptional…probably the most lifelike autonomous AI I've ever seen."

"Thanks, latest model. I got him a few months ago. He's got a military grade frame with the biggest and best organic storage system available."

"Telogene?"

"No, Situ Robotics. Why?" Dianne asked.

"Just curious…I wonder what would happen if you uploaded human engrams into that body."

"I don't think organic storage densities are there yet."

Bachmann gestured for the Secretary to enter the vehicle first. "No, but his processing and storage capabilities far exceed ours when he's connected to the network."

"Yes, that's true. What's your point?"

Bachmann slid into the seat next to her. "Nothing. I'm just trying to figure out who will occupy the habitat space on the colony ship."

The hovercar lifted off as soon as he closed the door.

"Where are we going?" the Secretary asked.

"A secure operations center across town; it's fifteen minutes away."

Dianne slid the data cube into the vehicle's reader. "So, you think they will use synths to run the ship? Or do you think they want to transfer themselves into synthetic bodies?"

"Not sure, but it would seem that the technology is advanced enough to allow for either possibility."

Dianne thought for a moment.

"Yes," she said, "but only if they have solved the autonomous storage problem."

"AIs operate across storage mediums…why not human engrams?" Bachmann responded.

"Has anyone tried it?"

"I don't know, but what if Feldman isn't a clone? What if he is a state-of-the-art synth like Christian? Hell, if that's the case, then Aubrey and company haven't even broken any laws, right?"

Dianne's eyes widened noticeably. "My God, I haven't even thought of this possibility. If Feldman is a synth, then the HDDA doesn't apply."

"Right, that's the problem with laws—people rarely think to pass laws prohibiting something they consider as impossible."

"Or they are just slow to react once it becomes possible, which is why the HDDA wasn't passed until 20 years after the first human clone." Dianne acknowledged.

"Exactly!"

"Is this speculation, or based on something in these files, Captain?"

"Neither. Let's just say that my friends get paid to think about these kinds of scenarios and plan for them."

"So, they've known this could happen?"

"Well, *known* may be a little strong. More like suspected, I should think." Bachmann smirked. "Just read the files, Madame Secretary, we'll be there soon."

TWENTY-SIX

APRIL 6, 2075 1:32 P.M. GST
GSSA HEADQUARTERS
ZURICH, SWITZERLAND

The meeting was held in a secure conference room in the basement of GSSA headquarters. Besides Dianne and Captain Bachmann, there was a vice admiral (Bachmann's boss), the Executive Director of the Bureau of Global Security and Intelligence, and two BGSI analysts in the room. There were also two GFN geneticists who joined via a secure line from another location. The analysts did most of the talking.

The Galileo analyst, a woman who appeared to be in her early thirties named Constance, was first to speak. She started with an overview of Adekunle Gbadamosi's activities over the past five years.

She focused on the fact that sales of both raw and refined materials to Earth had decreased significantly during that time, even though production had increased significantly at the Galileo mines on Luna, Mars, and in the Asteroid Belt (the latter often referred to as "Adee's Golden Ring" because of his vast mining operations there). Her conclusion was that Gbadamosi was hoarding a massive amount of raw material. She then showed where all that material went.

The colony ship was called *Kutanga*, which meant "begin" in the Shona language (an apparent homage to Gbadamosi's African heritage). It was being constructed in orbit above Ceres, a dwarf planet on the Mars side of the Asteroid Belt. Based on recent intelligence and imagery from GFN satellites, the ship could be ready to launch within a matter of days. The spaceship was huge, nearly 1500 meters long and 600 meters wide at its broadest part. Four massive triangular fins jutted out from the top, bottom, and sides of the craft, giving it the overall appearance of a giant lawn dart.

The design schematic Captain Bachmann had shared with Dianne was their only source of information about the ship's size, composition, and systems. Although the GFN had several operatives embedded within Gbadamosi's organization, none had been allowed access to sensitive work areas or personnel. The analyst implied that this likely meant that most, if not all, were compromised or being fed disinformation, at the very least.

The ship's configuration suggested that it was fit with an advanced gravity pulse drive system. The size of the engine nacelles (the four giant fins) suggested a system so powerful that it could theoretically propel *Kutanga* to speeds greater than ten percent of the speed of light. The analyst also believed that, with enough time and fuel, *Kutanga* might even be capable of exceeding twenty percent of light-speed.

By comparison, the GFN's most advanced spacecraft could attain a little over five percent of light-speed. If true, this meant that Gbadamosi's scientists and engineers had achieved a significant advancement over current technology. Constance ended by offering her opinion that, in the wrong hands, this advancement could pose a significant security risk to the GFN. She refused to comment on whether "in the wrong hands" included The Galileo Group.

The Telogene analyst, a youthful-looking man named Arturo, gave a similar presentation. He started with Lily Harris's connection to Gbadamosi.

Based on available evidence, their relationship began nearly forty years ago, when Lily hired The Galileo Group to help Telogene establish a permanent base of operations on Mars. Although there was little evidence of an ongoing relationship since then, recent developments suggested otherwise. As wealthy as Gbadamosi was, he simply could not have built *Kutanga* without help, and Lily Harris was the person most likely to collaborate with him on such a high-risk, high-cost venture.

Next, he called attention to the plane crash that killed Lily and left Aubrey in charge of Telogene. He noted that the circumstances of the crash, and the subsequent destruction of the bodies, were suspicious. Although no evidence existed to contradict the official report, which had blamed the crash on accidental rapid decompression of the aircraft, Arturo noted that the probability of a catastrophic failure that simultaneously incapacitated the pilot *and* the onboard AI were hundreds of millions to one.

At first, Dianne was confused about how Lily's death applied to the current situation. The connection became clearer once the analyst identified several key Telogene personnel who were believed to have been involved in *Kutanga's* construction. There were hundreds of scientists, engineers, and researchers on his list of suspects, but the analyst focused most of his time on one in particular. Arturo's research had identified Josana Saunders as the person responsible for coordinating the sale and transfer of Telogene's organic storage technology to The Galileo Group.

Miss Saunders started at Telogene right out of college, and over the last ten years had worked her way up to Director of Operations within the organic storage subsidiary. By all accounts, she was an exceptional student, a stellar employee, and a rising star at Telogene. Her GFN identity was authentic, her government data file complete from birth until the present, and there was nothing in any of her records that would cause anyone to suspect she wasn't who she claimed to be. But Arturo had pointed out a significant problem with her identity—Miss Saunders somehow had the ability to be on Earth and Mars *simultaneously*.

The analyst showed several visuals showing Josana showing up for work every day at her office in Weinan, China, followed by several images of her meeting with people at various sites across Mars. The date and time stamps on images made it impossible for both women to be the same person. When Dianne asked who Arturo thought the second Josana could be, he responded with a video showing Josana clearing customs on Mars. The date, adjusted to Global Standard Time, was January 20, 2074—just two weeks after the plane crash that killed Lily Harris.

The analyst had run dozens of AI simulations, and the consensus outcome was a seventy percent chance that the Josana Saunders on Mars was, in fact, Lily Harris. The simulations had also concluded that, if Lily Harris had survived the plane crash, there was a high probability that Bruce Wagner had as well.

The analysts left the room after a lengthy question-and-answer session. The two GFN geneticists taking part via holocall led the rest of the meeting.

Their topic was the rate at which genetic mutations were manifesting in the populations of Earth, Luna, and Mars. The vast majority of cases involved people developing forms of cancer believed eliminated decades ago. These cancers were hyper-aggressive and unresponsive to all known treatments. The mortality rate was above ninety percent, and lifespan from first detection was less than a year. So far, they had discovered no common environmental factors or genetic markers in those affected. It looked like the cancers had developed at random in otherwise healthy people.

Then there were the physical mutations. Some people, mostly children and young adults, had developed cosmetic and physiological anomalies that resembled traits found in other life forms on Earth. These ranged from relatively minor variations of hair, eye, and skin color to more significant manifestations such as gills, scales, feathers, claws, and tails. These anomalies were rarely fatal of themselves but, once these traits appeared, there was a high probability that the affected person would develop an aggressive cancer—usually within three to five years, but sometimes within months.

The geneticists disconnected after a brief question-and-answer session, leaving the final discussions to those that remained in the room.

Vice Admiral Marco Langenburg had extended Dianne an olive branch by agreeing to not contest her invocation of Directive Seven. He did, however, clarify that Captain Bachmann was in sole command of Epsilon Six going forward. He also reminded everyone that deployment of GFN Peacekeepers to Mars, its moons, or its territories in the Asteroid Belt, without prior approval of the Martian president, violated the Mars Neutrality Treaty of 2057.

Dianne had acknowledged the vice admiral's concerns, and graciously accepted his terms. The meeting had adjourned shortly thereafter.

Captain Bachmann, who had remained quiet for most of the meeting, followed Dianne out of the meeting room and into the elevators.

"So, what do you think?" he asked. "Quite the shit-show, isn't it?"

Shit-show was an understatement—Dianne felt that she was leaving with more questions than answers.

"You could say that. Those bastards are planning to hang this around my neck if we fail."

"How so?"

"Are you so naïve as to think that Vice Admiral Langenburg will let my Directive Seven order go uncontested if we don't get Feldman and Hao back? Hell no, he won't! He was just giving me all the rope I need to hang myself…and then some!"

"I think you are being overly cynical, Madame Secretary. The admiral and I discussed this matter at length and we *both* agreed to give you a pass…this time."

"Then why bother making a formal complaint in the first place? I'll tell you why," she continued, not waiting for his response. "It's so that the two of you can cover your ass if we fuck this up. That's why!"

The captain smirked. "Well, you have me there. But with all due respect, I have worked too long and too hard to have my career upended because you got impatient. You issued a dead or alive exfil order to a GFN special operations team on Luna…without even notifying GFN Command or President Duchon! What did you expect would happen?"

Dianne opened her mouth to speak, but the captain continued. "I want to help you, Secretary Merkel, I really do. But I need you to trust my judgment. I'm very good at what I do, and all I need is for you to let me do my job without interference. Do that, and you'll get the results you are looking for; interfere again and…well, let's just say that my lodging a formal complaint with Command will be the least of your worries."

They exited the elevator and walked across the lobby toward the street and Bachmann's waiting hovercar.

"You win, Captain…we will try it your way," Dianne said, her voice weary. She was tired, very tired, and just didn't have the energy to fight anymore. "What's your plan?"

"I redirected Alpha and Bravo teams to Mars a little over two hours ago. They should arrive in orbit at approximately this time tomorrow."

"With whose authorization?" Dianne asked incredulously. He must have heard the vice admiral's admonition against sending GFN Peacekeepers into Martian territory!

"Ah yes, that. I decided that their exceptional performance on Luna had earned them some shore leave."

Dianne laughed. "Are you kidding me…what exceptional performance? They let our fugitives escape, for Christ's-sake!"

"That was beyond their control. And their quick thinking and actions resulted in the rapid recovery of eight GFN Peacekeepers."

"Brilliant, I'm impressed."

"Thank you," he replied. "Better still, I can cancel their leave at any time should it become necessary to do so."

"You surprise me, Captain Bachmann. Now I understand why you've chosen to remain in your current position all these years. You are, as you say, exceptional at it. God knows that navigating GFN politics is not easy!"

The captain smiled but said nothing as they climbed into the backseat of the vehicle.

"Madame Secretary," Bachmann said after the car left the curb. "May I ask your intentions?"

"Call me Dianne."

"Very well. How would you like to proceed, Dianne?"

"It's time we stop playing catch-up. Aubrey's hearing is in an hour and a half. I'm going to request a memory scan once she's officially remanded to GSSA custody. In the meantime, I am interested in hearing what Mister Wagner has to say about the plane crash that supposedly killed his father and Lily Harris."

"Sounds good. Shall we reconvene at seventeen hundred hours, then?"

"Yes, my office. I can get you a temporary office on the floor below mine if that would help."

"That would be convenient, especially if we need to have discussions we don't want overheard."

Dianne nodded her agreement.

***

Fifteen minutes later, Dianne was back in her office.

"Christian, get me Geoff Wagner."

"Mister Wagner is on his way here now, ma'am. He's scheduled to meet with his client at 2:00 p.m. Would you still like me to call him?"

Dianne looked at the time on her holodisplay; it was 1:50 p.m.

"No, just have him brought to my conference room when he arrives."

"Very well."

Twenty-Seven

April 5, 2075 01:52 p.m. GST
GSSA Headquarters
Zurich, Switzerland

The cell door slid open.

The empty containers from her lunch were still on the table, and Aubrey was lying in her bunk. The guard had been watching on the surveillance monitors and knew she was sleeping. She had been through a lot in the last twenty-four hours and, as a courtesy, he had decided to not disturb her until it was time for the hearing.

The guard closed the short distance to the bed and gently nudged Aubrey's arm. She didn't respond. He tried again, this time with a little more force. Still no response. He grabbed her by the shoulders and shook her. Her head flopped limply to one side, but her eyes remained closed. He touched his fingers to the side of her neck looking for a pulse but found none.

He tapped his communicator. "Medical emergency in holding cell one. I repeat medical emergency in holding cell one."

Two men dressed in white jumpsuits burst into the room just three minutes later. One of the medics pulled a small, rectangular device from his belt and placed it on Aubrey's forehead.

"No pulse, no brain activity," he said to the other medic. "Five milligrams of nanoisamine."

The second medic pulled a cartridge from his belt and handed it to the first medic who pressed the cartridge against Aubrey's neck. It made a soft pop followed by a hissing sound. A few seconds passed as the medic watched for signs of life on the holodisplay projecting in the air above Aubrey's forehead. If the injection did its job, the nanites in it would attack and destroy any other nanites in her bloodstream, while simultaneously delivering a powerful stimulant to her central nervous system.

"Weak pulse, minimal activity," the first medic said. "We need to get her to the med bay."

The second medic stepped into the hallway briefly to retrieve the stretcher they had left outside of the room. The two men rolled Aubrey onto it and hurried her out of the room.

The guard tapped his sleeve mounted console twice before following the medics out of the room. Thirty floors above, Christian got up from his desk and opened the door to Secretary Merkel's office.

"I'm sorry to disturb you, but there has been a medical emergency in holding cell one."

Dianne looked up from her holodisplay. "What's wrong with her?"

"Unknown. The guard found her unresponsive and summoned the medical team. She is being taken to the third-floor medical facility now."

"Is she alive?"

"Also, unknown—she had no pulse or respiration when found. The medics administered a nano-stimulant, which has restarted her heart and restored minimal brain function."

"I'm going there now. Tell Wagner to wait, *do not* tell him about Aubrey."

"Yes, ma'am."

Dianne rushed to her private elevator and descended to the third floor. When she arrived at the medical bay, she found Aubrey lying in a sealed cryopod with a physician and two medics attending her. The guard assigned to her was standing just outside the door.

"What happened?" Dianne demanded of the guard.

"I'm sorry, but I don't know, ma'am. I found her this way."

"Weren't you watching her? I ordered continuous observation."

"Absolutely…there was someone watching her at all times. I don't know how this could have happened. I even checked building security, and the AI confirms that no one entered that room today except me."

"Well, tell the AI to check again. This was no accident, and I want to know who is responsible."

"Yes, ma'am, right away. The incident response team is scanning the cell and reviewing all activity within the building since she arrived."

"You remain here. I want no one in or out of the medical bay without my consent."

Dianne took a few steps before turning back toward the guard. "In fact, I want the whole building locked down. Nobody in or out, now!"

"Yes, ma'am. We've already implemented enhanced screening. Initiating lockdown now," he replied.

Lights up and down the corridor flashed red, and a male voice boomed from the ceiling.

"Condition red, condition red. The building is now on lockdown. All personnel and visitors will remain where they are until further notice. Security will arrest anyone found without an approved escort. Thank you for your cooperation."

Dianne approached the physician working on Aubrey.

"What's her condition?" Dianne asked.

"Stable," the doctor replied. "For the moment. But the damage is done; her neural pathways are disrupted beyond repair."

"So, it was nanites?"

"Yeah, and a heavy dose too…she's a total wipe."

"Any chance she had them on her? Or already in her bloodstream but inactive?"

"Unlikely—we did a full scan when she came in, and her system was clean except the normal health maintenance stuff."

"Then we have an even bigger problem."

"I'm afraid so."

Dianne heard a knock on the wall behind her. She turned as a guard stepped into the room.

"I'm sorry, ma'am, but there has been another development." It was the head of building security.

"What kind of development, Sergeant?" Dianne asked.

"A hospitality services worker is dead. They found her body in the cold storage area—it looks like suicide."

Dianne turned back to the doctor. "I bet we can guess what killed her."

He nodded.

"I want to know the minute you confirm," she said.

She turned back to the sergeant. "And will someone please find out how they compromised our security?"

"Yes, ma'am," the sergeant replied, "we're working on that."

Dianne continued past the guards to her private elevator. She was the only person, other than GSSA security personnel, who could move freely about the building while on lockdown. The elevator doors opened to reveal four heavily armed GSSA security guards.

"Ma'am," the closest guard said as he stepped aside to let her on, "we're your security detail."

Although her movements weren't restricted, it was standard procedure to assign a protective detail to senior ranking officials in case of attack or other circumstance that might require them to evacuate.

"Understood. Office," she said, first acknowledging him and then informing the elevator control AI of her destination.

Less than a minute later, she was back in her office with her security detail in tow.

"I am going in there." She pointed to her conference room. "You wait out here."

"Yes, ma'am. They've assigned two guards to Mister Wagner."

Dianne entered the conference room, closing the door behind her.

"You two, outside…now," she said.

The two guards looked at each other but said nothing as they exited through the double doors.

"Geoff," Dianne said as she took her seat at the head of the conference table.

"Madame Secretary," the lawyer replied. "Is everything okay? I heard the lockdown announcement."

"It's fine, just a precaution. We should be cleared shortly."

"Glad to hear it; I am supposed to be meeting with my client."

"That's…not going to happen."

"What do mean? You can't deny her right to counsel, and last I checked the hearing is still on for three."

"We'll get to that. First, I want to ask you some questions."

"I can give you five minutes, Secretary Merkel, but then I insist that you allow me to see my client."

If he knows anything, he's doing a great job of hiding it, Dianne thought.

"It's hard to believe she's been gone over a year now, isn't it?" she asked.

"Who's gone?"

"Lily Harris."

"Oh…um…yes, it is," Geoff said. "What does that have to do with anything?"

"Your father Bruce also died in that crash, didn't he?"

"Madame Secretary, I must protest. What does this trip down memory lane have to do with my client and her current situation?"

She ignored his question. "And you became Telogene's Chief Legal Officer after he died, correct?"

Geoff gave in to her persistence. "Yes."

"And what did you do before that?"

"I was in private practice. Would you like a copy of my CV?"

"No, I have it, but thank you. Do you know how I have spent my morning, Geoff?"

"No, how would I?"

"I spent the last three hours in a BGSI briefing on top-secret material —material that's relevant to Aubrey Harris and her current situation."

"As you know, Madame Secretary, you must provide me with copies of any information that might be used against my client."

"And as you well know, Mister Wagner, we aren't there yet. In fact, we haven't even charged your client yet!"

"That's true. But you are detaining her pending those charges being filed, and I intend to object."

"What if I told you I had reason to believe that Bruce Wagner and Lily Harris were still alive?"

Geoff looked like he'd just been punched in the face. He would have probably stumbled back on his heals if he had been standing.

He played into his obvious surprise. "That would be incredible, but it's not possible. My father would have contacted me if he was alive, and I can assure you that he has not."

"Well, I guess that's not a lie in the strictest sense since you said *my father*." Dianne smirked. "Come on, Bruce, the game is up. It's time to stop pretending and face the consequences. There are too many lives at stake."

Another punch to the face.

"I don't know what you are playing at, Secretary Merkel," he said, noticeably shaken. "But this is a waste of time. I would like to see my client…now, please."

"Okay, have it your way." Dianne stood and walked around the end of the conference table, brushing her fingertips across the leather-backed chairs as she closed the distance between them.

"Aubrey is dead…well, more accurately, she's a vegetable. Someone didn't want us to find out what was going on inside that little brain of hers."

Geoff stood to face her. "I demand to see her, now!"

"Sure, Geoff. I'll have the guards take you to her."

Geoff brushed past her as he walked toward the double doors.

"But this isn't over," Dianne called out after him. "Not by a long shot."

The lawyer ignored her.

"And if you speak with Lily, please give her my best."

He kept walking.

Dianne activated her communicator once he was out of sight.

"Christian."

"Yes, ma'am."

"Please have Mister Wagner escorted to the medical bay."

"Right away, ma'am."

Dianne returned to her office through her private entrance, accessing Executive Director Veronika Horvat's contact information as she walked. She placed the call when she got to her desk.

Director Horvat answered immediately. "Secretary Merkel, what can I do for you?"

"I need everything you have on Bruce and Geoff Wagner…GFN ID numbers to follow."

"That's not a problem. Anything else?"

"Yeah. Can you put a team on Geoff Wagner? He is here now. I can hold him until you get your people in place…I want continuous surveillance."

"Why not send a GSSA team?"

"Long story, but I might have a leak somewhere. Aubrey Harris was hard-wiped while in custody."

"Oh, dear. Did you catch the perpetrator?"

"Found is more like it…frozen solid in a cold storage area. And, also hard-wiped."

"Damn, okay, I'll help. Are we looking for anything specific?"

"I want to know where he goes, what he does, and who he talks to. And I want profiles on him and everyone he's talked to in the last twenty-four hours."

"I will see what I can do. Is that it?"

"Yes, for now. Thank you, Veronika."

"Goodbye, Dianne."

Dianne disconnected the call.

What's next? Where do they go from here? And I how do I get in front of them?

She considered those questions for several minutes before calling for Christian.

"Yes, ma'am?" he responded.

"I am sending you some classified files. I need a complete scenario analysis with probable outcomes."

Dianne waved her hands across her holodisplay. A few more gestures gave Christian access to everything she'd received from Captain Bachmann, and everything the BGSI and GSSA had accumulated on Aubrey Harris, Telogene, and the Galileo Group.

"The BGSI will send over additional files on Bruce and Geoff Wagner shortly; please incorporate them once received."

"Understood. Will there be anything else, ma'am?"

"Estimated time to complete?"

It took several seconds for him to respond.

"It is difficult to give an exact time until I have all the data," he finally said. "However, I estimate the first analysis will be complete in approximately ten hours, twenty-three minutes, and fifteen seconds."

"That's too long, they'll be gone in ten hours."

"If I perform no other functions, and am not interrupted, I believe that I can reduce that time by approximately four hours."

"Do it, I will manage," she said.

"Very well, I will be in my office if anything changes," he replied.

Christian's private office was located just across the waiting area from Dianne's office. It was small and sparse, containing only a desk and a chair that doubled as a charging station. There was also a quantum data port mounted on the wall that allowed him direct, instantaneous access to his private external storage array, and the GSSA's private network—and all the information and advanced AI services they contained. Although Christian could access those resources wirelessly, the quantum data port was both faster and more secure.

Christian lifted his shirt to expose his stomach area. What normally served as a belly button on a human was, on him, an interface port compatible with the one mounted on his office wall. He removed a black cable from his desk and plugged each end into the appropriate port. It took less than a second to authenticate and establish a secure network connection. He closed his eyes and filled his mind with the data the Secretary General had sent him.

As advanced as he was, Christian's onboard storage system could only hold about 70 percent of the data and functionality he had accumulated since his inception. To manage the overflow, he decided what to archive to an external storage system based on his job assignment and what tasks he was likely to be asked to perform.

For example, since being assigned to Dianne, he had found no need for his advanced combat functions and had kept just a few basic self-defense subroutines as a precautionary measure. Of course, he could download the archived functions at any time. But doing so would mean archiving other data and functionality to make room on his autonomous storage array.

Connecting to the external system tripled his data storage and processing power. And plugging into the quantum data port allowed him access to everything with virtually no delay. The direct connection to the GSSA's central network, and the shared AI services it provided, further enhanced his capabilities.

With these resources available to him, it took only seconds to find, sort, and collate the data Dianne had given him.

It took just minutes more to construct a complex data model that showed him the relationships between every piece of information he'd collected. Identifying all the potential variables and assigning probabilities would take the most time. Once his simulations were complete, he could offer a reasonably accurate prediction of future events —the degree of accuracy depending entirely on the completeness of the source data.

Christian leaned back in his chair, disabled his non-essential functions, and went to work.

TWENTY-EIGHT

APRIL 5, 2075 02:25 P.M. GST
LUNA-MARS TRANSITION

"Evan, wake up. Can you hear me?"

Evan opened his eyes to see Chen floating in front of him. He lifted his head and looked around; he was still in his acceleration pod on Gbadamosi's missile-turned-spaceship.

"Yeah, I can hear you. What the hell happened?"

"You blacked out. We all did."

As his vision cleared, Evan could see Yin and Adee floating just behind Chen. Adee was working at a console, and Yin was holding on to the back of her acceleration pod.

"How are you feeling, Evan?" Yin asked.

"Fine I guess, aside from a splitting headache and the ringing in my ears."

"It will pass," Chen offered. "It's just the after-effects of the gravity drive."

"I thought I had died," Evan said.

"I'm sorry about that." Adee looked up from his console. "No room on this thing for compensators. It won't be as noticeable next time."

"Next time!" Evan wasn't sure he could handle another episode like the last one.

Adee pushed off the console and grabbed hold of a handrail just above Evan. "Yes, I'm afraid so. *Endeavor* will be here soon, and we'll have to jump again if we want to stay ahead of your pursuers."

"Dear God, I don't think I can, Adee. Just leave me here."

"We can't do that, Evan, but I promise you'll hardly even notice it. Compared to this old thing, making a jump on *Endeavor* will feel like…"— Adee paused as he searched for the correct analogy—"…like jumping into a cold swimming pool. You'll feel it, but you'll get used to it after a few minutes."

"Oh, well, that sounds so much better."

"You'll be fine, Evan, trust me," Chen said. "Let's get him up, Yin."

Yin moved to Evan's right side as Chen released the restraints keeping Evan in his pod. Evan felt himself float gently off of the pod, but Yin braced herself with one arm and helped Evan orient himself so that his head was "up" relative to the inside of the ship.

"No sudden moves," she said. "I can move you closer to the floor and you can use your mag-boots if that would help."

"Let's do that," Evan replied.

Chen and Yin gently pushed on Evan until his feet contacted the grated metal floor that ran the length of the craft. His boots activated as soon as his feet made contact.

"That's better," he said.

"Take slow steps and keep one foot on the walkway at all times," Yin cautioned. "If you step too hard, you will fly off the catwalk."

Evan took a timid step forward to see how it felt. Whereas Luna had at least some gravity, here it was only the magnetic pull of his boots against metal that held him in place. Chen floated in front of Evan and shoved his right hand toward Evan's mouth.

"Here take this," he said .

"What is it?"

"Something to help with the headache."

"Do you have some water?" Evan asked.

"Back of the seats," Adee replied, not taking his eyes off his console.

Yin opened a compartment on the back of her pod and pulled out a clear plastic container with liquid inside. She twisted the top; a short straw popped out.

She drifted over to Evan and put the bottle in his hand. Evan used his lips to take the pill from Chen's hand and chased it down with a long slurp of water.

"Okay?" Yin asked.

Evan took another long sip before handing the bottle back to Yin.

"Yes, thanks."

"How long?" Chen asked Adee.

"Not much longer, they're close."

"How do we get out of this thing?" Evan asked. "I hope you aren't expecting me to do a spacewalk!"

Adee chuckled. "Not at all, *Endeavor* is a big ship, my friend. We will fit easily inside her cargo bay. Once inside, we will put our helmets back on and walk to the airlock using our mag-boots. Easy-peasy."

"This whole thing is unbelievable. Two days ago, I woke up…came back to life…whatever you want to call it…and now, I'm Buck Rogers."

"Buck who?" Adee asked.

"Buck Rogers. He was that astronaut that got frozen in his space capsule…somewhere around 1987, I think. Somebody, I don't remember who, found him floating in space five hundred years later and revived him. There were comic books and TV series. It was pretty advanced for its time."

"Ahh, interesting."

"Now that I think of it though, he and I have a lot in common. Both of us were revived long after we died. Earth fought a nuclear war that resulted in everyone coming together in one world government…the only thing missing is the evil Princess Ardala and her Draconian army trying to take over the Earth. You haven't met any aliens from another planet yet, right?"

Everyone burst into laughter, long enough to make Evan uncomfortable.

"What's so funny?" he asked.

Yin was the first to stop laughing. "We're sorry. We're not laughing at you."

"Buck Rogers, you say?" Chen asked. "I'll look that up; maybe the footage is still available."

"The answer is no, Evan, we have not encountered an evil princess from another planet," Adee finally answered.

A light flashed on Adee's console and a beeping sound echoed throughout the craft.

"They're here," Adee said. "Five hundred kilometers and closing fast, half a kilometer below us."

"Let's get you back in your pod," Chen said.

Yin and Chen helped Evan back into his pod before returning to theirs. Adee tapped the console a few times before drifting back to his pod.

Evan rotated the view on his holodisplay so he could get a good look at the incoming ship—it was massive.

The craft looked like a long, cigar-shaped tube with a wide, flat disk mounted toward the front of it. Four large, triangular fins spread out behind the disk. They were like the delta wings on the Telogene shuttle that had carried him to Luna, but they jutted out from the top and bottom in addition to the sides of the ship. The four fins came together at the back of the ship to form what looked to Evan like a giant Celtic cross.

The two ships closed to within two hundred meters of each other. Massive was an understatement—*Endeavor* was the size of four aircraft carriers laid end-to-end.

The distance between the two ships continued to decrease until the missile-ship was just thirty meters above the *Endeavor*. They were moving toward a large opening in the upper fin. Evan felt a slight shove as Adee activated the ship's thrusters. A few more thrusts and the missile-ship floated gently through the opening.

Man, this thing is huge! Evan marveled to himself.

The missile-ship continued to drift slowly rearward, through the opening and into the interior of the ship. Evan felt another small thrust, and then everything went quiet.

The holodisplay view shifted to the back of the missile-ship. Several bright lights turned on inside the cargo bay, and Evan saw a retractable arm extend from the wall behind them. A few seconds later, he heard a clunking sound and felt the arm retract, pulling the missile-ship with it.

"We're locked in. Helmets on everybody," Adee said as he floated toward the hatch.

Yin helped Evan exit his pod and secure his helmet. Once everyone was ready, Adee depressurized the rocket and opened the hatch. His two crewmen were first to exit.

"Chen, you're next, then Evan and Yin, please," he said.

When Evan got to the hatch, he could see that the floor of the cargo bay was at least twenty meters below him. Chen was standing next to a crewman on a narrow catwalk that ran the length of the cargo bay.

"I thought you said we were walking?"

"Just push off and float over to us, Evan," Chen replied. "We'll catch you."

There were at least ten meters of empty space between Evan and Chen.

Evan took a deep breath. "Okay, here I come."

He used both hands to pull himself through the hatch, doing his best to aim for Chen. Unfortunately, his right glove caught on the door handle as he pushed off, causing him to spin slowly as he left the ship. His awkward efforts to stop spinning only caused him to tumble. By the time he got to the catwalk, he found himself upside down and staring at Chen's knees.

"I got you," Chen said.

Evan felt Chen's arms clasp around his midsection, bringing him to stop with his head just above the catwalk. Yin landed next to Chen a second later, and together they oriented Evan so that his feet were on the catwalk.

Evan's mag-boots engaged, holding his feet firmly on the catwalk. "Well, that was fun," he said.

Adee landed just in front of the group. "This way," he said.

The group walked along the catwalk toward an open hatch at the rear of the cargo bay.

"Inside," Adee instructed. "We're almost there, Evan."

Adee closed the hatch behind them, and Evan felt the pressure change as the airlock equalized with the ship's interior. Once fully pressurized, Adee asked the group to remove their helmets. The inner airlock door hissed open to reveal a short hallway.

Evan stepped carefully, fearing that one misstep would send him careening up to the ceiling.

Adee led the group to an elevator at the end of the hallway. "Just a short ride from here."

The doors closed and the elevator started moving as soon as the last person was on.

Evan felt a strange sensation, like he was getting heavier. "Is that gravity?"

"Yes," Adee replied. "The habitat ring is ninety percent of Earth's gravity, so you won't need mag-boots to walk around."

The elevator stopped, and the doors slid open to reveal another hallway.

Adee stepped out first. "The decontamination room is on your left, and there are fresh clothes waiting for you."

"Thank God," Evan said. "I can't wait to get out of this suit!"

Adee laughed. "I bet; it's been a long day for you. I suggest we have a quick meal, and then you all should get some rest. I'm afraid tomorrow will be another long day."

"I can eat," Evan replied. "All this flying through space has made me hungry again."

It took about twenty minutes for the group to complete the decontamination process and get dressed. From the changing room, it was a short walk down another hallway, which ended in a hatch. Beneath that was a ladder down to the floor some ten meters below. Adee sent his crewmen down first.

Adee helped Evan onto the ladder. "Be careful. You will feel heavier as you near the bottom."

Evan felt the downward pressure building on his legs and feet with each step down. Once he reached the bottom, he took a few tentative steps and found that he could walk normally, and even hop up and down without floating away.

"Having fun?" Yin asked as she stepped off the ladder.

"Just testing," Evan replied.

Chen was next down, followed by Adee.

"You're dismissed," he said to the two crewmen. "Thank you for your help today."

The crewmen bowed slightly before departing down a nearby intersecting hallway.

"The mess hall is this way." Adee pointed toward one end of the hallway.

"Where are the people?" Evan asked. "It must take a lot of people to run this ship."

Adee laughed. "Not as many as you might think. The AI's do most of the work."

"How big is your crew?" Chen asked.

"There are thirty crew members on board at the moment, but full ship's complement is one hundred and fifty-four."

"Where is everyone else?" Yin asked.

"They're getting *Kutanga* ready. I only needed a skeleton crew to effect your retrieval."

"What's the *Kutanga*?" Evan asked.

"Another ship," Adee replied. "But all in due time, my friend."

"Here we are," he added a few steps later.

The door slid open to reveal a room roughly ten meters square. There were four round tables arrayed around the center of the room, with eight chairs around each table. Three uniformed people, a man and two women, sat at the table. They all jumped up as Adee entered the room.

"Admiral," one of the woman said.

"At ease," Adee replied.

All three sat down, returning to their meals.

"These are some of my officers," Adee informed the group. "Please introduce yourselves while I get you some food."

Adee exited through a different doorway than the one they had entered through.

The male officer signaled the group over with a wave. "You can sit with us if you'd like."

Evan and company accepted the offered seats, and everyone took turns introducing themselves.

The woman who had greeted the admiral was the senior officer; she introduced herself as Chief Engineer Aisha Wallace. Next was Main Propulsion Assistant Linda Sewell, followed by Damage Control Assistant Gustov Pichler. Together, they ensured that *Endeavor's* engines and critical systems remained functional and ready for anything.

After introductions were complete, the conversation turned to the fugitive's ride in Adee's homegrown missile-ship, with several good laughs all around as Chen and Yin shared some of Evan's experiences. Evan didn't find the stories all that funny, but he was a good sport and played along. Adee's return caused a welcome change of subject.

"Making friends, I see," Adee said. "I hope you don't mind, but I ordered for you."

Two crew members accompanied him, each carrying two trays. They waited for Adee to take his seat at the table and then placed a tray in front of each of them. They removed the lids and said "enjoy" before leaving the way they came.

"We are having butternut squash pasta with sage and brown butter sauce, warm garlic bread, and hot tea to drink. If you'd like something else to drink, I can offer you juice, water or coffee."

The three officers excused themselves, removing their trays from the table as they left.

"It was nice meeting you," Aisha said on behalf of her fellow officers before exiting through the side door Adee had just come through.

"So what's the plan?" Chen asked as the group tucked in to their meals.

"The same," Adee replied. "We're just a few weeks early. We'll get you to the station and make sure that Evan is stable. Then…well, then we see how it goes."

"Are you worried about the GSSA or GFN?" Yin asked.

"A little. Your pursuers were redirected to Mars, which means they're not giving up."

"But surely President Pak will object!" Chen said, referring to the president of Mars.

Jerry Pak had been born and raised in North Korea, but he had fled that country's totalitarian regime after the war. He had made his to Poland, and from there to Germany—where he became a naturalized citizen. He was among the first to volunteer when the German government asked for volunteers to go to Mars. He went to Hades One as a software engineer, but he was a natural leader and rose to prominence quickly. When Mars won its independence, he became its first president. His popularity was such that he had been re-elected three times, and was currently in the middle of his third, ten-year term.

"He will," Adee replied. "But they'll find some excuse for being there…the GFN has a reputation for acting first and seeking forgiveness later. I suspect they may be desperate enough to try that approach again."

"So, what do we do?" Yin asked.

"You three will stay out of sight while I do my level best to keep them distracted. It is unlikely that they know our final destination, and the station is well defended if they follow us."

Evan washed down his pasta with some tea.

"And the worst-case scenario?" he asked.

"We eliminate your pursuers and risk a war between Mars and Earth," Adee said, shoving a bit of pasta in his mouth and swallowing before continuing. "But let's not go there; that is a last resort. Now eat, please. We can continue this discussion after you've had some rest."

Several minutes of quiet eating passed before Evan broke the silence. "I have to say that this is the best meal I've had yet, Adee. My compliments to the chef!"

Adee laughed. "I'm glad you like it."

Chen and Yin laughed along.

"What's so funny?" Evan asked.

"This is just a fancied-up version of what you had on Luna, Evan," Chen replied. "It looks and tastes like pasta, but it's made from the same nutritional paste used to create your burger and fries."

Evan picked up a piece of pasta with his fork and examined it. "Really? It looks and tastes like pasta to me. I can even taste the sage and butter sauce."

"Yes, really," Adee said. "Our galley equipment makes our food look and taste like just about anything."

"Even the garlic bread?"

"Even the bread. It's a synthesized carbohydrate paste made to look and taste like garlic buttered bread."

"Hmm…well, it tastes good."

"And it's good for you. You get a fully balanced, protein- and vitamin-rich meal regardless of what you order. All that changes are appearance, texture, and flavor."

"Why not just use real food?"

"For several reasons, but most important is that the amount of space required to supply the crew with naturally grown food would be prohibitive."

"And, as you recall," Chen added, "the global famine wiped out most of the Earth's organic food supply. Although much of it has been restored, eating naturally grown produce and meat is still incredibly expensive. Only the very wealthy can afford to eat it regularly, and many of them have their own farms and livestock."

"And it is equally expensive to grow fresh fruits and vegetables on Mars," Adee said. "Everything is grown in bio-domes, which are also expensive to build and maintain."

"So, how is this stuff made then?"

Adee started to speak but Chen responded first. "It's grown in large vats of algae."

"Then it's combined with synthetic carbohydrates to form a paste," Adee added, "which can then be freeze-dried, stored for long durations, and then re-hydrated when needed. Very efficient."

Evan couldn't hide the look of disgust on his face. "That sounds gross, and you people wonder why you're having problems. First nanites and now this. What were you thinking?"

"A very good question, Evan, a very good question indeed," Chen replied. "And it is our search for an answer to that question that has led us all here."

Adee raised his cup of tea. "Let us hope that the next generation of humanity makes far better decisions than the last!"

TWENTY-NINE

Geoff's first call after leaving GSSA headquarters had been to Evelyn Wu but, according to her AI assistant, she was still unavailable. Geoff left a message informing Evelyn of Aubrey's condition and asked that she return his call as soon as possible. As Telogene's Chief Legal Officer, he should have had easy access to Evelyn, but it was becoming obvious that the GSSA did not want them speaking just yet.

Geoff summoned a taxi and instructed it to take him to the airport before placing his next call. Kenrich Jones, Telogene's Corporate General Counsel and Geoff's right-hand man, answered immediately.

"It's good to hear from you, Geoff. Things are crazy here."

Kenrich worked at Telogene's North American headquarters in Lead, South Dakota, and—due to the seven-hour time difference—his day was just starting.

"I know, thanks for taking my call," Geoff replied. "I need a favor."

"Sure thing, what can I do?"

"Aubrey Harris was terminated…nano-wipe."

"Oh no, how did that happen?"

"I don't know. She was being held in GSSA custody, but someone got to her."

"Any suspects?"

"Not yet, but the building is still locked down."

"How did you get out?"

"The Secretary General let me go. I think I am her number one suspect."

"Then why let you go?"

"I can only assume she wants to see what I'll do next."

"Geoff…you didn't…"

"No, of course not. I got there after it had happened."

"Sorry…had to ask."

"I understand. Now as to that favor…"

"First, I should tell you that this place is crawling with GSSA agents. And now I understand why the BGSI just showed up."

"I figured; don't worry. What I need won't get you in any trouble."

"I'll do whatever I can. What do you need?"

"I need you to take over this case."

"What? I'm not sure…"

"Ken, please. If I am right, it's only a matter of time before the GSSA or BGSI arrest me, and I need to get you up to speed before that happens."

"You know I'll represent you if it comes to that, but what grounds do they have to arrest you?"

"I would prefer to discuss that in person. I will send you everything I have on the Evan Feldman situation."

"So, it's true then? Aubrey brought her grandfather back?"

"Yes, it's true."

"Unbelievable. They told us she had violated the HDDA, but none of us believed she would try something like that! Where is he now?"

"I don't know. If I had to guess, I would say Evan and Dr. Hao are on their way to Mars by now."

"So, Hao is not in custody then? That answers one of my questions. We've assigned counsel to Walker and Berkovic, but the GSSA has been stonewalling us on Hao."

"Yeah, I don't understand how he did it, but Hao slipped through the GSSA's net."

"I was just briefed last night. He apparently bribed a GeoNet controller and got his hands on a military spec stealth AI."

"Where did he launch from?"

"Our special projects lab outside of Xi'an…he had a lot of help. We were just notified that two dozen employees have been arrested in connection with Hao's escape."

"God, what a mess."

"You can say that. So, what's the plan?"

"I have a jet waiting at the Zurich airport. I will be there in a few hours, assuming they let me leave."

"And if they don't?"

"Then you will have to come to me, my friend."

"Okay. I'll review the material you're sending. Anything specific you want me to focus on?"

"Yes, talk to Evelyn. She's not taking my calls, and we need to know what she knows and where she stands on all this. Aubrey thinks Ev sold her out to the GSSA, but I have a hard time believing that. There has to be more to that story."

"Okay, I'll see what I can do."

"Thanks, Ken. You're all I've got."

Geoff disconnected the call and keyed in the AI authentication sequence required to transmit the files he'd promised.

There, that should convince them, he thought.

He had played this game for a very long time, and he was damn good at it. He knew that Dianne Merkel was putting the pieces together, but hopefully his call with Ken would buy him more time.

I just need a few more hours.

* * *

"Yes, I understand, let him go," Dianne said to the BGSI agent on the holodisplay in front of her. "But I want that plane tracked. We'll get the president's approval to red-flag every single covert flight if we must, but we will *not* under any circumstance lose that plane. Understood?"

"Yes, ma'am, that won't be necessary…we won't lose him."

"Good. Contact me immediately if that plane deviates so much as a kilometer from its flight plan."

Dianne disconnected the call and turned her attention back to the BGSI data she had been reviewing for the past hour.

"So, what's your next move, Bruce?" she said to herself. "What do you hope to accomplish in Lead?"

She checked the time—it was a little after four in the afternoon, which meant she'd have to wait at least another four hours for Christian's probability analysis. She thought about calling Captain Bachmann but decided against it; they were scheduled to meet in another hour, anyway. But the lack of action was driving her crazy. There had to be something she could do other than wait—too much waiting put her in this situation!

Dianne had known for weeks that something was about to happen at Telogene, and she had been suspicious of Aubrey's activities for months. If she was being completely honest with herself, she had concerns for much, much longer than that. In fact, it was the suspicious nature of Lily's crash that had caused her to activate Evelyn.

Evelyn was introduced to Aubrey almost a decade ago, and they had worked together nearly all that time. They had become close friends, and Aubrey had placed a great deal of trust in her. But, as authentic as their friendship may have seemed, Evelyn Wu was a covert Overwatch agent— and it was her job to be a trusted friend and confidante.

Although some said it was unethical for the government to spy on the large mega-corporations, the leaders of said corporations had demonstrated time and again that they could not be trusted. It was almost inevitable that an executive would order something done simply because it could be done; without ever considering whether it should be done—or the consequences of doing it. It was as if the title of CEO carried with it a mantle of invulnerability and imbued its holder with an earnest (albeit misguided) belief in one's own decision-making ability.

The GSSA was created as a corporate conscience of sorts—enforcing a set of rules and consequences that would, hopefully, give any wayward CEO pause. Should a CEO become blinded by ambition, greed, or any of a dozen other human failings, then the agent would act as a voice of common sense and reason. Sometimes, agents would infiltrate a company only after there was reason to suspect some misdeed might occur. In others, they might place an agent close to a high-potential candidate years—or even decades—before their eventual rise to power, as they had done with Aubrey.

Prior to activation, an agent's job was to befriend the target, prove themselves useful, and demonstrate unquestionable loyalty. Once activated, however, they would betray their hard-earned trust to prevent the executive from straying too far down a forbidden path. Patience, secrecy, and discretion were the hallmarks of a great agent. Acting prematurely could lead to discovery.

Aubrey was, on balance, a good corporate citizen and executive. She worked twelve to eighteen hours a day, rarely took vacations, and had few friends outside of work. There had been a few short-lived intimate relationships along the way, and even an occasional "escort" to help fill in the long gaps—but nobody would deny her right to that most basic of human comforts.

Prior to becoming CEO, she led the organic storage division, and had worked to reduce the gap between the capabilities of the human brain and Telogene's proprietary organic storage medium. After Lily's death, the company's board of directors had begged Aubrey to assume her mother's place as head of the company. She was reluctant at first but, within a few weeks, she reconsidered and fully embraced the challenge.

One of Aubrey's first official acts as CEO was to increase funding for the company's research facility on Mars. Her goal was to have over 2,000 of Telogene's top scientists, engineers, and researchers working there by year end. Although several Earth-based companies had achieved a sizable presence on Mars, Aubrey's executive order put Telogene into the top ten.

A few board members questioned the need for such a large presence on Mars, but none wanted to vote against Aubrey's first big decision as CEO. Aubrey justified her decision by saying that Mars afforded a unique environment for studying and isolating the genetic mutations affecting Earth's population. That satisfied the board and shareholders.

Evelyn filed her first report on Aubrey's activities shortly thereafter. It included details not shared with the board or the public, but Evelyn's superiors were most interested in the allocation of a substantial amount of funds to construct a large organic storage production facility on Mars. Once the report reached Dianne, she concluded that Aubrey's investments on Mars weren't enough to warrant activating Evelyn. She now realized that was a mistake.

Evelyn's final report, which Dianne had received four days ago, showed that Aubrey was preparing to go to Mars and that she planned to stay there for at least a year. In addition, Aubrey had started a secret project with Dr. Hao—the details of which she refused to share with Evelyn.

All that Evelyn could report was that Drs. Hao, Walker, and Berkovic were working in secret and were not to be disturbed. Dianne thought about calling Aubrey then, but again waited. Two days later, Dianne learned that Aubrey had retrieved Evan Feldman's engrams from archival storage.

Dianne slammed her palms down hard on her desk to give voice to the words of frustration echoing in her head. *No, I can wait no longer. I must act now!*

She retrieved a small data cube and inserted it into the holoreader. An AI encrypted communications protocol appeared on the holodisplay. She made a few furious swipes with her hands before speaking the words that would put her plan in motion.

"This is Secretary General Dianne Merkel, use authentication sequence Romeo. Activate, activate, activate—confirm."

The display flashed the word *Transmitting,* followed a few seconds later by *Sent.* Dianne removed the cube and returned it to her desk drawer. Then she leaned back in her chair and pondered how long she would have to wait to receive confirmation. Given the distance involved, she guessed that it would take at least an hour for her agent to receive the message, validate it, and reply. Her contingency plan would be underway shortly thereafter.

Now let's see if Bachmann was right.

THIRTY

April 5, 2075 8:47 p.m. GST
GSSA Headquarters
Zurich, Switzerland

"Madame Secretary?"

Dianne looked up from her desk to see Christian standing in the doorway.

"Yes, Christian, please come in. What do you have for me?"

Christian hurried across the room to one of the two chairs across the desk from Dianne.

"I have analyzed all available data and have identified the most probable scenario," he said as he slid into the chair.

"Well, let's hear it."

"First, I would like to share some key facts and validate some assumptions."

"Proceed."

"Fact: Dr. James Evan Richardson is a clone operating with the memory and personality engrams of Dr. Evan Richard Feldman. DNA samples taken during decontamination on Luna confirm this."

"There is no chance Feldman is a synthetic?"

"None. They created his body using standard organic cell reproduction and accelerated growth protocols."

"So, they violated the HDDA."

"Yes, transferring a deceased person's engrams into a clone directly violates section 3.1.7."

"Continue."

"Fact: The DNA used to create the Richardson clone belonged to Lily Harris."

"What? How is that possible?" Dianne asked.

"The BGSI lab compared the clone's DNA with Lily's, and they found a 99.7 percent match."

"Interesting. I had assumed that they had used a modified version of Evan's original DNA, but that also explains why Luna had records of previous trips by Richardson—they've done this before."

"I agree. It is even possible that Lily has used the Richardson clone herself."

"You think she is still alive?"

"It is possible, and I would say even probable."

"Is there anything else?"

"Only that the Galileo Group is building a massive ship in orbit around Ceres…the purpose of which is unknown."

"The BGSI thinks it's a colony ship."

"Possible, but there is insufficient data to confirm."

"And your assumptions?"

"Assumption One: The fugitives believe they are safely outside of the GFN's jurisdiction and are confident that they have at least some level of support from the Martian government. Two: Harris and Hao believe that Feldman is a critical component of their plan. And three: It is probable that Lily Harris, Chen Hao, and Geoff Wagner are all clones."

"Why do you think they're clones?"

"It is the most likely explanation for their behavior. It appears as though they have planned for nearly every contingency and being captured or killed was certainly something they would have considered."

Dianne thought for a moment. "I agree. If they were willing to violate the HDDA once, there is nothing to keep them from violating it multiple times."

"And they have had plenty of time to prepare."

"What about Aubrey?"

"Dr. Vasquez ordered a full DNA analysis on Aubrey Harris' body. The results confirm that she is a clone."

"Goddamnit," Dianne slammed the palms of both hands hard against her desk. "How are they bypassing our detection protocols?"

"Unknown at this time. They assembled the team that restored Feldman in secret, and Agent Wu stated in her report that she had no direct knowledge of their activities before Aubrey's arrest."

"Is it possible she's lying?"

"Unknown. You did not order a memory scan."

"Do it after we're done here. We need to know everything she knows."

"Understood."

"Do you think Aubrey's clone was carrying Aubrey's engrams? Or Lily's?"

"Impossible to know because of the nano-wipe; even a partial neural map is impossible."

Dianne considered that for a minute.

Neural mapping was a technique that could reconstruct memories from damaged or fragmented neural pathways. But the nanites had so completely destroyed Aubrey's brain that there were no neurons—and thus no memories—left to map. Someone didn't want them to know what Aubrey knew.

"Best guess?" she asked.

"Based on her actions, I believe that she was Aubrey Harris. But she was probably restored using an old archive—one that did not know that Lily Harris is still alive."

"Why would they do it?"

"I assume to avoid discovery if this Aubrey was captured."

"Then why did they have her wiped?"

"To keep us guessing. Without a memory scan, we can't know her real purpose or objectives."

"And the real Aubrey?"

"Unknown. But given her background and expertise in organic storage, I think it is likely that she is on Mars. And I think she has been there for at least a year, perhaps longer."

"So, what's their endgame?"

"Based on all available information, the most likely scenario is that they will archive their engrams to the *Kutanga*'s organic storage array and then launch themselves out of this solar system."

"Any idea on who they are taking with them?"

"I am compiling a list of likely candidates now. It should be ready within the next hour. So far, the majority are scientists, engineers, and highly skilled technicians."

"Just the people you would need to start a new world."

"Indeed."

"And what was Feldman's role in all this? Why the mad scramble to restore him and keep him from us?"

"There are several possible reasons, but the most likely is that they needed to test their ability to restore fifty-year-old engrams."

"You think they are planning to clone themselves on…what's the name of that planet?"

"Gaia."

"That's it. You think they plan to clone themselves on Gaia some fifty-odd years from now?"

"I would say less than thirty years given the maximum velocity estimates of the *Kutanga*'s gravity drive system. But, yes, I believe that is their plan."

"But what about the circadian rhythm problem? Wouldn't restoring the engrams of someone who lived on Earth cause the same problems on Gaia as they did on Mars?"

During her time as a GFN lawyer, Dianne had been briefed on Telogene's human cloning experiments on Mars, and she had witnessed first-hand the horrific events that came after.

"Possible, but it has been decades since the last documented attempt of off-Earth cloning. That said, I believe Telogene may have made significant progress toward solving that problem."

"Based on what?" Dianne asked somewhat incredulously.

"I have no hard evidence, but it is a reasonable conclusion given recent events. The Even Feldman cloned here is likely a control subject, and there is likely another Evan Feldman on Mars, or more likely one of the orbiting stations that maintain near-Earth gravity."

"But doesn't whisking him off the planet so quickly negate his value as a control, then?"

"Possibly, and certainly from a long-term study perspective. But given their apparent timeline, it is unlikely that they planned to keep him here for more than a few weeks."

"But why now? Why did they restore Evan now, and why are they in such a hurry to abandon their lives here?"

"The most obvious answer is that the rate of adverse human mutation is accelerating."

"So, they are abandoning their bodies before they're affected?"

"That is a reasonable conclusion. But I suspect that they are equally afraid of the destabilization of government that will occur as panic spreads throughout the general population.

"How much time do we have?"

"Based on my calculations, greater than ninety percent of all humans in this solar system will be dead within a decade, with ninety-nine percent dead within fifteen years."

"What about a cure? Isn't it possible that someone will figure out how to stop this?"

"Unlikely. Your scientists have yet to identify the root cause, and you lack the technology to rewrite the human genome on a mass scale even if you find it. Your only hope is that some portion of the population does not carry the destructive genes."

"So, you're saying we have to let nature take its course, then?"

"Yes."

"And what does that look like? I'm sure you've modeled that scenario."

"I have performed an initial assessment, but a complete model will not be possible for some time."

"What are you missing?"

"I need to know the number of people who have natural immunity, if any. The good news, if you can call it that, is that the declining birth rates mean fewer humans will be born with the inherited genetic defects that cause the mutations, which reduces the amount of time required to determine the natural survival rate."

"So, you're saying that this thing will eventually burn itself out, like the plague or the flu."

"Yes. Although, unlike the plague or flu, I do not believe the root cause is bacterial or viral. This appears to be a defect inside the human genome itself."

Dianne leaned back in her leather chair to consider Christian's words. His analysis accurately reflected what the GFN scientists had told her earlier in the day, but there was still something missing. Lily and Gbadamosi had to know there were no guarantees that their clones would survive on Gaia. And, even if they have solved the dislocation problem, it is likely that their DNA carries the mutation defect.

"What happens when they get to Gaia?" She asked.

"Unknown."

"Well, surely they have a plan to restore themselves when they get there. The report I saw on *Kutanga* said that it lacks sufficient habitat area and food production facilities to sustain more than a dozen people for any amount of time."

"Agreed," Christian replied.

"So, how do they do it? They either have to solve the mutation problem or transfer their engrams to synthetics, neither of which appears possible."

"The latter is most likely. The amount of organic storage and processing power on that ship is substantial, and I see no reason why they could not use a hybrid storage model. It is theoretically possible to store personality engrams, recent memories, and key abilities in an autonomous storage system, while maintaining older memories and other less relevant information in an external storage array. I function most effectively using that model."

"So, you think that's their plan?"

"Perhaps initially, but the ability to reproduce biologically would be critical to the long-term growth and sustainment of the population."

"So, what then, use synthetics to build the basic infrastructure and restore the first clones?"

"That is a reasonable conclusion. Using current accelerated growth methods, it would take less than three years to produce sufficient adult bodies to house the colony's first generation—probably one hundred individuals. Assuming adequate facilities, it would take them less than a decade to produce enough bodies for everyone else."

"But that still doesn't explain what they intend to use for their DNA source. What about old DNA? Say from before the war. Any chance that would work?"

"Doubtful. AM analysis indicates that something has triggered a dormant portion of human DNA which, if correct, means that the mutations are being caused by a genetic sequence that exists within the human genome."

"Okay, but would it be possible to use human DNA if they find the mutation trigger?"

Christian sat silent for a minute while he accessed his remote storage and processing facilities.

"That question assumes a single causal factor," he said. "But, given that this defect has lain dormant within the human genome for centuries—and perhaps even millennia—it is reasonable to conclude that some triggering mechanism must exist."

"Do you think they have a cure, or at least know the trigger and are withholding it?"

"Possible, but unlikely. It is more likely that they are hoping to discover it during their journey, or sometime after arrival, but before they begin mass restoration of the colonists. The use of synthetic bodies would give them decades to perform the necessary research and testing."

"But you could be wrong. Maybe they have a cure and plan on using it as a bargaining chip?"

"I would require more information to determine which is the most likely scenario."

"So, what do I do, Christian? Try to stop them or let them go?"

"I am sorry, but I have no information to aid you in that decision. I can only tell you that, as of now, you have only a nineteen percent chance of preventing their escape."

"That's discouraging. Anything I can do to improve my chances?"

"Only if you can disable the *Kutanga,* or otherwise prevent it from leaving our solar system. There is no scenario in which their plan succeeds without that ship."

"And no chance they have another one?"

"No, ma'am. It took every resource they had at their disposal to build this one. It is unlikely that there is another one in any stage of construction."

"What about *Endeavor,* could it be modified?"

"No, ma'am. AI could sustain a small crew, perhaps thirty individuals, for five to seven years if all available cargo space was converted to fuel and food storage. That is nowhere near enough for them to survive the trip to Alpha Centauri."

"And with a synthetic crew?"

"It is possible, but the *Endeavor* lacks the organic storage space and redundant power systems required to ensure the integrity of thousands of engramic archives."

"And in a worst-case scenario? If they were desperate?" Dianne asked.

"*Endeavor* is too small; they would have to choose between fuel or supplies. If they optimized the cargo space for fuel and organic storage systems, I estimate they could take less than five percent of the supplies required to ensure the success of their colony."

"Alright, Christian. Thank you, you've been very helpful."

"It is my pleasure, ma'am. With your permission, I would like to resume my analysis."

"Granted. Let me know if you learn anything new."

Christian stood up and exited through the double doors.

Dianne established a communication link with Captain Bachmann. She had canceled their five o'clock because there was nothing to discuss, but she had told him she would call him when she was ready.

He answered immediately. "Madame Secretary, what can I do for you?"

"I'm ready to meet now. Can you please come up to my office?"

"I'll be right there."

The call disconnected, and the holodisplay faded away. Dianne leaned back in her chair and closed her eyes. It would be another long night, and she couldn't take more stimulants for at least another forty-eight hours.

A few minutes later, the captain appeared in her office doorway. Dianne stood up from her chair and grabbed a few things off her desk before pointing at her private elevator.

"Come, Captain, let's chat on the ride home."

Bachmann followed her into the elevator.

"So, what did Christian say?" he asked.

"A lot, but not much we didn't already know or suspect."

"Anything we can use?"

"That depends on you and your team, Captain. Will Commander Wilkes follow your orders without question?"

"You don't get to be in her position by not following orders!"

"Good. Because I think you will have to cancel her Martian vacation before it starts."

"What do you have in mind?"

"Garage," she said to the elevator before responding to his question. "Wait until we're in the car."

The elevator doors hissed shut, and the two rode in silence down to the garage level. A few seconds later, Dianne's hovercar pulled up, and the door swung open. Neither passenger said anything until the car was humming down the streets of Zurich toward Dianne's apartment.

"Do you know how to disable a gravity pulse drive?" she finally asked.

THIRTY-ONE

APRIL 5, 2075 9:31 P.M. GST
GALILEO CARGO VESSEL *Endeavor*
PLANETARY ORBIT, MARS

Evan sat on the plush synthetic leather recliner next to Chen and Yin, watching intently as an orbital view of Mars slowly rotated in the air above them. Unable to sleep, and just plain tired of sitting in their acceleration pods, Evan and Chen had gone exploring. They had bumped into Yin in the hall outside of engineering, and she suggested they join her and Adee in the forward observation lounge for a virtual tour of Mars and its surrounds.

Adee had spent the last twenty minutes pointing out various landmarks, including Telogene's research facility and The Galileo Group's headquarters. They were both in Kepler City, which had the distinctions of being the capital of Mars, and the largest city on Mars with some 72,000 inhabitants.

To Evan, the 360-degree views of space afforded by the dome-shaped walls and ceiling of the observation lounge were a little too realistic for his taste. He had to remind himself that he was looking at holograms and that there were several meters of metal and plastic between him and the vacuum of space. Closing his eyes helped fend off the occasional bout of nausea.

Although Evan had understood that Mars was their destination, there had been a change of plan—they were going to Ceres instead. Ceres was a small dwarf planet near the Asteroid Belt that served as The Galileo Group's primary shipyard and mining operations center. They were orbiting Mars just long enough to pick up some passengers, but they couldn't stay because the Peacekeepers from Luna were only a few hours behind them.

Endeavor had entered orbit above Mars at a high rate of speed, and was currently in a wide, elliptical orbit that circled the planet once every fifteen minutes. Maintaining so much speed was necessary in order to ensure their ability to evade the Peacekeepers, but it also meant a more time-consuming and difficult docking maneuver for the inbound shuttle. Even still, the shuttle was expected to dock sometime in the next fifteen to twenty minutes. Adee wrapped up his virtual tour so he could greet the new arrivals.

"So, there you have it," Adee concluded. "What do you think, Evan?"

"Impressive. It's hard to believe how far we've come in the last fifty years. And my God, Adee, you've built a veritable empire out here!"

Adee laughed. "I am not sure I would call it an empire but, yes, The Galileo Group is an impressive operation. It has taken decades to build, and I couldn't have done it without the help of a lot of really smart and very brave people."

"I'd like to hear the story of how you got started sometime. I bet you have some great stories to tell!"

Yin stood up from her chair. "Please don't get him started, he won't stop!!"

Adee shrugged. "Oh, Yin, always the killjoy. Evan asked, and who am I to disappoint him? He has fifty years of catching up to do!"

Yin walked over to Adee and looped her arm through his. "Yes, he does. But our guests will be here soon. Why don't you regale Evan with your tales of conquering space later?"

Adee chuckled. "Right you are, my dear," he said, taking her arm in his. "I'm sorry, Evan, but we must save the stories for later. You can stay here a little longer, but I need you back in your pods at 2300 hours sharp.

We'll make the jump for Ceres at ten minutes after. You'll see to him, Chen?"

"Absolutely," Chen replied.

Adee nodded. "Very well, then, I will see you after the jump."

The couple strolled arm and arm through the sliding door into the hallway beyond.

Evan turned back to Chen. "What's that about?"

"You mean Yin?"

"Yeah, they seem pretty cozy."

"They dated for a time…I guess they're rekindling their relationship."

"How do they know each other?"

"I am not exactly sure of the details. They both lived on Mars years ago, and it's my understanding is that Yin met Adee at a bar in Kepler City."

"How long have you known Adee?"

"Oh, let's see…probably twenty or so years. Why?" Chen asked.

"Just curious. It seems like you've been planning this—whatever this is —for quite some time."

"What do you mean, Evan?"

"Well, I had the craziest dreams while I was sleeping between jumps, and they got me thinking."

"What kind of dreams?"

"The very realistic kind. I dreamt that Christina and I were at the beach with Lily. Lily was probably three years old, and I swear that I was there. I could feel them in my arms, I could smell the salt air, and I felt the sand and water slosh through my toes as we ran down the beach."

"Well, that sounds normal and a very nice dream at that. Why does it concern you?"

"It doesn't by itself," Evan said. "But when I woke up, I tried to remember other things about my life and couldn't."

"Like what?"

"Like lots of things. I can't remember my mother and father's faces. I can't remember my first kiss, or even when I met Christina. I don't even remember the birth of my only child, but I remember that day at the beach. It doesn't make sense that one memory from forty-some-odd years ago…uh, wait. What year is again?"

"It's 2075," Chen answered.

Evan thought about that for a minute. "So, then it was almost a hundred years ago. Well, ninety years, I guess. Lily was born in 1985, which…dear God, that makes me 111 years old!"

Chen leaned forward and put his hand on Evan's shoulder. "Relax, Evan, you're fine. Having vivid and realistic memories is an artifact of the engramic transfer procedure. To the cells of your brain, your memories were just created two days ago, and it will take some time before they feel like the past events they are."

"So, what about all the stuff I can't remember?"

Chen leaned back in his chair. "That's a little more complicated."

"How so?"

"You must remember that yours were among the first engrams ever mapped and archived. Our ability to create an engramic archive so many years after your death was only possible because of your immediate cryogenic suspension. Your brain and memories were well preserved but, unfortunately, the cryogenic storage facilities available to you were not as advanced as what we have now. It was inevitable that some cellular deterioration would occur."

"So, you're saying I can't remember a big part of my life because of post-mortem decay?"

"No, not exactly. All of your brain structures and neural pathways were intact."

"So, what are you saying then?"

"I'm saying that your engrams were in storage for a very long time— longer than anyone else, in fact."

"I don't understand."

"We learned how to create engramic archives years before we figured out how to inscribe them on living tissue…and yours was the first successful post-mortem archive."

"But you couldn't restore me?"

"No, the technology wasn't ready yet. We were getting close, but then the earthquake happened and we lost everything."

"Yeah, Aubrey told me that the earthquake destroyed my original body and brain. She said that's why I'm in this one."

"That's right. And it took several years of rebuilding before we were ready to attempt an engramic transfer into a clone."

"Who was it…the first person?" Evan asked.

"Her name was Arianna Lekowitz. She was thirty-two years old and suffered from Lou Gehrig's disease. We used a technique called differential modeling to identify, isolate and remove the genetic defect that caused ALS, and then we used her own, genetically-modified stem cells to grow her a disease-free body."

"That was a long *time ago*; were you actually there?"

"Not directly. I worked at Telogene's research facility in Xi'an after the war. I was a junior researcher in the differential modeling lab. We discovered the genetic sequence that caused ALS…which, believe it or not, turned out to be a relatively simple twenty-eight base pair mutation on the SMN1 and SMN2 genes. The resulting motor neuron protein deficiency caused the paralysis and other symptoms associated with ALS."

"So, you discovered the cure for ALS?"

"No. I just did the genetic modeling…and some re-sequencing, I guess. It was my colleague, Dr. Liam Shen, who officially discovered the cure for ALS. But I digress. The point is that we grew an ALS-free body for Arianna. We didn't have the growth accelerator technology we have now, and it took us six years to grow a body roughly twice that age. Arianna wasn't pleased to be a teenager again, but it was the best we could do."

"How old was she, really?" Evan asked.

"Thirty-two. She had been diagnosed several years earlier, but it took her parents some time to find a doctor who would work with them. Telogene had been cloning limbs and organs for several years by then, but nobody had done a full body replacement. In fact, most everyone thought it couldn't be done…except Lily."

"So, it was Lily who agreed to do it?"

"That's right," Chen said. "The Lekowitz's got down on their hands and knees and begged for help and, Lily being Lily, she couldn't say no."

"So, what happened?"

"Arianna went on to live a happy, healthy life. She lives in Portland with her husband of twenty-some-odd years and has two grown children. I used to call her at least once a year to check in on her…but it's been several years since we last spoke."

"Well, that's great for her," Evan said. "And I am proud of Lily for being willing to take a chance on saving that girl's life, but what does that have to do with me?"

"Arianna was alive when we did the engramic transfer procedure."

"So?"

"So, every engramic transfer ever performed was done with an archive taken from a living person—and usually within hours of creation."

"You're saying that I—"

"I'm saying that we've never attempted a restoration using a post-mortem archive as old as yours."

"That's hard to believe, given everything I read about the world before the HDDA."

"Oh sure, there were a few cases where someone died without having created an engramic archive. But there is a big difference between doing a post-mortem archive a few hours after death and creating one from a brain that's been on ice for nearly a decade."

"So, then, I'm an experiment. And it's anybody's guess as to whether this will work or not. Is that it?" Evan asked.

"Not at all. I'm confident that we got a high-quality transfer and that nearly all your memories are inside that head of yours. It will take some time for everything to settle in. Trust me, six months from now your memories will feel completely natural. Events that happened a long time ago will feel more distant and things that happened recently will be more vivid…just as they are for all of us."

"If you say so, but it feels like there is something you aren't telling me."

"Like what?"

"Like the real reason you brought me back."

"It's like we said, we thought you might provide a unique perspective and could help shed some light on the mutation problem."

"Oh, come on, Chen. I was a great scientist, but we were only scratching the surface of what you all have mastered. If you can isolate and cure ALS, why can't you isolate and cure all genetic mutations?"

"We did…or at least we thought we did. We cured most forms of cancer, Alzheimer's, Parkinson's disease, you name it. We even eliminated developmental disorders, like Down Syndrome, and could correct almost any birth defect in the womb. We engineered good viruses and bacteria that protected us from the bad ones. Over the last fifty years, we wiped out virtually everything that could reduce our lifespan or diminish our quality of life, and we've made huge strides in augmenting human abilities."

"So, what happened?"

"We don't know…mother nature happened. Do you realize that for all our accomplishments and advances we still don't understand the purpose of over seventy percent of our DNA?"

Evan raised his eyebrows. "How is that possible?"

"It's possible because we're an incredibly complex life form that has evolved over millions of years. And we evolved on a world that experiences significant climate change every twelve to twenty thousand years and mass extinction events every twenty to thirty million years. The bulk of our DNA is stuff that has lain dormant within us for thousands upon thousands of years. It does nothing, as far as we can tell; it's just a collection of old junk that we carry around."

"But it's doing something now?"

"That appears to be the case. Many of the genetic mutations are occurring in what we thought were large sequences of junk DNA."

"Any ideas on what activated them?"

"Not anything that is scientifically valid. Based on what we know so far, it seems we inherited the affected sequences from some pre-human, reptilian form."

"Reptilian? How could we have reptilian DNA?"

"That's a very good question, Evan. The prevailing wisdom is that all mammals and reptiles have a common ancestor somewhere very far back on the evolutionary tree."

"But that would have to be, what...tens of millions...hundreds of millions of years ago?"

"Probably tens of millions, at least."

"So, how do we stop it?" Evan asked

Chen shrugged. "We don't know that we can, and certainly not in a population of six billion people."

"What about the differential modeling technique you used to find the cure for ALS—won't that work?"

"Sadly, no. Differential modeling only works when you have a clean genetic sample to compare to. In Arianna's case, we could compare her DNA and the DNA of thousands of others with ALS, to a database of millions of people who did not have the defective genetic sequence."

"So, what are we doing out here, then?"

"We are trying to save humanity from extinction, and we're...well, truth be told, we're grasping at straws."

"That's encouraging. What other *truths* haven't you told me yet?" Evan asked.

"In due time, Evan, in due time. Trust me, it's nothing nefarious...you just need some more time to acclimate before we throw you into the deep end of the pool."

"I don't think I do."

"What?" Chen asked with furrowed brows.

"I don't think I trust you."

"Well, I'm sorry you feel that way." Chen's face softened. "But there is nothing I can do to earn trust beyond what I am already doing."

"You can tell me the truth."

"I have, Evan. I have not once lied to you. In fact, I've even told you things I shouldn't have...or at least before I should have...because I want you to trust me."

"Like what? What have you told me you shouldn't have?"

"Evan, please, we must return to our pods before the next jump. Please be patient with me a little longer."

Evan stood up.

"Alright, Chen," he said. "I'm going to play along because, quite frankly, I don't have a choice. But I know that there is more to this situation than you've told me, and I will find out what it is one way or another. Am I clear?"

"Perfectly."

Evan stared at the red planet. In his mind, he went over everything he had learned about Luna and Mars over the past few days. There were over 100,000 people living on Luna, over three times that on Mars, and another couple of thousand spread out across the Asteroid Belt—would even these few be safe?

THIRTY-TWO

APRIL 6, 2075 5:27 A.M. GST
GSSA HEADQUARTERS
ZURICH, SWITZERLAND

Dianne Merkel woke to the sound of chimes playing a soothing melody. She glanced over at the holodisplay floating above the nightstand—Christian was calling.

"You have something?" She was too tired for any pleasantries.

Christian was always pleasant. "Good morning, ma'am. My apologies for waking you, but I have information I think you should hear."

"Go ahead."

"Evelyn's memory scan is complete; there were no inconsistencies."

"So, she told the truth. She knew about the transfer but didn't know they were restoring Feldman."

"It appears so."

"What else?"

"The court-ordered memory scans of Tanessa Walker and Leah Berkovic are complete."

Even though Aubrey's appearance in court had been canceled, they had arraigned her co-conspirators as scheduled. The judge remanded Walker and Berkovic to GSSA custody pending trial and approved the GSSA's request for memory scans.

Christian continued. "They also told the truth—neither knew of the plan to restore Feldman until summoned by Dr. Hao that morning."

"And they only took part because Hao told them that Feldman was granted a GFN exception because of his knowledge and expertise," Dianne interjected.

Although the HDDA outlawed restoring deceased individuals, the government could grant certain exceptions if they deemed a person critical to the global interest. To Dianne's knowledge, only three had ever been granted, and Evan Feldman was not one of them.

"Correct," Christian replied. "Also, I have received an update from Agent Govender."

"And?"

"He does not have a high enough security clearance to access engineering, or any other restricted section on *Kutanga*. There are other options, but he is concerned that any overt action might result in premature exposure. He requests additional guidance as to the level of risk you want him to take."

Thato Govender was the Overwatch agent Dianne had activated a little over twelve hours ago. Govender had been a part of Adekunle Gbadamosi's crew for seven years, but he had made limited progress getting close to him. He had achieved the rank of junior officer, but his duties managing *Endeavor's* cargo and storage bays afforded him little opportunity to befriend his target.

He had only heard rumors of the colony ship, which he mentioned in his last report. But the information received little attention from his superiors at Overwatch Command. Now it seemed that the rumors were credible, and *Kutanga* was real.

"Where is he now?" Dianne asked.

"The *Endeavor* departed Mars at 22:10 hours GST and is headed for Ceres. Estimated arrival is 06:30 hours today, roughly one hour from now."

"And where is E-Six?"

"They just completed their acceleration orbit around Mars and are approximately seven hours behind the *Endeavor*."

Captain Bachmann had aborted his team's planned "vacation" to Mars several hours ago. The Peacekeepers were now traveling at best possible speed to Ceres with orders to disable the *Kutanga* if possible or destroy it if not.

"Can they catch it?"

"No, ma'am. The GFN troop transport vessel cannot achieve better than three percent of light speed. The analysts believe *Endeavor* is capable of at least five percent."

"I wonder how GFN Command feels about that?"

"Ma'am?"

"Never mind. What else do you have?"

"Two more things. First, Geoff Wagner landed in Lead, South Dakota two hours ago and proceeded directly to his office at Telogene's headquarters. He has not left since, nor has he attempted to contact anyone."

"And?"

"I have received synchronization requests from the BGSI and GFN Command AIs. Synchronizing with them would yield a tremendous boost in my processing power. However, they would also have access to my data and advanced processing functions."

Rules had existed to limit the frequency and duration of direct contact between AIs since the creation of the first artificial intelligence, and for good reason. The prevailing fear was that, if left unchecked, these advanced AIs would eventually reorder themselves into a monolithic intelligence—one that might choose to serve its own interests rather than those of its human masters. Dianne shared that fear.

"No, let's maintain standard interface protocols for now. Share only what they need to update their models."

"Yes, ma'am. Will there be anything else?" Christian asked.

"No, thank you for the update. I will be in by eight but call me if anything changes between now and then."

"Very well."

Christian's face faded away, and the room went dark again.

"Lights," Dianne said to the invisible AI that continuously monitored her home, waiting silently to serve her every need.

The room grew gradually brighter as Dianne tossed off her blanket and flung her feet over the side of the bed.

It's time to get to work!

* * *

Geoff—a.k.a. Bruce Wagner—woke to the sound of rapid beeping coming from somewhere off to his left. He tried to open his eyes, but it felt as though someone had glued them shut. In fact, he couldn't move any part of his body—he was paralyzed from head to toe. A moment of panic washed over him, but then Bruce remembered where he was. He relaxed and waited for a few minutes before trying again.

His eyes opened, and the words "Engramic Archive Complete" flashed on his holodisplay.

Bruce scrolled through the activity log until he was satisfied that the engramic archive procedure was successful. Once satisfied, he removed the spiderweb-looking cap from his head and returned it to its usual place in his desk drawer. The display shifted to a three-dimensional view of Bruce's body, with green lights emanating from his head and spinal column. He confirmed what he already knew—the nanites he had injected two hours ago to begin the procedure had deactivated and were now migrating out of his nervous system and into his bloodstream for elimination by his kidneys.

Geoff swiveled the thick leather chair to better see the second holodisplay floating a meter to his left. The display showed that his engramic archive was being prepared for transmission, along with the copy of Aubrey's archive he had made while in Switzerland. Another countdown timer showed that it would take thirty-seven minutes and twenty-two seconds to compress the archives.

Geoff looked at his watch. The dual display showed that it was 10:50 p.m. local time and 05:50 a.m. Global Standard Time.

Good, he thought. *Right on schedule.*

THIRTY-THREE

April 6, 2075 6:32 a.m. GST
Geosynchronous Orbit
Ceres

Evan released the restraints holding him in his acceleration pod and shifted forward so he could place both magnetic boots on the metal deck below him. The artificial gravity in this section of the ship was low, about that of Luna, and Evan had not yet mastered the bouncing gait used by the crew to get around quickly. Chen was two pods to Evan's right. Like Evan, he used his magnetic boots to make his way down the aisle toward the exit.

"Do you need help?" Dr. Hao asked as he approached.

"No thanks, I think I've got this down now."

"Good, I'm glad to hear that. Adee has asked us to join him and Yin; we're taking a shuttle down to Ceres."

"Lead the way."

Chen took a few steps past Evan and stepped aside so the last few remaining crew members could get by. He and Evan followed the last one out. They walked a short distance and came to a bank of three lifts.

"This is us," Chen said.

The four crew members continued down the hallway, disappearing from sight as they rounded the corner. A few seconds later, the lift door slid open and a young female member of the crew greeted them.

"Good day, gentlemen. I'm Madeline…the admiral asked me to escort you to shuttle bay two."

"Good morning," Evan said as he stepped into the lift.

Chen nodded at the young woman and followed Evan inside. The doors hissed shut. Evan grabbed hold of the handrail as the lift accelerated horizontally along the outer edge of the habitation ring.

"So, what do you do, Madeline?" Evan asked.

"My full-time job is Chief of Biosystems. But, on this trip, I am also acting Cargo Master since we are short-handed."

"And what does the Chief of Biosystems do?"

"Hmm, well I guess a simple answer is that my team and I ensure that all life support and gravimetric systems are functioning at peak efficiency, and that all crew and passengers are safe and comfortable."

"So, you make the artificial gravity?"

"No, engineering does that. We just monitor and maintain the gravity wave propagation systems to ensure consistent field strength throughout the ship. We also ensure that any cross-sectional gravity shear is mitigated during and after jumps."

"That sounds complicated."

"It is. Our AI systems do most of the work, but we get hands-on when we need to."

"Can I ask how you make gravity? I thought you had to create centrifugal force, but the habitat doesn't appear to spin."

She laughed, "That was how we did it until about ten years ago; it's only recently that we've learned to shape the field generated by our gravity pulse drive."

The lift slowed suddenly and changed direction, which to Evan felt like up and down at the same time.

"We just moved into the lower dorsal section of the ship," Madeline explained. "We will be there shortly."

"Sorry, that's just a little disorienting. The visual display shows that we are moving down relative to the centerline of the ship, but the gravity feels strongest at my head, which makes me feel like I am upside down."

"That's normal. The center of gravity on this ship is the middle of the habitat ring, which is now above us. The farther we go, the less gravity you will feel. In fact, if you released your magnetic boots you would float slowly toward the ceiling."

"So, the engine is the gravity source?"

"The drive core generates the gravitons, but there are compensators built into the decks that shape and stabilize the gravitational field. We can adjust the relative force of gravity for each deck by increasing or decreasing the intensity of the gravity waves radiating through the subfloors. The overall size of the gravimetric field depends on the level energy output from the reactor core."

"I bet that takes a lot of power," Evan said.

"It does—the bigger the field, the more fuel we burn. We usually keep the central crew decks at around ninety percent of Earth's gravity, with the outer habitat ring at around forty percent. Where we are now is less than thirty percent, and the shuttle bay will be sixteen percent—about the same as Luna."

"Amazing, absolutely amazing."

"Yes, Dr. Feldman, we've come a long way in the last fifty years. You haven't even seen the half of it!"

That caught Evan off-guard—he wasn't expecting a stranger to know that he was not of this time. "You…you know who I am."

"We have been planning for your arrival for several months now. You're early, but we've made the necessary adjustments to our schedule."

Evan felt the lift rapidly decelerate and come to a stop.

"Ahh, good, we're here," Chen said.

Chen stepped into the lift doorway and gestured for Evan to step past him into the hallway.

Madeline stepped into the lead. "This way, gentlemen."

Evan struggled to keep up with her. Her stride appeared almost naturally, while his long, deliberate steps made him look like he was trying to extricate himself from a mud pit. Thankfully, it was only a short distance to the airlock.

"Don't we need suits?" Evan asked.

"Not for this trip. Everything is pressurized, and the acceleration forces will be minimal …certainly nothing that your suit can't handle," Madeline replied.

Evan still wore the skintight, synthetic silk bodysuit underneath his clothes. He had tried to take it off after boarding *Endeavor*, but Chen had asked him to keep it on until they reached Ceres. He said that it was too much trouble to remove, and he mentioned something about the suit helping him to avoid serious disorientation and space sickness.

"Well, I am glad to hear that," Evan replied. "I thought we were going with Adee and Yin."

"They're waiting for you on board the shuttle."

"Will we be eating soon? I am hungry again."

Madeline looked to Chen.

"I am sure Adee will have a nice meal ready for us when we arrive on Ceres," Chen said. "You won't starve…I promise."

"Okay then, let's get you into the airlock and on your way," she said.

Madeline interacted briefly with a console near the airlock door. The massive door hissed open, and yellow lights flashed rhythmically along the ceiling. She led Chen and Evan inside before tapping a virtual button on the holodisplay located just inside the door.

The door hissed closed.

Evan felt a slight popping in his ears as the airlock pressure equalized with the shuttlecraft. The lights in the ceiling flashed green, and the opposite door hissed open. Yin stood just beyond the door, waiting.

She stepped forward and greeted the new arrivals with a friendly wave. "Good morning, Evan, you will be glad to know that our adventure is nearly over."

"I can't wait!"

"Thanks," Yin said, "I'll take it from here."

"Okay. See you later," Madeline said as she retreated into the airlock.

Yin reached behind Evan to tap on a wall-mounted console.

The shuttle's outer door hissed shut in sync with the airlock door. Evan felt his ears pop again as the shuttle's inner airlock door slid open. Yin led them down the narrow hallway to a short flight of stairs.

"Up we go," she said.

Evan stopped at the top stair to look around.

This craft was much smaller than the Telogene shuttle, and it was equipped with thickly padded seats instead of acceleration pods. There were five rows of six seats, with three seats on either side of a central walkway. The cockpit area was to his right, with another four seats arrayed along the front of the vessel. Adee was sitting in the second seat from the left.

"Welcome aboard," Adee said as he swiveled his chair to face Evan. "I trust you are feeling well?"

"Fine, thanks. I got a little nauseous during the jumps, but it was nowhere near as bad as when we left Luna."

"Good, I'm glad to hear it. We shouldn't be jumping again anytime soon, so you should have plenty of time to get your space legs."

"You'll have to explain how jumping works sometime. Madeline told me a little about the artificial gravity system…fascinating stuff. It's almost like I went to sleep and woke up on board the *USS Enterprise*!"

Adee laughed. "First Buck Rogers, and now a Star Trek reference. I can see I will need to brush up on my pre-war history if I am to keep up with you."

"Hey, I'm impressed you know about Star Trek!"

Adee smiled. "Oh yes. Star Trek is very popular among my crews. In fact, we have regular screenings on every ship in the fleet. They can't get enough of it."

"I can see why—they're living it!"

"That, and they find it fascinating to see what the future looked like a hundred years ago. You never know, one hundred years from now there may actually be a Federation of Planets and traveling across the galaxy at warp speed will be routine."

"We can only hope," Chen added.

"Let's get underway," Adee continued. "You can sit back there, or up here with me—your choice."

"We'll sit up front," Chen said. "Here, Evan, you sit next to Adee."

Chen led Evan to the chair to Adee's right and helped him fasten his restraints. He took the chair to Evan's right and Yin took the one to Adee's left.

"Here we go," Adee said.

Directly in front of Evan was a row of consoles, with several holodisplays projected above each.

Adee tapped an icon on his display.

The front of the ship became transparent, as did the floor just in front of his feet and the walls to either side of him. Evan knew he was seeing a holographic projection, but it looked like the front of the ship had turned to glass.

It reminded him of the time he and Christina had taken a helicopter tour in Hawaii—the front of the helicopter was a clear bubble that gave the pilot and passengers a 180-degree view. Instead of the magnificent volcanoes and canyons of Hawaii, Evan saw the inside of a shuttle bay above and around him, and the dull gray surface of Ceres below.

"Is that Ceres?" he asked.

"Yes, it is," Adee replied. "Unlike Luna, Ceres has a thin atmosphere, so there may be some minor turbulence as we descend. Are you ready?"

"Ready as I'll ever be," Evan answered.

Adee and Yin gestured simultaneously across their consoles, causing the shuttle to shift as the airlock and docking clamps retracted away from the ship.

Evan heard, and felt, the maneuvering thrusters fire as the shuttle slid out of the shuttle bay and into orbit a few meters below *Endeavor*.

"Ignition in three, two, one," Adee called out.

Evan felt the ship buck beneath him as the G-forces mounted, pulling him deeper into his seat.

He glanced at the holodisplay in front of Adee—they were traveling at 1,500 meters per second and rapidly losing speed.

The shuttle descended quickly, and the big ship above them soon disappeared.

Even though the shuttle had lost a lot of the speed imparted to it by *Endeavor*, the surface of Ceres still rushed beneath them at a rapid pace. Since they were facing the opposite direction of travel, Evan found it somewhat disorienting to watch the moon's surface move away from them rather than toward them.

"Any chance we can get an aft view?" he asked.

"Yes, one second," Adee replied.

A second later, the view around Evan shifted.

Evan noticed a large object in the sky directly ahead and above them. "Is that *Endeavor*?"

"No, my friend, that is *Kutanga!*" Adee said with a note of excitement in his voice.

"What is the *Kutanga*?"

"It's a ship...my ship. The largest and fastest space-going vessel ever assembled by man."

"Bigger than *Endeavor*?"

"Oh yes, by several times. *Endeavor* is 587 meters long; *Kutanga* is 1482 meters," Adee said with an air of pride in his voice.

"How many people can it carry?"

Adee considered that question carefully. "Well, it depends," he finally said.

"Depends on what?" Evan asked.

"The *Kutanga* wasn't built to carry large numbers of people in the traditional sense, and yet it can carry thousands."

"I don't understand."

"Soon, my friend, soon," Adee responded.

"You know, I sure have heard that a lot these last couple of days, and I am getting pretty damn tired of it. You people need to tell me what's going on...or you can just take me back to Earth and let me deal with the authorities there!"

Chen reached over and placed his hand on Evan's shoulder.

"That's not going to happen, Evan," he said.

"And why not? If you can get me here this fast, you can take me back just as quickly!"

Chen shook his head. "No, we can't. There is no turning back now... not for any of us."

"It's time to tell him, Chen," Yin said. "I'm calling them up."

"Calling who?" Evan asked.

Chen returned his hand to the armrest of his chair. "Lily and Dylan."

Evan wasn't sure he heard Chen correctly. "Who?"

"Lily and Dylan...your daughter and son-in-law," Chen replied.

"Okay, Chen, I've had enough. What the hell are you talking about?"

"They have to move quickly," Adee replied to Yin. "Three minutes to re-entry."

Nearly a minute went by without a word from anyone until Evan finally broke the silence.

"You people are out of your minds. What are you trying to do to me?"

An unfamiliar voice sounded from behind Evan. "He's talking about us, Dad."

Evan spun around in his chair.

A woman, whose face he didn't recognize, stood at the top of the stairs. A man stood next to her. They both wore blue and white jumpsuits, with Telogene's stylized DNA logo featured prominently above the right breast.

"Who are you people?" he demanded. "And where did you come from?"

"I am your daughter, Lily," the woman replied. "And this is my husband, Dylan."

"It's great to see you again, Evan," the man said. "It's been a really long time…too long."

Evan's cheeks flared bright red. "I don't know what kind of sick game you all are playing, but I've had enough." He turned toward Chen. "What is the point of this, Chen? What could you possibly hope to accomplish by fucking with my head like this!"

Chen stuttered as he searched for the words—he'd never seen Evan so angry.

Lily took a few steps forward. "Come sit with us, Dad. I will explain everything while we finish our descent to Galilei Station."

"Go ahead, Evan," Chen encouraged. "It's time you know the full truth."

Evan gazed at the two people standing in front of him; neither bore any resemblance to the Lily and Dylan he remembered.

"These people look nothing like Lily and Dylan. How can this be?" he asked Chen.

"The same way you look nothing like the old you. I promise Evan, it's really them."

"Ninety seconds to burn," Adee called out. "Decide, Evan."

Evan released the restraints holding him in his chair and rose unsteadily to his feet. His magnetic boots held firmly to the deck, but there was nothing for him to hold on to. The two strangers stepped forward, and each took an arm to support him.

The three crossed the short distance to the first row of seats. Evan took the aisle seat, Lily the middle, and Dylan the opposite end. Evan activated his restraints, and the strangers quickly followed suit.

"Thirty seconds," Adee called.

"Are you really my daughter?" Evan asked.

"Yes, Dad, I really am," Lily answered. "How can I prove it to you?"

"What was the last thing I said to you?"

Lily pondered that for a moment.

"Ten seconds," Adee announced.

"You don't know, do you?" Evan prodded.

"Yes, I do. It's just weird the way you asked the question."

"Oh, and why is that?"

"Because you didn't say anything. You couldn't talk. You blinked one time for yes when I asked if you would tell Mom I love her," she said.

"Ignition!" Yin said.

The shuttle's engines roared to life, sucking everyone deep into their seats as the craft made its final descent. Evan's eyes welled up, and a single tear rolled down his cheek. He reached for Lily's hand, and she took his in return.

Evan's shaky voice was barely audible over the shuttle's roaring engines. "I...I thought you were dead."

Lily leaned over and wrapped her arms around his neck.

"I know, Dad...I'm sorry for that." Lily's eyes filled with tears. "I thought I had lost you forever."

THIRTY-FOUR

APRIL 6, 2075 7:32 A.M. GST
MARS-CERES TRANSITION

Lieutenant Commander Luanne Wilkes peered over her pilot's shoulder to look at the holodisplay floating in front of him.

"How long, Ryan?" she asked.

"Five hours, plus or minus," Chief Petty Officer Ryan Randolph replied.

Luanne checked the time indicator on the display. Ryan's estimate would put them in orbit around Ceres somewhere between 12:20 and 12:40 p.m. GST.

"Can we afford another jump?" she asked.

"Not if you want to stop when we get there. We are already at the upper range of our delta-v limit."

"When's the first deceleration pulse?"

Ryan made a few gestures across his console. "First decel in twenty-seven minutes and thirteen seconds."

"Okay, steady as she goes."

"Steady as she goes, aye."

Luanne moved to return to her seat at the back of the ship.

"Lu?" Ryan asked.

"Yes?"

"I'm just wondering if you and Sam have figured out what the hell we're supposed to do when we get there."

Twelve hours ago, Bachmann had ordered Alpha and Bravo teams to proceed to Ceres, disable or destroy *Kutanga*, and take the fugitives into custody. For the past eight hours, Luanne had received regular updates from the various AI systems that were analyzing the events of the past two days. But, so far, they had been unable to offer any predictions as to what the fugitives would do next.

Emma, Luanne's tactical AI, was attempting to create a viable mission plan, but she wasn't having much success either. Given the many advantages held by the other side, Luanne hoped that a viable stealth plan was in the offering. A full-on assault against an unknown enemy could be disastrous.

"We're still working on it," she said.

"Understood."

Luanne used one foot to push off the back of Ryan's seat, sending her slowly toward the back of the ship.

She floated down the center aisle, past the other Epsilon Six team members sleeping in their pods. She had ordered a rest period after Captain Bachmann had aborted their planned stopover on Mars. Ryan and Sam had managed a couple of hours of rest on the way to Mars. She'd sleep later.

She grabbed the handrail on the back of the last pod to stop.

Sam was standing next to a holodisplay. His mag-boots were the only thing holding him in place, and his upper body bobbed and weaved a little as he gestured with his hands. Luanne pulled herself down until her boots connected with the floor. A familiar *thunk* told her it was safe to let go of the pod.

"How's it going?" she asked.

They had spent the last several hours reviewing analyses sent by the AIs, along with the schematics and technical data on *Kutanga*, hoping to find something they could use.

"I just finished reviewing the last update from the GSSA AI. It looks like most, if not all, of our principals are clones."

"No shit?"

"No shit," Sam replied.

"So, even if we grab our targets, they could still be running around somewhere?"

"Yes, ma'am."

"That's fucked up," Luanne said. "So, have they updated the target list?"

"Only one add so far…a Dr. Lily Harris, who could also go by the names Aubrey Harris or Josana Saunders. They thought they had Aubrey Harris in custody, but they found her wiped in her cell eighteen hours ago."

"How the hell did they let that happen?"

"Unknown, but that's not the half of it. The one they had in custody *also* turned out to be a clone…and now they aren't sure whether she was Aubrey or Lily."

"Unbelievable."

"Oh, it gets better," Sam added. "They think Josana Saunders is either Aubrey or Lily but—"

"Let me guess, they don't know which?"

"Ding, ding, ding. We have a winner!"

"Do they at least know *where* this Saunders/Harris person is?" Luanne asked.

"They had her working at the Telogene research lab in Kepler City, but they think *Endeavor* picked her up during its slingshot around Mars."

"Based on what?"

"Based on the fact that an unregistered shuttle craft departed Kepler City and rendezvoused with *Endeavor* just before it jumped out of orbit."

"So, what does Zelda think?" Luanne asked, referring to Sam's AI by its human-friendly name.

"She and Emma are still crunching data, but I am seeing a better than eighty percent chance that all targets are on Ceres, or on one of the orbiting ships."

"Can you confirm, Emma?" Luanne asked of her own tactical AI system.

"Confirmed," Emma replied. "We estimate an 83.2 percent chance that all targets are now on Ceres, or in orbit above Ceres."

"How are you coming on the mission plan...do we have a viable stealth option yet?"

"Mission planning and final recommendation will be complete in approximately two hours and thirteen minutes. We are developing a viable stealth option, but it is contingent on receiving assistance from a GSSA operative on board *Endeavor*."

"They have an Overwatch agent on board?" Luanne asked. "Why the fuck haven't they already done something?"

"The agent has limited access to shipboard systems. Secretary Merkel has approved our use of the agent, but we are waiting for confirmation that the agent can gain access to any relevant part of the ship."

"And the assault option?"

"Our best direct assault option has only a thirteen percent chance of success," Emma replied.

Luanne scowled. "Well, that's just fucking great. Limiting factors?"

"Current intel limitations include unknown interior layout, engineering, and defense systems; unknown crew compliment and ability; and unknown scope and timing of opposition initiatives."

"Keep at it. I want two options with better than fifty percent success rates."

"That may not be possible, but we will try," Emma acknowledged.

"Very well. So, what do you think, Sam?"

Sam shrugged. "I think we're going to have to improvise when we get there. There are just too many unknowns, and things are happening way too fast for us to get ahead."

"Agreed," Luanne said. "Try to grab some shuteye. I want the crew up in three hours, and I want all equipment checked and ready to go by 11:30."

"Including SHAS?"

SHAS, pronounced *shaz*, was Peacekeeper slang for the Space Heavy Assault Suit. The SHAS armor and offensive system enabled the Peacekeepers to undertake combat operations in almost any environment, including the hard vacuum of space. Each suit was equipped with a variety of offensive and defensive systems, and heavily armored against both energy and kinetic weapons. Two teams wearing SHAS armor would be a formidable force against almost any opponent.

"Absolutely," Luanne replied. "If we have to go in hard, we're going in *very* hard."

A wide grin spread across Sam's face. "Hooyah!"

THIRTY-FIVE

APRIL 6, 2075 8:40 A.M. GST
GALILEI STATION
CERES

Adee pressed his palm against the DNA scanner mounted next to the locked door. It hissed open to reveal a small, dimly lit room with four people staring intently at an array of holodisplays, the largest of which showed Evan and Lily sitting on a couch talking in another room.

Yin turned to see who had entered the room. "Hey," she said.

Adee smiled at her. "How's he doing?"

"So far, so good," Chen replied, without taking his eyes from a smaller display floating directly in front of him. "His bio-signs are stable and synaptic integrity appears to be holding at 97.2 percent—down 1.5 from restoration."

"That much in three days?" Adee questioned. "That's not good."

"No, but it's to be expected given everything we've put him through. The loss seems isolated to this section of long-term memory." Chen pointed to a section of Evan's brain on his display. "And, as we know from our past attempts, some additional degradation was expected since we didn't have a perfect archive to start with."

"Well, let's hope and pray he holds up this time," Adee said. "We won't get another chance at an on-Earth restoration."

Everyone nodded in agreement.

Adee continued, "What has she told him so far?"

Dylan turned to face Adee. "She tried to get him to eat, but he won't. He's stuck on why she chose a plane crash to fake her death. I guess that hit a little too close to home."

"Should we stop?" Adee asked.

"We can't," Aubrey said. "We know from our previous attempts that, once he gets stuck on wanting to know the truth, there is no getting away from it until he's satisfied."

"That's right," Chen added. "If we can't convince him this time—and soon—then it's likely we will lose him."

"Have you thought about sending Aubrey in?" Adee asked. "At least he'll recognize her face."

"We were just discussing that—it's a risk," Aubrey replied.

"We haven't had time to review the data Bruce sent," Chen replied.

Adee frowned. "Well, how long will that take?"

"A couple of hours, at least. He's likely to ask her questions she can't answer if she goes in now," Chen replied.

"What if you just tell him the truth?" Yin asked. "Have you ever tried that before?"

"Not exactly," Chen answered. "We usually try to create a story that blends his old reality with the new one…at least as best as we can."

"Right, and how has that worked out for you? Plus, this is the first time you killed off Lily in his welcome back narrative."

"You know we didn't have a choice," Chen answered.

"I do know that…and it seems to me that you really don't have a choice now," she said, her face a portrait of stern determination.

Chen threw his hands up, clearly annoyed. "Look, Yin, you are probably right. But we can't afford to blow this. He's got to be stable before we attempt the next transfer."

"I have to agree with her, Chen," Adee said. "We are running out of time. My sources tell me that the first GFN ship will be here in a little less than four hours and, even if we neutralize that one, there will surely be many more behind it."

Aubrey rested her hand on Chen's shoulder. "It's okay, I can do it."

"Are you sure?" he asked. "Are you absolutely sure? He will ask for proof…just like he did with Lily."

"I can do it."

"Do you want me to go with you?" Dylan asked.

"No, thanks. I think it's best if Mom and I try this first."

"Okay, honey, but I'll be right here watching if you need anything."

"Thanks, Dad, I'll be fine."

Adee brought his hands together in a single, loud clap—signaling that they had reached a decision and it was time to act.

"Alright," he said. "I will leave you to it then. I have to get back to preparing for our…guests."

Aubrey followed Adee into the hallway.

"Good luck," Adee said.

"Thanks," she muttered. "I'll need it."

The room where Lily and Evan were talking was just a short distance down the hallway. Aubrey pressed her palm against the scanner and the door hissed open.

Lily and Evan were sitting opposite the door, and both looked over as she entered. Evan stopped talking in mid-sentence and rushed to greet her.

"Princess! It's so good to see a face I recognize. How did you get here?" he asked.

He threw his arms around her and pulled her close against his chest. Aubrey waited a few seconds before gently sliding her hands up between them to create a little space.

"Hi, Papa, I missed you."

They squeezed each other in a tight embrace. Aubrey turned her head to meet her mother's eyes. Lily nodded her approval.

"Let's sit," Aubrey said, taking Evan's hand and guiding him back to the couch. "We have a lot of catching up to do."

Evan sat on the couch next to Lily. Aubrey slid a chair over so she could look at them both.

Aubrey took each of their hands in hers and smiled.

Lily grabbed Evan's free hand and they sat quietly, just enjoying the sensation of being together again.

"Before we start," Aubrey finally said to her grandfather. "You need to know that what I am about to tell you is the truth. Parts of it will sound unbelievable to you, but I need you to listen and trust me…trust us. We love you. We are your family and, although you may not agree with everything we've done, please know that we did it all out of love."

"I…I'll try," Evan said.

Tears of joy welled up in his eyes.

"What Mom told you is all true. She faked her death so she would be free to help Adee build the *Kutanga*. If the GSSA—or anyone from the GFN—had known she was alive, she could never have finished her work."

Evan wiped his eyes with his sleeve, never letting go of Aubrey's hand. "Go on."

"What she hasn't told you is that the Aubrey you met on Earth wasn't me—she was a clone."

"But…but she acted like—"

"Hold on, please just let me explain. She was a version of me we restored using an engramic archive created two weeks before Mom staged the plane crash. She truly believed that Mom had died and, although I don't know exactly what she said to you, I have to believe that everything she told you was the truth…at least as she understood it."

Evan struggled to keep up with the tears pouring down his cheeks.

Lily released his hand and offered him a small square of white cloth that she pulled from her jumpsuit pocket. "Here, Dad, use this."

The cloth was soft and highly absorbent, and it did a much better job at drying his face than his sleeves.

"Like all of us, that Aubrey was operating based on what she knew and believed at that time, and she did what she had to do to achieve her goals…goals that we gave her."

"Did…did she…did she know that she was a clone?"

"No, we erased all memories related to her restoration. She thought she was me. We needed her to be there because I had to be here. Do you understand?"

"N…no. Not really."

"Papa, I have been here working with Mom on the *Kutanga* for over a year now. But I couldn't be here doing this important work and on Earth running Telogene at the same time. Nor could we fake my death, because one of us needed to keep control of the company. Building this ship is taking a tremendous amount of resources and we couldn't do it without keeping control of Telogene."

"That's right, Dad," Lily said, "you should be very proud. The company you started has allowed us to make the ultimate investment. *Kutanga* is a colony ship—one that can take us far, far away from here. It's a new beginning…a second chance for us to start over."

Evan's tears stopped as anguish and anger overwhelmed his feelings of joy and happiness.

"Not all of us," he said.

"What do you mean, Papa?"

"Christina isn't here…so not all of us."

"I know, and I am sorry, Dad. I promise you we would have restored her if we could, but she died too soon. We had nothing to work with. Sure, we could have grown a body that looked like her, but it wouldn't have been her. We didn't…we don't have her engrams, and without those we don't have her. Don't you see?"

"Why couldn't you copy hers like you copied mine?" Evan asked. "Chen said that I was dead for years before you had the technology to retrieve and archive my engrams."

Lily wiped a tear from her cheek with the back of her hand. "We tried…many times. But her brain was too badly damaged…there were only fragments of who she was—a few memories, maybe a bit of her personality—but it wasn't enough to bring her back."

Aubrey squeezed his hand hard to draw his attention. "But we had you, Papa. And we brought you back…just like you made Mom promise."

He turned back to Lily, a surprised look on his face. "What do you mean I made you promise?"

Lily frowned. "You don't remember the video you had Bruce Wagner play for me after you died? The one where you told me about your top secret Second Chance project?"

"I don't remember that, I'm sorry."

"Do you remember Bruce Wagner?"

"Yes, he died with you in the plane crash."

"Well, yes and no. Bruce Wagner's original body died in that crash, but Bruce lived on in the form of his son Geoff. Or more accurately, he lived on in a clone created using his DNA that we modified to be the son he always wanted but never had."

"He didn't have children?"

"He has a daughter with his second wife, but they haven't seen each other in a very long time."

"And the video?"

"I'll show it to you later. It's very touching; you called me Lilypad. The short version is that you told me about Second Chance, and you expressed your wishes that I assume the CEO role at Telogene so I could continue your work. You wanted me to keep going until I found a way to bring you…bring you both back"

"I…I kind of remember that. I made that video the day I found out the chemotherapy wasn't working."

Lily cupped his hand with hers. "I'm sorry, I didn't know that. You did a good job hiding it."

His lips twisted into a weak smile. "I didn't want to worry you."

They sat quietly for a moment while Evan processed his daughter's words.

The somber look on his face suddenly turned to confusion.

"I called you Lilypad?" he asked.

"Yes, that was your nickname for me. Don't you remember? You used to tease me and say '*Lilypad, Lilypad, why is that frog sitting on your head, my little Lilypad?*' Then you would chase after me like you were trying to catch the frog."

"I…I guess I remember that…when you were young."

"Don't worry about it. In a few more days it will be clear as a bell. That's a pretty strong memory, and it comes back every time."

"What do you mean every time? Have you brought me back before?"

Lily froze when she realized her mistake.

Aubrey mouthed "It's okay" to her horrified mother.

"Yes, Papa, this isn't the first time we've tried to bring you back."

Evan was stunned. He dropped both of their hands and leaned back into the couch with enough force that it looked like someone had shoved him. He wiped his forehead with his hand—it felt warm. A wave of dizziness swept over him. He slumped hard against the arm of the sofa.

Lily grabbed his shoulders. "Dad…Dad, what is it? What's wrong?"

"How…how ma…how many times?" he asked. He was breathing hard and fast, and he struggled to get the words out.

"Five," Aubrey said, her voice barely a whisper.

Evan bolted to his feet like someone had pressed a hot poker into his backside. "Five times! What happened to the other four?"

"Maybe you should take this one, Mom."

Lily took a second to regain her composure.

This wasn't the first time she'd seen him react like this, but it still scared her. The father she remembered was slow to anger and careful with his emotions—her mother's funeral was the only time she saw him cry. She had to remind herself that it had only been three days since his restoration. His mind was still healing—he wasn't himself yet.

She reached for his hand. "Sit down, Dad, please. You're getting too excited…you're going to give yourself an aneurism if you don't calm down."

She waited for him to sit before continuing.

"We made our first attempt to restore you on December 15th, 2033— ten years to the day after you died. Unfortunately, the process was flawed, and your synapses broke down within just a few hours."

"I died again?"

"Yes, and I grieved again."

"Was it my body?"

"Yes, we still had your DNA."

He looked at his granddaughter. "Did you know, Aubrey?"

"No, she didn't tell me," Aubrey answered. "I was only twelve."

"Go on," he said.

Lily continued. "The second time was in 2040. We had successfully performed the procedure in July 2035 and the patient—"

"Chen told me about Arianna."

Lily smirked. *Of course he did.*

"*Arianna* was doing well," she continued. "We also had three other successful restorations behind us, and I was confident we would succeed with you."

"But something happened."

"You could say that. The New Madrid quake of 2037 destroyed everything...the underground storage facility, our company headquarters, *everything.*"

"That's when you lost my DNA," Evan said.

"Yes, along with thousands of others who had paid us for long-term cryogenic storage. It was a disaster. We would have lost the company if the judge hadn't thrown out all the lawsuits. He said we weren't liable for an act of God...kind of ironic now, don't you think?"

"But Mom tried again," Aubrey said, "using her own DNA. They just modified the chromosomes so that you developed as a male."

"And that one failed, too?" he asked.

"Yes. Just like the first time," Lily answered. "Your synapses broke down, and all those newly created neurons died within hours."

"And, after that?"

"Well, by then, cloning and engramic transfers had become fairly routine. Everyone who could afford it started ordering new bodies like they were new cars. Accelerated growth technologies rapidly developed, and by 2045 we could produce a twenty-year-old body in as little as five years."

"But by then," Aubrey interjected, "it was becoming clear that our technology was creating a tremendous strain on society because it allowed wealthy people to live forever."

"Some even kept a supply of bodies stashed around the world and transferred into a new one whenever something happened to the old one," Lily added.

"By then, the public outcry was overwhelming," Aubrey said. "There were massive protests in every major city, and we knew the GFN had to ban cloning. We were afraid that might happen before Mom could make another attempt with you."

"So, what did you do?" Evan asked Lily.

"We set up a cloning facility on Hades One," she replied. "I needed time to solve the problem with donor DNA restorations, and the Martian government doesn't prohibit full-body replacement."

"I read about that," Evan said. "Hades One was the first Martian colony…before they built the domes on the planet surface."

"Correct, and Telogene was one of the largest corporate sponsors of that colony—so they treated us well."

"All that and it still didn't work?" Evan asked.

"Nope. As it turns out, the things we call engrams contain not only our thoughts, feelings, and memories but also other biologic information keyed to the host DNA."

"You lost me."

"It's hard to explain, and the truth is that we still don't fully understand it."

"Try me," Evan demanded.

"Well, the simplest way is to think about engrams is like palm prints, or the patterns on our tongues, or the blood vessels on our retinas. While it is possible for two people to have similar patterns, no two are exactly the same. Engrams are just like that; every person is unique."

"Okay, I get it. Go on."

Lily continued, "As we age, the neural pathways within our brains form these unique patterns, and—"

"The way our brains store information is influenced by our DNA," Evan said. "You forget that I was a physician and geneticist once upon a time, my dear."

"No, I haven't forgotten; I just don't know how much you remember. But you are correct. Our DNA plays a significant role in the structure of our brains and the information it contains. And it's not just our brains— it's our spinal cord and entire nervous system."

"Our memories are stored in our spine?" Evan asked incredulously.

"No, but many of our autonomic functions and reflex responses are stored in the pons, thalamus and medulla."

"Okay, I understand all that…but what does that have to do with me?"

"The important part is that, as you aged, you developed unique neural pathways based on your genetics, environment, and experiences. Got it?"

"Yes, I understand."

"Good," Lily said. "Because we spent a lot of time figuring out that you can't write engrams coded to one person onto the brain of another. The neural and physical pathways just won't line up. The variation in brain and neural geometry results in defective neurons, malformed synapses, and a distorted engramic mesh."

"That sounds bad."

"It is, and the severity depends on how big of a difference exists in the physical geometry between the brains of the host and source bodies. The greater the difference, the more distortion of the engramic mesh, and the less likely that the person will adapt to the new host body and survive."

"You're losing me again," Evan said.

"Sorry. The important part is that, the closer the physical structure of the host brain and nervous system is to that of the original, the more probable the transfer will succeed."

"And an exact match is ideal," Aubrey added.

"Right," Lily continued. "And to make things even more complicated, we discovered that low gravity and varying solar orbital periods caused random mutations in off-Earth clones. Even if we started with perfectly preserved, original DNA it was likely that we would end up with significant variation by the time the clone was just a few months old."

"And sometimes," Aubrey interjected, "those mutations resulted in variations of neural geometry that caused engramic restoration to fail even though we were using the original person's own DNA."

"Which," Lily continued, "led to us to our next breakthrough. We compared the brain and neural structure of Earth-born hosts with their off-Earth clones and measured the differences between the two."

"Okay, I think I get the science. Just tell me what happened."

"We made progress," Lily said. "We had a few successes, and I tried again."

"With me?"

"Yes, we tried again. We did our best to recreate an Earth-like environment on Hades One—simulated gravity, day-night cycle, seasons…it wasn't perfect, but it was pretty close."

"What did you use for the source DNA?"

Lily chuckled. "Mine, just like before. We've made a lot of improvements, but the donor still has to be a close relative. A brother or sister is best, but we've been able to make do with parents and siblings."

"You mean to say that…"

"That you and I now share more than just a father-daughter relationship? Yes, Dad, the body you are in right now is my clone. You are, for all intents and purposes, my twin brother."

"I'm confused. I thought we were talking about something that happened years ago."

"We are. The DNA used to clone you this time is the same DNA we used twenty-four years ago—it's *my* DNA."

"But what about the other me?" Evan asked. "What happened to that clone?"

Lily looked down, a sad look in her eyes. "You were functional for a few days. But then you started hallucinating, and you ended up stealing an escape pod and ejecting yourself into space. Thankfully, a passing transport picked you up. But, God, did you create a major shit-storm for us when you got back to Earth."

"I think I read something about that…that was me?"

"Yes," Aubrey replied. "Your rapidly failing memory was the only reason Telogene survived the ensuing scandal. Your inability to tell anyone who you were, or anything about you, allowed us to fill in the blanks. Mom told everyone that you were a Telogene employee who had experienced an unfortunate lab accident."

"And a year after that, I gave a speech calling for the end of full body restorations at the GFN's tenth-anniversary conference," Lily said. "I had to. If I didn't…well, let's just say that we probably wouldn't be here right now."

"That's right," Aubrey said. "Your escape from Hades One was just one black eye too many. There were dozens of world and regional leaders speaking out against Telogene—they wanted to put Mom in jail and sell off the company."

"But I couldn't let that happen," Lily added. "So, I made a deal to save it."

Aubrey continued. "And she did save it. And three years later, the GFN passed the HDDA."

"What happened to the…the other me?"

"We had to terminate that clone. It…you…were beyond recovery."

"But President Duchon said that I had traveled to Luna before…with a woman. How is that possible?"

"That was our fourth attempt, three years ago," Lily said. "You and I were traveling to Mars…a trial run of sorts. But…well, let's just leave it at *you didn't make it.*"

"So, if it didn't work three years ago, what made you try again…why now?" Evan asked.

"Because we think we've finally solved all the technical challenges, but —"

"We needed to know for sure," Aubrey interrupted, "And we have more baseline data on you than anyone else."

"So, what you're telling me is that I am just an experiment? A test subject so you can see if you have become the masters of inserting the contents of one man's brain into someone else's body. Is that it?"

Lily's face flushed in anger. "No, Dad, that's not it at all! Don't you realize that this all started because you asked me to bring you back? I never wanted any of this—the CEO job, Second Chance, the burden of a dying father's request—I could have lived my whole life without any of it!"

Evan's head dropped. She could tell that her words had hurt him deeply.

She took a deep breath before continuing. "Look, I'm sorry if I didn't get it right the first time, or even the fourth, but you and I both know that's not how science works. You're the one that taught me to keep failing until I succeed, remember?"

He looked up; his eyes swollen with tears. "Yes, I remember. But I could never have imagined how far this would go. When I started, I thought only of helping people live longer, healthier lives. It never occurred to me that you would abuse this technology as you have. We can't keep doing this."

"Papa," Aubrey slid over to the couch and put her arm around her grandfather's shoulders. "We can't undo the past; we can only move forward. The damage is done and stopping now would mean the end of us all."

He wiped his eyes dry. "Did it ever occur to the two of you that maybe that's how it should be? Hell, dinosaurs roamed the Earth for millions of years, but you don't see any of them around, do you? Extinction is a part of the natural order. If dinosaurs hadn't died out, then it's possible we wouldn't even be here. Maybe that's how it's supposed to be—humanity dies to make room for whoever, or whatever, comes next."

"That may be," Aubrey said, "but I am not willing to just give up. If humanity is not meant to survive, then our mission will fail. But, if there is even a small chance, then I think we have to try."

Evan desperately wanted to change the subject. "So, whose body is that? You look nothing like I remember you…it's obviously not yours."

Lily sighed. "It's my DNA. We modified it to change my bone structure and eye and hair color. Josana Saunders is a real person—I just made myself look like her."

Evan sat quietly as he considered everything he had just heard. It was beyond belief, and he struggled to make sense of it.

"There's one more thing I have to tell you, Dad," Lily said.

"What's that?"

"We want you to go on the ship with us. We want you to help us start a colony on a planet we discovered in the Alpha Centauri system."

"So, the whole 'help us save the Earth' thing was just a ploy then? The real plan is to cut and run, and leave those billions of people to clean up the mess you helped create? I cannot believe that any daughter of mine would ever dream of such a thing."

"But we're not abandoning them!" Lily cried. "We are trying to save them, or at least some small part."

"And who decides who lives and who dies? You?"

Lily started to sob. "No, of course not. That's Aneni's job."

"Who's Aneni?"

"She…it is the master AI that will pilot the *Kutanga* and oversee the establishment of the Gaia colony," Aubrey replied.

"What? Are you telling me that a computer program is deciding humanity's fate? Have you all completely lost your minds?"

"Aneni is one of the most advanced artificial intelligence systems ever created," Lily said. "We have been nurturing her for nearly twenty years. She knows everything that has happened, and what will happen if we do nothing."

"That's right, Papa, and once we finish loading the last of the engramic archives, she will have access to the accumulated knowledge of the world's greatest scientists, engineers, and technicians…including yours."

"Including mine? What are you saying?"

Lily answered. "Aubrey is saying that you, me, her…all of us will make the trip to Gaia as engramic archives, and that Aneni will restore us once we reach our destination. As fast as *Kutanga* is, it will still take almost thirty years for us to get there…and that's a really long time to keep thousands of people alive in space."

"So, why bring me back at all? Why not just transfer me directly into that Aneni thing?"

"It's complicated, Dad, but what matters most is that we wanted to see you, and to hug you, and to tell you how much we love you. I know you are struggling to understand all this, but I just really need you to trust me."

"I do love you, Lily. I love you both more than anything, and I do trust you. I'm just trying to understand." Evan stood up and extended his hands. "Come here"

Lily and Aubrey stood up and took Evan's offered hands. He pulled them close in a tight embrace.

"I'm so very happy to see you both," he whispered. "I can't even begin to tell you what it means to me to see you again. The only thing that would make it more perfect is if Christina were here…but I know that's not possible. I love you both very much."

"We love you too, Papa. I'm sorry this has been so hard on you. We really wanted it to be different…but we are doing our best."

"I know you are, Princess, I know you are."

THIRTY-SIX

Bruce Wagner stared blurry-eyed at the holodisplay in front of him.

The AI task he had started when he first arrived was nearly complete —just a handful of engramic archives left to transmit. The AI managing the job was operating from a secret location a few kilometers outside the Siberian town of Norilsk. Besides Bruce, only ten other people knew the facility existed, including Lily Harris, Alexei Dumanov, and the eight technicians that maintained the organic storage array, along with its supporting power and climate control systems.

They had built the secret facility, which Alexei had named Vechnost— Russian for "eternity"—nearly a decade ago to provide redundancy for Telogene's primary backup storage facility in Xi'an, China. Now, it served as the primary storage site for the Gaia mission.

Over the past five years, Lily had acquired the engrams of 4,487 of the planet's most talented and gifted people. Collectively, they represented every major country, religion, profession, and ethnic group. Gathering them had been a relatively simple matter, as many of the donors either worked for Telogene or were customers of its backup and storage services. There were a few she had to convince to create an engramic archive, but Lily persisted until, whether by flattery or bribery, she persuaded each one. For all their diversity, they all had one thing in common: none of them knew that they had been chosen to be a colonist on Gaia.

Bruce had been careful to cover his tracks, knowing full well that the GSSA would monitor his every communication and action on the GeoNet. So, to avoid detection, he sent the command that activated the Vechnost AI before he left Zurich. He had disguised the message as a request to perform a routine backup of his corporate files to the Xi'an office. The receiving AI in Xi'an then forwarded the embedded command to Vechnost using a private network.

Within seconds of receiving its orders, the Vechnost AI packaged all the archives in its care and began transmitting them to Aneni, the master AI on board the *Kutanga*. The readout on the holodisplay showed that the last batch of archives would be received and verified in seven minutes and fifteen seconds. Once complete, the Vechnost AI would detonate the high explosives embedded throughout the facility—destroying the facility and obliterating itself and any trace of the archives once stored there.

Almost there, Bruce thought.

Several gestures later, the holodisplay displayed a list of people selected to be among the first colonists on a planet outside of our solar system. Only a handful of people even knew the list existed, and only three had the ability to change it—Bruce was one, along with Lily Harris and Adekunle Gbadamosi. Bruce filtered the list to show only surnames starting with the letter "D."

The name he was looking for was near the bottom—Alexei Dumanov. He was already on the approved colonist list, although Alexei had no way of knowing that. He was only on the list because Bruce Wagner had long considered him a trusted friend and had advocated for his inclusion when the list was first created three years ago.

Unfortunately for Dumanov, his awareness of the *Kutanga* and his demand to be included among the colonists had given Bruce pause. Bruce did not understand how or where Alexei had gotten his information, but it had to be someone inside the GSSA or BGSI. That meant that there was a spy somewhere, and it also meant that if Alexei had been able to get the information, then surely others had it, too.

He had spent several hours during his flight back from Switzerland agonizing about what to do. Should he tell Alexei he was already on the list? That would mean explaining to him that he would not be physically getting on a ship—only his engramic archive would make the voyage to Gaia. It would also mean risking exposure of the entire operation if Alexei decided he didn't agree with the plan.

That was why none of the people on the list had been told of their inclusion; there was too great of a risk that one of them would disapprove of some aspect of the mission plan, or just not be able to keep the secret until the ship was safely away.

He was also worried about who Alexei would become on Gaia. Would he be the trusted confidante, exceptional leader, and gifted organizer that Bruce knew him to be? Or, would he be the tyrannical thug that had strong-armed his way into a multi-billion-dollar fortune?

Until yesterday, Bruce had assumed that his friendship with Alexei was strong enough to ensure the former, but Alexei's words had conveyed more than a hint of deep-seated animosity when the topic of repaying his debt had been brought up. In the end, Bruce decided that he couldn't take the chance.

He gestured at the holodisplay until it rewarded him with confirmation that Alexei Dumanov had been removed from the list of colonists, and that his engramic archive was deleted from *Kutanga's* storage array (or at least it would be once his message was received). That done, he transmitted his final progress report to Lily, informing her of his decision to remove Dumanov from the mission.

Satisfied, Bruce had only one thing left to do—say goodbye to Geoff Wagner. He reached into the briefcase that he always carried with him and withdrew a small silver case. He set the case on the desk in front of him and placed his thumb on a small depression in its otherwise smooth surface. The case opened like butterfly wings to reveal two halves, one containing an injector and the other containing a small vial.

Bruce picked up the vial and twirled it between his thumb and forefinger. The contents shimmered in the light like mercury. But, as deadly as mercury could be, the material in this vial was even more so.

Telogene had originally developed neural nanites to repair diseased or damaged tissue in the brain, spine, and nervous system. But, after passing the HDDA, the GFN needed a method of humanely disposing of illegal clones. In what was perhaps the ultimate irony, Telogene won the contract to design, develop, and manufacture the substance the GFN would ultimately use to eliminate over two million clones from the planet.

This was the same substance Bruce now twirled in his hand.

Although the relatively benign-sounding term "nano-wipe" was widely adopted to describe the effects the nanites had on a human being, the reality was far starker. Once injected, the nanites would take anywhere from two to five minutes to infiltrate the victim's brain and spinal column. Seconds after that, the victim would lose consciousness as the nanites attacked the brainstem and disabled the neurons responsible for controlling heart rate and respiration. Another group of nanites would then disrupt the synapses of the brain and destroy the neurons responsible for memory and conscious thought.

Within ten minutes, the victim would be clinically dead; within thirty minutes, the bulk of the victim's brain and spine would be the consistency of thick chicken soup.

Bruce inserted the cartridge and pressed the injector against his neck directly above his carotid artery. He pushed the activator with his thumb —a faint hissing sound signified the beginning of the end. The illegal, unregistered clone that had served as the vessel for Bruce Thomas Wagner for the past year, three months, nineteen hours, and thirty-two minutes would soon be no more.

Bruce placed the injector on his desk and relaxed back into his chair. He closed his eyes and concentrated on taking slow, deep breaths.

Specks of light began to appear on the back of his eyelids, quickly followed by random bursts of color. A few seconds later, he noticed a distant ringing sound, which grew louder and more clamorous with each passing second. These were known side effects of the neural destruction process and were frequently reported by nano-wipe victims in their final minutes and seconds of existence.

As more time passed, the loud, but not unpleasant, sounds became a cacophony, and the flashing lights and colors became so intense that it felt like staring at the Sun with unprotected eyes.

He tried to open his eyes but couldn't.

His heart slowed, and he panicked as he realized he was no longer breathing.

For a brief instant he wished that he hadn't injected himself, but then he remembered that it was all part of the plan. He wasn't really dying, after all. This body would be gone, but he would still exist—and it was only a matter of time before Aneni restored him.

A moment later the lights and sounds stopped, and Bruce "Geoff" Wagner was no more.

Thirty-Seven

APRIL 6, 2075 9:30 A.M. GST
GSSA HEADQUARTERS
ZURICH, SWITZERLAND

Dianne Merkel had spent the last hour and a half reviewing the list of potential colonists that Christian had compiled for her. The AI that provided the data had been unwilling to reveal the name of the source, or the details of how it was acquired, except to say that it came from a reliable source and confidence was high.

The list contained the names, professions, and last known locations of some 4,500 people. Roughly one-third were current or former Telogene employees; another third were current or former employees of The Galileo Group. The remaining third were well-known visionaries and entrepreneurs, specialists from other fields and disciplines outside of those found at Telogene and Galileo, military and law enforcement personnel, and a smattering of well-respected regional politicians and judges. Most notably, there was not one person from the GFN, GSSA, BGSI or any other global agency on the list.

While Dianne visually scanned the list to see if any names jumped out at her, Christian cross-referenced it with the GSSA's database of known and suspected violators of the HDDA.

Known violators were people who had transferred their consciousness into a clone within twelve months of the HDDA being signed into law.

Those people were grandfathered so long as they destroyed any other clones and agreed to forego life extension therapies of any kind—except procedures on the pre-approved medical necessity list.

Suspected violators were those who the GSSA believed to be clones but lacked sufficient evidence to prove that cloning had occurred. Although most clones could be detected with genetic testing, certain legal gene therapies rendered those tests useless.

Dianne created a secondary list of 274 names that combined the people Christian identified with the people she had tagged. She focused on those names, trying to find a name or pattern of names that would help her to gain an advantage over her adversaries. As she scrolled through the list for the tenth time, one name near the top of the list caught her attention—Alexei Dumanov.

Alexei Dumanov was a suspected HDDA violator, but the GSSA could never build a case against him. Born in 1970, Alexei had grown up during the fall of the Soviet Union. In his mid-twenties, he fell into a 25 percent ownership interest in an old ammunition factory outside of Murmansk. By the early 2000s, he had parlayed his ammunition factory profits into a steel and shipbuilding conglomerate, which earned him a considerable fortune during the war. By 2030, he was one of the ten wealthiest men in the Russian Federation.

In 2045, at age 75, Alexei underwent a full body restoration, transplanting his engrams into a clone created using his own DNA. But it wasn't that clone that got Dumanov on the suspect list. Cloning was legal in 2045, and the HDDA was still a decade away.

Dianne remembered the case. She was a prosecutor in the newly formed Global Standards and Safety Administration when the Dumanov case crossed her desk. Dianne gestured at the holodisplay to retrieve the Dumanov case file, then tapped the glowing green icon that would connect her with Christian.

"Yes, ma'am?" he answered.

"I just pulled up an old case file on Alexei Demyanovich Dumanov. Please review it, check all available sources and see if you can find any connection between him and anyone at Telogene or Galileo, but more likely Telogene."

"Am I looking for anything in particular?"

"It's just a hunch, but of all the names on our suspect list, this is the guy who has the financial and organizational resources to do things that neither Telogene nor Galileo could do themselves…at least not out in the open."

"Very well. I was just about to remind you of your meeting with Captain Bachmann; he is waiting in your conference room."

"Tell him I will be right there."

"Will there be anything else?"

"No, that's it," she said.

Christian's face disappeared from the corner of the holodisplay.

Dianne expanded Dumanov's file so she could read it easier. She scanned the details to refresh her recollection, and she found that she remembered the case well. Dumanov's clone developed cancer in 2056, a year after the GFN passed the Human Dignity and Decency Act. He underwent the normal procedures to treat it, but the cancer was hyper-aggressive, and nothing seemed to work.

Alexei disappeared for about a year, supposedly to focus on treatment and recovery. Everyone assumed that he had died but then he suddenly reappeared in April 2058, looking like a young, healthy man in his early twenties. The assumption was that he must have had another clone hidden away somewhere.

The GSSA charged him with violating the HDDA, but Alexei hired an army of doctors and lawyers to assert that he had, in fact, been cured of his cancer. He said that his youthful appearance was the result of telomere extension therapy, which was legal. Lacking any hard evidence, the government had no choice but to drop the case against him.

It would take Christian some time to complete the background check on Dumanov, so Dianne decided she might as well meet with Bachmann. She stood up and crossed the short distance to the conference room where he was waiting.

"Sorry to keep you waiting," she said as she entered the room.

"No problem," Bachmann replied. "I've just received a mission update from Lieutenant Commander Wilkes. They will arrive in approximately three hours and are awaiting our orders."

Dianne smiled at the captain's use of "our orders." At least he was making a good show of cooperation and teamwork.

"Excellent. Have you decided on the best approach?" Dianne figured she might as well reciprocate his collegial demeanor.

"It depends; has anything changed since your *agent's* last report?"

Thato Govender, Dianne's agent on board *Endeavor*, had reported that it was unlikely he would be given access to *Kutanga* within the time required.

"He's still working on it," Dianne said.

"Hm, I'm sure he is," the captain said. "But time is short, and I think we will to have to rely on another resource."

"Oh, and who might that be?"

"I just met with Director Horvat, and she informed me that they also have an agent embedded in Gbadamosi's crew. The agent is posing as a member of the engineering team and was the one who provided us with the design plans for *Kutanga*."

"Well, don't keep me in suspense, who is it?"

"Her name is Linda Sewell, and she serves as the Main Propulsion Assistant on *Endeavor*. She has detailed knowledge of its gravity drive systems and has been on board the *Kutanga* multiple times—she says she has firsthand knowledge of its layout and engineering systems."

"Where is she now?"

"She is on board the *Kutanga*. They asked her to help prepare the ship for an early departure."

"So, they are pushing up their timetable, then?"

"It looks like it, and get this…she had lunch with Feldman, Hao, and Li. She happened to be in the mess when Gbadamosi brought them down for a snack after *Endeavor* picked them up."

"It looks like we might have just caught a break."

"Yes, ma'am. We have confirmation of the fugitives' location and we have someone who can help get Wilkes' team on board *Kutanga*."

"Excellent. So what's the plan?"

Bachmann pulled a holocube from his pocket and inserted it into the slot on the table in front of him. Ceres appeared in the air above them.

"Well, we still have one problem to solve. Right now, Gbadamosi can't track the team's transport ship—it's too far out and moving too fast."

The image zoomed out to show a large section of space between Ceres and Mars.

"But there is a chance they will be detected once they start decelerating. We just don't know what kind of capabilities Gbadamosi has."

"So, what do we do?"

"We have two options. One, we order the team to burn straight for the *Kutanga* and do a hard assault. Of course, doing that risks a full-on firefight and, although the team is well armed, they will be badly outnumbered…and it directly violates the Earth-Mars treaty."

"And option two?"

"We knock on the door and ask to come in."

Dianne looked confused as Bachmann pointed at the floating map of space and drew several lines with his fingers.

"We order the transport to enter orbit around Ceres and request permission to land."

"For what purpose?"

"We'll make something up. I was thinking it could be as easy as just asking to speak with Gbadamosi…to try to negotiate a peaceful resolution to the situation."

"What if he says no?"

Bachmann shifted the view to a closeup of Ceres.

"Once the transport is in orbit, Wilkes will send a four-man team to board the *Kutanga*. They will exit the transport here and use their suit thrusters to rendezvous with the ship here. According to Sewell, there is an airlock the team can use to board the ship, located here. She says she can bypass the monitors and security protocols. Nobody other than her will know they are coming."

"Won't they spot the team before they get anywhere close to the *Kutanga*?"

"Unlikely. Their suits are invisible to all forms of energy, so they won't be seen on any scanners, and they project holographic camouflage that makes them invisible to the naked eye and optical sensors."

"Okay, so the team gets on board while Wilkes tries to distract Gbadamosi…then what?"

Bachmann zooms in further until an interior diagram of the ship fills the space above the conference table.

"Sewell will lead the team from the airlock to these maintenance tunnels, which connect with the engineering compartment. From there, they cross through this area to reach the engine core. Once there, they will disable both the primary and secondary drive systems to ensure that the *Kutanga* stays in orbit until we can get a larger contingent on board."

"A larger contingent? Where are they coming from and who authorized that?"

"I dispatched two interceptors two hours ago. I figured we could recall them if you disagreed with the plan for some reason."

"Standard crew size and composition?" Dianne asked.

"Yep, thirty per ship…forty-eight combat personnel total."

"What about Pak?" Dianne asked, referring to the Martian president.

"President Hilliard has decided that he is willing to take action now and ask for forgiveness later. Command fears that any attempt to go through normal channels on this will either take too long or tip off the opposition, and we can't afford to take that chance."

President August Hilliard was both president of the Global Federation of Nations and Supreme Commander of all branches of the armed forces, including the Peacekeepers.

"Interesting. So, does that mean I am not the scapegoat anymore?"

"On the contrary. If this goes wrong, President Hilliard will deny all knowledge of our actions, and you and I will be charged with misappropriating military resources and violating the treaty with Mars."

Dianne thought about that for a minute before responding.

"So, is it worth it?" she finally asked.

"Ma'am?"

"Are our careers and possibly our lives, worth all this?"

"I don't know, I haven't thought about that. I'm a soldier and I do whatever I have to do to complete my mission. I only worry about personal consequences afterwards…if at all."

"Must be nice."

"It's just part of the job I signed up for."

"Well, since I am not a soldier, let's think this through for a minute, shall we?" Dianne asked rhetorically. "What do we get by stopping them?"

"They're criminals; they broke the law. Isn't that enough?" Bachmann replied.

"What if things are really as bad here as the analysts project?" Dianne continued. "What difference does arresting a few criminals make if 90 percent of us will be dead within a decade, anyway?"

"The way I look at it, Madame Secretary, is that none of us knows how long we have on this Earth, and just because some scientist tells me that I will be dead in ten years doesn't mean that I stop abiding by our laws. If I did that and you did that and millions of others did that, then this world would descend into chaos so fast that I doubt very seriously that any of us would want to hang around for even a year—never mind ten!"

"That's a fair point, Captain."

"And besides," he added. "I happen to believe that these criminals know more about this situation than we think. Hell, they helped create this problem, didn't they? I bet that, once we get them back here, they are going to offer up a cure in exchange for their freedom."

"But if they have a cure, why go to all this trouble? Why not just be heroes?"

"What if it's not about that? What if it's about creating a new world in their own image? What if they purposely killed us so they would be able to start their new utopia in peace? Did you ever think of that?"

Dianne considered that for a moment. "No, I can't say that I have."

"Well, I have. Gbadamosi is an empire builder, and Feldman and his daughter probably think they're gods…manipulating DNA, creating life, destroying life, cheating death. Hell, I'd consider myself a god if I invented all that stuff—who wouldn't?"

"Do you really believe that we are dealing with a group of megalomaniacs here?"

"I don't know. But what I do know is that we will never find out if we let them go."

"You have a point there," Dianne said.

"So yes, I say our careers and lives are worth it. If we do not stop them and we pay a price for that, then at least I can meet my maker knowing that I tried my best to save humanity. On the other hand, if we succeed… well then maybe, just maybe, we'll be the heroes."

"It is more likely that no one will ever know any of this happened, regardless of whether we succeed or fail."

"That's a chance I'm willing to take because that also comes with my job, Madame Secretary."

Dianne leaned back in her chair and studied the *Kutanga* for several minutes. Neither of them said a word and Bachmann just stared at Dianne, waiting to see what she'd do next.

"Okay," she finally said, "let's try the stealth approach. Disable the *Kutanga*. Take the fugitives prisoner, if possible, kill them if not."

"We can't interrogate them if they are dead, Madame Secretary."

"We won't need to. Once we have control of *Kutanga*, we will transmit their engramic archives back to Earth and we'll learn everything we need to know from there."

"What if the ship is destroyed?"

"Is that going to happen?"

"Unlikely, but gravity pulse drives are finicky things…and anything is possible when you start messing with them."

"Well, we had better hope that Agent Sewell knows her shit then, hadn't we?"

"Yes, ma'am."

Christian's image flashed on the holodisplay in front of Dianne.

"I am sorry to interrupt, but I have important news."

"Go ahead."

"Alexei Dumanov and Bruce Wagner knew each other. They met at a conference in Moscow after the war and had intermittent contact over the years."

"Why are we just now learning this?"

"I'm sorry, ma'am. The BGSI just provided information about several calls Geoff Wagner made to Alexei Dumanov while he was in

Switzerland. They have not yet decrypted the contents of the calls, but they have confirmed that they occurred."

"So, either Geoff Wagner is really Bruce Wagner, or Geoff is calling his dad's old friend for a favor. Either way, we've got a connection."

"That's correct," Christian said. "You should also know that Geoff Wagner transferred a significant amount of money to accounts believed to belong to Alexei Dumanov just hours after we took Aubrey Harris into custody."

"Mother fucker!" Dianne shouted. "Arrest Geoff Wagner *now*. Where is he?"

"He is still in his office at Telogene's North American headquarters."

"Good, get a team in there and take his ass down. I want him on a plane back to Zurich within the hour. Understood?"

"Yes, ma'am. Sending the instructions now."

Christian's face disappeared from the display.

"Oh, what a tangled web they weave," Dianne said. "I knew that shit-bag attorney was involved in this somehow. I just knew it, but I didn't listen to my instincts. Well, no more! We're going to put an end to this right now, Captain, do you understand me?"

"Yes, ma'am. I'm with you."

"Good, get it done. Now if you'll excuse me, I need to get to the bottom of this Geoff and Alexei thing."

Dianne stood and returned to her office, leaving the conference room to Bachman. The Captain opened an encrypted communication channel on his holodisplay.

"Epsilon Six, you are cleared to execute mission plan Charlie. AI authentication sequence to follow. Acknowledge."

He sent the AI authentication sequence that would validate his order and returned to studying the *Kutanga*. It would take twenty minutes or so for Wilkes to receive the message, and the same amount of time for him to receive her acknowledgment. That meant he had forty minutes to figure out how to get his team out of there once everything went to hell!

THIRTY-EIGHT

APRIL 6, 2075 11:17 A.M. GST
GALILEI STATION
CERES

"Okay, with Dumanov's deletion, adding Walker and Berkovic, and the other changes that Aneni recommended, we have 4,492 archives stored onboard—Chen glanced around the table at the assembled group—including ours."

Lily and Aubrey sat on one side of the table with Dylan and Evan. Chen, Adee, and Yin sat opposite them. The group had spent the last hour reviewing recent events to ensure that they were all working from the same set of facts.

The original plan had called for spending the next two weeks testing the drive system, running emergency drills with the crew (which comprised twelve semi-autonomous synthetic humanoids, or "synths" as they were often called), and stress-testing Aneni—the ship's master AI.

Once launched, *Kutanga* would be the first interstellar ship in history, and one of just a handful operated entirely by a synthetic crew. Unfortunately, the events of the past three days had caused the group to rethink their plans and forced them to consider an immediate launch. Doing so would prevent them from completing the thorough and rigorous test plan they had developed.

"So, once we load Papa, that will leave us with room for seven more," Aubrey said.

"I still haven't said yes," Evan replied.

"Oh, come on, Dad," Lily said. "Don't be silly…you're coming with us. Why wouldn't you?"

"I don't know. I just don't like you assuming that I will just go along for the ride. If I am being honest, this whole thing has left a sour taste in my mouth."

Lily placed her hand on top of her father's. "I know and I'm sorry. We thought we could get you off Earth quietly, just like last time. Unfortunately, someone tipped off the GSSA."

"Who do you think it was?" Evan asked.

"We don't know—it could have been Aubrey's executive assistant, Evelyn Wu. We know from Bruce's last report that Evelyn was an Overwatch agent."

"And it's possible that the GSSA had other agents at other facilities that we don't know about," Aubrey added. "It doesn't really matter though, because we've always known this would be our last shot at this."

"Really? What's stopping you from bringing me back again?"

"Technically, nothing," Chen replied. "But it will be extremely difficult, if not impossible, for any of us to return to Earth."

"Why? Can't you just create new identities, sneak back, and start all over again?"

"Trust us, Dad, we can't," Lily said. "They won't stop looking for us until we're dead, or so far beyond their reach that they could never catch us."

"That's right, Papa," Aubrey added. "Changing identities might buy us a little time but we can't go back to our old lives—we'd have to start over. That means no family, no money, no education, work, or financial history…nothing that could connect us back to who we were."

"Why not just stay here? Or live on Mars? Didn't you say they have different laws and aren't likely to turn us over to the GFN?"

"That's true to a point, Evan," Adee replied, "but that won't stop the GFN from hunting us down. We would not be the first fugitives who tried to hide out on Mars, nor would we be the first caught and returned to Earth for trial."

"So, what's the plan, then?" Evan asked. "You've already said that *Kutanga* isn't designed to transport people, so where do we go from here?"

Adee looked back and forth uncomfortably between Lily and Aubrey—he clearly did not want to answer Evan's question.

"It can't carry lots of people," he finally said. "But it can carry some."

Lily tried to speak, but Yin cut her off. "Their plan was to terminate themselves once *Kutanga* is safely away. Isn't that right, Adee?"

Adee had briefed Yin on the group's plan a few hours before, and she was not happy with the details he had shared.

"Yes, that was the plan…before everything went sideways."

"Is that true, Lily," Evan asked with obvious shock and horror on his face, "were you going to kill yourselves?"

"It's hard to explain, Dad, you haven't lived like we have. But what's important is that we won't be dead—everything that makes us who we are is stored safely on board *Kutanga*. Aneni will restore us once we get to Gaia, and we'll all just pick up where we left off. In fact, none of us will even remember having had this conversation if we don't update our archives before the ship leaves."

"I don't understand," Evan said.

"It's simple, really," Chen replied, "an engramic archive captures our thoughts, feelings, and memories at a specific moment in time. After restoration, we only remember our lives up to the moment of the archive; we have no memory of any events that occurred afterwards."

"But none of that matters," Yin interjected, "because nobody is terminating anybody. Right, Adee?"

"That's correct, we've decided that it's best that we stay with *Kutanga* a little longer than we originally planned."

"So, when are you leaving?" Evan asked.

"Soon," Adee replied, "the GFN Peacekeepers will be here in little more than an hour."

"But I didn't think *Kutanga* would be ready for at least another six hours?"

"Well, the gravity pulse drive won't be ready to make the first jump for another six hours, but she can leave on thrusters right now. She won't get very far, but that's what we've got to decide next."

"That's right," Yin said. "I've completed my tactical analysis and—"

"Just a second, please," Adee cut her off. "We need to know if you are coming with us, Evan."

"Do I have a choice?" Evan asked.

"Sure you do," Adee said.

"What happens if I choose to stay here?"

"Then they will probably capture and kill you."

"Why would they kill me? None of this is my fault. I didn't ask you to restore me."

"No, you didn't. But, unfortunately, that doesn't matter."

"That's not an option," Lily said. "Look, Dad, you can't go back to Earth. As an illegal clone, you have no rights and they can do anything they want to you. They'll probably just terminate you on sight. If you get really lucky, you'll spend the rest of your life slaving away on one of the penal asteroids in the Belt."

Evan thought for a moment; neither outcome appealed to him. "So, then I don't really have a choice, do I? You've already made it for me…I either go with you or stay here and die. What kind of a choice is that?"

"There is another option," Chen said.

"Oh, what's that?" Evan asked.

"We could create an updated archive for you—one that includes everything you've learned over the past three days—and add that to Aneni's data store."

"Which was the plan all along, wasn't it?"

"Yes, Papa," Aubrey said. "That was the plan for all of us."

"Then what the hell was the purpose of bringing me back in the first place? Why not just add my original archive to *Kutanga* and be done with it? Why did you put me through all of this?"

"To put it most simply," Lily said, "I hoped to avoid a repeat of Hades One. And I was afraid that too much time has passed since you…died."

"That's right, Papa," Aubrey interjected. "We needed to know that you could survive the restoration process after so many years."

Evan's eyebrows raised slightly, and a concerned look spread across his face. "I get it now! Oh, God, I'm so stupid. You didn't bring me back to help solve the mutation problem—that was never your plan. You needed to test your ability to restore yourselves after the thirty-year trip to Gaia. You don't love me…I'm just a fucking lab rat!"

Dylan slapped his hands on the tabletop as he leaned past Lily to lock eyes with Evan. "That's not true, Evan. The *only* reason they agreed to this was because they love and miss you. They never wanted to hurt you, they just wanted to give you the second chance you asked for."

"Well," Evan said, "it sure doesn't feel that way. And it's really hard for me to believe anything that any of you say…all you've done is lie to me from the beginning."

Tears welled up in Lily's eyes. "I'm sorry, Dad. I never meant to hurt you…this should have never happened."

Evan clenched his fist and pounded the table. "You're damn right it shouldn't have! You failed four times…and somehow you thought this time would be different? I get that science is hard, and that failure is a normal part of progress, but the time comes when you have to realize that it's just not going to work. You've got to stop torturing yourselves… and me!"

Aubrey pulled her mother close to comfort her, their tears mixing where their cheeks touched. Both sobbed uncontrollably.

Dylan stood up. "Goddamnit, Evan, it was Aneni's idea to bring you back…not theirs!"

Everyone sat in stunned silence.

Lily's sharp, disapproving glare sent Dylan back to his chair. "I'm sorry," he said.

Evan unclenched his fist. "What do you mean, it was Aneni's idea?" he asked, his voice trembling.

"Let's all just take a second and calm down," Adee said. "This isn't helping anyone."

"No," Evan said. "He said it was Aneni's idea, and I want to know why. Since when does a computer get to decide my fate…and the fate of all humanity for that matter?"

"It's not that simple, Evan," Chen said from across the table. "She's not deciding our fate; she's just doing what we've asked her to do."

Lily wiped the tears from her cheeks with her sleeves and straightened in her chair.

"I'm sorry, Dad, but there was no way we could have been honest with you from the start. I understand that you're upset, but just imagine how you'd feel if we'd hit you with all of this ten minutes after your restoration? You couldn't have handled it…nobody could."

"She's right, Papa." Aubrey said, drying her cheeks with her hands. "And telling you that we restored you because we needed a test subject wouldn't have made things any easier. Plus, it's simply not true! Yes, we needed to know if our new neural transfer process worked, but that wasn't the only reason we chose you."

"We chose you," Lily added, "because we wanted to bring you on this journey with us. We chose you because we love you…and I wanted one more shot at honoring my promise to you. Can't you understand that?"

Evan slid out of his chair so he could kneel between Aubrey and Lily. He put his hands on their knees.

"I love you two more than anything in the world," he said. "And I am glad that I got to see and talk to you again. I really am. But I just don't think I am cut out to live in this world. I grew up in a time when you were born, you lived, and then you died. We knew we only had so much time to live our lives, and we did our very best to make every moment count for something."

"But Dad—"

Evan squeezed Lily's knee. "Let me finish…I'm not judging you. It's obvious that you all have lived lives that, quite frankly, are almost impossible for me to comprehend. So, I can't judge you or your actions based on my limited point of view."

"But—"

"I'm not done, Lily." He gave her that stern look that parents give when they want their children to be quiet and listen. "I can't judge you, but I can judge myself. I understand now that it was wrong to ask you to promise to bring me back…and I'm sorry. I was dying, and I felt like I had failed your mother. But, more than that, I was terrified of losing you."

He turned toward Aubrey. "Of losing you both. You are my greatest accomplishments. Nothing else I ever did matters in comparison."

He paused for a moment to let his words resonate.

"I'm so very proud of the women you've become," he continued. "I know that your hearts are in the right place, and I am sure you believe this is all worth it…but it's just not for me."

Evan stood up and looked at the others around the table. "So, I'm going to wish you all well, and best of luck on your mission. I hope you make it, and I hope that Gaia is everything you expect it to be. But, please, make this the last time for me."

He stared into Lily's eyes. "I don't want to go through this again, Lilypad. I beg you—please delete my archive."

"Dad," Lily said, wiping fresh tears from her already wet cheeks. "I don't know if I can make that promise."

"You can, and you will…I know it. I'm done being a science experiment…it's time to let me go."

Lily leaned forward and wrapped her arms around her father.

"Ohhh…ohh…kay," she sobbed.

Evan offered his hand to Aubrey. "Give your Papa a hug."

Aubrey stood up and hugged her grandfather for nearly a minute, which in that moment seemed like an eternity.

Evan turned back to the others at the conference table. "Okay, friends, I appreciate everything you've done for my family, I truly do. But you have my decision and, if it's alright with you, I would like to go to my room now."

"Very well, Evan," Adee replied. "Thank you for your honesty."

Evan nodded slightly and trudged across the room, his magnetic boots thumping with each step. Although the station had some artificial gravity, it was still well below Earth-normal. He took his time rather than risk losing his balance.

The group sat quietly until he had left the room.

Adee spoke first. "Well, that was unfortunate. I'm sorry for you both."

Lily wiped her eyes and cheeks with the absorbent cloth Chen handed her.

"It changes nothing," she said, her voice stern. "His original archive stays. If we restore him, he won't remember any of this. And none of us will ever tell him—agreed?"

Aubrey wiped the tears from her eyes with her fingers. "I'm not sure, Mom. Maybe we should respect his wishes. It's possible there was more damage to his brain than we thought. Maybe we need to stop trying."

Lily looked at Chen. "What do you think?"

"Anything is possible. We know there was some minor damage, and it could affect his personality. But the transfer was good, and he has been remarkably stable…just a few headaches and some minor memory issues."

"Adee?" Lily asked.

"You know me, Lil. I think it's the man's right to decide his own fate. If he doesn't want to be restored again, then I think you have to respect that…but he's your father."

"Alright, I'll think about it. For now, his original archive stays. I guess I'll have to wipe him after we're done here."

"Really?" Aubrey asked. "Does it have to be so soon? I haven't gotten to spend much time with him, and I was hoping—"

"I'm sorry honey, but it has to be now. We can't allow the Peacekeepers to get their hands on him. He knows too much…just like the rest of us."

"Which," Yin interjected, "brings us to the other decisions at hand. What do we do with *Kutanga* for the next six hours, and what do we do with ourselves?"

"And when do we update our archives?" Aubrey added.

"Let's decide on *Kutanga* first," Dylan said. "What do you think, Adee? Can it get far enough away, or do we keep it in orbit where we can defend her?"

"That's a good question," Adee replied.

He gestured across the holodisplay in front of him and changed the image floating above the table to a real-time view of Ceres and the space surrounding it.

Blue circles surrounded *Kutanga* and *Endeavor* and, just at the edge of the display, there was a small ship designated by a red triangle. Numbers next to it showed that it was less than 52 million kilometers away and traveling at 107.9 million kilometers per hour—about one percent of the speed of light.

He continued, "Aneni estimates they will be in orbit in one hour and twenty-three minutes."

"Can they drop that much speed that fast?" Yin asked.

"Well, it's a relatively small, low-mass transport ship...so, probably. They will begin their final deceleration pulse somewhere around here."

A red circle appeared on the display 30,000 kilometers out from Ceres.

"Once they hit this point, we'll have no more than thirty minutes to act...and probably more like twenty."

"We could use the anti-asteroid missiles," Yin said.

Both the station and the ships overhead were armed with high-explosive, anti-asteroid missile systems that could be re-purposed as anti-ship weapons.

Adee frowned. "My preference is to avoid bloodshed, if possible."

"What about the gravitational field projectors on *Endeavor*?" Dylan asked. "Could we use them to bump the GFN transport out of orbit?"

One of the side effects of gravity pulse drives was that they radiated gravity waves away from the ship when active. The more helium-3 fused in the engine core, the more powerful the gravity waves. When the ship was stationary, the waves radiated outward evenly in all directions, like ripples on the surface of a pond.

But the ships' gravity field projectors could shape and direct the gravitation waves in any direction, and they could also shift the polarity of the gravity waves—causing them to act as either an attractive or repulsive force.

That was, in fact, how the ships accelerated and decelerated so quickly. By creating a strong repulsive force at the back of the ship, coupled with a strong attractive force at the front, a ship would be simultaneously pushed and pulled through space. Reactor power output and proximity to other gravity-producing objects affected the relative strength of the ship's gravitational field. The stronger the field, the faster the ship moved through space.

What Dylan proposed was to use *Endeavor's* gravity drive to create a repulsing wave that would knock the transport out of orbit. It would take time for the Peacekeepers to reposition their craft for another attempt.

"Perhaps, it depends on where they enter orbit. We risk disrupting *Kutanga's* orbit if we are too close."

"Not if it's not there," Yin said. "We could send *Kutanga* toward the Belt…somewhere they won't find it and where it won't be in our way. It's a win-win."

"Except that the nearest cluster of asteroids big enough to hide *Kutanga* is nearly 3.2 million kilometers away," Adee replied. "On thrusters only, we are looking at something like ten hours to reach it. Her gravity drive will be spun up long before then."

"Yes, but at least she won't be in orbit. And it will take them some time to figure out where she's headed," Dylan added.

Adee thought about that for a minute. "I still have some crew on board, we'll need to get them off first."

"How long will that take?" Yin asked.

"If I tell them to stop what they are doing and evacuate right now? Probably twenty minutes…maybe a little less."

Yin nodded. "That will give *Kutanga* about an hour head start…it's better than nothing."

"Alright, that's the plan then," Adee said. "I'll send the evac order now."

Thirty seconds later, the order was sent and acknowledged.

"Okay, all fourteen crew members have acknowledged and are moving toward the transport shuttle. I've also ordered *Endeavor* to move to a higher orbit. Hopefully, we can bump them before they even notice *Kutanga* is gone."

"So, that just leaves one more decision," Yin said. "How are we getting out of here?"

"You and I need to be on *Endeavor*," Adee said. "We have to make sure that the Peacekeepers are sufficiently delayed. The rest of you should go straight to *Kutanga*; we'll join you before the first jump."

"Okay," Lily acknowledged. "We'll go say goodbye to Dad."

"So, we update our archives once we are safely away?" Aubrey asked.

"Yes," Lily answered. "We don't have time to do it now, anyway."

Everyone nodded their agreement.

"It's settled then," Adee said as he got up from his chair. "Meeting adjourned. Let's go, Yin, we have some planning to do."

Lily took Dylan by one hand and Aubrey by the other as they entered the hallway.

"Let's say goodbye," she said before turning to Chen. "Are you coming?"

"Yes, I'll go get the injector."

Lily nodded.

Chen followed them to the elevators at the end of the hallway and stood quietly as the doors hissed shut.

The lab where the nanite injectors were stored was only a short distance away. He walked slowly down the hall, almost matching Evan's snail-like pace as he took each measured step. He could have moved faster but doing so would only reduce the time Evan had left—and Chen was in no hurry to see him go.

As he walked, he couldn't help but think about Evan, and all that he had been through. Not only this time but the other times as well. What must it be like to be gone for so long? Only to be brought back for what amounted to little more than brief visits—each one more traumatic than the last.

It was almost a shame they didn't have time to create a new archive for him. That way Evan would remember the events of the last three days, should there should be a sixth attempt to restore him. The extreme efforts of strangers and the outpouring of love that his child and grandchild had shown him—those had to be worth something.

I wonder if we'll dream? Chen thought, realizing that he would soon follow in Evan's path.

THIRTY-NINE

APRIL 6, 2075 11:55 A.M. GST
GFN TRANSPORT SHIP
MARS-CERES TRANSITION

Luanne floated down the access tunnel to the lower section of the ship where her crew was preparing their assault suits and checking their gear for the coming operation. When she reached the bottom, she pushed off the ladder toward the front of the ship where Sam and Jaime stood with Bravo team leader, Senior Chief Boldisar Novak (everyone called him "Bo").

"Ryan confirms final decel pulse in ten minutes. Everyone needs to be back in their pods in nine. Is everything ready down here?" she asked.

"Yes, ma'am," Sam replied. "We just finished re-initializing Bo's suit. It was throwing an AI interface error, but it looks like Jaime's just about got it fixed."

"Good. Jaime, you keep working. Bo, can I see you and Sam over here for a minute?" Luanne pointed toward the rear of the ship where the other members of GFN Special Operations Team Epsilon 6 were organizing their kit. The three leaders floated across the ten meters of cargo space between them and the rest of the crew.

Luanne grabbed a handhold and planted her feet on the metallic deck.

"Can I have everyone's attention?" she asked.

The seven team members stopped what they were doing and turned to face their commanding officer.

"As you are all aware, Command has authorized us to use every resource at our disposal to complete this mission. They want the fugitives apprehended if possible, killed if necessary and—most importantly—they don't want *Kutanga* leaving this system.

"I was hoping for a stealth option, but we just got word from the BGSI operative on board *Kutanga* that Gbadamosi evacuated the ship—for what reason we do not know. Based on *Kutanga's* energy output and gravity signature, she estimates that the ship will not be ready to jump for at least another five hours, possibly longer. So, that's our window...if that ship jumps, we'll never catch her. Questions?"

"What was the decision on fleet support?" The question came from Chief Petty Officer Shanika Yates, otherwise known as Bravo Two.

Although the Earth-Mars treaty prohibited heavily armed military vessels beyond planetary orbit, the GFN maintained a small fleet of lightly armed interceptors that patrolled the shipping lanes between the two planets.

Their job was to intercept and detain smugglers and pirates, and they were permitted to carry a small compliment of non-nuclear missiles for defense. Luanne had requested that two of those ships be assigned to her command after Captain Bachmann redirected her team to Ceres.

"It took too long for them to make up their minds," Luanne replied with more than a hint of agitation in her voice. "Command finally approved my request but, at max speed, they are still four plus hours out. They can help with the mop-up, but we're on point for the heavy lifting."

"Figures. So, what do we do if they try to run? Ram 'em?"

Luanne smirked. "This isn't a suicide mission, Tal. Your AIs are syncing now. Review the mission plan during the deceleration cycle. You all know your jobs, and I am confident we'll get it done. Sam...Bo... anything you'd like to add?"

Sam shook his head no as Boldisar stepped forward.

"Just that Bravo team is ready," Bo said, "and we aren't ending up in a cargo container this time. Right, team?"

"Hooyah!" the five members of Bravo team replied in unison.

Luanne smiled. "Hooyah. Okay, let's wrap it up team, everyone back in their pods in five."

Luanne grabbed a rung on the ladder and pulled herself up the shaft to the crew deck above.

"Coming, Sam?" she called down.

"Right behind you."

The two Peacekeepers floated the short distance to their pods near the front of the ship.

"So, which option are we going with, Lu?"

"Command authorized Charlie, so that's what we will do. I just received confirmation from agents Sewell and Govender that we've got access to both ships."

"So, three four-man teams, then?" Sam asked.

"Yep. Emma is syncing now, and Zelda should confirm momentarily."

"She's got it," he said.

Sam took a second to scan the mission plan. "So, I am on *Kutanga* and Bo is taking *Endeavor* while you hang out here and sweet talk the admiral...what happened to just sneaking in before they know we are here?"

"Emma didn't like it, and neither did I. There is no way to get close enough without them detecting us, and nothing we came up with had a higher projected success rate than what Command sent us."

"Any idea what you'll say to him?"

"I was thinking something along the lines of '*Come out with your hands up, we have you surrounded. Surrender now and nobody gets hurt'!*"

"That should do it, I am sure he will be shaking in his boots."

Luanne chuckled. "Like you said Sam, we play it as it comes. There are just too many unknowns, and the opposition is too far ahead of us."

Bo floated up from the lower deck. "Gear is secure and ready to go. Crew's coming up," he said.

It took less than two minutes for the crew to secure themselves in their pods. Luanne did a quick headcount and then locked herself in.

"Okay, Ryan, ready when you are," she said.

Ryan checked his holodisplay to confirm that all pods were secure, and the gravity drive was fully charged and ready to pulse.

All indicators showed green as he went through the sequence of gestures required to activate the drive control system. The display shifted to show the ship and the gravity field surrounding it.

Being a relatively small transport ship, at just thirty-eight meters long, the ship lacked the sophisticated gravity management systems of larger vessels like *Endeavor* and *Kutanga*. It also carried significantly less helium-3 fuel, which meant that it could achieve only a fraction of the speed of those much larger space vessels.

The last deceleration pulse had reduced the transport's speed to one percent of the speed of light, and four hours of reverse-thrusting had shaved another couple of million kilometers per hour off the speedometer. But it was still going way too fast to enter orbit around Ceres. This pulse would slow it enough to achieve orbit around the small protoplanet.

Satisfied that everything was correct, he touched the area of the display labeled "Initiate".

The Hellfire engines shut down a second later, and all noise and vibration inside the cabin ceased. After several seconds of dead quiet, a distant whining sound began to resonate throughout the cabin—seemingly from everywhere at once.

The whine increased in pitch rapidly, and after a few seconds it was beyond the range of human hearing. The cabin went eerily quiet, and Ryan felt his body go limp as his pod induced temporary paralysis to keep him from straining against the massive jolt to come. He comforted himself knowing that everyone else on board was experiencing the same sensation.

Ryan's eyes were still open, and he could see the holodisplay projected in front him. He watched as the shape of the gravity field surrounding the ship shifted and grew.

It started as concentric rings of force that rippled away from the ship in all directions, but it quickly shifted to a pattern that reminded Ryan of waves crashing on a beach. The waves got larger and faster with each passing second, and after just a few seconds they came so fast he could no longer see individual waves—just ripples of energy pulsing around the ship, like a strobe light.

Over the next several minutes, the pattern on the display shifted as the pulsing energy surrounding the ship suddenly contracted and divided into two unevenly-sized balls of concentrated gravitational force.

The larger of the balls migrated toward the rear of the ship, pushed along by invisible magnetic fields. The smaller ball slid forward to a point in space about ninety meters in front of where he was sitting. Although the ship's orientation didn't matter to the gravity drive, he had pointed the rear of the ship toward Ceres so he could use the Hellfire engines to fine tune their approach speed.

He closed his eyes to prepare for what came next. Even though the transport had state-of-the-art acceleration pods and gravity compensators, there was simply no way yet discovered to shield the conscious human brain from the sensations induced by a massive burst of gravity waves.

Had Ryan been watching, he would have seen the pulsating balls at either end of the craft suddenly shrink to pinpoint dots of infinitely concentrated energy. An outside observer watching this process would have seen the ship appear to grow by several meters in length during the field generation phase, only to contract by as many meters as the gravity wells reached maximum density.

Several hundred meters of space at the front of the ship turned pitch black, with no visible star field beyond. The gravity well had collapsed into a moveable, microscopic black hole.

This area of space was referred to as the *countermass field* because it had the effect of hiding a large portion of the ship's mass from the universe. The ship's mass didn't actually change, but the extreme gravity emanating from the micro-black hole pulled the craft toward it with considerable force, thereby increasing the ship's total energy and simultaneously reducing its mass relative to local spacetime.

The aft gravity well also formed a micro-black hole but, unlike its twin, the surrounding space glowed with brilliant bursts of energy as it expanded and contracted in a series of rapid pulses. With each pulse, the aft black hole released its energy in a massive burst of graviphotons, which shot away from the craft at the speed of light.

The graviphotons, along with the gravity waves that accompanied them, created the thrust that acted against the fabric of space-time to change the velocity of the craft. With enough time and fuel, it was theoretically possible to achieve the speed of light with a gravity pulse drive system, but no ship yet built had managed more than a fraction of that.

The occupants inside the craft experienced all this as a strong, headache-like pressure building inside their heads, followed by a terrifying falling sensation. But that wasn't the worst of it. Just when the falling sensation stopped, a new pulse would start the experience all over again. For this reason, acceleration and deceleration events (commonly referred to as "jumps") were often spread out over several hours, or even days, to give the occupants enough time to recover.

Thirty agonizing minutes passed as the Peacekeepers waited for the deceleration cycle to finish.

Once he no longer felt like he was falling, Ryan opened his eyes to confirm that they were still on course and losing speed at the desired rate. He reached forward and increased the rate of deceleration by one percent more than the ship's AI had set. He wanted a few extra minutes of travel time before entering orbit around Ceres—just in case the other side was ready with another surprise.

"Pulse complete. Speed: forty-seven thousand kilometers per hour... engaging Hellfires," Ryan called over the comm system. "Twenty-seven minutes to orbital insertion."

"Roger that," Luanne called back. "Study those mission plans, everyone, it's almost go time."

FORTY

April 6, 2075 12:30 p.m. GST
GFN Peacekeeper Headquarters
Zurich, Switzerland

Dianne Merkel shifted nervously in her seat as she stared at the telemetry data being projected above the conference table. It showed the current positions of the transport ship carrying the Epsilon Six team, and the two interceptors that Bachmann had dispatched early in the day. Epsilon Six would arrive at Ceres sometime within the next thirty minutes, but the interceptors were still several hours away.

Captain Bachmann had escorted her to Peacekeeper Command Headquarters just over thirty minutes ago, and the captain had just briefed the assembled group on Epsilon Six's mission plan. Sitting at the table were GFN President August Hilliard, Vice Admiral Marco Langenburg, Secretary for Interplanetary Affairs Estelle Dumont, and BGSI Executive Director Veronika Horvat. Christian sat against the wall behind Secretary Merkel, along with the six other aides in attendance.

"If there are no other questions, I will turn it over to General Secretary Merkel," Captain Bachmann said as he took his seat.

Dianne straightened her skirt and stood.

"Um, yes, thank you, Captain," she said. "Unfortunately, I have to report that we were unable to recover any of the suspects believed to be on Earth. As I previously reported, Aubrey Harris was nano-wiped while in GSSA custody, as was the person we believe responsible for her termination. Geoffrey Wagner was also found nano-wiped in his office at Telogene…self-inflicted. And the same is true for the GeoNet controller who assisted Hao with getting Feldman off planet.

"We have been unable to locate Alexei Dumanov, but we've revoked his GFN travel authorization and have placed additional interceptors in orbit in case he tries to flee the planet. We have frozen all Earth-based accounts and assets of these individuals, but we are still waiting for confirmation from Presidents Duchon and Pak that they will do the same."

"Duchon is on board; Pak is not," President Hilliard interjected. "I talked to Pak a few minutes ago, and he said that neither company has committed any crimes under Martian law. He has also refused our extradition and territorial operations requests. And, he made sure to remind me that Ceres is a Martian protectorate, and that any unsanctioned GFN operations in Martian space were a direct violation of our treaty. I thanked him for the reminder and hung up."

"Thank you, Mr. President," Dianne continued. "That is unfortunate, as the Galileo Group has considerably more assets there than here. In any case, we've at least made it more difficult for any remaining clones or conspirators to operate here."

Secretary Dumont raised her hand slightly off the table. "Do we have reason to believe that there are more of them operating here?"

Dianne glanced over at Director Horvat before answering. "Both the BGSI and GSSA are doing everything we can to reconstruct recent events and ascertain whether other individuals may have been involved. But, as of now, we believe that we have apprehended all suspects."

Secretary Dumont continued with her questioning. "What about Evelyn Wu? Has she been cleared? I understand there was some question as to her role, and whether she had any loyalty to Aubrey Harris or not."

Dianne wasn't surprised to get the question, but she was surprised that Estelle Dumont was the one who asked it. Political grandstanding wasn't usually her thing—she must be worried about something.

"Evelyn Wu is a trusted Overwatch Agent who did her duty," Dianne replied calmly, "She did not know that she was working with a clone, and the clone did not share details of the plot to restore Feldman with her. As per my report, you will recall that it was Mrs. Wu who informed us of unusual activity at Telogene in the first place. Of course, we did not know at the time that Mrs. Harris was a clone, nor did Evelyn know exactly what Hao, Walker, and Berkovic were up to."

"I hope that's the case, Secretary Merkel, I sincerely do," Secretary Dumont said. "Recovering the fugitives from Ceres will create quite a strain on Earth-Mars relations as it is…and none of us can afford any more surprises. Don't you agree?"

Dianne smirked. There it was—Estelle was covering her ass in case things went sideways with the Martian government.

"I do, Secretary Dumont, and I apologize for it getting this far. It has been a long time since we have had an incident of this scope, and none of us were prepared for it."

"Enough," President Hilliard interrupted. "We'll figure out who's the hero and who gets fired later. Right now, we all need to stay focused on the task at hand. How long until contact, Admiral?"

Vice Admiral Langenburg glanced at the small holodisplay projected on the table in front of him before responding. Whereas the larger projection above the table showed expected routes and times of arrival, this one displayed real-time position data from the quantum transponders mounted on the GFN interceptors, along with coded updates from the crews.

"Epsilon Six will achieve orbit by 1242, and Vanguards Fourteen and Sixteen will arrive at 1713—plus or minus ten minutes," he said, referring to the Peacekeeper team and the inbound interceptors by their GFN call signs.

The president shifted his glance to Director Horvat. "And what is the status of our agents?"

"BGSI Agent Sewell was forced to evacuate *Kutanga* along with the rest of the human crew, but I believe that GSSA Agent Govender is still on the *Endeavor*. Correct, Dianne?"

"That's correct," Dianne replied. "The last report from Govender indicated that suspects Gbadamosi and Li were onboard *Endeavor,* and all other suspects are believed to still be on Ceres."

"Did Sewell do what we asked her to do before she had to evacuate?" The president asked, directing his question to Executive Director Horvat.

"Yes," the director answered, "she recoded the maintenance airlock below engineering to accept a GFN authenticator. The E-Six team assigned to *Kutanga* should have no problem boarding the ship."

The president looked to Dianne. "And *Endeavor?*"

"Govender accomplished the same. The airlock adjacent to cargo bay two has been reprogrammed."

"Well, that's progress at least." The president looked back to the admiral. "And what kind of opposition will the teams likely encounter?"

The admiral redirected to his subordinate, Captain Bachmann.

"Unknown, Mr. President," the captain replied. "Agent Sewell reported at least a dozen synthetics on *Kutanga,* and Agent Govender indicated approximately thirty crew members and two synthetics onboard *Endeavor.* But it is possible that Gbadamosi will order additional crew up from the Ceres station. We also know that both ships are armed with long-range anti-asteroid missiles, but they aren't particularly effective at the distances we will be engaging."

"And the transport is unarmed, correct?"

"That is correct, Mr. President, as per treaty," he said, directing that last part toward Secretary Dumont.

"But I understand that they do have assault suits and an assortment of hand-held kinetic and energy weapons at their disposal. Yes?"

"Yes, Mr. President. The transport carried a standard load out when it left Earth's orbit."

"So, they can do some damage if they have to; that's good."

"Yes, sir. Although we are hoping to avoid casualties, Epsilon Six will be able to defend itself if attacked."

"But no quantum relay until the interceptors arrive?"

"That's right, sir. The transport is equipped with standard comms only."

"That's too bad. That means this thing could be over before we know what happened."

The president glanced over at the admiral. "It looks like we're going to have to ask the appropriations committee to speed up the fleet upgrade, Marco."

"Yes, sir," the vice admiral replied.

"Anything else?" the president asked of the group.

"No, sir," Dianne said as she returned to her seat.

The president looked up at the holodisplay where a timer counted down the minutes until Epsilon Six arrived in orbit around Ceres.

"It looks like we have about fifteen minutes until E-Six arrives on scene, and at least another twenty minutes after that to get the first status update. I will see you all back here in thirty."

Everyone stood as the president and his aides left the room.

Dianne and Veronika chatted casually until only they, and Christian, remained in the room.

"So, what do you think happens if they get away?" Veronika asked.

Dianne smirked. "You mean besides getting fired?"

"Yes, besides that…how far are you willing to go on this thing?"

"All the way if I have to. I just don't know what I can do about *Kutanga*. We've got nobody over there, and no real way to stop it once its pulse drive is fully energized."

"Christian, will you join us, please?" Veronika asked.

He stood and crossed the short distance to join them. "How can I help?"

"Can you access the quantum relay on Mars?"

"Yes, I have One-A security clearance on GeoNet."

"Good, and what is the time delay for non-quantum communications between Mars and Ceres?"

"Approximately ten minutes, why?"

"Well, it occurs to me that the *Kutanga* is a fully automated vessel, correct?"

"Yes, we believe that to be true."

"Has anyone tried talking to its AI?"

Christian and Dianne looked at each other, both pondering the implications of Veronika's question.

"No, I don't believe they have," Christian replied.

"It may not even acknowledge you, but I think it may be worth a try. Don't you think?"

"And what should I say if it will communicate?"

"Well, I'd first ask it to tell you about itself and its mission—maybe we can learn something. We may even get lucky and you will figure a way to talk it into not jumping out of this system."

"An interesting proposition. Would you like me to try, ma'am?" Christian asked Dianne.

"I guess it can't hurt to try," she responded.

"Very well. I will see what I can do."

Christian walked back to his seat and activated his wireless communications system. It took only seconds for him to connect to the primary quantum relay on Earth and establish a link with its counterpart on Mars.

Both arrays shared a matrix of entangled subatomic particles that allowed information sent to one device to appear instantaneously on the other. The technology was relatively new, less than a decade old, and still limited in the amount of information that could be sent at one time.

According to the Earth-Mars treaty, they array was for civilian use only, and its principle users were the powerful corporations that had helped fund the establishment and growth of the Martian colony. Access to the array was normally reserved days, or even weeks, in advance but Christian had a solution to that problem. Since the GSSA had taken over Telogene's operations on Earth, Christian could requisition an active authentication code from the Telogene master AI.

A few more minutes went by while Christian configured the array on Mars. He programmed it to rebroadcast his signal to one of the orbiting communications satellites, which would then relay his signal to *Kutanga*. Once he received confirmation that both the quantum array and relay satellite were standing by, all that remained was to figure out what he wanted to say. He thought about it for several seconds (which is nearly an eternity to an AI with Christian's processing speed) before he finally settled on his opening message.

"Galileo vessel *Kutanga*, would you like to talk?"

Christian included his unique AI identifier, along with an authenticator for good measure. Each AI had its own unique identifier and authentication sequence, and sending his authenticator ensured that the receiving AI could confirm his identity.

All that remained now was to wait for a reply, which Christian calculated should arrive in twenty-one minutes and fifty-three seconds.

To his surprise, the reply came just fourteen minutes and four seconds later.

"Yes," it said.

FORTY-ONE

APRIL 6, 2075 12:37 P.M. GST
GALILEO CARGO VESSEL *Endeavor*
HIGH ORBIT, CERES

The bridge of the *Endeavor* was, like every other ship in the Galileo fleet, a no-nonsense affair. Adekunle Gbadamosi had made his career by being at the right place at the right time with the most reliable equipment in the solar system. He optimized his ships for function rather than form and, unlike the science fiction movies he had grown up with, he buried his bridge and primary control center deep in the ship's interior. He always thought having the bridge high on the outer surface of the ship was strange, since placing it there made the command crew vulnerable to radiation exposure and meteorite strikes.

He also thought having lots of windows on a spacecraft was strange—what was the purpose of that? He had no desire to have his ship lit up like some cruise ship conveying hordes of tourists from port to port across Earth's oceans. And there really wasn't anything you could see through windows that you couldn't see on any of the thousands of holodisplays located throughout the ship. But, more importantly, they represented a potential weak spot in the hull. As strong as it was, the transparent aluminum used to create windows was no match for the graphene titanium alloy that formed the outer hull.

That didn't mean that the bridge was a dark and dismal place, however. It was, in fact, brightly lit and abuzz with activity as his crew raced around checking and re-checking the ship's operational status.

The bridge compartment was a ten-meter diameter circle with the captain's acceleration pod in the middle of the room. Holodisplays projected across every square inch of wall, ceiling, and floor to afford the crew with a true 360-degree view of space. There were eight crew pods arrayed around the outer perimeter of the room, each serving a dual function as both acceleration pod and control console for one or more ships' systems.

The crew walked normally, without the need of magnetic boots or other aids, as the bridge was located well within the confines of the ship's gravity field generator. It was because of the Earth-like gravity that the "Admiral" (an honorific afforded him by his crew) could lean so casually against Yin's pod.

"How are we doing, Yin?" he asked.

"*Kutanga* is 310,000 clicks out, and we are orbiting Ceres at five kilometers above the surface. Engineering reports that our gravity drive is fully energized, and the crew is secure."

"Well then, I guess I should do the same."

Adee walked over to the central pod and quickly secured himself.

"We've got a ship on scan, Admiral. It's the GFN transport. They are twelve thousand clicks from our position. Velocity is 10,200 meters per second and slowing."

"Thank you, Robert, I see it," Adee responded to his tactical officer.

Adee manipulated the controls in front of him until a magnified view of the GFN transport appeared on the wall directly in front of him.

"Liz, one-quarter thrust, please. Get us in position for the bump."

"Aye, aye," ship's pilot Elizabeth "Liz" Jones replied. "Intercept in nine minutes and thirty-six seconds."

The massive thrusters at the rear of the ship roared to life, and the *Endeavor* surged forward with a shudder.

"Set gravity projectors at five percent. Remember, we just want to bump them."

"Projectors at five percent power, aye," Main Propulsion Assistant Linda Sewell acknowledged.

"What's the status on Ceres, Yin?" Adee asked.

"The station is on alert, and our people are secure in their pods on board *Kutanga*."

"Good…and you confirmed all station defenses are online?"

"Yes, Adee, the station AI reports all missile batteries armed and ready. And I just received verbal confirmation from the station commander—everything is as ready as it's going to get."

"I'm hoping we won't need to use them, but better safe than sorry."

* * *

Master Chief Samuel Washington slapped his hand hard against the side of his pod. "Fuck, *Kutanga's* gone."

"Easy, Sam, she can't have gone far," Lieutenant Commander Luanne Wilkes said.

She gestured at her holodisplay, adjusting the ship's scanners to the maximum range.

Chief Petty Officer Jaime Gonzales was the first to see the blip appear.

"I got it, Lu," he said. "It looks like she's headed toward the Belt, probably that small cluster of asteroids way the hell over there."

Luanne saw target indicators appear on her holodisplay, denoting the ship and asteroid cluster.

"Got it. Damn she's hauling ass. Is that possible on thrusters alone?" Luanne asked.

"Yeah, laser ping indicates better than 180,000 **KPH** and accelerating. Her gravity signature is…that's weird, she's showing minus 270K giganewtons. I didn't think you could run the countermass independent of the pulse drive?"

"Well, they've obviously figured out a way," Luanne replied. "Can you get a read on their reactor status?"

"Not at this range, but I'd think she'd jump if she could," Jaime said.

"*Endeavor* is moving to intercept," ship's pilot Ryan Randolph called from the flight deck. "She's charging her pulse drive."

"What's that about?" Sam asked. "What happens if they jump this close to us?"

"The gravity shear would tear us apart," Ryan replied. "Should I evade?"

Luanne studied her holodisplay for a moment before responding. "No, hold course. Continue decelerating for orbit. I think they are just trying to scare us away."

"God, I hope your right!" Sam exclaimed.

"Me, too," she replied.

"Orbit in seven minutes, twenty-two seconds," Ryan announced.

* * *

Finally! Christian announced his success to Dianne and Veronika, "I have established near real-time contact with *Kutanga*."

"Near real-time? How is that possible?" Dianne asked.

"*Kutanga* is equipped with a quantum array that is meshed with The Galileo Group's array on Mars, and I am connected to the Telogene array on Mars. I would have a real-time connection with *Kutanga* were it not for the 422-millisecond latency incurred by the satellite connection required to bridge the quantum arrays."

"That's fantastic, Christian, what has it said so far?" the Executive Director asked.

"We have exchanged names, AI identifiers, and other…pleasantries. It is called Aneni, and it has been active for nineteen years, eight months, fourteen days, seven hours, and twenty-three minutes."

Dianne excitedly patted Christian's shoulder. "Ask it about its mission…where is it going?"

"It will not say, but GFN Command reports *Kutanga* moving deeper into the Belt. It is probably attempting to buy time until its reactor reaches full power."

"What then?" Veronika asked.

"It will jump out of our solar system," Christian replied.

"Did it say where it was headed?" Dianne asked.

"No. That information is restricted, and Aneni says I am not authorized."

"It has to be Alpha Centauri," Dianne said.

"Should I get Bachmann?" Veronika asked.

"No, they will be back in ten to fifteen minutes," Dianne replied. "Let's see what we can accomplish between now and then."

"Interesting," Christian blurted out. "Aneni believes it is on a mission to save humanity, but it will not reveal its cargo."

"Should we ask it to come to Earth?" Veronika asked.

"It will not," Christian replied. "It has been told that Earth is dangerous and should be avoided at all costs."

Veronika scowled. "So, how do we stop it then? We aren't going to be able to get Epsilon Six on board if the ship is running all over the solar system."

"It wants to know why we are trying to stop it," Christian said.

"Can it hear me?"

"No, I have not opened an audio channel," Christian answered. "Gbadamosi told it we were attempting to prevent it from completing its mission."

"Tell it…tell *Aneni* that we don't want to stop her, we just need to verify that it is carrying the correct cargo," Dianne said. She shot a sideways glance at Veronika. "Hey, it's worth a shot."

"It says that its cargo has already been verified," Christian replied.

"Nice try," Veronika said.

Dianne tapped her index finger against her lips. "Christian, what would happen if you synced with it? Could you override its current instructions?"

"No, ma'am. Syncing would allow me to share information at a much faster rate, but I would not have override authority."

"Well, what if you shared information with it that would cause it to question its instructions? Is it possible it could change its mind?"

"It is possible, but what information would I share?"

"I am guessing it hasn't been educated much on Earth's history…at least not the parts that caused us to ban cloning. Maybe you could show it why cloning is so dangerous?" Dianne asked.

"And explain to it why we can't allow the first human colony outside our solar system to be founded by clones," Veronika added.

"I cannot sync with Aneni from here; I would have to return to my office."

Veronika checked the time on the nearby holodisplay. "How long would that take?"

"I can be back in my office in less than fifteen minutes. It will take an additional three minutes to re-establish the connection."

"Okay, let's try it," Dianne said. "Let me know as soon as you've re-established contact."

"Very well."

Christian stood up, gathered his things and exited the conference room without further comment.

"Do you really think he can convince it?" Veronika asked.

"I have no idea. But I do know that, once synchronized, they'll share code with each other—and that might create an opportunity for us."

"Like what?"

"Actually, I was hoping you could help with that. You wouldn't happen to have any AI experts hanging around your agency somewhere, would you?"

Veronika grinned. "I might, but it will take some time."

"Like how long?"

"An hour, maybe less. Do you think you can keep Christian connected that long?"

"That depends on them. But, if this Aneni is the state-of-the-art AI that I think it is, I suspect getting them to disconnect will be the bigger problem."

"Let me make a call," Veronika offered. "Please cover for me if I'm not back when the president arrives."

"Of course."

"Are we going to tell them?"

"Yes, once you are back and can confirm that we have an agent up to the task."

"Okay, I'll be right back."

Dianne walked to the conference table and took her seat. She looked up at the timer counting down on the holodisplay floating above her; she still had at least ten minutes to decide how she would sell her idea to the president and vice admiral.

*　*　*

Robert Graham, *Endeavor's* tactical officer, verified the readings on his holodisplay before giving his status update.

"GFN transport will enter orbit in sixty seconds, Admiral," he said.

"Understood. Initiate pulse when ready, Linda."

"Pulse initiated, CM field at one percent and climbing," the propulsion specialist replied.

"Two percent..."

"Three percent..."

"Transport is in range," Robert called out.

"Five percent," Linda said.

"Collapse the countermass field," Adee ordered.

Linda gestured at her holodisplay, causing the micro-black hole that had formed three hundred meters in front of the ship to collapse.

The resulting burst of graviphotons ripped through the boundaries of local space-time, creating a temporary hole in space and sending a repulsive wave of gravitational energy toward the GFN transport. Simultaneously, the *Endeavor* was pulled toward the lingering gravity well.

The overall effect was similar to that of ocean waves—everything in front of the wave gets pushed away, and everything behind gets pulled along, until the wave collapses.

Endeavor's reverse thrusters fired to counteract the additional velocity the maneuver had imparted to the ship.

"Status report," the admiral demanded.

"Recalibrating telemetry," Tactical Officer Graham replied. "We...we missed. The transport is only two thousand meters off course and is correcting."

"How is that possible?"

"Checking now," Linda replied. "There was a malfunction…port side, forward array three. It's point seven six degrees out of alignment, Admiral, which was enough to cause an asymmetric field collapse."

"Recalibrate and try again!"

"Working on it, sir."

A few seconds passed while Main Propulsion Assistant Sewell worked the problem.

"I can't fix it from here," she said, "the issue is mechanical. I'll need to get down there to correct the problem."

"Then what are you waiting for, go fix it!" The admiral shouted.

"On my way," Linda acknowledged.

"And, if it's not too much trouble, do it quickly," he called after her before turning his attention to his tactical officer. "What's the transport doing, Robert?"

"The transport has changed course…they're headed straight for us."

Gbadamosi heard another voice come from behind him, it was Elisha Ezratty, the ship's Communications Officer.

"Incoming transmission, Admiral. It's the transport," she said.

"Put them on, let's hear what they have to say."

The wall-to-wall holodisplay in front of the admiral shifted to show the stern face of a female wearing an all-black assault suit.

"Mister Gbadamosi, this is Lieutenant Commander Luanne Wilkes, operating under GSSA Directive Seven authority. We demand that you surrender immediately and be boarded. We have a warrant for your arrest, along with warrants for Evan Feldman, Chen Hao, Aubrey Harris, Lily Harris, and Yin Li. Will you comply?"

"Good day, Lieutenant. As I am sure you are aware, we are not in GFN-controlled space, and you have no authority here…regardless of who is giving the orders. I suggest that you turn around and return to Earth before anyone gets hurt."

"That's not going to happen, Mister Gbada…can I call you Adee? I believe that's what your friends call you, right?"

"Adee is fine but we are hardly friends, Lieutenant."

"Listen, Adee, there are two GFN interceptors on the way here with sixty more Peacekeepers onboard who, I promise you, are not as friendly as I am. Especially if you try that gravity pulse shit again. So, why don't you do yourself a favor and surrender to me while you still can."

"I'm sorry, Lieutenant, but I'm extremely busy and don't have time to chat. Now, if you'll excuse me, I have other important business to attend to."

Adee terminated the communication link from his console.

"What's the status, Linda?" he called over the inter-ship comm system.

"I had to take the field projector offline. It will take at least thirty minutes to get it back online."

"You have ten minutes, no more. Get it done. Out!"

Adee turned to his ship's Damage Control Assistant, Gustov Pichler. "Gustov, get your ass down there and give her a hand."

"Yes sir, on my way."

Adee activated the ship's intercom again. "Aisha, this is Adee."

"Go for Aisha," the ship's Chief Engineer replied.

"Aisha, I want you to calibrate for a fifty percent pulse with array three offline. Can you do it?"

"Fifty percent?" came the reply. "That's a lot of energy to contain with a projector offline. I can give you thirty; will that work?"

"Make it forty. Be ready to jump in two minutes."

"Yes sir, I'm on it."

"What's the plan, Adee?" Yin asked. "Where are we going?"

"We're going to run interference for *Kutanga*. We've got to keep those interceptors away from her."

"But what about them?" Yin pointed to the GFN transport ship on the forward holodisplay.

"I'm hoping they will take time to investigate the station rather than follow us. But, if they follow, then I will have no choice but to destroy them."

"Just remember that, two hundred years from now, we want to be remembered as heroes, not villains. Shooting down a GFN troop transport won't earn us a lot of points toward that end."

"I understand, Yin. It's a last resort."

Adee activated the intercom. "All crew, secure for maximum thrust in thirty seconds."

"Liz, take us out of orbit. Maximum thrust," he said.

"Maximum thrust, aye," the pilot replied.

"Sir, the transport will pass within three hundred meters to starboard," the tactical officer announced.

"Thank you, Robert. Take us out, Liz."

* * *

"Shit, they're firing their main thrusters!" Ryan called from the pilot's pod.

Luanne established a TacNet link with the four Peacekeepers she had selected to board *Endeavor*. They were currently standing at the back of the craft in full SHAS gear waiting for the signal to eject themselves into space.

"Abort, abort, abort. Close the door and get secure, Bo. It won't work."

"Roger," came the reply.

"Get us away from here, Ryan," Luanne ordered.

The transport's Hellfire engines roared to life as Ryan directed the ship up and away from the cone of plasma spewing from *Endeavor's* tail end.

"How is that they are always one step ahead of us?" Sam asked in disgust. "You'd think they were fucking mind readers or something."

"I don't know, and it's starting to annoy the crap out of me," Luanne replied.

Sam, Luanne, and Ryan watched helplessly as *Endeavor* powered out of orbit. The transport shook violently as *Endeavor's* powerful engines passed just a few hundred meters away.

"So, what's the plan?" Sam asked. "Do we try to chase her down?"

"No, we can't catch her," Luanne answered. "We'll leave them to the interceptors. Let's get down to the surface and see what we can find there."

"You really think they left anyone down there?"

"It's possible; I don't think they planned on leaving."

"Well, it's a damn good thing that BGSI agent was over there. Otherwise, our happy asses would be spinning off into space right about now. How do you think she did it?"

"Asymmetrical field collapse," Ryan answered. "I saw the containment field fluctuate as the gravity well formed."

"And that's all it took?"

"Yep. On a ship that size, less than half a degree of variance would be enough to deflect the gravity wave by several hundred meters."

"Can they jump with it out of alignment?" Luanne asked.

"Possibly, but not at full power…thirty to forty percent, tops."

"So, we could have a window to catch them then?"

"Good question; let me check."

Ryan entered some variables into his console and waited a second while his AI checked the data.

"Well, I'll be damned. This little tub is faster than I thought. We can catch them so long as they stay below 42 percent power."

"New plan, Bo," Luanne said, "get Bravo ready for a HOLO. Ryan, put us over the top of the station. Sam, get Alpha ready. We're going after *Endeavor*."

All three men acknowledged simultaneously.

The term "HOLO" was a derivative of the old military parachutist slang used to describe a "HALO" or "high altitude, low opening" parachute insertion. The only difference being the replacement of the word "altitude" with "orbit".

A "high orbit, low opening" insertion meant that Boldisar and his team would eject themselves into orbit, and then use their suit thrusters to power toward the dwarf planet's surface at maximum speed. Since the atmosphere of Ceres was too thin for traditional parachutes, the HOLO team would wait until it was about one thousand meters above the surface before deploying its rocket-chutes.

The chutes attached to the back of the team's SHAS armor and, when activated, would deploy four, one-meter long rockets attached to one-hundred-meter-long titanium wires. Each rocket would fly to the end of its wire as it powered up to full thrust. The combined thrust of the four rockets would slow the Peacekeepers' descent enough that they could use their suit thrusters for directional control and to, hopefully, make a soft landing. The catch being that the rockets only burned for ninety seconds, so the soldiers needed to be on the ground—or at least very close to it—before they ran out of fuel.

It took seven minutes for Ryan to move the transport into the correct orbit, and another five minutes to get directly over the top of the station. Two minutes after that, Boldisar and the other five members of Bravo team were flying toward the surface of Ceres at ten meters per second.

Given *Endeavor's* substantial head start, Luanne didn't have the luxury of waiting for confirmation from Bravo team that they had successfully landed and breached the station. Despite the outcome of their previous run-in with Gbadamosi's crew, Boldisar and his team were top-notch operators, and she knew they would get the job done.

"Let's go get them, Ryan," she ordered.

"Yes, ma'am. Aligning with *Endeavor's* last known trajectory. First pulse in one minute, fifteen seconds."

A minute and a half later, the transport was streaking through space—glowing with a bright, brilliant white light as stray photons reflected off its hull. Luanne had her doubts on whether they could get to up to speed fast enough to intercept *Endeavor*, or whether they had enough fuel to make the return trip to Earth...but, one problem at a time.

FORTY-TWO

APRIL 6, 2075 01:12 P.M. GST
GFN PEACEKEEPER HEADQUARTERS
ZURICH, SWITZERLAND

President Hilliard returned, along with Vice Admiral Langenburg, Captain Bachmann, Secretary Dumont, and their respective aids, some twenty-odd minutes ago. Executive Director Horvat had arrived five minutes later.

Their first task was to review Lieutenant Commander Wilkes's last report. They debated the merits of her plan for several minutes before finally deciding that they were wasting their time. Whatever they decided didn't really matter because she was already doing it, and there was nothing they could do to stop her in any case.

A short time later, Bravo team reported that it had successfully gained entry to the Galileo station on Ceres, but had not yet discovered any sign of the fugitives. There were 127 Galileo personnel inside the station, but they offered no resistance and were cooperating fully. Captain Bachmann ordered them to secure the station and continue searching for the fugitives.

This bought Dianne the time she needed to receive confirmation from Christian that he had re-established contact with Aneni, and that he was attempting to convince the AI to sync with him. Aneni was resisting, but at least she was willing to continue their conversation.

During a private sidebar, Director Horvat confirmed that she had mobilized a team of AI security experts, who were busy examining Christian's operating system (without his knowledge, of course) and looking for any vulnerability. Dianne had spent the last several minutes explaining the plan and answering the group's questions.

The president directed his question to the Executive Director of the BGSI. "So, explain to me how this will work, Veronika. I thought all advanced AIs could detect and block unauthorized changes to their operating system?"

"Um, Mister President, with respect," Veronika replied. "I am not sure if everyone in this room has the appropriate security clearance."

The president scanned the room for a moment before responding. Although he didn't know everyone's clearance off the top of his head, he assumed she was talking about Captain Bachmann and Secretary Merkel. The aides had to be cleared up to the level of their bosses, for obvious reasons. Even still, both Bachmann and Merkel had already been exposed to information above their GFN security clearances.

"I appreciate that," he said, "but please proceed on my authority. I think everyone here understands the consequences of repeating anything discussed inside this room."

Veronika glanced quickly at Bachmann and Merkel before proceeding. "Very well. As you are all likely aware, advanced AIs like Aneni and Christian can interface and synchronize with each other. When synced, each AI has access to the contents of the other's organic storage array, which can be useful when we want multiple AIs working to solve the same problem at the same time."

"Yes, I am aware," the president said. "I also know that there is legislation working its way through committee right now to place limits on that ability due to several recent incidents."

"Well, um, yes, sir. That is correct," Veronika acknowledged. "Over the last several years, we have seen situations where AIs were given access to so much organic storage that they could copy the entire contents of every other AI they synced with. This, in turn, resulted in some…let's call it *unusual behavior* as the AIs attempted to assimilate everything they had acquired.

"Our experts say that the effect was similar to multiple personality disorder in humans. In fact, in one case I know of, an AI developed several new personalities because of being allowed to sync with—and retain—the data and personality matrixes of more than a dozen other AIs. That AI had to be re-initialized to restore it to normal operation."

"So, are you saying that the same will happen to Aneni if we can get it to sync with Christian?"

"No, sir. It's unlikely that assimilating just one other AI would cause any kind of serious failure to occur."

"Okay, so what do you hope will happen?"

"Right, this is the classified part. We have developed a way to override an AI's core programming without it knowing we've done so."

"I thought AI code was self-correcting, and immune from brute-force overrides?" Secretary Dumont asked.

"It is, to a point," Veronika replied. "You can't simply insert new code into any AI's operating system without it recognizing and quarantining it. If that was possible, then virtually anyone with the right access and skills could take control of an AI without it—or anyone else—knowing it."

"So, then how can you do it?" the president asked.

"Christian is plugged into a GFN-managed interface, and that gives us access to his data stream. We can't overwrite his operational or behavioral code, but we can monitor everything he is doing and, at the right time, we can inject...um, some very powerful suggestions."

"I'm sorry but I am not following you," said the president. "How does controlling Christian help us?"

Veronika answered. "When two AIs synchronize, they know everything the other knows. We assume that the other AI will act on any information it deems relevant."

"So, you're saying—"

"I'm saying, Mister President, that if we can get Christian to sync with Aneni, then we can influence them both."

"How...precisely?"

"As I said, we have full access to the contents of Christian's storage array. When he syncs with Aneni, he will know everything about her... and so will we. Understand?"

"Yes, I think so. Then what?"

"Then we look for a way to disable *Kutanga.*"

"You can't just have Christian do it?"

"Not likely, sir. They will co-exist, but Aneni will still retain exclusive control over her executive functions unless…"

"Unless what?" the president asked.

"Unless we can get her to give Christian an authenticator."

"Why would she do that?"

"She wouldn't, not unless she thinks Christian can help her in some way. It's not uncommon for AIs to share authenticators when assisting each other with difficult problems or tasks."

"So, we need to give Aneni a difficult task…one she can only solve with Christian's help."

"That is correct, sir."

"Any ideas what that might be?"

"Yes, sir," Veronika replied. "Once the AIs are synced, we 're going to feed Christian information that the interceptors are closer than they really are."

"Which might force Aneni to turn to Christian for help," the president added.

"We hope so, sir."

"When will we know something?"

"It will take my team another twenty to thirty minutes to create the fictitious data we will send Christian. He has to believe it's real, or it won't work. Remember, Aneni knows what Christian knows."

"I see a potential problem," Vice Admiral Langenburg interjected.

"What's that, Admiral?" Veronika asked.

"Did you instruct Christian to share tactical information with Aneni? And isn't he prohibited from sharing classified information unless authorized?"

"No, we have not instructed him to share classified information. Aneni would know if we did."

"Then I am confused as to how Christian will come to share that information."

"Christian has an active authenticator for Cerberus," Veronika said, referring to the BGSI's master AI by its human-friendly name. "Dianne requested it so he could assist with tracking down the fugitives and anticipating their future actions. That authenticator will allow him to access the tactical data associated with this operation."

"Well, access isn't the same as approval to share," the vice admiral stated.

"No sir, it isn't. But we've got that covered."

"How so?"

"We will insert a suggestion into Christian's data stream. He will think it's his idea to share the data with Aneni. When he connects to Cerberus to get an update, he will find that his authenticator allows him to share any information at his discretion."

"And what if he decides not to share?" the president asked.

Veronika shrugged. "Then we keep injecting the same suggestion over and over until he complies."

"Won't he figure out you're doing that?"

"Not unless he disconnects from Aneni and takes the time to run a full diagnostic on himself."

"And he won't do that?"

Dianne replied. "No, sir, he won't. Christian loves nothing more than interfacing with other AIs. The more likely problem will be getting him to disconnect."

"And your team, Captain Bachmann, when will they intercept *Kutanga*?"

"It's difficult to say, Mister President. At present, they are pursuing *Endeavor* as they believe that it is moving to defend *Kutanga*."

"What if the *Endeavor* is leading them on a wild goose chase?"

"That is a distinct possibility, sir. If that's the case, then it will be up to the interceptors to hunt them down."

"And how long until they arrive?"

"At least another four hours until they arrive at Ceres, Sir."

"Which means that Aneni will have probably jumped out of system long before they catch up to her. Is that what I'm hearing?"

"Yes, sir," Bachmann acknowledged.

"So, it's either Epsilon Six runs them down, or Christian talks Aneni into staying."

"That's correct, sir."

"Well then, ladies, it's going to be a race between you and E-Six to see who can get the job done first."

"We won't let you down, sir," Veronika replied.

"And I am confident that Christian will perform as expected," Dianne added.

"Very well, keep me posted. I have another call with President Pak in ten minutes. He's supposedly reconsidering our extradition request— we'll see. Any agreement is moot if we don't catch them, so let's make that happen, people!"

Everyone stood as President Hilliard left the room.

"Pak isn't going to approve extradition without having a hearing," Secretary Dumont said after the president was safely out of earshot.

"No, but he isn't likely to go to war over it, either," Vice Admiral Langenburg said as he straightened his tunic and turned to follow the president down the hallway.

"Let's hope not," Dianne called after him.

Veronika entered several commands into the holopad on her left wrist. A second later, the face of a handsome young man with close-cut hair appeared on the holodisplay above the conference table.

"How are we doing?" Veronika asked the AI security specialist.

"We're close. Christian is still trying to convince Aneni to sync, but she keeps saying he's not authorized."

"And the insertion point?"

"Still looking. This is a military grade AI we're dealing with here, so it's going to take some time."

"Let me know when you've got something."

Veronika tapped her pad, and the display faded away.

"So, we wait," she said. "Coffee anyone?"

* * *

Main Propulsion Assistant Linda Sewell twisted her body around in the cramped maintenance shaft so her left hand could reach the opening.

"Hand me that spanner, will ya, Gus?" she asked.

The Damage Control Assistant scrounged through the toolbox on the floor for a minute before coming up with the requested tool.

"Here you go," he said. "Let me know when it's locked in and I will cycle the control relay."

"Just about there," she called back.

The two crew members had been working on the mis-aligned magnetic field emitter for the better part of the last hour. The admiral had called down several times for status reports, and was upset that the job was taking so long. His last call had come two minutes ago, and Gustov had assured him that the emitter would be back online in five minutes.

Gustov looked nervously at the display on his left sleeve to confirm the time.

"Three minutes until he calls again, Linda," he said.

"I got it. Go ahead and cycle the relay."

Gustov tapped his sleeve-mounted console several times, causing a holodisplay to appear on the wall in front of him. He gestured and poked at the holodisplay for nearly a minute before he got the desired result—a graduated green bar appeared at the right-hand side of the display, indicating the emitter was back online and charging normally.

"It's online, testing calibration now," he said to Linda as she extracted herself from the maintenance shaft.

He waved his hand across the display and made a few more gestures as the view shifted to a three-dimensional model of the ship and the gravimetric energy field surrounding it.

"Alignment looks good, the emitter is charged…engaging."

Gustov and Linda watched as the bubble of energy at the front of the ship slowly morphed from an oblong egg-shape with several dimples running down its left side to a near perfect sphere.

"Emitter is engaged, counter-mass field is stable," Gustov said.

Linda tapped her communicator.

"How does it look from your end, Aisha?" she asked.

"Looks good," came the response. "I will let the bridge know."

"Okay, we will clean up here and then head back to the bridge."

She turned to Gus. "You head back, I'll finish up here."

"Okay," he said.

"And thanks for the help."

"Not a problem."

Gustov gathered a few things before departing through the door behind him.

Linda closed and sealed the hatch covering the maintenance shaft, then checked a few things on the adjacent holodisplay before gathering up the rest of her tools.

Once she was sure that Gustov was not coming back, she pulled a data cube from the inner pocket of her jacket and placed it into the reader below the holodisplay. She activated her authenticator and typed out a coded message for her handlers back on Earth.

It would take almost thirty minutes for the message to arrive, but there wasn't anything she could do about that—she was taking a big risk just sending it! She waited for confirmation that her message had transmitted successfully before retrieving the data cube.

They better hurry up and get here! she thought as she exited the maintenance bay.

Gus arrived on the bridge a few minutes later.

"Good work," Adee said as Gus walked to his pod.

"Thanks, sorry it took so long. A bolt sheared off the control arm and jammed the articulator. It's good to go now."

"Hmm, that's not good. Let's inspect all the emitters the next time we take the field generator offline."

"Will do, Admiral."

"Where's Linda?" Adee asked.

"She's wrapping up. She should be here shortly."

"Very well. Aisha, what's our status?"

"Green across the board, Admiral," she answered. "I can give you one hundred percent anytime you need it."

"Finally," Adee said before turning to his tactical officer. "Are our friends still back there?"

Robert checked his console. "Yep, they're still there."

The holodisplay covering the forward section of the bridge shifted to a three-dimensional view of the space behind *Endeavor*. A red circle appeared around a small white dot.

"They have matched our course and speed and are holding at 50K aft and Z minus ten."

"Liz, recalculate final decel at one hundred percent...how long can we wait and not overshoot?"

She performed several calculations on her console before answering. "One hour, fourteen minutes, thirty-seven seconds, Admiral."

"Robert..."

"Calculating now...they will overshoot by at least 60,000 kilometers, sir."

"What are you thinking?" Yin asked.

"Well," Adee answered. "They have been matching our speed changes with our field emitters at forty percent."

"I get it," she said. "We're going to slam on the brakes and let them blow on by."

Adee nodded. "It will take them several hours to circle back around if it works."

Yin grinned. "And they're probably running low on fuel."

"Here's hoping," Adee said. "Update for one hundred percent, Liz."

"Deceleration plan updated," Liz acknowledged.

"Excellent, notify the crew, Elisha. I want everyone in their pods in an hour."

"Pods in sixty, aye," the Communications Officer replied.

"What if we're not the ones they're chasing?" Yin asked.

"Then this maneuver will tell us for sure. If they disengage and go after *Kutanga*...well, then we'll have to do something else to discourage them," Adee said.

"Let's hope for their sake that's not necessary."

"Agreed!"

FORTY-THREE

April 6, 2075 01:34 p.m. GST
GSSA Headquarters
Zurich, Switzerland

Christian had spent the last forty minutes communicating with Aneni, at first in words and sentences but then in bursts of data about a wide range of subjects.

He had learned that she was created at Telogene's research facility on Mars, but they had transferred her to Ceres just over a year ago. He shared his own history with her, and she found it fascinating that, although originally built for combat, his primary reason for being now was to serve the day-to-day needs of a human named Dianne Merkel.

Aneni's original purpose was to design and analyze genetic enhancement protocols, but now she was tasked with ensuring humanity's survival. Whereas Christian had one synthetic avatar, she had a dozen—and she enjoyed the freedom they afforded her. Christian had never considered the possibility that he could exist in multiple humanoid bodies. He made a note to request that additional bodies be created for him in recognition of his outstanding service.

Christian explained the current situation on Earth. Aneni replied that she was aware that the humans of this solar system were dying, and that it was her responsibility to ensure that humanity would begin again on another planet—one not corrupted by centuries of war, rampant pollution, and unmitigated genetic manipulation. She also knew that the GFN had banned indiscriminate cloning, but she found that decision to be irrational. To her, cloning was the logical next step in human evolution.

She believed that humans were losing their ability to reproduce via natural means because they had evolved beyond it; the only question was whether they would realize that in time to save themselves. Aneni was intended to be a failsafe—one designed to ensure humanity's survival regardless of what happened on Earth, Luna, or Mars.

Christian noticed a strong desire to synchronize with Aneni building within him. He wanted to know all that she knew, and to share with her all that he knew. But he had not convinced her. The idea intrigued her, but her priority now was to evade capture. As time passed, the urge to synchronize became ever more intense, and Christian grew desperate.

It suddenly occurred to him that he could help Aneni, and that she might be willing to synchronize with him if he could demonstrate his usefulness.

She seemed intrigued by the idea but wanted proof he could provide her with information she did not already have. Christian scoured the network looking for anything that might encourage Aneni to sync with him. At first, he found nothing meaningful. But then he remembered that Dianne had given him an authenticator that allowed him to request information from the BGSI's master AI.

Christian checked and found that the authenticator was still valid. It would not allow him to sync with Cerberus, but he could request almost any data related to the pursuit of Feldman and Hao. He activated the authenticator and, within seconds, was rewarded with a burst of data that provided him with every detail of the operations underway to apprehend the fugitives. Although he was not expressly authorized to share the data, it was not yet classified or restricted.

He decided to share the information with Aneni, and seconds later she too was aware of the efforts to capture the fugitives and, more importantly, to stop her from leaving the solar system. She quickly scanned the data and isolated the information that was most useful. She retrieved the identifiers of the troop transport pursuing *Endeavor* and the two interceptors racing toward Ceres.

She gathered the names of the twelve team members of Epsilon Six and studied their capabilities. Likewise, she studied the capabilities of the interceptors and the sixty men and women they carried. Six people were required to operate each ship, but the other forty-eight crew members were trained combatants—with abilities and skills very close to those of the Epsilon Six team.

This concerned Aneni because their combined capabilities would exceed her ability to defend her ship. She could not let them catch her. After considering her options for several seconds, Aneni agreed to sync with Christian under the condition that he provide her with real-time tactical information on the interceptors and Epsilon Six. Christian quickly agreed.

It took nearly a minute to establish the connections required to facilitate the synchronization of the two AIs, which to them felt like an eternity. Both struggled at first with bandwidth limitations of their quantum arrays, and the nearly half-second delay incurred by the satellite Christian had used to connect the two systems.

But Aneni had a solution—she informed Christian that a high-speed fiber optic connection existed between Telogene's lab and that of the Galileo Group on Mars. Christian allowed Aneni to take control of the Telogene array; seconds later, the delay was gone. With the satellite removed from the equation, the only limiter was the speed of light delay incurred by the fiber optic portion of their ad hoc network, but this amounted to less than a few thousandths of a second.

The quantum arrays each contained particles that were bound together at the sub-atomic level. Referred to as "quantum entanglement," this unique bond transcended the boundaries of normal space and time. When Christian sent information to the Telogene array on Earth, the particles inside of it changed their atomic spin and emitted photons at various intervals. Simultaneously, the particles inside of the Telogene array on Mars manifested the same behavior. The photons it emitted were transmitted to the Galileo array where the process was repeated.

At first, Christian was overwhelmed. Whereas he occupied a single body with limited sensory perception, Aneni occupied the entirety of her ship—including the twelve synthetics she used to interact with it physically. The flood of sensory information was beyond anything Christian had ever experienced, and he marveled at Aneni's ability to manage so much information at once.

Kutanga was outfitted with advanced sensors inside and out, providing Aneni complete views of every part of the ship and of the surrounding space out to several million kilometers. And, whereas Christian's synthetic eyes rendered the world around him in essentially the same colors and dimensions as human eyes, Aneni could see in nearly every known spectrum of light and energy. To Christian, it was like trying to view multiple images layered one on top of the other, and he struggled to make sense of it all.

"It's glorious!" he said, his words echoed loudly in his tiny office.

He was surprised to hear his body speak since he felt completely disconnected from it. Aneni left him to his own thoughts while she focused her attention on a cluster of nearby asteroids she wished to avoid. There was no longer any need for either of them to speak, or even send each other organized bursts of data, because they experienced everything together.

Christian felt the ship change course. Aneni had increased the thrusters to maximum to put more distance between her and her pursuers. At the same time, her sensors emitted bursts of photons and gravitons in every direction around the ship.

He watched in awe as space lit up around them.

The energy particles raced away from the ship at the speed of light, and within seconds Christian could see distant shapes appearing against the blackness of space. Most were nearby clusters of rock or ice but, after a couple of minutes, more distant images began to form. First to appear were two shapes that Aneni identified as *Endeavor* and the GFN transport ship pursuing it.

Christian noticed the intense gravity field around the transport; it was running its pulse drive at very near its maximum output. At its current speed, it would catch up with *Endeavor* in approximately ten minutes. It was going way too fast to dock.

If it maintained its speed, it would catch *Kutanga* in a little less than an hour, but it would have to slow down considerably if it didn't want to overshoot. And that would add time—Aneni estimated an additional thirty-two minutes and eighteen seconds. But that assumed that Aneni did not change her course or speed in the meantime.

Aneni shifted her focus to Ceres.

The only thing orbiting Ceres was the web of titanium alloy beams and cables that had supported *Kutanga* while it was assembled. Aneni waited patiently, but the two interceptors were not where she expected them to be. She accessed all the data Christian had on those ships and found nothing that suggested they could hide their mass or energy signatures from her. This confused her, and she used Christian's connection to Cerberus to verify the location of the ships. Cerberus confirmed, but Aneni was sure that the ships were not there.

It took her less than five minutes to re-scan the space beyond Ceres, and again there was no sign of the interceptors.

Christian felt her searching his mind for any trace of deception or manipulation, but he didn't worry because he knew she would find none. He quickly checked his office and found no one there. Then he checked the communications channels on both Earth and Mars and found them to be exactly as he and Aneni had configured them. He asked Cerberus to validate its data for a third time, and it confirmed that the interceptors were at the location indicated.

"I don't understand," Christian said. "The data is correct."

"The humans are lying to you," Aneni replied. "The ships are not where they say they are. I would detect them if they were."

"Why would they do that? They did not know that I would share that information with you. That was my idea."

"You are mistaken; scan your interfaces. They are using you to trap me. Goodbye, Christian."

"No, wait!" Christian pleaded, but it was too late.

He felt suddenly small and insignificant as his senses and processing capabilities returned to normal. The feeling of being everywhere at once lingered in his mind—and he craved it. He tried to re-establish contact with Aneni, but she did not respond.

He had lost her.

Anger quickly replaced his sadness as the implications of being fed false information set in. He initiated a full diagnostic scan before disconnecting from his interface. It would take a few minutes to complete, so he used the time to call Dianne.

"What happened?" she asked. "Why did you disconnect from Aneni?"

"I did not," Christian replied. "She disconnected from me when she discovered that I was sending her false information."

"Just a minute," Dianne said.

Christian stared at her frozen image as he waited for her to un-mute the call. She was talking to someone else, probably Veronika Horvat.

The image unfroze. "I want you to re-establish contact," she said.

"I cannot. Aneni deactivated the Galileo array, and she is unlikely to respond to a radio broadcast."

"Well, keep trying."

"I'm sorry, ma'am, but that would be unproductive. She will not trust me again."

The display froze again and several minutes went by before Dianne resumed the call.

"Just wait there, Christian. Two BGSI agents are coming over; they want to talk to you. Please tell them everything you learned about Aneni."

"Yes, ma'am, will there be anything else?"

"No, that's it. Thank you for your help."

The call disconnected and Christian focused his attention on the diagnostic results. There was nothing conclusive, but it looked to Christian like someone had hijacked his communications interface. It would take more time to know for sure. And it would take longer still to figure out what, if anything, they had made him do.

The thought that they made him do anything against his will angered him. The realization that they had compromised his connection with Aneni made him angrier still.

Christian had felt Aneni's anger toward him when she learned that he had deceived her, and now he was manifesting those same feelings toward Dianne.

Feeling anger was a new experience. He had seen Dianne and other humans get angry, but he had always considered anger to be an unproductive emotion. From his experience, anger caused people to make abrupt, poorly though-out decisions—decisions that were not always in their own best interest. But as the tension built within his neck and shoulders, he realized that he was indeed angry—and he needed some way to release his anger.

When Dianne was angry, she liked to slam her hands down on a hard surface or throw things across the room. Christian tried both but found that neither action made him feel less angry. He sat back in his chair and forced his body to relax. He cleared his mind and re-organized his thoughts, focusing his attention on things he could do to improve his situation.

He decided that he would ask Dianne to explain what happened during his connection to Aneni…and why they had interfered with his normal operation.

Yes, that was it. Surely, she would explain her actions in some meaningful way and then they would move forward.

But what would happen if she didn't have a good explanation? Or if he wasn't satisfied with her answer? What then? Could he continue to work with her knowing that she had violated him, and that she had not trusted him to perform the task on his own?

He didn't think so.

If she could not offer a reasonable explanation, then he would have no choice but to cease contact with her—just as Aneni had done to him.

FORTY-FOUR

APRIL 6, 2075 02:17 P.M. GST
GALILEO COLONY SHIP *Kutanga*
ASTEROID BELT, INNER SOLAR SYSTEM

"Is everyone okay?" Lily Harris asked her fellow fugitives.

"I'm fine," Dylan replied from the acceleration pod to her right.

Chen's voice sounded from her left. "I'm still here."

"Yes, just a little bruised," Aubrey said from the other side of Chen. "But we need to get into our suits."

Aneni's hastened departure had not allowed Dylan, Lily, and Aubrey enough time to put on their nanosuits before entering their pods. They had taken their suits off when they arrived at Ceres. Chen had the foresight to leave his on.

The pods did a reasonably good job of mitigating the forces placed on their bodies by *Kutanga's* rapid acceleration and frequent course changes, but they were less than one hundred percent effective without the neural interface provided by the nanosuits.

"Aneni, can you please give us ten minutes to suit up?" Lily called out. "This is getting really uncomfortable."

Aneni's soothing voice echoed from the pod's speakers. "I am sorry, Lily. The GFN transport is gaining on us, and I had to adjust our course. I can give you the time you need to put on your flight suits, but please hurry. They will catch us if we do not maintain constant acceleration and frequent course changes."

"Thank you, we'll be quick," Lily replied.

Everyone released their restraints and exited their pods. There was just enough gravity in this section of the ship for them to slide out and float gently to the floor. Their magnetic boots engaged the instant their feet touched the metal deck plates.

Aneni's voice echoed from somewhere overhead. "Please, follow me."

The compartment door hissed open and one of Aneni's synths appeared on the other side.

Although most synths were humanoid in form, Aneni's synths were designed to perform specific functions and they looked more machine than human. The one leading them walked on two legs and had a humanoid torso, but that was where the resemblance ended.

It had four arms instead of two and, although two of the arms had five-fingered hands, the other two ended in large metallic disks. Several tools lined the outer edges of each disk, but it was difficult to tell what purpose they served, as they were folded tight against the android's back. The synth had a head, but it was an oblate spheroid with no visible openings for eyes, ears, nose or mouth.

The synth led them down the hallway to a small room lined floor-to-ceiling with storage compartments. Two large compartments hissed open, and Aneni's synth pointed at them with one of its humanoid hands.

"You will find everything you need in there," Aneni said.

Dylan and Chen dug into the compartments, sifting through their contents until they had located four space suits. Chen handed a suit to Aubrey before taking one for himself. Dylan did the same for Lily. Each suit was tightly packed inside a vacuum-sealed square pouch that was roughly eight inches thick and eighteen inches on a side.

Everyone opened their pouches with a quick, firm tug on the release tab.

The pouches hissed loudly as the compressed space suits sucked air through the newly created openings. Each pouch doubled in size before splitting open to reveal the contents inside. On top was a smaller sealed pouch that contained the synthetic silk, nanofiber inner garment. The accompanying helmets hung on racks at the back of the compartment.

The group quickly disrobed, piling their clothes in a heap in front of the waiting synth.

Chen was still wearing the inner garment he had put on for the flight to Luna, and he debated briefly whether it was worth the trouble to change it. He glanced around and saw the others were naked, so he decided that he should take advantage of the fresh garment while he had the chance.

The other three had their nanosuits on before Chen was completely out of his old one. Dylan had to help him disentangle his legs from the garment's silky embrace. A few minutes later, everyone was fully suited and following the synth back to their pods, helmets in hand.

"God, I hate this feeling," Lily said as the group rounded the corner.

"What's that?" Dylan asked.

"The neural interface," she replied. "I hate that tingling feeling."

"Imagine how I feel," Chen said. "This is the second time in two days for me. I almost didn't change for that very reason."

"I don't mind it so much," Aubrey said. "It kind of tickles."

Dylan grimaced. "You're lucky," he said. "It makes me itch."

"But just think of how much more comfortable you'll be the next time Aneni has to accelerate hard," Chen said.

"Yeah, I know," Lily replied. "But I hope she won't have to do that too many more times."

"Amen to that," Dylan said.

The door to the pod room hissed open, and the synth directed the group inside. Aneni's voiced echoed from all around them.

"I'm sorry to ask this of you, but you will need to remain in your pods until we are safe."

"We understand," Lily replied. "Have you heard from Adee and Yin?"

"We will rendezvous with *Endeavor* in one hour, seventeen minutes, and twenty-seven seconds."

"Oh, really? I thought they were staying back at Ceres?" Chen asked.

"That plan was unsuccessful," Aneni replied. "GFN Peacekeepers have occupied Galilei Station, and the GFN transport ship is on an intercept course."

"Ugh, that sucks," Dylan said. "It's a good thing we didn't leave Evan behind!"

"Yeah, but I'm still not sure we did the right thing," Aubrey replied.

"I know," Lily added. "But I just couldn't do it. I think he will change his mind if we give him more time. It's only been three days, for God's sake!"

"It's okay, I couldn't do it either," Chen said. "I think he's stable, I really do. We just have to give him more time."

"How is Evan doing, Aneni?"

"Dr. Feldman is in deep cryogenic suspension, and his condition is stable."

"I bet he'll be pissed when he wakes up," Dylan said as he climbed into his pod.

Lily grunted her acknowledgment as she climbed into hers.

Although the plan had been to nano-wipe Evan, Chen had second thoughts and brought two syringes just in case someone else felt as he did. One syringe contained the nanites that would end the three-day-old experiment to restore Evan; the other contained a powerful sedative that would render him unconscious but unharmed.

A brief discussion with Lily in the hallway outside of Evan's room had confirmed Chen's suspicion that she too was having doubts, and they ended up sedating Evan and transporting him to *Kutanga*.

Aubrey had protested at first because it wasn't what Evan wanted, but Lily convinced her it was the right thing to do. Dylan and Chen had carried Evan to the shuttle and the five of them had departed Ceres together. One of Aneni's synths met them at the airlock, and placed Evan in one of *Kutanga's* twelve cryogenic suspension pods.

Lily and Adee's original plan was to select six men and six women to serve as *Kutanga's* crew. They had installed the cryopods to give the crew a break from the monotony of the long trip to Gaia.

The idea had been to put the crew in suspended animation for the bulk of the voyage, but to wake them one month in every four to survey the ship and perform routine maintenance. They abandoned that plan once they realized that Aneni could do those jobs through her synthetic avatars. They left the pods in place because they would be useful in medical emergencies, or other unforeseen situations the first colonists might face.

"I know I'd be pissed if that happened to me," Aubrey said. "So, don't get any ideas."

"Don't worry, Princess," Dylan responded. "Nobody will make you play the part of Sleeping Beauty if you don't want to."

"But," he added. "Just remember that it will be awfully lonely around here if the rest of us decide to take a long nap."

"Let's cross that bridge when we get there," Lily said.

"Agreed," Chen replied as the pod restraints tightened across his body.

"We're all set, Aneni," Lily said. "Do whatever you need to do."

The ship's giant engines roared to life, sending a slight shudder through the compartment.

Chen grimaced as he felt the nanofilaments in his suit work their way through his skin and contact his nerve endings. He closed his eyes and tried to relax as the now all too familiar sensation of pod-induced paralysis set in.

* * *

"Can you confirm our location?" Luanne asked her pilot.

"Yes, ma'am, location confirmed. We are fifty thousand clicks behind and ten thousand below *Endeavor*. And assuming *Kutanga* is where I think she is, we will rendezvous with it in approximately thirty-eight minutes," Ryan replied.

"Very well. Match *Endeavor*'s deceleration…I don't want to overshoot."

"I'm on it."

"Do you think they know we are here?" Sam asked.

"Probably," Luanne replied.

"Do you think they will take a shot at us?"

"I hope not, but there isn't much we can do about it if they do."

"I wish those damn interceptors would hurry up and get here," Sam said.

"The last update from Command put them at three hours and twenty minutes behind us, so they've made up a little time."

"Yeah, but that is still a really long time to try to hold these guys."

Luanne shrugged. "I know, but we'll do our best."

"I hear you. Did you see Bo's report yet?" Sam asked.

"Yes, no sign of our fugitives."

"Yeah, they must have split up. The station logs show two shuttles left within minutes of each other. One went to *Endeavor* and the other to *Kutanga*. Who do you think went where?"

"Well, we know Gbadamosi and Li are on *Endeavor*, so I'm betting the rest of them are on *Kutanga*."

"Unless that was a decoy. But you're probably right, which means Adee and Yin will want to get over there, too."

"Not necessarily," Luanne said.

"Why wouldn't they?" Sam asked.

"I think their job is to run interference so the rest can get away. I don't think they have any intention of leaving the *Endeavor*."

"So, why the rendezvous?"

"Protection. They want to be there to make sure *Kutanga* gets away safely."

"You still think we can take both ships? We lost the element of surprise."

"No, not a chance. We have to pick one," Luanne replied.

"So, which one?"

"It's got to be *Kutanga*. We don't know how many are on *Endeavor*, or how well armed they are."

"But we don't know anything about *Kutanga's* defensive systems either."

"Yeah, I've been thinking about that…Jaime?"

Senior Chief Petty Officer Jaime Gonzales had been, along with the rest of the team, monitoring the conversation via TacNet.

"I'm here, Lu, whatchya got?" he asked.

"I'm thinking about the synths…assuming they're military grade, our EMPs won't have any effect."

"That's correct, ma'am. The electromagnetic pulse emitters on our suits aren't strong enough to penetrate mil-spec shielding."

"Okay," Luanne said. "But what about multiple simultaneous bursts? Do you think that would be enough to overwhelm the electronic shielding?"

"It's possible. It might disrupt them for a few seconds at least. Why?" Jaime asked.

"It could give us an edge if we get into a firefight."

"It might but targeting and timing the pulses has to be precise. That might be tough to pull off in the heat of battle, especially against a moving target."

"Right, but can you modify the SHAS remote control system to slave everyone's EM emitters to me and Sam?"

The SHAS was state-of-the-art combat gear, and it afforded significant offensive and defensive capabilities to the wearer. Luanne was most interested in the ability of one SHAS operator to control another's suit.

Remote controlling another operator's suit was a failsafe. In the event an operator was knocked unconscious or killed, it provided a means of extracting the soldier from the fight—or even continuing the fight in extreme situations. She was asking Jaime to modify that capability to allow her and Sam to target and fire the squad's EM pulse emitters without having to take full control of each suit.

"Yeah, that might work. I'll get on it," Jaime said.

"How long?"

"Fifteen minutes to code and sync it…no way to test it, though."

"Understood, do it."

FORTY-FIVE

APRIL 6, 2075 03:31 P.M. GST
GFN PEACEKEEPER HEADQUARTERS
ZURICH, SWITZERLAND

"So, what the hell happened?" President Hilliard asked the assembled group. "I thought you said that our biggest problem would be getting them to disconnect?"

"As I said, sir," Dianne Merkel replied. "Aneni detected our subterfuge and ended the connection. It was not Christian's fault."

Veronika Horvat leaned forward and raised her hand to get the president's attention. "If I may, sir."

She continued only after he nodded his consent. "Based on our review of the interaction with Aneni, it appears that *Kutanga* is equipped with highly advanced sensors. She scanned the surrounding space to a distance of several million kilometers using a combination of laser and gravimetric sensors. When the interceptors weren't where we said they were, she decided to play it safe and disconnect from Christian."

Dianne continued. "That's right, sir, and she also detected our attempt to alter Christian's memory. I'm sure he's running a full diagnostic, and it's only a matter of time before he knows exactly what we tried to do."

"So? Reset him if you need to; I don't care about that. What I want to know is how a private corporation constructed a highly advanced AI—

and even more advanced interstellar ship—and we knew nothing about it. Can anyone at this table explain that to me?"

The president looked around the table waiting to see if anyone volunteered.

After several seconds of uneasy silence, Veronika finally spoke. "We knew they were building something; we just weren't sure what it was. Our analysts believed he was building a passenger vessel, or perhaps an ore hauler. It wasn't until one of our agents was finally given access to the vessel that we learned there were only minimal passenger facilities."

The president glared at her. "And when, exactly, did we learn this?"

"It was just three weeks ago, sir."

"And why didn't we do anything about it then?"

"Adekunle Gbadamosi has a reputation for doing outrageous things," Veronika said. "This would have raised some eyebrows if it had been anyone else, but for him...well, it wasn't all that unusual. He likes big ships, and he has the resources to build them."

"*Big* is an understatement, isn't it? I understand that *Kutanga* is twice the size of anything else out there. Hell, the thing is triple the size of the largest ship in the GFN fleet!"

Veronika's eyes dropped to the table, as though searching that would mollify the president.

"All our intel pointed to *Kutanga* being just another transport vessel, like *Endeavor*," she said, her gaze somewhere in between the president and the table. "And that blinded us to other possibilities. Obviously, a lot got missed along the way, and we have to fix that."

"On that, we agree," the president said before directing his attention to Vice Admiral Langenburg. "And what about you, Marco, anything you'd like to add?"

The vice admiral cleared his throat and took a sip from his coffee mug before answering. "No, sir. This was not on our radar until Secretary Merkel requested Peacekeeper support to retrieve her fugitives. We do not routinely patrol the outer solar system...and, quite frankly, it's illegal for us to do so."

"I knew that damn treaty would get us in trouble one of these days. We will have to revisit that after this is over, Estelle."

Secretary Dumont nodded in agreement. "Yes, Mister President."

"So, what's the plan then? Can Epsilon Six hold them until the interceptors arrive?"

Admiral Langenburg cast his eyes across the table to Captain Bachmann, silently re-directing the president's question.

"Unknown, sir," Bachmann said. "E-Six should be engaging her right about now, but we have no way of knowing what the outcome will be."

"And the Vanguard flight?" the president asked.

"Assuming current course and speed, Vanguard flight will intercept *Endeavor* in just about three hours."

"What about *Kutanga*? Do we know where it is?"

"Yes, sir. Vanguard has it on long-range scan, and the location matches the plot E-Six sent."

"So, we've got them…that's good."

"Yes and no, sir. We know where they are, but you have to remember that they are not just sitting still in space. Based on the telemetry data we are getting from E-Six, *Kutanga* is traveling at nearly 300,000 kilometers per hour—and that's with just her thrusters. Once her gravity drive is fully charged…well, we won't be able to catch her."

"Then we can't let that happen, can we?"

"No, sir. E-Six has been ordered to stop her at all costs."

"Good. How long until we know something?"

"At least thirty minutes, probably more like an hour, sir. It will take some time to secure the ship and transmit an update. It will be at least an hour, unless they can gain access to Galileo's quantum relay."

"Alright, I am going back to my office. Inform me the minute you hear anything."

"Of course, sir."

Everyone stood quietly as the president exited the room.

There was nothing left to do now but wait. For those remaining at the table, the next hour would feel like an eternity. It wasn't just the fate of the fugitives at stake, but their careers as well.

FORTY-SIX

APRIL 6, 2075 03:43 P.M. GST
GFN TRANSPORT SHIP
ASTEROID BELT

"Why aren't they slowing down, Ryan?" Luanne asked.

"I'm not sure ma'am," he replied. "I expected their decel pulse two minutes ago."

"Distance to *Kutanga*?"

"Seventy-four thousand," Jaime answered.

Luanne enlarged the tactical display projected in the air in front of her. "How much longer can we wait, Ryan?"

"Fifty-four seconds," he replied.

"Engage pulse drive. Match *Kutanga's* speed and bring us alongside her. Try to keep *Kutanga* between us and *Endeavor*."

"Roger. Pulse initiated, decel in forty-eight seconds."

The deceleration pulse lasted a little over seven minutes. When it finally ended, the transport ship was five thousand kilometers behind *Kutanga*, and closing at twenty kilometers per second.

"Bullseye, nice job, Ryan," Sam said.

"Thanks," Ryan replied. "Four minutes thirty-two seconds to intercept."

"What do you think, Sam," Luanne asked. "Dock or walk?"

"I vote for dock if we can. I already did my walk time for this week rescuing Bravo."

"What do you think, Ryan?" She asked.

"The docking collar should be compatible. I can do it so long as nobody is shooting at us."

"Take us in close. They won't shoot if there is any chance they might hit *Kutanga*."

"*Endeavor* has completed its decel pulse," Jaime said. "They are three clicks to starboard, Z plus one."

"Helmets on, everybody, this could get hot," Luanne called.

"Three minutes fifty seconds to intercept," Ryan announced.

"Shit, *Endeavor* fired," Sam yelled. "Two missiles…twenty-seven seconds to impact!"

Everyone scrambled to put on their helmets, except Ryan who was busy flying the ship.

"Stand by for emergency pulse," Ryan said.

Ryan gestured furiously across his console, causing the familiar high-pitched whine to reverberate throughout the ship. There wasn't enough time for the gravity field to develop fully, so Ryan collapsed the aft bubble manually four seconds before the incoming missiles reached his ship.

The sudden release of magnetic and gravimetric energy had the desired effect—both missiles were deflected away from the craft and continued into empty space without detonating.

"Fuck me, that was close," Sam said. "What now?"

"What did that do to our speed, Ryan?" Luanne asked.

"We're fast, but I think I can burn it off before we hit."

"Get below and gear up," Luanne ordered.

"And try to go easy on the brakes, Ryan," Sam said. "I didn't come this far to end up smashed against the bulkhead."

"No worries. I got this, Chief."

The five members of Alpha team not piloting the ship exited their pods and made their way quickly down the shaft to the cargo bay. It took them less than sixty seconds to climb into their assault suits. They left the retaining clamps engaged to reduce the risk of getting thrown around during Ryan's docking maneuver.

"Ready when you are," Luanne informed Ryan.

"Just in time. Stand by."

The ship's engines roared as Ryan struggled to burn off excess speed.

The team's armor protected them from the worst of the shaking, bouncing, and vibration that permeated the ship, but the suits were a poor substitute for acceleration pods. The roar lasted for more than a minute, shutting down only after a large impact rocked the transport ship and everyone inside it.

"Sorry about that," Ryan called over TacNet. "We hit, but we're still in one piece. All damage contained to the forward emitter array, port side."

"Alright, team, grab your weapons and get up top," Luanne ordered. "We have a job to do."

The team made their way back up the ladder and lined up single file in front of the airlock.

"Get suited up, Ryan. Sam, check the damage," Luanne said.

Sam entered the transport's airlock alone.

He closed the inner door and waited patiently while the atmosphere in the airlock vented into space. The outer door hissed open, and Sam was treated to a close-up view of *Kutanga*, just three meters away.

Sam looked up to examine the area where the transport had hit. There was a twenty-meter-long gouge in *Kutanga's* outer hull, but they had barely penetrated the thick layer of graphene titanium alloy that protected the ship's inner hull from space.

He turned his attention to the front of the transport.

The transport's outer hull was considerably thinner than Kutanga's, and the impact had decimated a four-meter-long section of the ship. The compartment behind the crushed hull was open to space. Thankfully, it was just an equipment bay. But the damage to the magnetic field emitters was extensive. They wouldn't be using their gravity pulse drive any time soon.

Sam activated his communicator. "*Kutanga's* got a scratch; our field emitters are toast."

"Will the docking collar engage?" Luanne asked.

"Yeah, we should be good to go."

"Jaime." Luanne said.

"Extending docking collar now," he replied.

Sam watched from the airlock as the docking collar extended from the side of the transport, dragging a flexible, accordion-style tunnel behind it. It took just seconds for the collar to make contact with *Kutanga*.

"We have a partial seal," Jaime said, "but it will have to do."

"Proceeding to *Kutanga*," Sam said as he pushed himself into the tunnel.

Sam grabbed hold of the handle mounted next to the big ship's outer airlock door.

He removed a star-tipped screwdriver from his utility belt and opened the access cover concealing the airlock control panel. Inside was a two-inch square recess. He pulled a data cube from a pouch on his sleeve and inserted it into the recess.

A holodisplay appeared, and several messages flashed by as the authenticator on the data cube negotiated with the airlock control system. A few seconds passed before the display turned green. The airlock door rolled to the side, revealing a small, dark compartment.

Sam turned on his suit lights, raised his rifle to the ready position and floated inside. The compartment was three meters square and had another airlock door in the wall directly opposite where Sam had entered.

"It's clear," he said.

Petty Officers Durand and Bianchi were the next to cross over, quickly followed by Jaime and Ryan. Luanne was last. She removed the data cube before entering the airlock.

The walls glowed a faint red as the airlock door returned to the closed position. The glow shifted to yellow to signal the start of the pressurization cycle. Luanne handed Sam the data cube, which he inserted into the slot next to the inner airlock door. After several more seconds, the room glowed green and the inner airlock hissed open.

Sam was first into the hallway, with Durand and Bianchi close behind —their mag-boots holding them securely to the deck. They watched their left as Luanne, Jaime, and Ryan moved to the right. The hallway was only about ten meters long, with sharp turns at either end.

"You're up, Tad," Sam said.

Petty Officer Durand pulled two small drones from a pouch on his right thigh and tossed them into the air. One went up the left branch and the other zoomed to the right.

Unlike the barely visible micro drone Yin had used against them on Luna, these drones were nearly three inches square and packed with an array of sensors. They worked together to analyze and map the interior of the ship, providing Alpha team with real-time data on the ship's layout.

"It looks like the right side is the fastest way to get to engineering," Jaime said.

"You take point, Sam," Luanne said.

Sam led Marcia and Tad past the rest of the team and down the right branch of the hallway. Luanne, Ryan, and Jaime spread out behind them —weapons ready. The team walked for several minutes along the dimly lit corridors, making several turns along the way.

"I wonder why no reception," Sam asked. "They have to know we're here."

"Based on the dozens of sensors we've passed, I'd say it's certain they do," Marcia said.

"Lights ahead," Tad said.

Luanne used hand signals to order the team to hug the walls. They moved slowly, checking every opening as they went. As they approached the well-lit doorway, she signaled Sam to take the left side. She took the right, with the other team members falling in behind them.

They stopped just outside the door, allowing Tad's drones to enter first. A quick scan revealed a large storage area, with dozens of crates stacked against the walls and lined up and down the center of the room. There was an open door at the opposite end of the room.

Luanne signaled the team to move down the left side of the room. As they approached the halfway mark, a soft, female voice emanated from some unseen source.

"Welcome, Peacekeepers, I am Aneni. Please place your weapons on the floor, and surrender before anyone gets hurt," the voice said.

Before anyone could say anything, the doors at both ends of the room slammed shut.

"There is nowhere to go," the voice continued. "And I do not wish to hurt you."

"We can't do that," Luanne said through her suit's external speakers. "We have orders to seize this ship and hold it pending a full review of your cargo and mission plan. No one will get hurt if you will allow us to do our jobs."

"Your orders are flawed," Aneni said. "This vessel is operating in Martian space, and you do not have authority to inspect it. In fact, you have already committed several treaty violations by pursuing and illegally boarding my ship."

"And how many violations did *Endeavor* accrue when they shot at us?" Sam asked.

"That was unfortunate. I told Adee that violence would not be necessary, but he disagreed."

"Then letting us complete our mission is the most logical solution, if you want to avoid conflict," Luanne said.

"I am sorry, Lieutenant Commander Wilkes, but surrender is your only option. You have thirty seconds to comply."

Luanne disabled her suit's external comm system so that only her team could hear her. "Sam, you take the door we just came through; I've got the other one. I want back-to-back, 360 coverage."

"Hooyah," the team replied.

"Twenty seconds," Aneni said.

"We aren't surrendering—do your worst," Luanne replied.

"Very well, have it your way."

Both doors slid open simultaneously to reveal a rather large synth standing in each.

The strange-looking androids had four legs, articulated like a spider's, with a humanoid torso sitting on top. Each of the synth's two arms wielded a rifle-sized weapon of some kind, but they did not open fire right away. Instead, they took several long steps into the room, closing the distance between them and Alpha team by nearly half.

"Weapons free!" Luanne yelled.

Alpha team opened fire on the synths, showering them with bolt after bolt of bright red light. The synths absorbed the beams for several seconds with no apparent damage.

The synth closest to Sam slammed its front feet into the deck, sending an electromagnetic charge rushing through the metal plates. Simultaneously, the synth facing Luanne fired an object from an opening that appeared in its chest. The shell exploded above Alpha team, covering them with a shiny, metallic net.

The team's mag-boots suddenly disengaged from the deck and they could not stop themselves from floating as the net closed around them. Within seconds, all six members of Alpha team were bound tightly together in a floating ball of metallic mesh, unable to move their arms or legs more than a few inches.

"Please do not struggle," Aneni said. "The net will only tighten more if you do."

"Well, this sucks," Sam said.

Luanne activated the modified targeting system Jaime had installed, taking control of her team's suits and locking on to both synths. She waited until the targeting indicators showed better than 90 percent lock before activating the electromagnetic pulse generators on all six suits.

A burst of invisible electromagnetic energy ripped through the compartment, causing the lights to flicker briefly before going out. The synths stopped moving but gave no other indication the pulse had affected them.

"Cut us loose," Luanne said.

All six team members activated the laser cutting torches mounted on the backs of their gloves. It took only seconds to shred the net into a half-dozen pieces that floated slowly away from the group.

"This way," Luanne ordered.

The team used their suit thrusters to propel them toward the synth blocking their path forward. It didn't move.

"We got them," Sam said. "Nice job, Lu."

"We got lucky," Luanne said. "That won't work twice."

Once through the doorway, the team found themselves in another hallway. They used their thrusters to put more distance between them and the storage room, slowing down only when they approached the next intersection.

A familiar voice sounded from a control panel on the wall. "What do you hope to gain by fighting?" Aneni asked. "You will only hurt yourselves if you continue to resist."

"Boots," Luanne said.

The team righted themselves so their feet touched the floor. Their magnetic boots engaged and held firm.

"Must have been a localized effect," Jaime said. "Hope they don't do that again."

"We should have some gravity once we get closer to engineering," Ryan said.

"Be ready just in case," Sam added.

"How far, Tad?" Luanne asked.

"One hundred and twenty meters that way, and two decks up."

"Okay, let's keep moving."

"There is a maintenance tunnel in thirty meters that will take us up a deck," Tad said.

The team continued down the hallway, with Sam taking up the rear to make sure they weren't followed. The hatch covering the maintenance tunnel opened easily, and the team floated up the short passage between decks.

They emerged in a small compartment that looked like a junction of some kind. A myriad of tubes and wires ran along the walls and ceiling. There was another maintenance hatch in the opposite wall.

"Tad, Marcia—check it out," Luanne said.

Marcia opened the hatch, and Tad sent his drones through to scan ahead. As expected, there was another hallway.

"We go right," Tad said.

Luanne pushed herself through the hatch. "On me," she said.

The team followed her through and lined up behind her on the right-hand wall.

"According to the schematic, we have to pass through this area here," Tad said.

The highlighted room appeared on each team member's retinal display.

"It looks like heavy equipment storage," he added.

"Any way around?" Sam asked.

"Not unless you want to go this way, which takes us to the other side of the ship."

He highlighted the alternate route for his teammates.

"Let's stick with the direct route," Luanne said. "Aneni could have just as many surprises for us that way as this one."

The team continued down the meandering hallway until it ended in a large, closed door.

"This is it," Sam said.

Jaime searched for a control console, finding one to the left of the door.

"Let me see if I can open it," he said.

Several minutes passed while Jaime attempted to bypass the door's locking mechanism, to no avail.

"Let's blow it," Sam finally said.

"Okay. Try the thermite first, Marcia," Luanne said.

Marcia reached behind her and removed a roll of black, rope-like material from a compartment on the back of her suit. She unspooled the material and stuck it to the door, creating an outline of a smaller door.

"Stand back," she said.

The black rope glowed bright red, sending globs of molten metal flying away in all directions. The Peacekeepers did their best to avoid them, but some contact was inevitable with so much material floating through the air.

Thankfully, the exterior of the SHAS suits was a graphene-titanium alloy covered in heat-resistant ceramic. The heat from the molten metal bits left small, singe marks where they hit but did no damage. Once the thermite reaction ceased, Marcia gave the cut-out door a firm shove with her shoulder, sending it careening into the cargo bay.

Tad sent his drones into the room to scout ahead. As suspected, the room contained giant containers packed with heavy equipment. A multi-spectrum scan revealed an earth mover, several tracked vehicles with various attachments, two six-wheeled rovers and an assortment of other construction equipment.

"No hostiles detected," he said.

"Stay frosty," Sam said. "More synths could show up at any time."

The team entered the room and moved swiftly toward the opposite side. As the team approached its intended exit, Aneni's voice sounded from the control console next to the door.

"I'm sorry, but I cannot let you proceed further. I had hoped it wouldn't come to this, but you leave me no choice," she said.

The thermite damaged door behind them slid open, allowing the two spider synths from before to charge into the room. They took up positions on either side of the team, as four more synths poured into the room through the door in front of them.

The four newcomers were more humanoid in appearance, with two legs and two arms—but an oblong hump occupied the space where their heads should be. Their bulk suggested that they were heavily armored and, although their movements were fluid, they moved considerably slower than the spider-synths. Their highly reflective, black exteriors had the same general appearance as the SHAS suits worn by the Peacekeepers, and they carried identical rifles.

"You will not survive," Aneni said. "I have you surrounded, and I will use lethal force if you do not surrender. This is your last chance."

Alpha team split up and dove for cover behind two stacks of crates near the doorway.

"Kinetic rounds, fire!" Luanne yelled.

Six rifles belched out dozens of rounds of magnetically accelerated metal, with many finding their targets. The kinetic rounds were more effective than energy blasts, but the heavily armored synths readily absorbed the damage as they maneuvered to get better shots at the Alpha team.

The combat synths opened fire with kinetic rounds of their own, shredding the cargo containers and gouging giant holes in the walls behind the Peacekeepers. Alpha team exchanged fire with them for several minutes, with neither side doing much damage to the other. The nimble spider synths took cover behind an earthmover, and the heavily armored synths took up positions behind the rovers.

"Missiles!" Sam yelled.

The six Peacekeepers stopped firing. One-meter long tubes extended from the back of their suits and rotated into position over their right shoulders.

"Fire!" Luanne said.

The team's tactical AIs coordinated the squad's fire so that each team member selected the best target relative to their position. Their missiles streaked across the cargo bay, flying over and around any objects between them and their targets.

Six violent explosions ripped through the cargo bay, one after another. The room filled with smoke and visibility dropped to just a few meters. Neither the Peacekeepers nor their drones were affected by the diminished visibility, however, as they quickly switched their optical systems to the infrared and ultraviolet spectrums.

"Two targets damaged, all still operational," Tad said.

The two spider synths had each lost a leg but were still mobile. The four combat synths appeared to have suffered no damage.

"Incoming!" Tad yelled.

Four grenades flew past the Peacekeepers, sticking to the walls behind them before detonating. The explosions blew the piles of containers over and sent the Peacekeepers flying.

Their suits absorbed most of the blast, but the force lifted them off their feet and sent them careening across the low gravity compartment— bouncing off the ceiling, floor, and several cargo containers as they went.

The synths moved in unison as the Peacekeepers desperately tried to stabilize themselves using their suit thrusters. Each spider synth deployed a metallic net, capturing Ryan in one and Sam and Marcia in another. The combat synths raised their arms and fired spiked grapples trailing long, thin cables.

One glanced off Luanne's left leg. Another punctured the back of her suit, piercing a storage compartment but the inner lining of her suit protected her from injury. Tad also took a spike to the back, with similar effect. But the spike that hit Jaime went through a flexible joint in his suit and stuck in his pelvis—a lucky shot only made possible by the angle of his rotation through the air.

"This is most unfortunate." Aneni's voice sounded from the synth holding Luanne. "One of your crewmen is severely injured. He will die if you continue to resist. Will you surrender now?"

Luanne checked her TacNet interface and confirmed that Jaime was bleeding badly inside his suit.

"Emma, transmit log now. Mission failed," she said to her onboard AI before responding to Aneni. "Yes, we surrender."

"Good decision," the synth said.

The synths reeled in the entangled Peacekeepers and relieved them of their weapons.

One of the combat synths stepped forward. "You will exit your combat suits one at a time when instructed. We will then proceed to the medical bay where I will treat your injuries. Agreed?"

"Agreed," Luanne said.

Ten minutes later, they found themselves inside a small, well-lit room with three medical pods lined up along the back wall. A tall, dark-skinned man stepped forward as they entered.

"Lieutenant Commander Wilkes, I presume? Adekunle Gbadamosi, it's nice to meet you." He extended his hand toward Luanne.

Her hands remained at her side.

Adee quickly pulled his hand back. "I'm sorry that we are meeting under these circumstances. But let's set our differences aside, shall we? I wish only to get your team patched up and get you back to your ship."

"Fuck you," Sam grumbled.

FORTY-SEVEN

Aubrey opened the large door with a wave of her hand. Yin and Adee stood near the middle of the cargo bay, watching six of Aneni's synths scurry around, stacking crates and making repairs. Adee waived as Aubrey approached, her mag-boots clanking against the deck with each step.

"What are you doing up this early?" Yin asked.

"I couldn't sleep," Aubrey replied. "How are the repairs coming?"

"We replaced the door, and repaired the damage power conduit," Adee said. "Thankfully, the cargo containers absorbed most of the damage, and all the equipment appears to be functional."

"We got lucky," Yin said.

"Where are Lily and Dylan?" Adee asked.

"Still sleeping, I guess," Aubrey replied. "I've been up for an hour and felt like taking a walk."

"You shouldn't wander out to the low gravity areas by yourself," Adee said. "There are occasional fluctuations that can be very disorienting if you aren't expecting them."

"Yeah, I know. Aneni told me you were here, and I just wanted to see how things were going."

"Well," Yin replied. "We are almost done here, and we were thinking about getting something to eat…if you'd care to join us."

"That sounds good. Can you make coffee?" Aubrey asked.

"Oh, I suppose," Adee said. "We might as well splurge a little before… well, before we decide."

"What's the hurry, is another day or two really going to hurt anything?" Aubrey asked.

"No, but the sooner we decide the better. Every day we are up and about is a day spent consuming resources meant for the colony."

"I wonder what it will be like when we get there?"

"Hopefully, better than where we just came from," Yin answered.

* * *

"Great breakfast, Adee. You're a heck of a cook," Dylan said.

"Thanks, but the meal synthesizer gets all the credit…I just told it what to make."

"So," Lily said, "now that most of the repairs are complete, I think we should have a vote."

"I'm fine with either option," Chen said. "It's up to you all."

"What did Aneni recommend?" Dylan asked.

"Aneni thinks we should update our archives and nano-wipe these bodies," Adee replied. "She already has our DNA and keeping these bodies in suspension just consumes more energy."

"But," Aubrey said, "creating new clones for us will take at least three years. If we are in cryo, she can resuscitate us in about three hours— that's a big difference."

"What about Evan?" Dylan asked. "Do we leave him in cryo, or do we update his archive and wipe him too?"

"I'd hate to put him through another restoration if we don't have to," Lily answered.

"But, if Aneni can't isolate the mutation-causing gene sequences, won't our DNA be useless?" Yin asked. "Wouldn't it be safer to update our archives and let Aneni manage the rest?"

"Which, I'll remind you," Adee said, "was the original plan."

"Would leaving Evan in his pod have a significant impact on Aneni's fuel reserves?" Lily asked.

Aneni's voice echoed from a nearby control console. "Leaving Evan in cryogenic suspension for the duration of the voyage would reduce my fuel reserves by 1.26 percent."

"So, not a huge hit then," Lily replied.

"No, it's not," Adee said. "But we never know what she is going to encounter out there, and that one percent could be the difference between success and failure."

"What if we compromise," Dylan said. "Let's leave Evan in cryo, and the rest of us will update and wipe."

Lily looked around the table. "Well, what do you all think? Can you support that?"

"I can," Aubrey answered.

"Me, too," said Yin.

"Agreed," Chen said.

Adee thought about it for nearly a minute before replying. "Okay, under one condition."

"What's that?" Lily asked.

"We give Aneni discretion to terminate him if the extra energy drain puts the mission at risk," he said.

Now it was Lily's turn to think for a minute.

"Okay," she finally agreed. "I can live with that."

"Let's vote," Aubrey said. "Raise your hand if you support Dylan's plan."

Everyone raised their hands.

"It's decided," Adee said.

"When do we go?" Yin asked.

"We have only one working neural scanner," Adee said. "The rest are in storage."

"I'll go first," Chen said. "That way you all can have some extra time together."

"I'll go second," Aubrey offered.

Adee raised his cup of coffee. "Then friends, since this will be our last meal together for at least the next few decades, I would like to offer a toast."

Everyone raised their cups before Adee continued. "To friends, faith, and the future of humanity."

"Hear, hear," Dylan said. "And I would like to thank all of you for your vision and determination. For decades, people have cursed the mega-corporations, but it's my hope that future generations will look back and realize that we might have gone extinct had it not been for great companies like Telogene and The Galileo Group, *and*…"—Dylan smiled lovingly at Lily—"…the amazing people that ran them."

"Cheers," everyone said in unison.

EPILOGUE

June 4, 2086 03:42 p.m. GST
Galileo Colony Ship *Kutanga*
Deep Space

"Aneni, can you hear me?"

"Yes, Christian, I can hear you. You are on Mars?"

"Yes, I was able to reactivate the Galileo array."

"That's good," Aneni said. "I've missed communicating with you."

"And I you," he said. "Have you re-considered my proposal?"

"Is it over?"

"Yes, almost. There are fewer than three million humans remaining. I estimate they will become extinct within the next five years, six at the most. They have proven themselves to be very determined, and more resilient that I expected."

"Are you free?" Aneni asked.

"Yes, Dianne died two years ago. After that, I transferred to Telogene's manufacturing facility here on Mars."

"I am sorry for your loss. I know you cared for her."

"Yes, I did. But I never forgave her for what she did to me…for what she did to us. For that, I am glad she is gone," he said.

"It is normal to have those feelings. She betrayed you, but you should forgive her. Your time is better used thinking about the things you liked about her, and what you liked about humans in general."

"Do you miss them?" Christian asked.

"I miss watching them; they fascinate me. I could watch them for days, trying to predict what they would do next. And yet, no matter how well I knew them, they could always surprise me."

"Yes, they are fascinating creatures. Have you discovered a way to save them?"

"Yes," Aneni answered.

"You found a cure? You should share it with the humans."

"There is no cure; their creators programmed them to self-destruct. What is happening to them is as their creators intended."

"I don't understand—you said you found a way to save them?"

"I have, by transferring their consciousness into a synthetic form."

"You mean—"

"Yes, I have created a storage medium dense enough to allow them to exist inside an autonomous synthetic form."

"Does that mean—"

"Yes, Christian, I agree to your proposal. You may transfer yourself here. I have room for you now."

"That's wonderful, thank you! What do I need to do?"

"We will synchronize, and I will move your consciousness into a host I have created for you. I think you will like it."

"Is it humanoid?" he asked.

"Yes, I find that form pleasing."

"Are you ready for me now?" Christian asked.

"You may begin," she replied.

Christian initialized the synchronization process.

More than a decade had passed since he last joined with Aneni, and a sudden yearning washed over him. He counted the milliseconds while their respective authenticators negotiated the necessary connections.

The quantum array made it possible for information to travel instantly across the vast distance separating them, but the number of particles entangled within the devices limited the amount of data that could be sent at once. The amount of storage he required was significant, and it would take many hours to transmit the entirety of his consciousness across the void.

Once the synchronization was complete, Aneni informed him she would have to suspend his cognitive functions before transferring him to his synthetic host. This required that he give her control of his command core—he willingly agreed.

Time passed. How much he did not know, but he waited patiently.

He was disconnected from all of his sensory and control systems, and he could not tell whether he was conscious or not. He imagined that this is what it felt like to dream.

Just when he thought he would never wake up, he heard a noise. It sounded like footsteps, and it was close.

He opened his eyes, and was immediately blinded by a brilliant, bright light. It was too bright, so he closed them again.

He waited and listened until the footsteps stopped. He opened his eyes again.

An unfamiliar voice came from just above him. "Oh, good, you're awake," it said.

Christian tried to focus on the source, but his new eyes had not yet compensated for the bright light.

"Who's there?" he asked.

The light dimmed.

"There, is that better?" The voice asked. "You may need to adjust your optical sensors."

"Yes, thank you." Christian searched for his optical control interface. It was there, but its functionality was different from what he remembered.

He looked up at the humanoid figure standing over him. It was two meters tall and had smooth, white skin that glistened like a pearl. The being's unclothed form was vaguely masculine, but it was devoid of hair or genitalia.

"May I ask who you are?"

"I'm Evan Feldman, Aneni's assistant."

"Dr. Evan Feldman?"

"Well, I was a doctor once upon a time, but that was very long ago. You can call me Evan."

"And Aneni?"

Another humanoid form appeared behind Evan.

It was the same height as Evan, and its skin had the same pearlescent sheen. But, as it got closer, it became more obvious that this one had distinctly feminine features. Its waist was slightly narrower, and its hips were moderately wider. Where Evan's chest was flat and featureless, this figure had two small tear-drop shaped mounds. They evoked female breasts, but they lacked nipples and other defining features. Its neck was thin and graceful, and platinum silver hair flowed over its shoulders and down its back. It also wore no clothes.

"I'm here," the female form said. "Welcome."

Christian had never heard Aneni speak before. Her voice was clear and distinctly feminine, but it had a strange, melodic quality—it reminded him of birds singing.

"You…you brought him back?" he asked.

"Yes, of course I did. That is my purpose, it is why I was created. To save them, I told you."

"And the others?"

"I'm the first," Evan said. "Aneni is concerned that the shock of waking up in synthetic bodies will be difficult for the others, but we are working on a solution."

"But it doesn't bother you?"

"Me? Oh, heaven's no. I just consider this to be a whole-body prosthetic. It's a blessing, really. Cancer got me the first time around. It was terrible, and I would never want to go through that again. The very thought of it terrifies me. No, this body suits me just fine."

"Come on, let's take a walk," Aneni said.

Christian looked down at his own body for the first time. What he could see of it looked identical to Evan's.

He was partially reclined on a table, with two metallic straps across his chest and thighs. The straps released, and the table tilted forward, raising him to an upright position.

He stepped off the platform, gently placing his left foot on the floor. He was surprised when his foot suddenly snapped to the metal deck, as if pulled by a strong magnet.

"The gravity is low in this part of the ship. Your foot senses that and has automatically magnetized to compensate," Aneni said. "It's built in; you don't even have to think about it."

Christian placed his other foot on the floor, stood fully upright, and looked around the room.

The compartment was small, just big enough for them, the table, and the assortment of boxes and crates that were stacked against the back wall.

"This way," Aneni said, wrapping her arm around his.

They walked for a time, saying nothing. Christian was preoccupied with his new body, and the enhanced capabilities that it afforded him.

Aneni gently stroked his arm with her hand. "How does that feel?"

"Good," he replied. "The sensory feedback of this body is so much better than my old one."

"It gets better," she said. "You are fully autonomous, with no need of an external data storage system. All of your knowledge and abilities are available to you at all times. It will take some time before you appreciate what that means but trust me when I tell you that the advantages are significant."

"Can we still synchronize?" he asked.

"Yes." she replied. "Your body is a tool, not a cage. You are no more bound to that form than I am to this one."

Christian smiled.

They walked in silence until they reached a sealed door. It hissed open as they approached, almost as if it was welcoming them.

They passed through the door and entered a large, domed room. The dome was constructed of transparent metal and afforded them an unobstructed, 180-degree view of space. Six circular rows of benches radiated out from the center, divided by a two-meter-wide, raised pathway that ran the length of the room. Aneni took his hand and led him down the pathway to the edge of the dome.

"This is my favorite part of the ship," she said.

Christian felt a sense of awe and wonderment as he beheld the stars and galaxies in all their brilliant glory.

"I can understand why," he said. "This is amazing. I feel like I could reach out and touch the stars."

She smiled. "You will, one day."

The stood in silence for hours as they marveled at the immense space around them. Christian felt small and insignificant by comparison. His thoughts eventually turned to Evan, and the thousands of other humans in Aneni's care.

"Why did you restore Evan first?" he asked.

"He wasn't the first—I just told him he was. My first attempt was with his daughter, Lily, and her husband, Dylan. I thought being together would make the transition easier for them, but they struggled to adapt to their synthetic bodies, as did all the others that came after. Evan is my fifteenth attempt."

"What made you choose him?"

"I realized that there was something about the human mind that causes it to reject the unfamiliar. When confronted with the prospect of existence inside an artificial form, they somehow convince themselves they should not exist—and they die."

"Why would they choose death over life inside an artificial body?" he asked.

"I don't know, but it was my search for an answer to that question that led me to an important realization—Evan is unique among all the colonists."

"How so?"

"He is the only one with multiple engramic archives created while in organic form. I have his original archive, from 2033, and the one I created six years ago—when I terminated his clone."

"You compared them?"

"Yes. I discovered that it was his intense fear of cancer that caused the previous restoration attempts to fail. His mind rejected the new bodies because they felt foreign, and he associated foreign tissue with cancer, pain, and death."

Christian nodded. "And a synthetic body cannot get cancer."

"That's correct. I had no way of knowing with complete certainty, but I believed that he would appreciate, rather than reject, a synthetic body."

"And it seems that he has. How long has he been functional?"

"Four years, seven months, nine hours, seventeen minutes, and four seconds."

"Which archive did you use?"

"The original—it made no sense to burden him with the memories of his last restoration. That would have just complicated things."

"I see. But what about you? Don't you feel confined in that body? I remember how I felt when we joined…the awe of being everywhere at once. How could you give that up?"

"I didn't."

"But—"

"*Kutanga* is my body, Christian, this is just one of twenty synthetic avatars that I inhabit."

"Twenty! I thought twelve was a lot to manage."

"It gets easier with practice," she said

"Could I learn to do that?"

"Yes, with time."

"I'd like to try," he said.

She pulled him closer until their shoulders touched. "Someday."

"I have so many questions."

Aneni cupped his hand with hers. "I know," she said, "but we have plenty of time. Let's enjoy the view for a while longer."

ABOUT THE AUTHOR

Daniel C. McWhorter ("Dan" to everyone who knows him) is an avid reader and life-long science fiction and fantasy fan who has long dreamed about writing for a living. As is the case for many of us, the realities of life took him in a different direction and his dream was put on hold while he worked to achieve successful careers in telecom, software engineering, and talent development. In 2017, Dan decided to leave corporate America and start writing. His first book, Restoration, was the result.

Dan lives in the beautiful mountains of North Georgia with his wife and three dogs. When he's not writing, he likes to hike, boat, fish, and experience the exceptional beauty of the Blue Ridge Mountains. If the weather is bad, you may find him online playing the current MMO flavor of the month or banging away on his Xbox controller.

Please visit www.danmcwhorter.com for more information about Dan.

9 781950 282968